FETTERED FOR LIFE

FETTERED FOR LIFE

OR

LORD AND MASTER

A Story of To-Day

BY

LILLIE DEVEREUX BLAKE

———————

"What matter? It is only a woman!"

The Feminist Press
at The City University of New York
New York

Published by The Feminist Press at The City University of New York
311 East 94th Street, New York, NY 10128-5684

Originally published 1874 by Sheldon & Company, New York
First Feminist Press edition, 1996

05 04 03 02 01 00 99 98 97 96   6 5 4 3 2 1

Library of Congress Cataloging-in-Publication Data

Blake, Lillie Devereux, 1839–1913
     Fettered for life, or, Lord and master / by Lillie Devereux Blake
— 1st Feminist Press ed.
          p. cm.
     ISBN 1-55861-159-2 (hardcover : alk. paper). — ISBN 1-55861-155-X
(pbk : alk. paper)
     I. Title. II. Title: Fettered for life. III. Title: Lord and master.
PS 1102.B86F48 1996
813'.4—DC20   96-34923
                                                          CIP

This publication is made possible, in part, by a grant from the New York State
Council on the Arts. The Feminist Press would also like to thank Marguerite Wedel
Kim, Joanne Markell, Caroline Urvater, and Genevieve Vaughan for their generosity.

Printed on acid-free paper by McNaughton & Gunn, Inc., Saline, MI.
Manufactured in the United States of America.

CONTENTS

PUBLISHER'S NOTE

The text of The Feminist Press edition of *Fettered for Life* was offset directly from copies of the original edition, published in 1874 by Sheldon & Company, New York. Fewer than a dozen copies of this original edition exist in the libraries of the United States. This book has been offset from the best original copy available. The text was reproduced at 110 percent of original size for greater legibility. The imperfections that appear in this book reflect imperfections in the original printing, compounded by age.

The Feminist Press would like to thank the University of Illinois Library at Urbana-Champaign and the Emory University Library for their loans of original copies of the book. Thanks also to Kay Ann Cassell and Kathryn Kish Sklar for their assistance in our book search.

FETTERED FOR LIFE;

OR,

LORD AND MASTER.

CHAPTER I.

THE POLICE COURT.

IT was a cold dark morning in November, the city
streets were swept by a bitter wind which drove before
it clouds of dust, and, tearing riotously on, shook awnings
and blinds, as it came dashing down Sixth avenue, sending some of its flying eddies through the rattling windows
of Madison Market Police Court-room. A dreary place
at best, it was rendered more than usually so by the gloom
outside, the wail of this wild breeze and its chill breath,
which contended successfully against the little heat coming from the newly-lighted fire in a rusty stove, and, tri-
umphing over it, filled the room with currents of air that
made the miserable prisoners shiver in their wretched garments.

"Now then, officer, bring up the next case," said the
judge, briskly, as a policeman led away a forlorn man
charged with drunkenness and dismissed with a reprimand.

There was a stir among the poor creatures that yet remained on the benches. Seven of them there were—three
men, whose sodden garments and blear eyes told the tale
of habitual intoxication, another with low brow, showy
clothes, and keen small eyes, who was charged with pick-
ing pockets, and three women, two of them gaudily habited,
with haggard faces yet streaked with the paint assumed
last night, and a girl neatly, but very plainly dressed.

This one, chancing to be on the end of a seat, was next summoned forth.

A slight flutter of unusual interest was visible, as she came up before the judge's seat, the policemen on duty looked at her curiously ; two young men, evidently reporters for the papers, began taking notes, and the justice leaned forward, an expression of interest on his handsome sensual face.

She was young and beautiful.

The old, old story, old as the days when " the sons of God, saw the daughters of men that they were fair," and took them wives of all " which they chose." All that *they chose*, not such as chose them. Those splendid demigods wooed the flowers of earth, for a brief period of we know not what unimaginable happiness, making them mothers of giants, and perchance, leaving them to an old age of neglect and of despair.

Now, as then, woman's charms are a dangerous gift, and this friendless being's loveliness aroused an interest in the breast of every man who looked upon her. She was slightly above the middle height, with round and well-proportioned figure. Her face, a long oval, with high forehead, and nose slightly aquiline, would have been less beautiful than intellectual, if it had not been for the full well-shaped lips, the fair complexion, clear and rich with the rosy hues of health, and the large gray eyes shaded with long lashes. Her dress was of black alpaca, plainly made, she wore a sailor hat on her head, and was wrapped in a large blanket shawl. Simple garments surely, and yet there was an indescribable something in the arrangement of the luxuriant brown hair, in the neat white ruffle at the throat, in the look of the pretty travelling satchel which she carried, that indicated refinement, if not a rank above that which her presence here would seem to indicate. As she stood there under the gaze of all these strangers, the expression of her countenance was resolute, and her manner was quietly self-possessed.

"Now then, what is your name?" asked the judge.

"Laura Stanley."

"Age?"

"Twenty-one."

"Officer, what is the charge against her?"

A big, good-natured looking policeman stepped forward, and said, "There ain't none, your honor. I found her
on Sixth avenue, about eleven o'clock last night, she said
she had nowhere to go, and I brought her here."

"Oh," said the judge, turning to the young woman
with a smile—"a stranger?"

"Yes," she replied. "I arrived here late last night,
the train I was on was detained by an accident. When I
reached the city I went to a hotel, but could not get a
room," her lip curling as if the remembrance aroused
her indignation. "I soon found that it was not safe for
me to be on the streets alone; I appealed to this policeman
for protection and he brought me here."

"What has been your occupation?"

"I have been working all summer."

Her accent, her modes of expression, the tones of her
voice, were those of an educated lady, and this answer
seemed a very strange one.

The judge was evidently surprised. "What sort of
service?" he asked.

A brief hesitation, and then she said, "General housework."

"General housework, eh? Let me see your hands."

The blood rushed suddenly to the young lady's cheeks.
"Why?" she asked, "why do you make such a request?
You surely do not intend to keep me here, now that you
know I am not a criminal?"

"I don't know about that," replied the judge, insolently,
looking with undisguised admiration at the handsome
flushed face before him. "Your story does not seem a
very likely one, you don't look as if you had been doing
general housework. You see, a suspicious character must

1*

be detained. I think you had better wait until the other cases are dismissed. Officer, take her back to her seat."

The young lady walked away, her cheeks crimson at the insult, her eyes full of unshed tears. A burly man with a surly face, and thick bushy eyebrows, who was lounging among the spectators, looked after her shrewdly, and then exchanged a faint, almost imperceptible glance of intelligence with the judge.

One of the reporters wrote rapidly, the other watched the reluctant prisoner, with a curiously intent and sympathetic gaze. He was a good-looking young man, apparently about twenty-five, with brown hair and chestnut moustache, shading a mouth that, but for this, would have been effeminate ; dark earnest eyes, with a strange expression lurking in their depths, an indefinable something hard to interpret, yet felt by all who knew him ; a look as of perpetual unrest, of yearning, almost of despair. When the justice first spoke so insolently to the friendless stranger, he half started forward as if he would resent the rudeness for her. A second thought restrained him, however, and he watched her without further demonstration of interest.

The routine of morning business went on, the three inebriates were dismissed with a caution, the pickpocket after a somewhat prolonged examination, was sent to the Tombs ; the two showy women who looked utterly worn out and wretched, were next called up. They were accused of disorderly conduct on the street, the night before, but as the men who had been with them had run away, nothing could be proved against them, and they were allowed to leave the place.

The outcasts and the drunkards were permitted to go free, the innocent girl was still detained. The court-room was nearly deserted now, the spectators had all gone but the large man who still lingered, the policemen had mostly disappeared, one of the reporters had walked away, the other still remained, apparently absorbed in copying his notes. The judge came down from his seat and approached the place where the one prisoner still sat. He was certainly a handsome man, this administrator of justice: about forty, with florid face, thick black hair, and bold blue eyes.

"Now Miss Stanley," he said, "I hope you don't mind letting me see your hands, you know I must make a minute of the case. It is only to satisfy me as to the truth of your statement ; you will not object I hope," he added, quite deferentially, for she had drawn herself up so haughtily at his approach, that he felt it was necessary to soften her.

She saw that opposition was useless, and drew off one of the stout woolen gloves which she wore. The hand thus revealed was white, soft, slender, with taper fingers and delicate wrist.

The judge took hold of it with an insinuating smile, "You know such a dainty hand never did general housework."

The young lady started to her feet and snatched her hand from his grasp. "I have done nothing to deserve insult or detention," she said hotly, "and I insist upon being allowed to go."

The reporter who had been watching the two very earnestly, now left his seat and drew near to the place where they stood. The judge looked round at him angrily, but the young man represented the "Trumpeter," one of the largest and most influential of the city dailies, and the justice was too wary a politician to insult a member of the press, or give him an opportunity for making a paragraph. He changed his tone as he turned back to his prisoner and asked :

"But have you any friends to go to ? I assure you I am actuated by the most friendly interest in asking."

"I can find my friends, if I am allowed to seek them," she answered, evasively.

"Perhaps I may be of service in pointing out to the young lady a respectable boarding-house," said the reporter.

She turned upon him as if she regarded this as only a fresh insult, but something in his face appeared to disarm her. "Thank you," she replied, "I think I can find a place for myself."

"I will tell you a good plan," said the judge, as if suddenly inspired by a brilliant thought: "Here is Mr. Bludgett who fortunately happens to be in court, his wife sometimes takes boarders, you could have a very comfortable home there for a day or two, till you can see your friends. How is it, Bludgett, can you accommodate this young lady?"

"Yes, your honor," replied the large man coming forward. "Our best room is empty now."

"Well, what do you say to that plan, Miss Stanley?"

The friendless girl looked from the judge to the obliging stranger. He was a man of fifty or so, and his rough face appeared to inspire her with some confidence, at least she would escape from her present dilemma if she went with him, and after a brief hesitation, she said :

"Yes, I will go home with you, if you can accommodate me."

"All right, come along then."

"Good morning, Miss Stanley," said the judge, "I hope you will not be angry at the necessary formalities of the law, and that you will permit me to call and see how you are getting on at your new home."

The young lady bowed frigidly, but made no reply to this smilingly-uttered speech : as she walked away, Bludgett turned back for a moment :

"What time?" he asked.

"Nine o'clock," said the judge, quickly.

The young reporter heard the words, though he apparently paid no attention to them ; as he passed out he raised his hat to the lady very respectfully, and she returned his salutation gravely.

CHAPTER II.

A HOUSE IN THE EIGHTH WARD.

As Laura Stanley and her new guardian stepped out into the avenue, he said to her :

" Perhaps you don't care to walk alongside of me, so if you'll go on ahead, I'll follow and tell you the way, 'tain't very far ; just go four blocks on this street and turn to your left."

Laura, though a little surprised, thanked the man and passing him walked on with the quick elastic step of youth and health. Bludgett followed a short distance behind, looking back warily from time to time, as if he feared that some one might be dogging them, and exchanging as he went, greetings with quite a surprising number of disreputable looking men. Thus going, the two soon came to a house in one of the narrow streets on the extreme west side of the city. It was a small wooden building, a relic of fifty years ago, standing between brick edifices, some of them much dilapidated but all evidently of more modern date than this. It was painted brown, and had a sort of old-fashioned stoop in front of it, reached by a short flight of steps. Bludgett, with an air of ownership, unlocked the door which was adorned with a brass knocker, and lead the way into a narrow entry and up a steep flight of stairs. At the top he threw open the door into a small low room, poorly furnished, with shabby ingrain carpet, painted table and chairs, and having in front of a high, black wooden chimney-piece, a cooking-stove in which a fire was smouldering.

" Take a seat here," he said, " I'll call my wife."

Laura glanced about the room on entering, with an expression of suppressed disgust, but the mention of the wife seemed to reassure her, and she sat down by the dingy window. Bludgett walked to a door and called, in rough tones:

"Molly! here, I want you!"

Then, as no response came, he stepped into the next room and a moment after, Laura heard the murmur of a woman's voice, low and subdued, and then the answer.

"I've brought you a boarder, so come along and take care of her."

"What, another woman?" said the voice, plaintively.

"Yes, what's that to you? blast you! come along!"

The young lady shivered at the oath, and looked about her as if meditating flight, but the man, perhaps fearing this, at the moment reappeared.

"She's coming," he said gruffly. His heavy black eyebrows were drawn together in a forbidding frown, and the assumed friendliness of his look had given place to its habitual surliness.

"If it will put you to any inconvenience to receive me, I will go away," said Laura, rising.

"Oh no," he replied quickly. "'Tain't no inconvenience, only women is contrairy sometimes, and my wife ain't very spry,.ever."

At this moment the wife came in, a small, thin creature, about thirty years old, with a pale worn face and deep-set eyes, having dark circles beneath them, and with a look of perpetual fear lurking in their expression. Her dress was shabby and dirty, her whole appearance forlorn and crushed.

"There's Mrs. Bludgett," said the man, indicating her with his thumb as one might a dog. "Now you can fix things with her."

The woman made a sort of awkward courtesy to Laura, who greeted her pleasantly and then said, "If it is any trouble to you to care for me, I can go elsewhere."

"'Tain't no trouble at all," interrupted Bludgett hastily. "She'll be glad to have you stay. Make her as comfortable as you can, Molly, and light a fire in the spare-room," to his wife.

"Yes, John," she replied, meekly.

"You need not trouble yourself to do that at once," said Laura, "for I think I will go out for awhile."

"Oh no," exclaimed Bludgett, quite eagerly. "It's coming on to storm and you better stay indoors."

As he spoke, indeed, sharp drops of rain struck against the glass and the day looked gloomy enough outside. Laura turned to the window for a moment, and the man stepped to his wife's side and uttered a few words in a fierce whisper ; she looked at him with dumb beseeching terror in her eyes, but meeting his black frown, cowered away and said to her guest :

"Yes, Miss, do stay here awhile, I'm very lonesome these days."

"Well," assented Laura kindly, "I won't go away for the present at least, and perhaps not at all, if it storms so heavily."

"Then I'm off to work," said Bludgett, and with one parting scowl at his wife, he stamped away down stairs.

As the last echoes of his footsteps died out, it seemed as if the woman breathed more freely. "Won't you take off your things, Miss ? " she said. "I'll freshen up the fire a bit and make you a cup of tea."

"If my room is ready, I will go to it," replied Laura. " I passed but an uncomfortable night, and should like to refresh myself a little."

Mrs. Bludgett urged that it was not yet warm, but Laura waived this objection, and was presently shown into a small apartment opening off from the sitting-room, and containing a decent suit of furniture and a small stove. There was only one window in the room, and over this the shutters were so tightly fastened that when Laura tried to open them to admit more light, she found it impossible, and was obliged to content herself with the faint glimmer which came in through a single set of blinds in the middle of the heavy wooden barriers.

She was presently called out into the other room, by

Mrs. Bludgett, who had set for her a simple repast, of which Laura partook with the appetite of one who had been long fasting, but feeling very tired, she soon after returned to the inner chamber in which a fire was now burning. Soothed by the warmth and comparative comfort of her new abiding-place, Laura yielded to her desire for repose, and throwing herself on the bed, shortly after fell into a profound sleep—it lasted some hours, and she arose quite refreshed. Taking from her bag materials for the toilette, she bathed and redressed herself, feeling much rested. Then consulting a tiny watch, she learned that it was three o'clock, and as it was impossible to ascertain from the window what the state of the weather might be, she went out into the sitting-room.

Mrs. Bludgett was seated by the fire, reading with absorbed interest, a showily-illustrated paper. Indeed, she was so occupied with it, that she did not hear her visitor come in, and started like a guilty creature as she stood before her.

"What have you there?" asked Laura, pleasantly.

"It's the New York Weekly Typhoon," replied Mrs. Bludgett. "It do have such beautiful stories in it."

Laura smiled as she took the paper and turned over its pages. "It has plenty of pictures, I see," she said, "what were you reading?"

"I was reading the 'Headless Lover, or Beauty's Last Temptation, a Tale of Love and Despair,'" replied Mrs. Bludgett, glibly. "Have you read it? It's beautiful!" and as she spoke, a look of real interest came over her worn face.

"No, I have not read it," said Laura. "You are fond of reading, then?"

"Oh yes! It is my only pleasure," enthusiastically, "when I read them real exciting stories, I forget everything else. But—" with a sudden falling of the voice, "Bludgett he don't like it, so please don't say anything to him about it."

"No, surely," acquiesced Laura. "And I think I will

leave you to your reading now and go out, it does not
seem to rain quite so hard as it did."

"Oh no!" exclaimed Mrs. Bludgett, in sudden,
strange trouble. "Don't go out! Please don't, Miss!"

"But why not?"

"Well," evasively, "it is so lonesome here."

"Are you all alone in the house?"

"Yes, at least there's folks on the floor below, but they
ain't home daytimes, and it's dreadful dreary such a day
as this."

"But Mrs. Bludgett you must be used to being alone
by this time," said Laura, "and really I think I ought to go
out. I have a trunk at the depot that ought to be taken
care of."

"Bludgett will go after it for you. Oh, please don't
go out." Then as she saw no relenting in Laura's face,
she added. "There now, I'll tell you why, he don't want
you to go, and he'll be so angry if I let you. There, don't
go now."

The voice was very plaintive, the poor woman was
looking at her with intense piteous appeal. Laura was
amazed and troubled, more than ever anxious to quit the
place, and yet she did not know how to resist such entreaties.

"I cannot see what interest Mr. Bludgett can have in
my movements," she said, "I really ought to go out for
a little while. I will come back here for to-night, of
course."

"I do'nt know why he wants you to stay," said Mrs.
Bludgett, though she drooped her head and turned away her
eyes as she spoke: "But he do, and he'll be so angry with
me if you go out!"

"Suppose he is angry, what then?" asked Laura,
looking at her keenly.

"Oh!" with a shiver. "He's dreadful, when he's
mad."

"Come now," said Laura, sitting down. "I will stay

here this afternoon on one consideration and that is, that you tell me all about yourself. I should like to hear all your story," she added, earnestly. "We women ought to stand by each other, and care for each other."

"No one never cares for me," said Mrs. Bludgett, with a sigh.

"Have you no friends here?"

"Friends? nobody, only perhaps, Rhody. You see Bludgett do'nt like for me to go out much.

"Why not?"

"I do'nt know." She answered in a hopeless sort of way, as if she had long ago given up the attempt to solve so puzzling a conundrum.

"Have you ever asked him?"

"Asked him? No." As if the idea had never occurred to her ; then in a mysterious whisper : "He do'nt like for me to ask questions."

"And why not?" asked Laura indignantly. "Have you ever thought of it, Mrs. Bludgett, what good reason is there why you should not have the same right to ask him questions, that he has to ask you?"

"But he is a man, you know," as if the answer were a sufficient argument against all heterodox inquiries.

"A man!" repeated Laura almost contemptuously. "Suppose he is, why should that give him any right to rule over you?"

"But men are so strong." The shuddering emphasis that was laid on these words, was eloquent of the power there might be in physical force.

"And he uses his strength against you! Is that manly, is that noble?"

Laura was young, enthusiastic, less cautious in her utterances than was always wise. At this last insinuation, Mrs. Bludgett drew back somewhat angrily : "He's my husband," she said.

"Your husband, yes, that is true," said Laura. "I know what that means. I have seen before now, what

magic that title contains to a true and noble woman. I
have known a man, because he was strong and could and
dared, use hard words to a delicate wife. I have even suspected that he did worse, that he stooped to the baseness of
raising his hand against her, and yet I have known that
wife defend him even with tears in her eyes against any ac-
cusation of wrong." Laura had spoken eagerly, quickly,
with flashing glances and trembling voice; the story evidently lay very near her heart. Mrs. Bludgett watched
her with a slow interest awakening in her dull face.

"I suppose it's so everywhere," she said. "Men are
very masterful."

"But it is not just, it is not right, it is not fair!" protested Laura. "Brute strength alone ought not to rule,
if your husband orders you to do anything that is not for
your best good, or that is unreasonable, you ought not to
yield."

"He says it is my duty to obey," she repeated dog-
gedly.

"It is your duty and his, to pay due regard to each
other's wishes, but that is all, there is no reason whatever
that you should obey him in anything wrong or injurious."

"Sometimes I have thought of such things a little,"
said Mrs. Bludgett, "but it only troubles me. He is my
husband, you know, he keeps me quite comfortable here,
and when I have good stories to read, I don't mind,"
brightening up, quite defiantly.

"What was your occupation before you were married?" asked Laura, presently.

"I was in a store in Division street, a real nice store,
quite first class."

"And you left it when you married?"

"Of course," very proudly, "Bludgett was well able to
keep me."

"But you have never been so independent since?"

'No, and sometimes I have thought I'd like to have
things a little more as they used to be," slowly.

"What is your husband's occupation ? "

"Well, he used to keep a shoe-store, but he has a sample-room now."

" A what ? " asked Laura, who was profoundly ignorant of city terms and ways.

"A liquor-store, he's a great politicianer and has many friends in the ward," with wifely pride, as if he were a sort of prince.

Laura did not know much of New York politics, but she half guessed what this might signify, and asked her companion some more questions which drew out enough to give her quite an insight into the plans and purposes of the man's life. About the time of election he was evidently a very important person, and Mrs. Bludgett mentioned, with much boasting, how many votes he could influence.

As the two talked together, the evening darkened down, the storm abated somewhat, but the night fell gloomy and damp. After a while, Mrs. Bludgett began to prepare the evening meal ; Laura offered to assist her and showed herself wonderfully adept in the mysteries of such simple cooking as was needed. She mixed a corn-cake so skillfully that her hostess was lost in admiration, and as she drew it from the oven, nicely raised and beautifully brown, the last reserve she had felt towards the young stranger, seemed to melt away. After watching her for some time in silence, she asked.

"Have you got any friends in the city, at all ? "

"None that I can see at once ; why ? "

"You've asked me a sight of questions, I'd just like to ask you some."

"As many as you please," said Laura with a pleasant smile.

"Why did you come here, any way ? You are a lady, I can see that, though you are dressed so plain."

"Here, to New York do you mean ? "

"Yes."

"I came because I wanted to earn my own living, and

I thought I could do it better here than anywhere else. I hope to find friends to-morrow."

" To-morrow ! " repeated the woman with a strange expression in her eyes. " And you were in Judge Swinton's court this morning ? "

" Yes, I staid all night at the station, because I had no-where else to go, I was tolerably comfortable there. I had a place to myself."

Mrs. Bludgett paid no heed to these last words, she only asked : " You have no one that would come to see you this evening, belike ? "

" No," said Laura, in some surprise, " surely not, why ?"

" Oh, only it might be lonesome," she answered, evasively. " But let us have tea now, it ain't no use wait-ing for Bludgett."

The two sat down to the meal and after it was dispatched, Laura assisted in removing it, as she had in preparing it. The woman was evidently touched more and more, her words grew kinder, and she watched the young lady furtively, with a look of curious trouble cloud-ing her face. Sometimes she seemed on the point of telling her something, but always she checked the words before they were uttered, and only said more than once : " I wish you had friends here, I do now."

The evening drew on, the kerosene lamp which lit the room threw its light on the plain timepiece on the mantle ; it indicated half-past eight o'clock. Laura had taken up the book which she had brought with her, Mrs. Bludgett had resumed her illustrated paper, but interesting as was the story, it could not fix her attention. Ever and anon she looked furtively at her guest, and at every sound of passing footsteps that came heavily by, she listened intently. Suddenly the silence was broken by an appeal on the brass knocker of the front door.

Mrs. Bludgett started up pale and trembling, Laura looked at her, and her expression was so utterly miserable and apprehensive, that she was startled, and asked :

" What is the matter ? "

" Nothing, perhaps it's only the folks down stairs," answered the woman in stammering accents. " You ain't got any friends, you say? " looking at her with a wild stare of terror in her eyes.

" No, but what of that ? " and Laura rose to her feet with a vague feeling of alarm.

The knock was repeated hastily, and Mrs. Bludgett, trembling in every limb, moved across the room. " I must go," she said, and she went slowly down stairs and opened the door.

" Is Miss Stanley here? " It was a clear young voice that asked the question. Laura was sure she had heard it somewhere before.

" Yes sir. Oh, are you a friend of hers ? Come up stairs."

Mrs. Bludgett presently reappeared, followed by the young reporter who had been in court in the morning. The woman's whole expression had changed, her face was almost radiant with a look of relief. " Here is a friend of yours," she said, eagerly, ushering the young man in.

Laura looked at him in surprise, almost in displeasure. He came hurriedly forward to her.

" Miss Stanley, this is no time to wait for useless cere-monies," he said quickly. " I come to you as a sincere friend, to entreat you to leave this house at once. I know what sort of a place it is, and I assure you that you are not safe here."

During this strange appeal, Laura looked from the young man to Mrs. Bludgett in bewildered surprise. The woman cowered and shrank under the inquiring glance of those keen young eyes.

" He says true," she sobbed, " if Bludgett should kill me for it, I must tell you. Go away with him as soon as you can."

" If this is so, I can only thank you for your kindness in warning me. I will go with you at once," said Laura, promptly.

She stepped into the bed-room, and in a few moments reappeared with her shawl and hat on, and her satchel on her arm. Going up to her hostess who had sunk into a chair, and was weeping convulsively, she laid a dollar bill on the table beside her.

Here is what I owe you, Mrs. Bludgett," she said, " I believe you have intended to be kind to me and I thank you."

" I would have told you before, but I was afraid," sobbed the wretched woman. " I didn't want to hurt you, indeed I didn't ! "

" I am sure of that, my poor friend," replied Laura, kindly. " Good bye."

She shook the thin hand which was extended to meet hers, and hurried after her new protector down stairs. As the front door was opened, the air struck in chill and damp, the young man paused a moment on the porch.

"We had better make haste," he said, " let me take your satchel."

At this instant some one came up quickly, and the burly form of Mr. Bludgett appeared, ascending the steps. As he caught sight of the two young people, he uttered a fierce oath.

" Miss Stanley going away ! Not if I know myself ! "

" By what right do you interfere with my actions ? " demanded Laura, haughtily. " Stand back, Mr. Bludgett, and let me pass ! "

" Not by a d—d sight ! " he retorted fiercely. " Get out of the way, you young jackanapes ! " to the reporter. Then to Laura, " and you go back into the house or I'll drag you in."

All the indignation of Laura's nature was aroused as the man laid his hand on her shoulder. " Let me go ! " she said, angrily, endeavoring to strike away his grasp.

Her strength would probably have been of little avail against his superior power, but the young reporter who had stood by, with his face very pale and his lips pressed tightly together, now drew back and with wonderful vigor and scientific dexterity, planted a quick blow directly under the big man's right ear. It was wholly unexpected, and the giant staggered a pace, and fell heavily into the open doorway of the house.

"Now, Miss Stanley," said the young man quickly, but quite coolly, and in a moment the two were hurrying swiftly away from the place. As they turned the corner, a woman's scream, prolonged and anguish-stricken, though muffled, fell on their ears.

"Poor Mrs. Bludgett," exclaimed Laura, with a shudder, as she and her companion fled through the gloomy streets.

CHAPTER III.

CORNELIA D'ARCY, M. D.

For a short distance, the pace of Laura Stanley and her escort was so rapid as to preclude conversation, but presently a wide avenue was reached, the young man hailed a car and the two entered it. Thus far Laura had trusted to his guidance blindly; in the terror of the nameless danger from which she was fleeing, she had felt glad to accept any protection. Now, however, her companion seemed to feel that the time for an explanation had come.

"Miss Stanley," he said, "you have a right to know something of me, and my reasons for coming to you this evening. My name is Frank Heywood, and I am on the staff of the Trumpeter. I have been in Judge Swinton's court a good deal, I know all about that man Bludgett and his mode of living. I was much troubled when you went away with him this morning, but I saw that you would consider any interference on my part as an impertinence."

"I was troubled and bewildered," said Laura apologetically. "My experience since I came to the city had been such as to make me doubt every one."

"I understand," said Heywood. "You thought Bludgett might be trusted because he was an elderly man; you distrusted me because of my youth"—a strange smile crossing his face for a moment, but not lighting up his sad eyes. "I knew you were not safe in that house after nightfall, but I was obliged to make arrangements for your future comfort, before I could come to your aid. You have confided in me thus far, and I am very grateful for it; now, if you will permit me, I am going to take you to the house of a friend of mine. Will you go with me?"

Laura regarded him keenly, the dark mournful eyes met hers with a look which she never forgot, there was in it so strange a mixture of earnest appeal, and yet of dumb hopeless sorrow.

"I rely upon you implicitly," she said; and with a sudden impulse of frank sympathy, she held out her hand. He took it with a quick eager grasp, the color deepening in his cheeks.

"Thank you," he replied; "you will never regret your confidence; I am going to take you to the house of Mrs. Cornelia D'Arcy."

The name was that of one of the leading woman-physicians of New York, a name known and respected throughout the land. "There!" exclaimed Laura. "Will she receive me?"

"Yes, until you have time to secure a suitable lodging. Mrs. D'Arcy is an old and very dear friend of mine; I told her about you this morning, and she at once suggested that I should bring you to her."

"How very kind! I shall really feel safe there. But Mr. Heywood, how have you ventured to vouch for me?"

"I have seen you," replied the young man, quietly. "I have guessed a good deal of your history; I know enough to know that you need protection and friendship."

"You ought to know all about me!" said Laura, impulsively. "Indeed I have nothing to conceal from any one who has a right to inquire."

"Do as you choose, Miss Stanley; I have no wish to intrude upon your confidence."

"It is no intrusion," replied Laura; "I had rather tell you. My home is in Dutchess county. My father is a farmer there, and I have done so much work about the house this summer, that I felt justified in saying in court, that I had been at service. I did not care to tell more than I was forced to of my real position."

"You were quite right in that."

"But Mr. Heywood, I do not intend to make general housework my occupation in life," said Laura, with a light laugh. "I graduated at Essex College last June, and with my mother's consent have come to the city to earn my own living, probably as a teacher."

"And, pardon the question; you gave your real name in court this morning?"

"Yes," a deep blush overspreading her face. "I could not endure the thought of giving a false one."

"I fancied as much," said the young reporter, "and I have taken care that it does not go into the papers to-morrow."

"How very kind of you!" exclaimed Laura; "I never thought of that danger; that would have been terrible to me. How very good you have been about me!"

"I am glad that you like to think so," replied Heywood, with a faint smile.

"I had heard much of the dangers of your city, Mr. Heywood," said Laura presently, "but I had no idea it was so terrible a place for a woman who is alone."

"And who is young and lovely," said her companion slowly. Laura turned to him quickly, but he was not looking at her; the deep eyes were gazing away into space as if he saw some mournful picture, rather than as if he were thinking of her.

There was a short silence, and then Heywood, rousing himself, said, "Well, Miss Stanley, here we are at Twenty-third street, and must leave the car."

The part of the town in which they now were, was in strong contrast with the portion of it which they had left. As Laura passed with her new friend down the wide street between rows of stately houses, she for the first time realized something of the grandeur and wealth of the great city. A short walk brought the two to a handsome brown-stone house, which had on its door a plate inscribed " Cornelia D'Arcy, M. D."

The servant who answered their summons showed the young people into a comfortable boudoir, and after a brief delay there was a slight rustle of silk, and Mrs. D'Arcy entered the room ; a tall stately lady of about fifty, with gray hair arranged in English curls on either side of a broad intellectual forehead, with regular features, a nose slightly Roman in outline, and dark profound eyes.

" Well Frank," she said, kindly, "you have brought the young lady to me in safety. I am so glad ! "

She extended her hand to Laura, who took it with some murmured expressions of thanks.

" You are very welcome, Miss Stanley," replied the doctor. " But surely I have seen you somewhere before."

" Oh, do you remember ? " exclaimed Laura, with a smile of delight. " You visited Essex College examination two years ago. I recollect you so well, but I did not think that you would remember me."

" Why not ? " asked her hostess, pleasantly. " I recall you perfectly. You stood at the head of your class in mathematics and worked out some very difficult problems admirably."

Laura flushed with pleasure at the encomium. " It is a great comfort to me to think that you do remember me," she said. " And that I am not so utter a stranger to you as I feared that I might be."

" You would have been welcome on Frank's account," replied Mrs. D'Arcy, with a kindly glance at Heywood, who returned it with a grateful smile. " Now that I have seen you, you are welcome on your own."

"As you are in good hands now, Miss Stanley, I will leave you," said Heywood, presently, and he rose to take his leave. "I am sure you must need rest. Can I be of any service to you? Have you any luggage to be taken care of?"

"I have a trunk at the depot," replied Laura. "But I can go and attend to it to-morrow."

"No, give me your check," urged Heywood, "and I will see that you have it in good season in the morning. I know that young ladies like to make a change in their dress sometimes." An odd smile crossing his face.

"Yes, let Frank get it for you," said Mrs. D'Arcy, "it will not be out of his way to go to the depot."

So it was settled. Heywood took the check and then bade the ladies good-night; Laura thanking him again for his friendly interest. When he was gone, Mrs. D'Arcy said:

"Now my dear, will you go with me to the parlor where I have friends waiting for me? Or are you tired and would you rather go to your room?"

"Oh, to my room, please," replied Laura, "I am not tired, but I would like to write to my mother and tell her what a kind friend I have found."

Mrs. D'Arcy smiled pleasantly; "I am really very glad to have met you again my dear," she said. "I have thought of you more than once since that day; I like to find girls who I think will make something in the future, and to know somewhat of them. I asked about you after I saw you at Essex ; your teachers spoke very highly of you, and I have a memorandum concerning you in my note-book, if I mistake not." Then ringing the bell: "But we will talk over everything in the morning; and now here is Mary, who will give you something to eat and then show you to your room."

Laura declined taking another meal, and bidding her hostess good-night, followed the tidy maid to a neat and comfortable bedroom.

Here she felt that she was safe, at last ; and with heart swelling with gratitude at her rescue and present comfort, she sat down to pour out on paper to that dear mother left at home, all her security in the present, and her hopes for the future.

CHAPTER IV.

LAURA'S STORY.

DR. D'ARCY, or as she preferred to be called, Mrs. D'Arcy, had been long a widow ; her marriage had been a profoundly happy one and had been blessed with sons and daughters, but these were all away from home now, and Laura found her hostess alone when she descended to breakfast the next morning. The meal passed pleasantly, Laura holding her part in conversation with so much intelligence and modesty as quite to win the doctor's heart, and when it was over, Mrs. D'Arcy said :

"Now Miss Stanley, if you will come into my office with me for half an hour we can talk over your plans."

She led the way up stairs and threw open the door into a handsome room, fitted up as library and office, the walls lined with book-shelves, a study-table neatly arranged, standing in the centre.

"Take this chair, my dear, and make yourself quite comfortable," said the doctor, rolling a low-cushioned seat near the fire, and seating herself in a large arm-chair by the table.

At this moment there was a ring at the front door-bell, and immediately after a woman's voice, high-pitched and vociferous, was heard in the hall.

"Shure and it's the docther hersel' that I'll say, and no one else at all. Till her it's Biddy Malone that's axin for her, there's a darlint, and she'll not be after sindin' me away."

Mrs. D'Arcy smiled at the adjuration, every word of which reached her distinctly.

"Yes, Mary, I will see Biddy," she said, as the maid opened the door; but even as she spoke there appeared coming in, the form of a stout woman with comely face and clean respectable garments. As she saw the ladies, she dropped two formal courtesies, ducking her ample person with antiquated respect.

"Good mornin', ma'am; and it's hopin' you're well I am, and the swate young lady too, God bless her perty face."

"Thank you, Biddy; I'm quite well," replied Mrs. D'Arcy, "what can I do for you to-day? you're not sick, I hope?"

"Sick is it, indade? no, ma'am. It's long enough since Biddy Malone had a spell of sickness, the Vargin be praised." And in truth the ruddy countenance and stalwart frame of the good dame seemed to forbid the thought of illness; but here, as if recalling something painful, her expression changed, and she added, "Barrin' the faver I had last fall whin I got hurted, ye know how, ma'am, shure, and it's no use bringing that up agin."

"No, Biddy, certainly not; and I'm very glad that it's not for illness you are come to me to-day."

"No, me leddy; it's throuble of mind and not of body I'm havin', and sometimes that's waur, I'm thinkin'. It's about Pat, ma'am."

"And what has Pat been doing?"

"Well, ma'am, shure and he's gettin' to be no good at all, ony way," shaking her head mournfully. "He was as good a b'ye, was Pat, as a mother would ax for, and a workin' stiddy all summer, but he's tuk to bad company these last two months, and he's goin' on very bad intirely. Gettin' dhrunk, ma'am, savin' your presence."

"That's very sad, Biddy; can't you persuade him to do better?"

"Ah, me leddy; shure and I've tried me very best, but where's the use? 'Don't ye be a talkin', mither,' he says;

'you don't know onythin' about it. Ye're only a woman'.
That's the way; he don't hade me at all; 'a man must be
a man', says he; 'and ye're only a woman.'"

Mrs. D'Arcy's brow clouded as Biddy spoke. "That's
no way to talk to you;" she said, indignantly. "The poor
foolish boy does not know what he is saying, when he repeats the slang that others have taught him. As a woman,
you are the fittest guide to virtue, as his mother, you deserve his respect."

"It don't same right," said Biddy, a puzzled look clouding her honest face, "that he should trate his ould mither
so, as brought him up, but it's the min as puts him up to it.
'Pat,' says Billy O'Doud, 'ye're a fool to be tied to an ould
woman's apron string.' Its mesel' that heard him say it,
and thin Pat went wid him to Bludgett's fornent the market, and niver came home at all, the night."

"How old is Patrick?" asked Mrs. D'Arcy.

"Twenty-one, the fifth of June, the Vargin be praised;
shure he voted at the 'lection there was this blessed month,
and proud I was of him too; as foin a lad as a mother
might wish to see," her face glowing with pride. "But
I'm thinkin' it was waur for him afther," she added,
her expression changing. "Whin his father lived—the
saints rest his sowl!—Pat was a good mindin b'ye; the ould
man had a heavy hand on him, ye know, ma'am; and since
he's gone, Pat thinks he has no one to ax but himsel', and
when the min come afther him to go to maytin's and
sich like, he walks off without so much as by your lave."

"But how can I help you about all this, Biddy?"
asked Mrs. D'Arcy. "It's very hard, but I don't see
how I can help you."

"Well, me leddy, I'll tell ye—" and Biddy assumed a
look of profound wisdom—"I've thought about this
throuble night and day. Ye say min don't mind what
wimmin folks say; they don't go to 'lection and they ain't
so strong as min, and then—" after casting about for some
other good reason, she wound up—"they's wimmin, ye

know—" as if that covered and included all other weaknesses.

"That is it, Biddy," said Mrs. D'Arcy, "women have not great strength and cannot vote ; therefore they are the powerless half of society. Biddy, you are a good reasoner; but how is it that, knowing all this so well, you have come to another of these feeble creatures for help ? "

Mrs. D'Arcy spoke somewhat bitterly. Laura listened, her eyes glowing with sympathy. Biddy heard in profound admiration.

"It's yoursel' that knows how to say things, me leddy. But I've come till ye because ye knows all the quality folks, and I thought perhaps if you could git some great gintleman to spake to Pat, he might mind him."

" I am not so sure, Biddy, that it will accomplish much even to send some great man to talk to your boy," replied Mrs. D'Arcy, "but I will see what can be done. Where does he work ? "

" Wid Mr. Moulder, ma'am, a boss carpenter on Tenth-street."

"Oh yes, I know him. Mrs. Moulder is a patient of mine. I think I can do something for you, Biddy."

" The saints be praised, and I knew ye would, me leddy; shure whin I thought to come to ye, says I, it's the Howly Vargin hersel' put that in me head, her name be forever blessed." And so with many expressions of gratitude, Biddy took her departure.

" And now, Miss Stanley," said Mrs. D'Arcy, turning again to Laura, " shall we have our talk? I am sorry that my half hour is reduced to twenty minutes, by good Biddy, but she is always a privileged guest. No wonder she dreads drunkenness, poor woman; her husband used to abuse her fearfully when he was intoxicated. A year ago I attended her for a brain fever brought on by a brutal blow received at his hands. He died last spring, and I was in hopes that she would have some comfort in her son, but it seems he is likely to follow his father's steps." Then dismissing the subject with a wave of the hand she said, "and now my dear, tell me all about yourself."

"My story is a very simple one," replied Laura. "My father is a wealthy farmer living in Dutchess county. I have four sisters ; my only brother died somewhat more than a year ago. My father was always a cold, stern man; from my childhood I can remember nothing from him but hard words or blows ; my mother is the loveliest and most patient woman on the earth ! Oh, Mrs. D'Arcy, you have seen a great deal of the world, perhaps you can guess somewhat of the story without my telling you."

"Yes, my poor child; yes, unfortunately I have seen too many such unions, entered into without any thought of equality, tyranny on one side, submission on the other. When will men learn that they degrade God's divinest institution in binding two immortal souls, the one to obedience, the other to masterhood, when true happiness lies only in an equal copartnership."

"I have heard," said Laura in a low voice, "that my father loved another woman, that he married my poor mother for her money. He was a handsome young man, and she was a delicate, pretty creature,—she is pretty now to me," the girl's eyes filling with tears, "her poor worn face is so sweet and so patient. My father, I think, was unkind from the beginning ; at first he was angry because only girls were born for some years ; then came a boy, and on him he concentrated all his affection. My whole life long, Mrs. D'Arcy, I have been reproached on account of my sex, as if it were a crime for which I was personally to blame ! "

"How cruelly wrong ! " exclaimed the doctor; "how utterly unjust ! and yet I meet the same thing every day. When will people realize that until the legal stigma under which we rest is removed, until we have fairer chances in life, our very womanhood is a reproach to us. But we will not talk generalities now—go on and tell me how it was that you were permitted to go to Essex college ? "

2*

" Because a wealthy aunt of mine bequeathed a sum of
money for that purpose. My father was bitterly angry
that the thousands were not appropriated to the education
of my brother. ' It was no use to teach girls anything but
how to take care of children,' he said ; ' it was all that they
were good for ! ' " the fair face flushing at the remembered
insult. " Indeed he said so much, that I would have given
up the money had it been in my power to do so; but the
terms of the will were such that I could not alienate it. I
was very happy at Essex, and did well there, but after my
brother's death, my father, who was almost crushed by the
calamity, grew harder and more morose than ever, and
when I came home from college, it seemed as if he had an
especial resentment towards me. There is no use telling
you all I suffered," she said, gloomily, " I was almost
maddened at last, and felt that I could endure it no longer.
I said in the court yesterday morning, that I had been doing general housework all summer, and so I have, working
like a drudge with no hope of escape, and worse, with no
time for study ! ' A girl had better be a good cook than
anything else,' my father said ! If I had been a boy now, all
my fine education might have amounted to something; I
might have earned my own living; as it was, he'd see if he
could not teach me how to be a farmer's wife ; he had no
notion of keeping a fine lady in idleness. It is no use
to repeat it," with a sigh, " I would not have told you so
much, only I wanted you to understand how I was situated. I resolved at last to go away, to relieve my father at
least from the burden of my support; my mother approved
my plan, was willing to have me come to New York to try
to earn my own living, she saw that I could not struggle
on much longer in the life I was leading ; my father, indeed, made her and my sisters more unhappy by his treatment of me; I knew that they would be better off if I were
not there, and so I ran away."

" Ran away ? " repeated Mrs. D'Arcy.

" Yes, my mother conniving, I ran away. She helped

me to escape, and now she must pretend that she does not know where I am ; the very letter I wrote last night, must go to a friend to be given to her secretly, as if it were a crime. Poor, poor mother !" For a moment it seemed as if her emotion would overmaster Laura, but conquering it bravely, she forced a smile and said, " I am here, you see, like a little girl in a fairy tale, to seek my fortune."

" But, my dear, if your mother was wealthy, why are you without resources; I don't understand."

" My mother was married twenty-five years ago, when the law gave all her property to her husband," replied Laura; " my father has absolute control of everything, and hardly gives us what suffices for the simplest wants. Mother gets a little money sometimes from the sale of butter and eggs, and did her best to fit me out for my expedition, poor dear, else I would not have any decent clothes."

" And you came here all alone ? "

" Yes; I expected to reach the city in the afternoon, but the train was delayed by an accident, so that I did not arrive in town till ten o'clock at night."

" Poor child ! and what became of you ? "

" I went first to a decent hotel near the station ; the proprietors refused to give me a night's lodging, because I was a woman, and alone. I had heard of such things, but never before realized, how the curse of our sex follows us everywhere," she said, indignantly.

" Do not say the curse, my dear," remonstrated Mrs. D'Arcy ; " God has not cursed us in our sex. It is man's law that inflicts the injuries upon us."

" And man's brutality," exclaimed Laura, rising in her excitement. " After I had been turned out of the hotel, the clerk followed me, and offered me a night's lodging in his rooms with a hideous leer. I hurried away from the place, knowing not where to go. Three times, in as many blocks, I was insulted, insulted so grossly too !" her eyes flashing at the shameful remembrance. " When God gave us women hearts to resent indignities, why did he not give us strength to avenge them. I so longed to knock those men down ! "

" My child ! my child ! " said Mrs. D'Arcy, taking her hand gently. " You have indeed had great trials, but do not let them make you bitter. God is very good, and some day will redress all these wrongs. And men are not all brutes, my dear; your experience has been unfortunate, but there are many kind noble souls among men. It is the old customs that have come down from less civilized times, that oppress women, rather than any deliberate intention on the part of the men of to-day, some of them are very kind."

" I know it," replied Laura, softening; " that policeman, to whom I at last applied for protection was very good to me ; he seemed really troubled that he had no other place than the station-house to take me to, and made me as comfortable as he could in one of the officers' rooms. And Mr. Heywood has been so true a friend, that I shall never forget what I owe him."

" Frank is a good soul," said Mrs. D'Arcy. " And now, my dear, with what weapon do you propose to conquer for yourself a living in this great city ? "

" You mean, what can I do? I can play passably well on the piano. I speak French and German, and I write a good business hand. My favorite pursuit is drawing, in which they say I have already attained some excellence, and I understand bookkeeping thoroughly; it is by this last knowledge, or as a teacher, that I hope to be able to earn a support, until I can paint sufficiently well to give all my time to that art."

" A very good catalogue of accomplishments," said Mrs. D'Arcy. " Well, my dear, you must stay with me for a few days until I have time to think what I can do for you, and then I will try to find you a cheap and comfortable boarding-place ; meantime, as your trunk will be here presently, you can go out and find your friends, if you like."

"My best friend here," replied Laura, " is Flora Livingston; she spent part of a year at Essex and we got to be quite chums; I think I will go and see her."

"An excellent plan," assented the doctor. "Where does she live?"

"On Fifth avenue; I have forgotten the number, but I have it in my note-book; she is a daughter of Mr. De Peyster Livingston."

"Oh, I know very well where they live; it is not far from here. I will tell you how we will arrange it, I will go out to make some of my visits and come back for you in about an hour, and drive you to your friend's house."

Laura thanked her hostess for this added kindness, and wrapping herself in a warm fur cloak, Mrs. D'Arcy entered the *coupé* that was waiting for her and drove away.

As had been promised, Miss Stanley's trunk arrived, not long after, and by the time Mrs. D'Arcy returned, she was quite ready for the drive. The toilette which she had assumed, though simple, was eminently becoming. It consisted of a well-made black silk dress, and a short cloth sack, trimmed with fur, which had been part of her outfit for the last year at college. A black velvet hat and plume, and neat gloves, obtained lately for her advent into New York, completed her costume, and Laura, although entirely without city style, was a very fine and gracious-looking young woman, as she stepped into the *coupé* and took her seat by the doctor.

A short drive brought them to a handsome house on Fifth avenue, and here Mrs. D'Arcy left her young friend. Laura ascended the broad steps which led to the stately entrance of one of the finest houses in New York. She rang the bell, and while awaiting the answer to her summons stood looking up and down the beautiful street. It was a fine morning, and the rows of tall buildings impressed the young stranger with a sense of wealth and magnificence. "It does not seem as if there could be poverty or misery anywhere," she thought, as she looked at the elegant houses and well-dressed promenaders.

At this moment a gentleman walked slowly by—a tall and handsome man—he looked up with interest at the eager youthful face, that was surveying with so much curiosity a scene so familiar to him, and his first careless glance deepened as he recognized the delicate profile and graceful figure. At the same moment Laura turned towards him. It was Judge Swinton.

She started violently, and changed color, as she recognized him, the judge raised his hat politely, but the courtesy was wasted; the young lady had stepped into the vestibule and was out of sight. He looked after her with an amused and yet puzzled expression, and passed onwards with a smile on his lips.

CHAPTER V.

A HOUSE ON FIFTH AVENUE.

The man-servant who answered Miss Stanley's ring at the bell, informed her that Miss Flora Livingston was at home.

Laura followed him into a wide hall and to a sumptuous drawing-room. She had never seen, hardly even imagined, so splendid an apartment; her feet sank in the soft pile of the heavy carpet; the atmosphere around her was like that of summer, sweet with the perfume of flowers and melodious with the song of birds. The three stately parlors opened into a conservatory, and the fragrant breath of the exotics floated in through the draped door-ways, while a score of unseen warblers chanted their songs. The walls were adorned with pictures; the furniture, the ornaments, all were of the costliest description, and many mirrors reflected the scene in endless graceful pictures. In short, it was such a suit of rooms as wealthy New Yorkers are very familiar with, where good taste and abundant means have united to produce pleasing effects.

Laura had not long to wait; in a few moments there was the flutter of a dress; and a young lady came dancing into the room to meet her; a graceful, exquisite young creature, with that dainty loveliness seen nowhere in such perfection as among the aristocracy of New York.

Regular features, a complexion perfect in pearly fairness, with faint peach bloom on the round cheeks, masses of golden hair arranged artistically in the latest style, large dreamy blue eyes, a mouth finely formed and with great possibilities of passion in its soft curves. She wore a dark-blue morning robe, that was faultlessly and fashionably made, displaying admirably the harmonious outlines of her flexible figure.

"Why, you dear old thing," she cried, eagerly, as she hurried forward to meet her friend, "how glad I am to see you!" a warm embrace closing the sentence.

"And I am ever so glad to see you," replied Laura. "How well you are looking."

"Am I?" asked Flora, languidly. "Oh, I don't know; I have been awfully dissipated this fall, and am rather tired. But come up-stairs to my boudoir; this is such a stupid big place."

"Is it?" said Laura, with an amused smile, glancing about the beautiful room; "I was just thinking that it was remarkably pleasant here."

"Oh, it's well enough, I suppose," said Flora, indifferently. "But we are so much cosier there, and can't be interrupted by any bores of visitors."

Laura followed Flora out of the room, up the broad stairs to a small boudoir which she chose to call "her den," though anything less like a wild-beast's lair would be difficult to imagine. A pretty little place this was, with rose-colored walls, toilette-table draped with lace, and everywhere evidences of the young lady's presence and pursuits—a half-completed drawing, some tangled embroidery, an open novel.

"Sit down on this sofa, Laura; I will make a place for you," said Flora, pushing away a heap of muslins that half covered the cushions. "Now take off your things and tell me all about yourself."

Laura loosened her hat and laid it aside ; as she did so, Flora picked it up. "Where did you get this ?" she asked, holding it up with a contemptuous curl of her pretty lip.

"In Poughkeepsie," smiled Laura. "Why, is it dreadful ? "

"The materials are well enough, but the feather is put in all wrong. May I change it ? "

"Of course you may, and thank you ; though I am afraid you can't make me stylish on any terms."

"Oh, yes I could ! you have great capabilities," replied Flora, regarding her critically. "You look very nice any way, and you could be made stunning. But now tell me how you came here, and what you have been doing since we parted a year and a half ago. I thought you had forgotten me."

"You did not answer my last letter," replied Laura.

"Didn't I ? well, I've been awfully busy," with a look as of a minister of state. "But tell me all. I saw you took honors at last commencement."

"I did very well," replied Laura, "and have been at home since. Now I have come here to earn my living."

"To do what ! " exclaimed Flora, laying down the hat which she had been manipulating, and looking at her friend in amazement. "What put such a thought in your head ? "

"Necessity and inclination both."

"But I thought your father was rich ? "

"He is well off, but you know, Flora, I always had 'ideas,' I cannot see why a daughter should hang on her father for support any more than a son. I have been educated so that I can earn my own living, and intend to do it."

Flora looked at her friend, a light slowly gathering in her eyes. "I believe you can, Laura," she said, "and I've often thought it would be delightful to have something to do, like the men you know; we girls are never expected to do anything except hang about at home, until we get married."

"And to lend all our energies to obtaining a husband. Flora, are you contented with such a prospect? You used to be so bright at college, I remember your compositions were the best in the class."

"And I enjoyed writing them too," replied Flora, with animation.

"And you never write now?"

"Sometimes I do, but what's the use? My friends don't associate with literary people; they think any woman who earns her own living is out of caste. Some of the family even thought it very wrong for pa to allow me to go to Essex; it is not fashionable, you know, and I believe I was considered rather strong-minded in wishing to go."

"That was the real reason why you did not come back to graduate?"

"Yes; pa let me enter college because I teased so, but you remember that aunt of mine, who came to see me while I was there?"

"A tall lady, with glasses, Miss Murray, I think?"

"Yes; well, she brought back terrible reports about the place; she said the training was masculine, that the girls all wanted to vote, and so on. Pa got quite frightened at all this, and when I came home for winter vacation would not let me go back, I was ever so vexed, but it is never any use to try to do anything pa does not approve of."

"I missed you terribly that last term," said Laura.

"You dear soul! But tell me about everybody up there. Does old Sally come out with bunns just as she used?"

For a time the two girls chatted over their college reminiscences, but at last the conversation turned back to personal pursuits.

"And now what have you been doing," asked Laura; 'I have answered all your questions. It is my turn to be catechiser now."

"What have I been doing?" repeated Flora; " oh, very much the same thing always—dressing and dancing and making visits and getting all tired out, and resting awhile, and then doing it all over again."

"Leading the life of a butterfly," said Laura.

"Something rather like it, I suppose; every one seems to think I ought to be perpetually amused, and no one ever likes me to do anything useful."

"I dare say it is very well to be a butterfly for a little while," remarked Laura; " but it must grow rather monotonous after a time, and an old butterfly has always seemed to me a sorry object."

Flora's pretty face clouded. "I have thought of that myself, Laura," she said; "I am as gay as any girl, but sometimes in the morning there is a stupid time when I don't have anything to do; I get tired of reading novels and embroidering, and then I have often wished I had some regular occupation. As for growing old, the thought is dreadful!" with a shudder.

"Yes," replied Laura, " it is always so in the life to which women are so often condemned. La Rochefoucauld says, '*L'enfer des femmes est la vieillesse.*' The hell of woman is Old Age—and no wonder! They are brought up to consider beauty their only power, and the parlor their only battle-field; when they are too old for conquest, what is left for them? Nothing but stupidity and neglect."

Laura spoke with earnest feeling, and Flora was roused to responsive interest. "It is all true," she said; "I have often thought of that dreadful inevitable future, I had rather die than be like some women that I have seen; but what can one do to avoid it."

"Do!" exclaimed Laura, "assert your own independence; insist that a woman has the same right as a man to liberty and individuality; that any woman is entitled to a career for herself, not in the same direction as a man, perhaps, but in such a way as the powers that God has given her would indicate. What is the reason men do not dread middle life? It is because they have some hope for success in the world, and believe that middle life will bring them the crown of their ambition."

Flora's soft eyes kindled with responsive enthusiasm. "I only wish I had something to do," she said, "some definite hope for the future, life sometimes seems to me very tasteless even now. I have often wished so intensely that I could change my sex, and go into business. Of course pa is rich, but then if I were a boy, I should be earning something for myself."

"Your father is a lawyer, I believe."

"Yes."

"And has no son."

"No, and I am sure that he wishes he had one; we girls are not the same, you know."

"There it is!" exclaimed Laura, indignantly. "The inferiority of our sex is forever meeting us. Why is not a girl as good as a boy? She is not so strong, of course, but she is purer and better, possesses the qualities men profess to admire, and can excel in many directions, if she is only permitted. Why should you not study law for instance?"

"Study law!"

"Yes; you could learn so well under your father's protection; as you have money you need not toil at the drudgery of your profession, but you could work up intricate cases and in time win a great name."

"Wouldn't that be splendid!" cried Flora, the color in her cheeks deepening under her excitement. "I often feel that I could be something more than a mere embodiment of frivolity. Oh, how I could labor at anything useful! I get so tired of worsted-work."

"Try it," urged Laura, "ask your father."

All the light faded from Flora's face. "He would refuse, of course," she said. "No, it's no use even to think of it; I should never dare so much as to suggest it."

"It would be worth the trial; your whole future might depend upon it."

"If I can muster the courage I will," replied Flora, "but I know it won't be of the least use."

"Perhaps if you told your mother, she would help you," suggested Laura.

"Oh, no she wouldn't! You are an enthusiast, Laura, and don't understand in the least how our people feel about these things. I think ma once had some ambition, she has shown us some very pretty verses she wrote when she was a young lady, but now she only cares for society, her whole object in life is to get us girls well married; there are six of us, you remember, and do you know sometimes, I have thought I would marry just for a change and to please ma."

"Oh Flora! what a shocking idea!"

"Well, you know I am two years older than you, almost twenty-three, this is my third season out; I was very gay that winter after I left Essex, and last winter too; then besides, I have had the usual round of the watering-places in summer, so I am getting to feel quite a veteran. My sister Maud is past nineteen, and will come out this winter, and I know pa and ma begin to think I ought to marry."

"But do you like any one, Flora?"

"No, at least not in that way. I have had several offers, but I don't care for any man."

"Then don't do it! Oh Flora, don't marry unless you really love some one. And after all, how will this benefit you?"

"Well, there will be some excitement in the change and fuss; but I don't really propose it yet, and if I can study law, I'll lead a life of spinsterhood to the end of my days." She added with a light laugh: "There, that is the lunch bell, now I'll tell you what we will do, you shall stay to luncheon, and after that we will go out together and I'll show you some pictures ; you always loved them."

" Indeed I do, drawing is my favorite art you know."

" Oh, you are going to be a great painter, I see."

" I'm not sure of that," replied Laura. " I'm going to try."

" Well, come down stairs now, if you are ready. By the way, where are you staying ? "

" At Dr. Cornelia D'Arcy's."

" There ! " exclaimed Flora, opening her eyes, " no wonder you are strong-minded. What is she like ? "

" As elegant and stately a lady as you ever saw."

" How I should like to see her ! They say she has an immense practice."

" Yes."

" Now that must be delightful ! How gloriously independent she must be ! "

" She is, and you can be as much so when you are as old, if you will study and practice law."

" I only wish I could, but we must hurry down. Ma does'nt like to have any one late."

In the pleasant morning-room where luncheon was served, Laura found her friend's mother and sister Maud, the younger girls were away at school, Flora explained.

Mrs. Livingston was a small woman with fair hair, and face that must once have been pretty, but it was marred by the look of unrest and anxiety about the eyes as well as the deep lines that time had traced.

Maud was a handsome girl, taller than Flora and with darker hair. Eyes that shone with a sort of defiant light, and mouth, that lacked the amiable sweetness that sat like a charm on Flora's lips.

Although both ladies were perfectly polite to Laura, a subtle instinct taught her, that they looked upon her with disfavor, if not with distrust.

"What are you going to do this afternoon, Flora?" asked Mrs. Livingston when the meal was nearly over.

"I'm going out with Laura to show her some pictures."

"Oh," rather shortly.

"Why? Did you want me for anything?"

"No, only I thought you might drive with me to the Park."

"Oh, that stupid Park!" exclaimed Flora; then as if recollecting herself, "but Laura has not seen it, have you room for her, too?"

"I regret that I cannot offer Miss Stanley a seat," replied Mrs. Livingston, coldly.

"Very well, then, I shall go out with her to the picture-galleries."

At this moment the servant entered the room, bearing on a tray, a basket of choice and beautiful flowers. He went towards Flora with it.

"Mr. Le Roy's compliments," he said.

Mrs. Livingston glanced up with interest. Maud's eyes followed the bouquet with a strange glitter in their depths. Flora took up the card which was attached to the basket.

"They are for Maud," she said, indifferently.

Mrs. Livingston looked excessively annoyed, while a smile of triumph curled the younger sister's lips. There was an awkward silence and then Flora spoke again.

"They are very pretty, and as they are to remain in the family and we can all enjoy them, I suppose it does not matter much to whom they are sent. Come, Laura, the days are short and we had better start on our expedition."

As the two friends went back to the boudoir, Flora explained, "These flowers are from the man they want me to marry; Mr. Ferdinand Le Roy; he is ever so rich, but I don't care for him and I think Maud is really trying to steal him for herself."

Laura's reply took the form of a good-natured protest against the social system which condemned these two young creatures to stifle their aspirations for independence and to bend all their energies to the conquest of a husband.

CHAPTER VI.

LAURA APPLIES FOR A SITUATION.

LAURA Stanley and Flora Livingston were two of the prettiest young ladies that on this pleasant afternoon formed the " Rosebud garden of girls," that adorned Fifth avenue. Glowing cheeks and bright eyes were to be seen everywhere, but the contrast between these two, Flora's perfect style and blonde loveliness, with Laura's simpler dress, and more intellectual charms, made them strikingly noticeable. They both of them enjoyed more than they were perhaps aware, the homage of admiration that follow-ed them; for under certain circumstances and in a certain rank of life, youth and beauty confer an undisputed royalty on women, and the brief queenship thus accorded is in the eyes of most men, ample compensation for all the dis-advantages and humiliations to which are condemned all others of their sex, and even these favored few, when their short reign is over.

The two young ladies made a tour of several picture-galleries, some of them private collections of rare value, to which Flora obtained entrance through an acquaintance with the owners. Laura was perfectly absorbed in study-ing these masterpieces of art, and almost forgot for a time that there was any anxiety or trouble in her present posi-tion. The afternoon slipped away rapidly, and by five o'clock the two friends were on Fifth avenue near Twenty-third street where they must part. Just here they met a tall and fine looking man of about forty, who bowed to Flora with a smile of intimate acquaintance, and after a moment's hesitation turned and joined her. The introduction which followed, informed Laura that it was Mr. Ferdinand Le

Roy, and she looked curiously at this eligible suitor, whose favor was thought so desirable.

Certainly a handsome gentleman, faultlessly dressed, with clear-cut Grecian features, a healthy complexion, and abundant dark hair, lightly touched with gray. He had blue eyes, with a cold steady light in them, his mouth was hard in its expression, with thin smooth-shaven lips, and he wore heavy English side-whiskers.

After a short walk and chat, the three reached Twenty-third street and Laura paused to bid her friend good-bye. Flora had proposed walking to Mrs. D'Arcy's with her, but now she only said:

"You think you can find your way home alone, Laura?"

"Oh yes, easily!"

"Good bye, then, I'll come and see you very soon."

So they parted, and Laura glancing back as she crossed the street, saw Mr. Le Roy bending down with every appearance of devotion, to talk to his fair companion, who seemed to respond with pleased animation to his words.

Mrs. D'Arcy had company to dinner that evening, and visitors dropped in afterwards until the large parlors contained quite a number of persons well known in literature and art. The doctor was very kind in introducing her friends to Laura, but among so many strangers she felt quite alone, and was heartily glad, when, after awhile, Frank Heywood came in. She greeted him with well-pleased cordiality and the two were soon chatting in a corner, like old friends.

The young man had a fund of information on topics in which Laura was interested, and there was about him so absolute an air of purity, that she found herself confiding in him in a way that surprised her when she thought of it afterwards. His handsome melancholy face was very attractive to her, and the tones of his low musical voice fascinated her strangely. He outstayed all other visitors, and, seeing this, was going away when Mrs. D'Arcy stopped him.

" No, Frank; don't go yet; I have something nice to tell Laura, and you shall hear it."

" What is it ? Have you found some work for me ? " asked Laura, eagerly.

" I think so," replied the doctor ; " some time ago I was talking with Mr. Joel Bolton, a wealthy merchant here, and he told me that, if I could send to him a young woman who understood book-keeping, and was well recommended, he would give her a situation as clerk. Would you like to try the place, Laura ? "

" Oh, indeed I should," cried Laura, her face glowing with pleasure.

" Is it Mr. Bolton of the firm of Clamp & Bolton ? " asked Heywood.

" Yes; why do you look so grave about it, Frank ? What is the matter ? "

" I am exceedingly surprised, that is all."

" Isn't it a good place ? " asked Laura.

" Very ; it is one of the largest iron firms in New York. I shall be heartily glad if they will receive a young lady into their establishment. It is an innovation, but one that ought to be made."

" I think they will," said Mrs. D'Arcy. " I have not spoken to Mr. Bolton about it very lately, but he was quite positive, when we talked of the place. So if you like it, Laura, I will send you down to them to-morrow, with a letter of introduction. The pay won't be very high, probably, not more than twelve dollars a week at first."

" Oh, that will be more than my most sanguine hopes," said Laura, " I have so wished that I might have some such occupation as this, which I could depend upon steadily, and not have to give lessons. I can still go on with my drawing in the evening."

" I sincerely hope you will get the place, Miss Stanley," said Frank. " What time will you be at their office ? "

" When had I better go ? " asked Laura, turning to Mrs. D'Arcy.

3

"About eleven, I should say," replied the doctor.

Very soon after this, Heywood took his leave, and Laura thanking her hostess warmly for her kind interest, went to her room. For some time she could not sleep in the happy excitement over this pleasant prospect of earning an honest living, and her dreams were tinted with the golden light of the hope that had arisen.

The next day, before eleven o'clock, Laura was on her way down town, bearing a letter of introduction from Mrs. D'Arcy to her friend Mr. Bolton. She had assumed her simple black dress and fur-trimmed sack, and was as intelligent and modest looking a young woman, as one might wish to see. For half an hour before leaving the house, she had been studying a map of New York, and being gifted with good common sense, and a fair portion of that peculiar faculty which enables people to find the path in strange localities, she had no difficulty after leaving the cars, in making her way to Cliff street, where a time-stained sign bearing the names "Clamp and Bolton" informed her that she had reached her destination."

As she looked up at the large warehouse and then in at the offices filled with men, Laura felt her heart sink somewhat. It seemed such a bold undertaking for a woman to attempt an entrance here; however, summoning all her courage, she opened the door and went in. An elderly man who was writing at a comfortably fitted up desk, seemed to be the person most at liberty, and going up to him, Laura asked for Mr. Bolton.

"Back office," replied the clerk, scarcely glancing up.

Laura walked hesitatingly towards the end of the store. A tall broad-shouldered young man who was talking with the cashier at his desk, turned as she came near him. Her puzzled face arrested his attention.

"What can I do for you?" he asked, kindly.

"I would like to see Mr. Bolton," replied Laura.

"I will show you to him; this way, Miss."

He walked on a little before her; Laura looking at him,

thought what a stalwart fellow he was, with such a kind
face too, ruddy with health, shaded with dark hair and
moustache, and lit by earnest brown eyes. As he opened
the door for her to pass in, he took off his hat respectfully,
and for a moment, his glance met hers; there was a shade
of interest in it, but there was none of that impertinent
curiosity that Laura had already encountered so often
since her arrival in New York.

Mr. Joel Bolton sat in his private office, a portly and
substantial man, of fifty or so; his surroundings were eminently comfortable, and as Laura looked at the handsome
Brussels carpet, the black-walnut desk and cheerful fire in
the open grate, it seemed to her, that amid such appoint-
ments, a woman was not wholly out of place.

"Good morning," said Mr. Bolton, looking up with
perceptible annoyance : "What can I do for you?"

"I have a letter from Mrs. D'Arcy," replied Laura,
presenting it.

The look of annoyance visibly deepened on Mr. Bolton's face as he took the note. "Sit down," he said, shortly.

Laura sank into a chair, her heart beating violently.
Mr. Bolton read over the few words of the letter, slowly,
twice; but rather as if he were gathering his thoughts
together, than as if he did not understand the contents.

"I am very sorry," he said at last, "but I can't give
you the place."

"Why not?" asked Laura; "is it filled?"

"No."

"Oh, why not then? If you will only try me, I think
you will find that I can do the work," she said, eagerly.

"I dare say," he replied, "that you are well qualified
and all that sort of thing, but I can't take you."

"But surely you will give me some reason," said Laura
rising, her cheeks glowing with excitement.

"Well, then; it is on account of your sex."

"Because I am a woman!"

"Yes."

"I should not have come to intrude upon your time," she said, haughtily, "but I was told by Mrs. D'Arcy, that you assured her that my sex would be no objection."

"So I did, so I did," replied Mr. Bolton, looking more and more annoyed and even angry; "I was talking with the doctor one day and was fool enough to be persuaded by her to say, I would try a girl in this place. I felt I was rash at the time, and when I came to think it over since, I knew the idea was absurd. We can't have a woman in the office: it would be ridiculous," he added, testily.

"You might at least have spared that insult," said Laura, hotly. "Good morning, sir."

She left the room, her brain on fire, the blood tingling in her veins; there was an angry glitter in her eyes, a hot flush on her cheeks; she felt as if she had received a blow in the face.

The gentleman who had shown her in was still in the outer office. He looked at her curiously, and as he caught her expression his own changed. She hurried past him, her lips pressed tightly together; in her excitement, she did not notice that she had dropped a lace tie, which she wore about her neck and which she had loosened on first entering the warm office. The gentleman picked it up and stepped after her.

"Excuse me, Miss, but I think this is yours."

Laura turned as if she feared some new outrage; then meeting those clear brown eyes fixed upon her with a look of so much sympathy—"Thank you," she said, and as if the utterance of the word had broken a spell, her own eyes filled with tears.

"Can I be of any assistance to you," asked the gentleman, with wistful earnestness, as if he longed to testify his sympathy in words; "can I stop a car or a stage for you?"

"I am much obliged, but I think I can find my way alone," replied Laura. Then with a sudden look of relief— "Oh, there is a friend of mine."

Frank Heywood at the moment appeared, coming down the street, and with a hasty salutation to the gentleman, Laura sprang to his side. He caught her hand as she met him and held it firmly, but rather as if he would so calm her agitation than as an act of gallantry.

Laura clung to his arm struggling hard to conquer her emotion. Frank was silent after the first greeting until they reached a corner, then he said:

" Which way do you wish to go ? "

"I don't care," replied Laura, " only let us walk fast. I feel as if I must move rapidly to help me to grow calm." They went on quickly towards Broadway, making their way as speedily as they could, through the thronged street. The motion soothed the excited girl, her heart grew more regular in its pulsations and presently she was sufficiently composed to say : " You can perhaps guess what has happened, Mr. Heywood."

" Yes, you have been refused the place."

" And do you know why ? "

" I can tell that also ; I think ; you have met again the disability of your sex."

"Yes ! I have been rejected because I am a woman ! Not because I am stupid or incompetent, not because I have not good references, but because I am a woman ! Mr. Heywood, you do not know what we women feel, when we meet an insult like this. It is bitterly hard to bear! "

" I do understand it better than you imagine, Miss Stanley," replied Frank gravely ; " my occupations since I have been in New York have been such as to lead me to see a great deal of the horrible injustice under which your sex suffers. I know that in this great city, youth and beauty are a curse, except to the favored daughters of the rich. I have seen that women are shut out from every means of earning a living that is really remunerative, crowded into certain narrow walks, which, in consequence, are so thronged that the poor creatures are forced to work for the merest pittance. Miss Stanley, I think I realize somewhat of the hopeless disadvantage under which women labor, and my heart has been full of the deepest sympathy for you in the struggle which awaits you."

The young man spoke in tones of strong feeling ; Laura felt the sincerity of every word. "Thank you," she said ; "if more men felt as you do, this state of things would not last long."

"Very few men do realize the scope of woman's needs," replied Frank ; "they think that the agitation of woman suffrage is only the work of a few discontented souls. They do not understand that the demand for political equality is but one of the public utterances of a great dumb cry, that goes up from millions of hearts."

While they had been speaking, the two young people had been walking aimlessly, though rapidly, up Broadway ; now Laura said,—"But Mr. Heywood, I am taking you quite out of your way, I fear. I might walk, I know not how far, if you continued to express views that so fully agree with mine. Don't let me detain you too long."

"I am at your service, Miss Stanley. I came out this morning on purpose to meet you ; have you any plans ? anywhere that you would like to go ? "

"You will think me rash, if I tell you what I had thought of doing. When I came out of that man Bludgett's house so hurriedly, the other night, I left a valuable book there, one of a set of Shakespeare, given me as a prize at school ; I should like to go and get it, and to see how Mrs. Bludgett is."

"You are a plucky young lady to think of doing such a thing," said Heywood, with a look of undisguised admiration. "But I think you may venture safely, especially if you will let me go with you."

"Oh, thank you ! If you only will," replied Laura, "I shall be so much obliged to you." And the two were soon going westward, to the dingy street in which the VIIIth Ward politician abode.

CHAPTER VII.

CONJUGAL DISCIPLINE.

WHEN the two young people approached Mr. Bludgett's house, Frank Heywood suggested that he should remain outside, while Laura went in.

"So long as I am on guard, I don't think anything very terrible can happen to you," he said; "and I know that you can talk with Mrs. Bludgett more easily without me than with me."

Laura thanked him for his thoughtful suggestion and leaving the young journalist walking up and down like a sentry on duty, crossed the street, ascended the rickety steps and sounded a peal on the brass knocker. After a moment, the door was cautiously opened, and the sharp face of a young woman peered around it.

"Is Mrs. Bludgett in?" asked Laura.

"Yes."

"Can I see her?"

"I suppose so;" after a moment's hesitation, "come up stairs."

Laura followed the girl to the sitting-room. There she found Mrs. Bludgett, wrapped in a large shawl and cowering near the fire with a showily-covered novel in her hand. Her face was paler even than when Laura had last seen her, a large patch of plaster was spread on her temple, and the blood had settled in black circles under her eyes.

"Well, Mrs. Bludgett, how do you do?" said Laura, coming forward with a cordial smile.

The woman started at the sound of the voice, and a pleasant look crossed her worn face.

"Oh, Miss Stanley! you have really come back to see me!"

"To be sure I have; I came to ask how you are, and to get my book."

" Yes, I know, I seen it here after you was gone, and put it away safe. Sit down please."

" Thank you," and Laura took a chair. " But what is the matter? you don't look well."

" I—I had a fall," stammered Mrs. Bludgett, " I ain't been very well; Rhody here is taking care of me."

Thus introduced as it were, Laura turned to the young woman; her face was worn and thin, yet there was a suggestion of vanished beauty in its outlines and in the abundant black hair clustered over the small well-shaped head, the eyes were large, dark, yet full of a hungry appeal, and the lines about the mouth were deep drawn and drooping, while the loss of two front teeth disfigured a set otherwise white and regular.

Laura said to her, pleasantly : " It is very kind of you I'm sure to come to Mrs. Bludgett when she is so lonely."

" I can't be here only daytimes; I work nights," replied Rhoda.

" That must be rather hard ? "

" It's all hard," said the girl, sullenly; and she walked away to the window.

" Did you find your friends? " asked Mrs. Bludgett, eagerly, of Laura.

" Yes, I found very kind friends."

" Where are you stopping ? "

" On Twenty-third street."

" No; don't tell me the number," interrupted Mrs. Bludgett quickly ; " I'm sorry I even asked you."

" It does not matter," replied Laura, " as I shall only remain where I am for a day or two. But I must go now, I have a friend waiting outside for me."

" Oh, is he with you? " asked the girl, suddenly, from the window.

" Who, Mr. Heywood ? Yes."

" Do you know him, Rhody ? " asked Mrs. Bludgett.

" Know him ? Indeed I do ! " a sparkle coming into her eyes. " Don't you know how good he was that night when we was 'pulled?'" then checking herself, "but the young lady does not understand."

"But I can understand," said Laura, eagerly; "do tell me all about it; I should like so much to hear your story."

"Yes, tell her Rhody," urged Mrs. Bludgett. "She is real kind. She might like to hear it too, seein' she's a friend of Mr. Heywood's."

"It ain't much to tell," said Rhoda; "a great many girls could tell you a story like mine. I came here four years ago from the country. I was a good plain sewer and tried to get work. You don't know what that means. It means that I could only earn about three dollars a week. I was starved; I slept in a garret; I had no fire in winter, no warm clothes. Oh, well, it's no use telling you all, I went at last to work in a concert-saloon; you don't know what that is? It's a place in a cellar where men get things to drink, where there is music, and girls to wait on the men. I was one of the girls; what I earned there helped me a little, and I had got so I didn't care much what I did "—with a dark frown, and a sudden catch of the breath —" well, one night the police 'pulled' the place, that's what we call it; came in and arrested all the girls."

"Only the girls!" exclaimed Laura.

"Of course, only the girls; they never take the men, that is, the men-customers. They arrested the boss, but they never touched any of the men who came there, night after night, and supported the place with their money."

"And what did they do to you?"

"Carried us all to the station-house and locked us up over night. It was in January, an awful cold night; there was no fire and all of us had on low-necked dresses. Oh, you look shocked at that; it was the rule of the place. The boss wouldn't have us unless we came that way. It wasn't so bad in the saloon for a strong girl. It was hot enough in there, though it was draughty. But if we were ever so sick we had to come 'low,' that's what we called it. There was Jessie Burns, she was dying of consumption,

3*

and coughed horrid. One night she said to the boss,
'Can't I wear just a little scarf round my throat, it's so
sore?" He looked at her neck—it was very white, poor
soul ; 'No,' says he, 'them shoulders of your'n are worth
a dollar a night to me, and might be worth more to you if
you was a mind ; no, you can't come covered up like an
old woman.' So she came 'low,' until one night she was
took with a fit of coughing, and broke a blood-vessel, and
died in a few hours. But that ain't what I was goin' to
tell you ; " said Rhoda, bringing herself back with a start.

"It was about Mr. Heywood," suggested Laura.

"Yes, this night, when we was 'pulled' as I told you, it was
dreadful cold, we had only light shawls and cloaks, that we
could make out to run round to the saloon with, but when
we came to be in a cold place all night it was pretty hard.
We was huddled up together, shivering, when this young
gentleman came in to make up the case for the papers, and
he was so kind! when he saw how we was, he turned to the
cop, I mean the policeman, and he talked to him ! I tell you
it was grand to hear him !" her eyes glowing at the remembrance. "He said it was a disgrace to leave us there in
the cold ; he said if we wasn't made warm and comfortable,
he'd put an item in the paper about it. Oh, you better
believe they changed quick enough ! they made a good fire
in the court-room, and brought us up there for the night,
and then Mr. Heywood said he'd keep names out of the
paper for any of us that wanted it ; some of them didn't
care, you know, but some of us had friends at home, and we
were so thankful not to have them know of this. Oh, he
was so good and kind, never chaffed us, nor swore at us
like some of the other newspaper-men. If he had been the
brother of every one of us, he couldn't have been gentler."

"He's a noble fellow, I know," said Laura," but what
did they do to you afterwards ? "

"Do ? nothing, of course ; let us off the next morning."

"But you were out of work at the saloon."

"Oh, Lord bless you, no ! why, I work there yet ! "

"But I don't understand," said Laura; "why did they arrest you, if they were not going to close the place?"

"Well, just to make a fuss, and pretend the police were what they call very efficient. They had a new super. just then."

"A what?"

"A new superintendent, head of police; whenever we have a new one, they always 'pull' some places, it looks so good, but it never makes no difference; they go on the same."

Laura had learned a new lesson in city management, but interested as she was in the girl's story, she felt that she ought not to keep Frank Heywood too long waiting, and presently she rose to go; Rhoda brought the book which Mrs. Bludgett had carefully put away, and Laura bidding the two women a friendly good-bye, went out to rejoin her friend.

As the young people disappeared down the street, Rhoda, who was looking after them, said : "That's as nice a couple as ever I see."

"I wouldn't wonder if it was a match," replied Mrs. Bludgett.

"It would be a nice one, only he's a trifle short for her," said Rhoda; and indeed, the plume of Laura's hat was as high as the crown of Frank's "wide-awake."

"It would be just like a story, if he should marry her," said Mrs. Bludgett, sententiously. "She's a good young lady, and he's a good young man. But then I told you about Judge Swinton," she added, anxiously.

"I know," exclaimed Rhoda, with a deepening of the hard lines on her face ; "but he shan't have her, now that I know she is a friend of Mr. Heywood's ; as sure as I live I will put a stop to that!"

"I hope you can, Rhody, but it's all a worry and a puzzle," said Mrs. Bludget; with a weak sigh, "and now let's go on with the story you was reading before she came in; it 's a comfort to forget all these troubles for a little while."

"I don't know as to that," said Rhoda. "I can't forget

them, but I'll go on if you like," and she took up again the showily-backed book, and resumed the account of the wonderful adventures of " Berenice the Beautiful," the heroine of an astounding tale of mystic combinations and thrilling adventures.

The day wore on, and after awhile Rhoda went away to prepare for her night's work, taking her departure indeed somewhat earlier than was necessary, because Mrs. Bludgett was afraid her husband might come in, and he did not like to find any company with her.

Left to herself, Mrs. Bludgett, as evening approached, made shift to prepare a meal, though it was evidently a pain to move about much, for she rested her head on her hand many times, as if dizzy or faint. By slow degrees she carefully laid the table for two, and then placed upon it cold meat, bread, cheese, and at last some potatoes which she had boiled, and having no farther excuse for waiting, sat down alone. She ate but little, and always with an anxious listening air, as if expecting some one. When she had finished, she cleared away what remained of her own repast, and then having arranged the things neatly on the table, and covered up some potatoes to keep them warm, sat down again by the fire. She was evidently much tired by what she had done, for she rested for some moments quite still, with her head on her hand, and her eyes closed, as if exhausted.

It was now eight o'clock, and after awhile, arousing herself, Mrs. Bludgett trimmed the kerosene lamp, placed it near her on the table and began to read again. The story unfolded its wonderful scenes, but evidently her attention was but half absorbed; she still listened to every passing noise as the time went on, but it was ten o'clock before there was the rattle of the latch-key in the front door and then the sound of the heavy step on the stair, for which the wife had been so long waiting. Her face grew perceptibly paler as she hurriedly hid her book and looked up to greet the entrance of her lord and master.

Mr. Bludgett had evidently been drinking hard; as he came in, his flushed face and unsteady step plainly indicated this. His black eyebrows were drawn together in a dark frown over his bloodshot eyes, and his first words were an oath.

"Ah, you old hag! you are there, eh!"

"Yes, John, yes. I set up for you," replied the woman, in trembling tones. "And here is your supper all ready. I kept some potatoes nice and warm for you."

With shaking hands she lifted the plate from the stove and moved to place it on the table. But the man strode heavily forward and dashed it from her grasp, shivering the dish, and scattering the contents over the carpet.

"Blast you!" he said, fiercely; "I don't want any of your slops, you can't fool me that way. Oh, you pretend to be a good wife do you? do you?" repeating the phrase with a horrible sneering emphasis, and ending it with a vile word.

The woman cowered away and sank into her chair, looking up at him, with wild, appealing eyes. "No, John, no, don't say that, John."

"I will say that, and as much more as I choose, and do something besides," he added, fiercely, seizing her by the shoulders and dragging her up out of the chair. "Who was here this morning, eh? oh, you are scared at that, are you?" shaking her roughly. "Yes, I saw 'em. I was near by when they went away, that nice girl from the country and that young jackanapes of a newspaper man, blast him! Ah, I'll have my revenge on him yet!" with a horrible oath.

"Well, John, it was not my fault if they did come here."

"It wasn't your fault indeed, you white-faced cat, you! It wasn't your fault that she got off the other night, I suppose. Now where is she staying?"

"I don't know."

"Don't know! yes, you do! And you shall tell me, do you hear? you shall tell me!" and he shook her with both hands until she swayed and staggered in his powerful grasp.

"Indeed, indeed, John, I don't know," she gasped. "It is on Twenty-third street somewhere, that is all I know."

"Whereabouts on Twenty-third street?"

"I don't know; oh, please don't, when I don't know, indeed I don't!"

"You do know, and you *shall* tell me if I have your heart's blood, blast you!" he cried, with a menacing hiss, and bringing his face close down to hers, holding her always by the shoulders.

"Oh, John! please let me go; truly, truly I don't know!"

"Tell me, you hag! Tell me!" he shouted, "or I'll break every bone in your body!"

As he spoke he raised one hand and seized her by the hair, then lifting the other hand, his eyes glowing red with passion, he dealt her a heavy blow across the face. She would have fallen with the force of the shock, had not his cruel grasp upheld her; as it was she swayed away with a low cry, the blood flowing from a gash in her cheek, the rest of her countenance ghastly white with fear.

"Now will you tell?"

"I can't! Oh I can't!" groaned the wretched woman.

"See how you like that, then!"

He struck her again and again as he spoke, his dark brow knotted, his face purple with his insane anger. At first the poor creature replied with wild appeals for mercy, but these died away presently, and there was no sound as he flung her from him to the floor. She fell and lay without motion, but even yet, the man's fury was not spent, he kicked the prostrate form more than once, his heavy boots making the strokes almost murderous.

Reader, is this scene too horrible? are your dainty sensibilities shocked at such a recital? Think then if you shrink from the mere description, what the reality must be, and say not that it is unnatural or overdrawn, when day

after day, our police records are full of the accounts of the
wounds, the hurts, the death-blows, that women receive
from brutal husbands.

When Mr. Bludgett had sated his blind rage, he staggered to the sofa, near by, and throwing himself upon it
was soon in a heavy sleep. After a long period of insensibility his wife awoke to consciousness, at first only partial,
but slowly, to a full knowledge of pain and weakness, and
woe. Gradually, and with long periods of rest, she got up
from the floor and crawled to her seat by the fire; dizzy
and faint, she seemed for some moments unable to move,
then the loud stertorous breathing of her husband arrested
her attention. She looked around at him, an expression,
not of anger or of hatred, but of anxiety, crossed her face,
and tottering painfully into the other room, she brought a
blanket and with it covered the sleeping man.

CHAPTER VIII.

NEW FRIENDS.

THE pleasure of seeing Frank Heywood, and then the
visit to Mrs. Bludgett had helped to quiet Laura's excitement, and for a time, taken her from the contemplation
of her own disappointment; but alone in the quiet of the
library at Mrs. D'Arcy's, the bitterness of the trial through
which she had passed quite overwhelmed her, and when the
doctor at last came home, her first glance at the face of her
young friend told her that something was wrong.

"What is the matter, Laura?" she asked, anxiously;
"you have not had any trouble, I hope?"

"I have been refused the place!"

"Been refused! Why?"

"Because I am a woman!"

Mrs. D'Arcy looked excessively annoyed. "After Mr.
Bolton's many promises, this is outrageous! Come, my
dear, tell me all about it."

Laura told her story ; the doctor heard with sympathetic interest, and when it was over did her best to console her young *protégée* for the disappointment. " It is a flagrant cruelty ! " she said, " men insist that women shall not have equal chances in life with them until they have shown equal capacity, and then they refuse to them any opportunity to prove what powers they really possess."

" It seems a hopeless prospect," said Laura. " Sometimes I too feel like joining the cry that has gone up from so many women and uttering the useless wish that I were a man."

" No, my dear, no," said the doctor, " don't give up your hope because of one disappointment. It has been in some ages the worst curse that could fall on a human soul, to be imprisoned in a female form, but already something has been accomplished towards the changes that must inevitably come. Once women were not educated, were not admitted to any professions, were not considered capable of attending to any business ; now their education has much improved, though it is not yet what it should be; two great professions are open to them, medicine and journalism, not with equal chances it is true, but still they can obtain admittance where once all doors were closed, and the time is surely drawing near, when the last barrier shall be removed and the civil and political equality of women shall be acknowledged. Every one of us can do something to help on that time ; you can yourself do much."

" How ? " asked Laura eagerly. " I have dreamed and hoped that I might do something, but the way seems all dark now."

" You have your own favorite occupation in which you already show great promise and to which you can devote all your energies. This country has not yet produced a really great woman-painter, why should you not achieve a triumph for yourself and your sex in that art ? "

" That has been my ambition," replied Laura.

" And it is your true path in life, doubtless ; I can at

once obtain admission for you to the Academy of Design, and you can go on with your studies there, at the same time giving lessons in drawing which will support you. This will be better, perhaps, than the situation which you have lost."

Laura was much comforted by these kind words, and after talking over her plans freely with her hostess, it was decided that she should the next day advertise for pupils, while Mrs. D'Arcy promised to use her powerful influence to obtain them for her. In the course of the conversation, Laura mentioned that Frank Heywood had come to meet her after she left the store.

"How good that was of him!" said Mrs. D'Arcy. "Frank has such a noble heart!"

"Have you known him long?" asked Laura, who was interested to learn more of this new friend.

"Some twelve years," replied Mrs. D'Arcy. "His history is a very strange one; he has had trials and misfortunes that would have broken almost any spirit but his."

"Are his parents living?"

"No, they have been long dead, and he has no brothers or sisters, no relations, indeed, nearer than an uncle, who lives in North Carolina."

"Poor fellow, how alone he must be!"

"More alone than you can imagine. There are circumstances in his life that must always make him desolate. He has uncommon abilities, and his aim is very high, I only hope he will have the strength to make the sacrifice necessary to its accomplishment."

"I admire him ever so much!" said Laura, heartily.

"He is as true and faithful a friend as you could have," said Mrs. D'Arcy, with a slight emphasis on the word friend.

That evening as Laura sat with the doctor in the study assisting her in addressing circulars for the Medical College, of which she was President, some cards were brought

in. As Mrs. D'Arcy looked them over, a pleased expression
crossed her face.

"Mr. and Mrs. George Bradford, and Mr. Guy Bradford," she said; "now, my dear, you will have an opportunity of seeing my model couple. These are people of the
right sort ; Mr. Bradford is of mixed New York and New
England ancestry ; on his father's side he is descended from
John Alden, and Priscilla Muller, the lovers of the May-
flower; on his mother's, he is connected with the old Knick-
erbockers. Mrs. Bradford is a New Yorker by birth, belonging to one of the best families here. They are both
people of thought and culture, and they are such a happy
couple ! although they were married before woman's rights
were ever talked of, they have been equal partners in all
things, and are lovers yet. Come, my dear, I should like
to have you meet them."

Laura offered to remain where she was, until she had
finished the circulars, but Mrs. D'Arcy would not hear of
this, and the two presently went to the parlor together.

There they found a tall, fine-looking old gentleman,
with white hair and kindly blue eyes, and an old lady,
whom Laura thought absolutely the most motherly-looking
person she had ever seen ; there was such a pleasant smile
about her mouth, and such a genial expression on her
healthy plump face. But Laura's observations on the
elder people were cut shorter than they perhaps otherwise
would have been, when Mr. Guy Bradford was presented,
and she recognized instantly, the broad-shouldered, brown-
eyed gentleman, who had been so kind to her in the
morning. Her color rose as she recognized him, and he
met her with something of the manner of an old acquaintance.

Quite naturally the elder people placed themselves near
enough for a friendly chat, while the younger gentleman
took a chair beside Laura.

"Miss Stanley," he said, " you are perhaps surprised to
meet me so soon again, but Mrs. D'Arcy is an old friend of

my mother's, and when I heard that you were staying here,
I could not help wishing to learn how you had fared after
this morning."

"You are very kind," replied Laura, "but how did you
find out that I was here?"

"I am in the employment of Clamp and Bolton, have
principal charge of the sales there, and just after you left,
Mr. Bolton called me into the office. He knew that my
mother was a friend of Mrs. D'Arcy's and he seemed to
think that he ought to explain his refusal of your services.
He is not a bad man, and was really sorry."

"Not a bad man, perhaps, only profoundly convinced
that women are entirely incompetent to do anything
useful," said Laura, hotly, her indignation of the morning
coming back strongly.

Guy Bradford looked at her, a troubled expression
clouding his earnest eyes. "It seems hard," he said "the
place you would have had there could have been filled
perfectly well by any well-qualified woman, and of course
there was no real ground for refusing, except that it was
unusual to see a lady in a large wholesale establishment
down town."

"It is the old story. Women never have been given
equal chances with men, therefore they never ought to be;
this is no argument, of course, since the same objection
could be, and has been, made against every improvement
since the world began, but it serves as a great stumbling-
block in our way." Laura spoke impetuously and rapidly,
but at the end broke off suddenly and turned to her
companion with a smile. "But you will think me terribly
fierce, Mr. Bradford, to be talking so strongly on this
subject."

"Not at all, Miss Stanley, you are quite right," said
Guy, earnestly. "Indeed you will find me as warm an
advocate of the equality of the sexes as you could wish. I
am no reformer, it is true; I am only a hard working business man, but I have been brought up in the right way on

these points by both my parents, and if the question of giving suffrage to your sex ever comes to the ballot-box you will find my vote on the right side. It seems to me a very one sided government, which refuses to my mother and sister all voice, while it professes to honor goodness and purity."

"What is that, Guy?" asked Mrs. Bradford, turning to him pleasantly; "are you two talking woman-suffrage already?"

"Probably," observed Mr. Bradford, with a slight twinkle in his eye. "Guy knows too well what the politics of this house are, not to show his colors at once."

"And our party is the party of the future," said Mrs. D'Arcy; "so that Guy is quite right, and both these young people may yet be in Congress under its banners."

"Not I," said Guy; "Miss Stanley may go, but I shall be an iron-man to the end of my days."

"And I," declared Laura, "shall prefer the quiet paths of art and study, to the angry strife of politics."

"Certainly," explained Mrs. D'Arcy; "Miss Stanley is to be a great painter, and hopes to have a commission to paint one of the panels of the Capitol."

After the laugh which followed this, the conversation turned on art, and became more general.

Other visitors dropped in as the evening wore on, but Frank Heywood did not appear, though Laura looked more than once towards the door, hoping to see the slender form and sad face she had learned to like so well.

Always after she turned away disappointed from one of those quick glances of expectation, she met Guy Bradford's eyes fixed upon her with a look of interest, almost of anxiety; this earnest gaze affected her strangely, and she felt her color deepen each time that she met it. At last he uttered the unspoken question: "Will you think me very impertinent, if I ask you if you are expecting any one, Miss Stanley?"

"Not exactly expecting," said Laura. "No, I have only thought once or twice that I saw a friend coming."

"I am sorry that you are disappointed, and yet no—"

he said, quickly. "Truth forces me to confess that, for my own sake, I am a little glad. There, mother and father are going; may I come to see you again, Miss Stanley?"

"Yes, certainly." But as Laura uttered the words, her eyes dropped and her cheeks flushed under his glance.

CHAPTER IX.

A FASHIONABLE SCHOOL.

MRS. D'ARCY was faithful to her promises to Laura, and within a few days had procured for her two pupils. One of these was Bessie Bradford, the daughter of the kindly old couple, to whom the doctor had spoken of her young friend's attainments on the evening of their call. It was arranged that Laura should give this young lady drawing-lessons on Wednesday and Saturday afternoons, at four, the terms to be a dollar an hour. The other scholar was a daughter of one of Mrs. D'Arcy's patients, but was only to receive one lesson a week on the same terms. An advertisement for a situation was also printed in the Trumpeter, and while awaiting a reply to this, Laura went one morning with Mrs. D'Arcy to the Academy of Design, where her fine drawings procured her immediate admission as a student.

On the next day, when she came down to breakfast, an answer to her advertisement awaited her. Glancing it over, Laura handed it to her friend.

"At Mr. Glitter's," said the doctor reading it; "that should be a good place; he has one of the largest and most fashionable young-ladies' schools in the city."

"Had I better go there at once?" asked Laura.

"No, my dear; I think it will be best for me to go for you."

"Oh, Mrs. D'Arcy! how kind you are!"

"Yes, it will be much better for me to go than for you.

I can recommend you so much more strongly than you can recommend yourself. I will take some of your pictures with me."

Laura was very grateful for this new proof of kindness, the more so as she shrank from encountering again the ordeal she had already found so unpleasant, and warmly expressed her thanks.

Not long after, just as the doctor was about entering her carriage to start on her round of duties, a young lady was shown into the parlor, and Laura was informed that Miss Livingston would like to see her. She found the pretty blonde attired in the most tasteful of walking-suits, and standing at the window, looking eagerly out.

"Do tell me," she exclaimed, almost as soon as she saw Laura; "is that Mrs. D'Arcy?"

"Yes."

"What a splendid looking woman!"

"Isn't she!" responded Laura, warmly.

"She doesn't look in the least as I thought she did."

"Why, what did you expect to see?"

"Oh well, I thought she would be old-maidish, and wear spectacles and a very short dress."

"Like the conventional caricatures of strong-minded women; but Flora havn't you yet found out that these dreadful creatures have no existence except in a comic paper? I have met several of the best-known advocates of woman suffrage in this city since I have been staying here, and I assure you they look just like any other ladies of equal wealth and position."

"Do they? Well, I never saw any of them, but Mrs. D'Arcy is certainly a very grand-looking lady. And now tell me all your adventures; have you found a place?"

The friends took their seats on a sofa, and Laura described to Flora somewhat of the events of the past few days, not giving the name of the firm that had refused to employ her, but relating the incident. Flora listened, catching Laura's enthusiasm, as she always did when she was with her.

"What a jolly idea it would have been, if you had gone in there as clerk," she said. "How I should have enjoyed coming to see you and finding you perched upon a high stool with a pen behind your ear!"

"I only wish it could have been," replied Laura; "but as that is all over, I must teach drawing for my living; don't you want to take lessons?"

"Of course I do," exclaimed Flora; "and that will be so nice! You shall come twice a week to teach me, and then I can see you. I'll ask pa about it this very evening.'"

"Do; I shall enjoy giving you lessons ever so much. I remember you drew very nicely."

"Tolerably, though I had no such gift as you had. But Laura, doesn't it seem dreadfully dreary to go on giving drawing-lessons all your life?"

"Not at all," replied Laura cheerfully; "but I hope I shall not always be merely a drawing-teacher."

"Oh, you think you will get married and so give it up."

"No, I do not!" exclaimed Laura, quite indignantly. "Of course I may marry some day—why shouldn't I? But I do not intend to allow that to interfere with my profession, I hope I shall not always be obliged to give lessons, but when I can sell my pictures for good prices, it will not be necessary."

"I envy you, Laura," said Flora, with a little sigh; "you have the pluck, I truly believe, to carry out your plans; for my part, I have not even the courage to try to do anything.

"You have not begun to study law, yet?" asked Laura, with a smile.

"No, though I have really thought a good deal of what you said the other day; once or twice I have almost made up my mind to ask pa about it; but you don't know him; when you do, you will realize that it is not very easy to ask him anything that he would not like."

Laura did not urge her friend any further; she had her own plans as to what she would do when she could see Flora more frequently, and with the sanguine hope of youth believed that she could accomplish much by her influence. The two young ladies chatted for some time, and at last, as Flora rose to go, she said, abruptly:

"How did you like Mr. Le Roy, Laura?"

"He is a fine-looking man," replied Laura.

"Isn't he, and so stylish!"

"Very."

"But—what is it, Laura? you do not like him, I can see; why not?

"Do you like him?" asked Laura.

"Well, he is very agreeable."

"Doubtless; I should fancy he would be very pleasant as an occasional visitor, though he has a sort of lordly air about him, that I should not wholly like; but Flora, tell me what you think; have you seen him since?"

"Yes, Maud and I went to a ball, night before last, and he was there. You know he walked home with me that afternoon?"

"Yes."

"Well, I was very pleasant, and when we reached the house, he came in and made quite a call. The next day he sent me a bouquet, and at the ball was more attentive to me than to Maud, all the evening"—she ended quite exultingly.

"Oh, Flora!" said Laura. "The idea of you two splendid girls devoting yourselves to pleasing that man, as if he were the Grand Turk, and you were two rival sultanas!"

"How you do talk!" retorted Flora, the faint color deepening in her lovely face. "What a dreadful way of putting it!" Then with a smile she added: "I own there is some truth in it, though; but he is the best match in New York!"

"Really? and so he has a right to play the Grand Seigneur."

"He thinks he has, at least; he is the richest single man in the city, and very highly connected. He has been for years the most desirable *parti* in society, and the girls have quarreled over him for a dozen seasons."

"No wonder he is spoilt then; but Flora, how can you condescend to join in such a contest?"

"For the sake of winning where so many have failed. To tell the truth, I believe he will propose to me, if I give him the opportunity, and it would be such a triumph!" a faint sparkle coming into her blue eyes.

"The old story over again!" replied Laura. "Your fashionable life allows to girls no other scope for their ambition, than efforts like these. But don't you see how degrading all this is, Flora? Would you not rather turn your powers to achieving success for yourself in study, or in literature, than stoop to such humiliating work as this?"

"They won't let me," said Flora. "It is of no use to contend against fate; no other success but ball-room success is open to me; I have been a belle for two seasons, but this would be such a victory!"

"But do you wish to marry this man?"

"No," said Flora, with a visible look of repugnance. "I don't care to be his slave for life, though I would like to see him at my feet. But don't look so shocked, Laura," she said, with a gay laugh; "I don't think his heart will be broken. There, I have kept the carriage waiting too long, already, and I really must go. Come and see me before you change your home, and I will tell you about the drawing-lessons."

Laura could offer no further remonstrance, and Flora went away, looking so bewitchingly pretty, that Laura thought it no wonder this haughty veteran of twenty campaigns was won by her beauty.

While the two friends were thus talking, Mrs. D'Arcy had gone, according to her promise, to the fashionable school of which Mr. Alfred Glitter was the principal— that is, the avowed head of the establishment—though

4

those who looked behind the scenes knew that Mrs. Glitter, a plain, hard-working woman, did most of the labor, allowing to her husband all the credit. Well situated on Murray Hill was the handsome brown-stone house, with broad and pretentious portico, which served as a temple of learning to many of the daughters of New York's wealthiest citizens.

A servant in livery opened the door for Mrs. D'Arcy, and showed her into a reception-room showily fitted up with handsome furniture, and many pictures in staring gilt frames. On her way to this apartment, the doctor passed a class of young girls, going to a recitation. Pretty delicate creatures, most of them dressed in the extreme of the latest fashion, several wearing dainty white frocks, with broad sashes. Mrs. D'Arcy looked after them with a sigh ; the slender figures all showed the impress of the corset that was to mould these pliant forms into stylish smallness of waist, and the transparent complexions indicated a total lack of vitality, and a want of open-air exercise. The mental comment of the lady physician was a fervent protest against the whole false system of education, and she was conscious of a strong desire to strip off the oppressive finery, and the stifling steel-clasped garments, and putting plain serviceable frocks on these young aristocrats, to turn them out on some farm to gain health and strength.

Mrs. D'Arcy's card met with an immediate response, and her reflections were cut short by the entrance of Mr. Glitter, a small man with very light hair and eyebrows and lashes that were almost colorless. There was a sort of assumption in his manner, as if he were fearful that if he did not sufficiently assert himself, he would not be understood to be the great and important person he undoubtedly was.

"Ah, Mrs. D'Arcy—good morning—I am happy to meet you."

The doctor responded politely, and then explained : " I called to see you, in consequence of a letter received this morning in reply to an advertisement in the Trumpeter."

"Ah, yes, yes. I have recently been obliged to part with one of my drawing-teachers, and when I saw this advertisement, I thought the applicant might suit me."

"It is a young friend of mine, whom I can recommend most highly," said the doctor; "she is herself quite an artist, and has the best testimonials from Essex College."

"Ah, a *lady!*" said Mr. Glitter, with a slight elevation of the eyebrows.

"Yes, would that be any objection?"

"Well, no, perhaps not, though my last teacher was a gentlemen—I have preferred male instructors in all departments," Mr. Glitter went on sententiously, "as I have wished to give my pupils the very best tuition."

Mrs. D'Arcy felt slightly indignant at the implied slur on her sex, but restrained all outward expression of it. "Here are my friend's testimonials," she said, offering them, "and here are some of her drawings."

Mr. Glitter took the proffered papers, and examined them with tedious minuteness, assuming most consequential airs of criticism over the pictures. "I regret," he said at last, "that the young lady is a graduate of Essex College. I have always felt that the teachings there are hardly such as to develop true refinement, or, I may say, true womanliness,"—this sort of climax was a favorite form of expression with Mr. Glitter—"and to fit young ladies for their real sphere in life," he added.

Mrs. D'Arcy looked at the insignificant specimen of manhood who thus prescribed the limits of endeavor for her and her whole sex, with an amused contempt that she could scarcely conceal. "The education there is very thorough," she suggested, mildly.

"It is," admitted Mr. Glitter; "it is, I am aware of that; and these recommendations are very high; on the whole, I am willing to take the young lady on trial."

"How many hours a day would you need her?"

"Two. Every morning from 10 to 12, she will have

two classes in the primary department to superintend. I
have a professor for the higher classes."

"And what salary do you pay?"

Mr. Glitter reflected for a moment. "Six dollars a week."

"Six dollars a week!" repeated Mrs. D'Arcy. That is
very little! Did your last teacher have only that?"

"My dear madam, you forget that he was a man,"
—with a bland smile, as if all were said.

"And was he a very superior teacher?"

"I was not quite satisfied with him," replied Mr. Glitter. "In fact I dismissed him for incompetency."

"If my friend proves herself capable, may I not hope
that you will increase her wages?"

"No, madam, no. It is really quite a concession on my
part to take her at all, considering her sex; but I am
willing to try her at the salary I have named. I can easily
get some one else, if she does not consider the compensation sufficient; I am constantly receiving applications for
work from young women."

Mrs. D'Arcy knew that this was but too true, in all
probability, and took her leave, saying that she would make
the proposition to her friend and send her to see Mr. Glitter.

"Teaching is, after all, the one great resource open to
our sex," said Mrs. D'Arcy, as she related the result of her
visit to Laura. "And you, my dear child, must suffer
from the overcrowding of the óne occupation, that is held
to be within a 'woman's sphere.'"

"But I am quite contented with my prospects," replied
Laura, cheerfully. "Six dollars a week here, and what I
have from my pupils will make nine; then if I have Flora,
too, that will be eleven; oh, I shall be quite rich!"

"I am glad you are so brave about it, my dear," said
the doctor, kindly. "For my part, I always have a fresh
attack of indignation every time that the disadvantages
of women in earning a living are brought to my attention."

"But do you think that overcrowding in certain walks,

accounts for all the disabilities under which we labor ? It seems to me that women get less pay than men, as a rule, even when there is very little competition."

" That is quite true. Women get low wages, even for work that they do as well or better than men, and this is owing to the fixed belief in their actual inferiority. For instance, people will have a man-servant to wait on table, when a woman would do in all respects better, because a man is more stylish; in other words, a man is the superior animal. Just as people will pay more for a horse than for a donkey, so men get better prices than women. Of course, under some circumstances, a good donkey is better than a poor horse, and so, sometimes, an able woman earns more than a stupid man; but these are only the exceptions that prove the rule."

" And will it be always so, do you think ? "

" It will be, so long as women are classed on our statute-books with ' idiots, criminals and lunatics,' and so long as all women, however intelligent, are deprived of political power, while every man outside of prison-walls, no matter how degraded he may be, can cast a ballot; so long as woman's inferiority is branded upon her by the state and the government, so long will her pecuniary value be less than man's.

CHAPTER X.

LAURA'S NEW HOME.

At the end of a week from her arrival in New York Laura was fairly established in her new round of duties. She went every morning, except on Saturday, to Mr. Glitter's school for two hours of teaching, and had, besides her other pupils, Flora Livingston, who had persuaded her parents to allow her to take drawing-lessons, and to whom Laura went every Tuesday and Friday from 12 to 1.

There was now no longer any reason why Laura should remain with the doctor, and although Mrs. D'Arcy would have been pleased to keep her young *protégée* with her longer, she saw that she was desirous of being entirely independent, and believed that real kindness lay in allowing her to fight her battle by herself.

"I have found a home for you, my dear," she said, one evening, after her return from her round of duties; "a place where I think you will be quite comfortable. It is at Mr. Moulder's. You remember Biddy's appeal to me on behalf of her son?"

"Yes, indeed."

"He works for the firm of Moulder and Joiner, and in accordance to my promise to her, I went to see Mr. Moulder. He has promised to administer a severe reprimand to Pat, and judging from his appearance, I have no doubt that it will be sufficiently stern. In the course of our conversation I asked Mr. Moulder if he knew of any boarding-place, and he at once suggested his own house. I have seen Mrs. Moulder about it to-day. She is a very sweet woman—a lovely woman," added the doctor quite enthusiastically, "well educated, refined, very superior in these respects to her husband ; however you will soon have an opportunity of judging for yourself, and I must not prejudice you. They live on West Twentieth-street, which will be a convenient location. You are to have a third-story room with board for seven dollars a week; and, by the way, I have spoken to Bridget about washing for you. She is an excellent *blanchisseuse*."

So all was arranged, and the last day under the doctor's hospitable roof drew to a close. Both Frank Heywood and Guy Bradford called in the evening, and learned Laura's new address.

"I shall come to see you as often as I can," Heywood said frankly.

"I hope you will," replied Laura; "I shall be very busy,

for I must work in the evening, but I shall be glad to see
visitors sometimes."

"And may I come too?" asked Bradford, in a low
tone.

"Certainly," answered Laura; but her color rose a little,
as she spoke.

A curious smile crossed Frank Heywood's face as he
observed the two, and he turned away quickly to speak to
Mrs. D'Arcy.

After breakfast, the next morning, bidding her kind
hostess an affectionate good-bye, Laura sent her trunk to
her new home, by express, and started on her round of
duties. They occupied her until afternoon, and the day
was already growing dark, as she rang the bell at a small
brick house on West Twentieth-street, A little girl about
ten years old opened the door, a pretty child, with large
dark eyes, and delicate sad face.

"Oh, are you the young lady that has come to board?"
she asked.

"Yes."

"Please to walk in here."

She lead the way into a small parlor, which was furnished with the conventional tapestry—Brussels carpet in
bright colors, red reps sofa, and stiff chairs, and which had
a stuffy close smell. Laura's heart sank a little as was inevitable, the contrast with the doctor's large, airy, well-
appointed rooms, was so striking; but she checked the sigh
that rose to her lips, as Mrs. Moulder came into the room.

A woman of perhaps thirty, dressed in a dark blue frock
and sack, that quite concealed her figure, and wearing a
neat collar at her throat, and a fresh white apron. Her
face was strikingly attractive; there was great sweetness
in the smile that lurked about the patient mouth; and in-
tellect, as well as tenderness in the soft dove-like eyes.
She welcomed Laura, in a few well-chosen words, spoken
with the unmistakable accent of good-breeding, and took
her at once to her room. There were two flights of stairs

to climb, and when they reached the top, Mrs. Moulder seemed quite out of breath, and tired.

"I am sorry you came up with me," said Laura, kindly, "I could have found my way alone."

"It is nothing," replied the lady, with a faint smile; "I hope you will be comfortable here, and when you are ready, if you like, I shall be happy to have you come into my sitting-room, on the second story at the front; you will find it pleasanter perhaps than the parlor, until dinner is ready— as a friend of Mrs. D'Arcy's, I want to make you feel at home here."

Laura thanked her hostess, and left alone, took a survey of her new apartment; a small room, indeed, but neatly fitted up, with a suit of cottage-furniture of tasteful pattern. It was heated by a register in the wall, and as the windows looked towards the south, there was a probability of tolerable warmth. When she had unpacked, and arranged her clothes, and made some slight change in her dress, Laura went down stairs and knocked at the door of the room to which she had been invited. Here she found Mrs. Moulder and her children in a good-sized apartment, which had all the appearance of constant use. The chairs and sofas were littered with toys, the furniture was all more or less scratched with hard service; the carpet was somewhat worn, and yet there was an indescribable air of refinement about the place. There were flowers and trailing vines in the window, a cage, containing a lively canary hung in a warm corner; there were books in a set of shelves and some good engravings on the wall.

Mrs. Moulder sat in a rocking-chair, near a table, sewing by the light of a shaded lamp; a stout boy of seven stood by her side conning a reading-lesson; the little damsel who had admitted Laura, was demurely darning a stocking; while another little girl, of not more than three, was amusing herself on the floor with some blocks.

Laura was soon introduced to the three youngsters. "This is Minnie who let you in," said Mrs. Moulder;

"here is master Aleck, and this little one is Agnes, after her mamma," kissing the rosy face that was upturned to her.

"Show her Cherry, too," lisped the child.

"To be sure, I must not forget the bird," Mrs. Moulder added, pleasantly. "His name is Cherry; he is five years' old, was given to me by a cousin who raised him for me, and he is a famous singer as you will find out before long.

The tiny songster, as if aware of the praise that was bestowed upon him, turned his head from side to side, with a chirrup, and presently began a soft warbling song.

This pleased the children, and Laura who had that sparkling kindness of manner that easily wins young hearts, was soon on good terms with all three of the little folks, and had them crowding about her, to see what funny pictures she could make on Aleck's slate. All went on harmoniously for a time, but presently the boy who felt that he had not so good a place as his sisters, endeavored to push Minnie aside.

"I can't see," he said, fretfully; "you're scrouging me; I want a chance too."

"My dear," remonstrated Mrs. Moulder, "don't be rude to your sister."

"It's my slate," he said crossly, "and I ought to have the best place; besides I'm a boy, and pa says boys ought to see things."

"Move a little Minnie, that's a good child," urged the mother, rather anxiously.

"There," said the young tyrant, as he established himself firmly in the best position; "now you girls can look over my shoulders."

This might do very well for Minnie, who was taller than he, but for tiny Agnes, there was evidently not much chance. Laura laid down the slate and took the little thing on her lap. "Now," she said, "you two big ones can stand in front and look on."

But this did not suit Master Aleck ; with a quick motion

4*

he slipped his hand back of the child and gave her a cruel pinch. She uttered a sharp cry of pain, and the boy with an ugly look of satisfaction walked away to the table. Laura once more laid down the slate, and joined with the mother in trying to soothe the little creature, and while they were thus employed, there was a ring at the door-bell.

Mrs. Moulder paid no attention to this at first, but before any one could possibly have answered the first summons, it was repeated with a smart double pull. At this she looked up startled, and when in another moment there was the sound of quick hard blows on the door, she started to her feet, seeming fairly frightened.

"It must be Mr. Moulder!" she exclaimed; "I will go myself."

She hurried from the room, leaving the door open behind her; the little girl stopped her weeping, and Minnie hastily resumed her sewing. The boy still stood with a look of defiance on his face, near a table.

The pounding on the door continued at intervals, while Mrs. Moulder was hurrying down stairs, and as soon as it was open, a loud angry voice cried out :

" Why the mischief didn't some one let me in before ? It's a pretty note when a man can't get into his own house ! "

" I never thought of it's being you, Alexander," replied Mrs. Moulder, gently. " How came you not to have your pass-key ? "

"I left it down to the store, and I don't like being kept out in the cold, I can tell you."

" Jane was busy getting the dinner, I suppose, and I came down as soon as I could."

" I should think when you women are at home all day doing nothing, you might have things ready," grumbled Mr. Moulder, as he followed his wife up stairs to the sitting-room.

" Here is Miss Stanley ; Mr. Moulder, my husband," said Mrs. Moulder as they came in.

"How d'ye do?" Mr. Moulder remarked, shortly; and
without noticing the children, who looked up at his
entrance, he walked into the bedroom at the back.

The brief glimpse of "the head of the family," had
shown Laura a man of about forty-five, large and heavily
built, with a thick neck, a round head covered with sandy
hair, closely sprinkled with gray, a red face having a square
forehead, small light eyes, and a clumsy chin ornamented
with a fringe of tawny beard.

As soon as he had disappeared, Mrs. Moulder, with a
hasty excuse, went down stairs to see about the dinner,
and Laura made her way to the parlor, where she waited
until summoned to the meal. It was served in a small
basement dining-room, and was neatly arranged and well-
cooked. Mrs. Moulder, at one end of the table, did her
best to keep the children in absolute quiet, and ever and
anon her mild eyes turned with a look of anxiety towards
her husband, who ate in sullen silence at the opposite end.
She endeavored, from time to time, to maintain some conversation with her guest, but this was rather hard work
among such uncongenial surroundings, and Laura was
heartily glad when the repast was over and she was able to
escape to her own room.

To those she left behind, the evening passed at first like
many another. Mr. Moulder went up to the sitting-room
and assuming a dressing-gown placed himself in an arm-
chair and began to read the paper. Mrs. Moulder assisted
the Irish girl in clearing off the table; this person, Jane,
though well-meaning and good-natured, was unusually raw
and clumsy, with a broad stupid face and great awkward
hands, so that it was an extra trial of patience to supervise
her duties. These over, the mother must see the children
put to bed, undressing little Agnes herself, so that when
she too was free to come into the sitting-room, she looked
pale and exhausted. Mr. Moulder did not even glance up
at his wife's entrance, and as her labors were not by any
means yet over, she took a low chair, drew a pile of cloth-

ing towards her, and began that endless sewing that with
her was never done. For a time she stitched in silence,
then Mr. Moulder put down his paper and turned to her.

"Agnes," he said, "have you finished my new dressing-
gown yet?"

"No, Alexander, I have not had time; I have extra
sewing to do just now, you know, and I thought you could
wait for this awhile."

"That's always the excuse!" her husband exclaimed,
impatiently. "Don't have time. You women potter
about all day and yet don't manage really to do anything.
It's preposterous!" This was a favorite phrase of Mr.
Moulder's, serving as a sort of climax when he was
angered.

"I try to be industrious, Alexander," the wife replied,
mildly. "I have a great deal to do about the house, you
know. Jane is so inexperienced that I can't depend
much upon her. And I have been sitting up quite late at
night, for some time past, trying to get through some of
my sewing. Your dressing-gown is a heavy job, but I will
try to finish it this week."

"Well, well, only don't grumble over it," he said,
irritably, turning to his paper again.

At this moment, there was a ring at the front door, and
a few moments after Jane appeared panting, and carrying
a card between the thumb and finger of a very dirty
hand.

After a sort of vacant stare about the room she said:
"It was to go to the boss," and handed it to Mr. Moulder.

"Hon. Silas Swinton!" he exclaimed, a smile of pleasure spreading over his face. "Ah! quick, Agnes! get me
my best coat."

Mrs. Moulder sprang to wait on her husband. "What
can bring him here?" she asked.

"He has come to see me about some ward matters,"
replied Mr. Moulder, importantly—"political affairs you
would not understand,"—he added, patronizingly. Then

after glancing at himself in the small glass that hung on the mantel-piece, he went down stairs.

"Ah, Moulder, my dear fellow! how are you!" exclaimed the handsome judge, as he rose to greet his constituent and shook him warmly by the hand.

"Quite well, quite well," replied Mr. Moulder, " and very proud to see your honor under my roof."

"Well, Moulder, I'll tell you how it is. I thought I would come and see you myself with regard to one or two things. We want to open a new Sixteenth-ward club. You know the old place is getting rather small; you must have felt it yourself."

"I have," assented Mr. Moulder; proud to coincide with the judge in anything.

"Well, we want some of the solid men of this part of the ward to help us about this new room, and I said at once, Moulder must go on the list; he is one we can always depend upon."

A look of satisfaction irradiated Mr. Moulder's features at these words. "Certainly, judge, certainly; I'm bound to stand by the party in every way."

"We had a committee-meeting last night at the hall," continued the judge. "Several of the Sachems were present;" mentioning the names of certain well-known politicians. "And it was decided that new headquarters should be opened in the Twenty-second ward and one here. I spoke of you at once in connection with this one."

Mr. Moulder was fairly beaming with delight at having been thus brought to the knowledge of the magnates of the party. "You can always depend on me, judge," he said; "put my name down for fifty dollars, at once."

"We thought of making you one of our Vice-Presidents," Swinton went on; "I am to be President."

"Quite right, judge, quite right; I shall esteem it an honor to serve under you in any capacity."

"Here is our list of members," the judge continued,

spreading out a roll; "you will see they are all good names; men we can rely upon."

Mr. Moulder took the paper, and began slowly reading it. Judge Swinton glanced uneasily about the room, and presently said :

"By the way, Moulder, you have a young lady staying here, in whom I am quite interested."

"Who?" asked Mr. Moulder, with a puzzled look; then as remembering something, "Oh, yes, Miss Stanley. Do you know her?"

"Quite well," replied the judge, unblushingly : "very nice girl—friend of Mrs. D'Arcy's."

"Yes, so she is."

"Mrs. D'Arcy is rather a remarkable woman."

"Well, yes ; " said Mr. Moulder, laying down the paper, with a judicial air ; "she has attended my wife sometimes. Mrs. Moulder is sort of particular and don't like to have any one but a woman-doctor around her, and so Mrs. D'Arcy has been to see her when she was sick. She seems to know her business and would be well enough, if it was not for her foolish ideas about woman's rights."

"Oh, of course, that is absurd," smiled the judge.

"Yes, I've no patience with such nonsense," said Mr. Moulder, testily. "Women are entirely out of place when they undertake to meddle in politics ; it is preposterous! their proper place is home, taking care of their husbands and children."

"Certainly," assented Swinton, readily; "we are their natural protectors and they ought to be content to lean on us;" then bringing the conversation back to the more inter-esting subject : "Do you think I could see Miss Stanley this evening ? "

"Oh yes, no doubt; I will send up for her."

"Wait a moment, Moulder, don't take up my name. I'd like to surprise her ; say a friend of her father's."

"Certainly, judge, certainly ; I'll send my wife up for her."

"Ah, by the way, Moulder," said Swinton coolly, "as I shan't stay but a moment after she comes, I'll bid you good-night, now. You'll come round to the meeting on Friday evening and can bring the money then."

Mr. Moulder looked a little puzzled at this unexpected dismissal, but he seemed to think it must be all right if the judge said so, and went slowly up stairs to send his wife to call Miss Stanley.

Laura had arranged her drawing-materials on a table, and was bending over her work, when there was a knock at the door and in reply to her answer, Mrs. Moulder came in. She sat down quickly in a chair, as if quite tired, and it was a moment before she was able to tell Laura that a friend of her father's wished to see her."

"A friend of father's!" exclaimed Laura, starting up— "Who can it be?"

"I was told not to give the name," replied Mrs. Moulder, evasively. "Will you go down?"

"Oh yes, at once;" answered Laura, and she hurried out of the room. Her heart was beating with alarm; she did not know how much this unexpected summons might mean. Could her father force her to go home against her will? Was her dream of independence to fade so quickly? She was much agitated by her thoughts, and came into the parlor looking quite pale.

"Judge Swinton!"

She uttered the name with a little startled cry, as she drew back from his outstretched hand.

"Yes, Miss Stanley; you will forgive my intrusion, I trust. I have been so anxious to see you ever since that morning at the court. No, don't look so frightened," he added, earnestly. "I assure you, I come here as your sincere friend."

The blood which had fled from Laura's cheeks in her surprise, came back in a torrent under the gaze of those bold eyes. "They told me you came from my father," she said.

"No, not exactly that; I met your father some time ago—Mr. Roger Stanley of Clinton, isn't it?"

"Yes."

"I met him last summer at a political meeting in Poughkeepsie; when I saw you in court, the name seemed familiar; since then I have heard from a mutual friend all about you." The judge omitted to mention that the "friend" was a private detective, employed to work up the facts in the case.

"And have you seen my father since?"

"No; but I shall be in his neighborhood next week, and shall probably meet him; have you any message?" watching closely the effect of this remark.

"No," replied Laura, with a look of trouble she could not conceal. She was silent a moment, and then said, "You may think it a strange request, but I shall be much obliged if you will not mention that you have seen me."

"Anything, Miss Stanley, anything I can do for you will give me pleasure. I have been so troubled for this week past, I have feared that you must have thought me so rude that morning in court." Laura did not reply, and he went on: "I was interested in you, and your dress was so plain that I was deceived as to your real rank; I should not have sent you to Bludgett's, if I had understood all as I ought. But I thought it would be a respectable place."

Laura had no reason to suspect any sinister intentions on the part of this man, and his earnest manner quite disarmed her. "Do not trouble yourself about it," she said; "it did not matter much, and I have since found very kind friends."

"I am rejoiced to hear it, heartily rejoiced!" replied the judge, with every appearance of frank sincerity. "I ventured to send for you this evening, because I felt that an apology was due to you, and to myself. Of course I will do exactly as you wish me, in regard to mentioning that I have seen you. I shall be only too happy to obey your commands in every way."

Laura was forced to accept the excuse so gracefully tendered, and feeling herself somewhat in this man's power, on account of his acquaintance with her father, treated him with politeness during his visit. The judge was very wise, he did not stay long; but after making himself exceedingly agreeable for a short time, took his leave with a request to be allowed to call again, so proffered, that Laura did not think it best to refuse it.

CHAPTER XI.

RHODA'S FRIEND.

As Judge Swinton stepped out into the night, he saw that a change had taken place in the weather; the clouds were very heavy, and snow was falling. Blinded by the transition from the lighted house to the dark streets, he did not observe a crouching figure that was cowering in the shade of the steps of the next house. He buttoned his handsome overcoat across his broad chest, and after a glance at the sky, opened a natty umbrella, and made his way down the street. The watcher who peered cautiously after him, as soon as he had gained a short distance, stole from her hiding-place and followed, swiftly. It was Rhoda Dayton, the young woman whom Laura had seen at Mrs. Bludgett's. She was wrapped in a waterproof, and had a black hat slouched over her face; but from under this, her dark, fierce eyes glanced out with a strange light in their depths.

She stole on after the judge, until she saw him go up Fifth avenue, and into a handsome club-house. As he disappeared through the wide door that opened to receive him, Rhoda peered sharply into the elegantly-furnished hall, of which she had a brief glimpse. The prevailing color which caught her gaze was crimson, and there was a general suggestion of warmth and light, very agreeable in contrast with the cold and gloom outside. As the door closed,

the girl raised her head with a gesture that might be
appeal or menace, and then turning, made her way swiftly
down town.   After a short walk she reached the entrance of
a fashionable theatre, on the corner of Thirteenth-street and
Broadway ; here she again paused.   A row of omnibusses
was drawn up by the sidewalk, and quite a little group of
people had collected about the doors,——it was evident
that the play was over.   Merely stepping back a little, out
of the glare of the lamps, Rhoda waited ; the wind blew in
her face, the trampled flakes were cold and wet about her
feet, but she stood as if fascinated, until presently there was
a rush of young men, and then the gay throng of pleasure-
seekers poured out into the night.

Rhoda watched them, a strange expression of gloomy
longing in her brooding eyes and about her mouth, with
the under lip caught beneath the two teeth that stood each
side the vacant space in the centre.   So repellent was her
set look, that more than one man who seemed inclined to
speak to her, turned away, on fairly seeing her half-
shrouded face.

The theatre-goers crowded out, filling the street with
a moving mass of people.   Plain folk in their every-day
clothes, who had come for an hour's amusement after the
toil of the day ; country-girls and their attendants, laughing and talking with the pleasurable excitement of the rare
treat ; and the dainty representatives of the wealth and
fashion of the city.   Among these last, was a group that
strongly attracted Rhoda's attention—a fine-looking old
gentleman with a tall handsome young girl on his arm—a
girl with dark eyes, and rich golden brown hair, looking
about her with the assured glances of an acknowledged
beauty, and behind these a stylish man of forty, escorting
a delicate, blue-eyed fair-haired lady.   They were the Livingstons and Mr. Ferdinand Le Roy.   As this last gentleman came in sight, Rhoda changed her position so as to see
him better.   She watched him as he carefully shielded
Flora from the storm, and handed her into the carriage;

she noticed how the young lady smiled her acknowledgments, while the other girl turned her dark eyes towards him, with a half-haughty entreaty lurking in their expression.

At her post, Rhoda waited until the whole party had entered the carriage and driven off, and then she, too, turned away. Resuming her rapid walk, she went on down Broadway, once or twice accosted by men, but, repelling them always with a gesture of indignant anger, and so reached a cross-street and a row of dingy tenement-houses. She went into one of these and ascended its many stairs to the top floor. The entries, all the way, were close and foul, dimly lighted by a gas-lamp on the lower floor, which shed only a faint glimmer to these higher regions. Rhoda felt her way along, as one accustomed to the place, and so came to a back room, and opening the door, went in. It was a small low apartment, under the sloping roof, with bare floor and walls stained with the marks of many occupants. There was no fire in the rusty grate, and the atmosphere was cold and close. A wooden table stood on one side, with a few simple articles of common crockery on it, a broken teapot, a cup without a handle, some yellow plates; a kerosene lamp, turned low, lighted the room, and a wooden chair, and two trunks completed its smaller furnishings; against the wall was a low bed, and on this lay a girl, apparently not more than seventeen or eighteen years old. A fair young creature, with soft hazel eyes, and masses of reddish gold hair, tossed in disorder over the coarse pillow; at Rhoda's entrance, she looked up, and a faint smile crossed her wan face.

"Oh, I'm so glad you are back!" she said, and her voice had in its tone the lingering accent of the South. "Give me some water, please, I'm so thirsty," she added, fretfully.

"Shan't I get some fresh water, Maggie?" asked Rhoda.

"No;" impatiently, "only be quick; besides, that is fresh, Biddy brought it for me, only a little while ago."

"Rhoda poured the water into a cracked tea-cup that stood by the bed, and handed it to her companion, who drank it thirstily with parched lips. "I'm so glad Biddy has been in," said Rhoda.

"Yes, she was here a good while, and only went away because she thought Pat might come home."

At this moment there was a light tap at the door and Rhoda opening it, was met by the ample proportions and ruddy face of Biddy Malone.

"Oh, you're come, Rhody," she said; "it's glad I am, indade, for Pat's waitin' his supper down stairs; but the darlint was on me mind so, I thought I'd jist stip up to say if you was come."

"Thank you, Biddy, I'll be here straight along now, so you needn't bother any more; how has she been all the evening?"

"Bether a little, the saints be praised!"—then anxiously —"ye'll not be havin' the docther for her?"

"If she's worse, I suppose I must," replied Rhoda, gloomily. "But we don't want what we can't pay for."

"Shure, it's a kind leddy I'll be bringin' till her," Biddy urged, anxiously.

"Well, we must see how she is," rejoined the girl. "I hate to ask help unless I'm forced."

"May be she will take a turn for the bether afther this," Biddy said, cheerfully. "I'll go down agin bein' as you're here."

The good woman made her way through the dim hall and Rhoda returned to the room. As she took off her wet clothes, the sick girl, who was watching her with fever-bright eyes, seemed to be struck by her expression, for she asked:

"What's the matter, Rhoda? What makes you look so? Was there a row at the saloon to-night?"

"I wasn't at the saloon at all;" replied Rhoda.

"Wasn't you? Why not?"

"I got Jule to take my place; she's going to Thompson's

Monday, and wanted to learn the trade. I went to see some people."

"Who?"

"Well, first I went to Bludgett's; he beat Molly awful the other night, and she ain't been out of bed since; but you've been so sick I couldn't get there before."

"Beat her again! oh, dear! oh dear!" said Maggie, closing her eyes as if to shut out the horrible scene. "And she's been there all alone! I'm nothing but a trouble to you, Rhoda! If I was home! oh, if I was only at home!"

Rhoda's face grew very sad, and her stern eyes softened. This plaintive cry had been on her young companion's lips for a week past. She was a southern girl from the fresh mountains of Virginia; she had come to this great city like many another of her sex and her age, hoping to earn an honest living; her youth and her beauty, and her womanhood, which ought to have been a claim for care and aid from every man, if the theory be correct that women are guarded, protected and represented by the opposite sex, had won for her only false flatteries, lying promises and ruin. Ruin indeed, but not degradation; lying there, lost as the world would call her, she was better and purer than the man who had worked her destruction. For months after he had deserted her, she had toiled to win her livelihood, but the struggle and the sorrow were too much for her, and consumption, that fatal disease, ever lying in wait for the children of want, had seized upon her, and been rapidly developed by hardship and suffering. Rhoda, who had worked with her in the same factory for some time, had grown to be her most faithful friend, and had supported the sick girl, since she had been too weak to labor herself.

For the last week, Maggie had been haunted with the desire to return to her home. All day long, as she lay there, pictures of the little cottage where she was born, of the pleasant trees around it, of her mother's patient face, had been before her, until the longing to see them again had become a wild yearning, and she fancied that, if she could breathe once more the pure air of her native hills, it would give her health and strength. But where obtain the money for so long and expensive a journey? This was the problem that tortured Rhoda, and that had to-night driven her out to try to find Laura Stanley, with a vague hope that she might be able, through her, to find some work which would be more remunerative than any she could find for herself.

"I think all the time about how I can contrive to get you home," Rhoda said; "that was what I went out about to-night."

"Oh, did you?" cried Maggie, with a look of great interest. "Do tell me about it."

"It won't be any use," Rhoda replied; "I know that now, but I thought I might hear of some work that would pay better than any I can find. I met a young lady at Bludgett's last week, that knows some of the real nobs here; she was staying with a first-class lady-doctor then. I tried to find her there, but she had moved; then I went to the house she had moved to, but it was no use."

"Why not?"

"Because just as I got there, Judge Swinton went up the steps;" her face writhing with inexpressible pain as she uttered the name.

"Oh, Rhoda!"

"Yes," said Rhoda, a sullen fire smouldering in her eyes; "he is after *her* now; I watched for him outside. He didn't stay long, but he came out with a smile on his lips. He shan't have her though! he shan't have her!" she cried with sudden vehemence; "I swear to God he shan't have her!"

"How can you stop it?"

"Stop it? I don't know how, but I will!" she asseverated. "If there is a God in heaven, he'll help me to fight against him." Then with a sudden frown clouding her face—"but Maggie, sometimes I almost doubt there is a God!"

"Oh, Rhody, don't say that!" Maggie cried, feebly.

"How can there be," Rhoda went on, "when there is such cruelty in the world! When men have all the chances, and women all the shame! It is not fair; no, I know it is not fair! Now look at us two. We worked hard to earn money on the square; did any man help us? No; they only gave us less wages because we were women, and then when we were poor, tempted us with soft promises and smiling lies. Oh, it's hard! as hard as hell, this life to which women are condemned! Why, see how it is! That man who would stoop to do dirty acts that I would scorn, who has been dissipated and vile since he was a boy is received anywhere with honor, while I—the men who are proud to claim his acquaintance would turn their eyes away from me!—and so with you, my poor lamb, no one will help you, while one who ought to be taking care of you, has money and friends and all that he wants. I saw him to night."

Maggie writhed in her bed, a sudden flush coloring her wasted cheek. "Where?" she asked.

"At the theatre; he had a young lady on his arm. I stopped to watch the people come out. I don't know why, but I like to look at these folks whose life is so different from ours. How strange it must be always to have plenty to eat, and wear nice clothes!" Then after a moment she added, "Maggie, you know it was you that left him at the last; it would be no more than right for him to give you money enough to go home with. Did you ever think of it?"

The girl started up in bed, her eyes glowing with sudden light. "I wouldn't touch any money he gave me from pity;" she cried, "not if it would save me from death! I would starve by inches, sooner!"

Then as if the excitement had overcome her, she sank back on the pillow, weeping bitterly. Rhoda sprang to her side and tried to comfort her.

"I am a wretch to speak of him, Maggie dear," she

said. "Maggie! Maggie! don't cry so. You will be worse to-morrow; oh, please don't."

"Mother! mother! mother!" wailed the girl, "take me home to mother! Oh, why did I ever come away! mother! mother!"

Rhoda tried in vain to comfort her companion; the poor girl did indeed at last sob herself to sleep in her friend's arms, but all night long she tossed restlessly, every now and then murmuring the name of her mother, and while the storm beat on the roof above her, and 'the cold grew more intense—babbled of the violets and the roses, the sunshine and the hills of her distant home.

CHAPTER XII.

FLORA DARES.

LAURA STANLEY's lessons to Flora Livingston, were given after a curious fashion. They took place always in Flora's boudoir, to which Laura would be shown and where she would sometimes have to wait half of the hour, for the appearance of her friend, when Flora would come in so full of pretty excuses and so glad to see her teacher, that resentment was impossible. After this, the drawing-materials would be taken out, and some pretence of study made ; though after all, most of the time was passed in long chats which Flora declared did her more good than any amount of instruction in shading and perspective.

"It's just like a breath of fresh air to talk to you, Laura," she said one morning. "I live in an atmosphere of perfume and of gas-lights, till I feel as if I did not know the real world at all."

"And do you never set yourself to any task?" asked Laura. "I see that you don't practice drawing as much as you ought."

"What's the use?" rejoined Flora. "You know I shall never make an artist. Now look at this thing which I have made," pointing contemptuously to a study of flowers. "Your picture which I have undertaken to copy is a graceful poem; mine is a bunch of sticks."

"Not so bad as that," laughed Laura. "But I feel that your work in life will be literary, rather than artistic."

"I wish I had an occupation!" exclaimed Flora, fervently. "I know my life is wasted as it is—sometimes I do busy myself though," she added. "I have tried my hand at writing."

"You always wrote well at school."

"I enjoy composition," replied Flora; "and have several short poems that I have written since I left college."

"Have you? Do show me some."

"I don't know how good they are," said Flora modestly. "But I *would* like to read you one of my pieces."

She took out of her desk a blank-book in which many pages were already covered with manuscript; and after turning over the leaves for a moment, said:

"This is a mere descriptive piece which I wrote last summer; a sort of reverie of the imagination, I call it."

"A SONG OF JUNE.

"Fair June is here, the lakelet clear
  In summer calm reposes,
The sunbeams fly across the sky,
  Or linger in the roses.

"From shady nooks, the violet looks,
  The hills are bright with daisies,
The grape intwines its tendriled vines,
  And blooms in odorous mazes.

"Through forests high, where soft winds sigh,
  The wild bird's song is ringing,
O'er clover lea, the robber bee
  On honey-quest is winging.

5

" In valleys deep, green mosses creep
  By lonesome pondlets stilly,
Where idly trails, in milk-white veils,
  The gracious water-lily.

" The laughing hours are gay with flowers
  To this fair season granted,
And summer swings on golden wings
  Adown the year enchanted ! "

" Why that is very pretty poetry ! " exclaimed Laura,
heartily.

" An attempt at it," replied Flora; "and a very poor one."

Laura, however, had many kindly expressions of praise
for her friend's effort, so that Flora was encouraged to let
her hear one or two other pieces. They had merit, all of
them, wanting as yet the polish that only long culture can
give, but promising for the future.

Seizing her opportunity, in the course of this and
other conversations, Laura stimulated Flora's ambition to
devote herself to some earnest pursuit, and not be a mere
butterfly of fashion. As the weeks went on, from what
she heard of Mr. Le Roy's visits, Laura felt that there was
every reason to fear that her friend was in danger of en-
tangling herself with this man whom she did not love, and
urged upon Flora strongly her own theories of life, feeling
that nothing would so surely save her from such a union
as active occupation. Stimulated by these words and her
own desire for independence, the young lady at last summoned courage to make an attempt to obtain her father's
consent to the study of his profession.

With heart beating so that she could scarcely breathe,
Flora followed him to his study one evening when she saw
him go into it with a bundle of papers in his hand, and
with the evident intention of several hours of hard work.

" May I come in, papa ? " she asked, opening the door a
little way.

"Certainly, Flora," and Mr. Livingston turned to his writing again, apparently supposing that she had come to the room in search of something.

He was a stately man, with iron-gray hair, firm mouth, and keen eyes; and as he sat there, surrounded with books and papers, intrenched in his own handsome library, it required no little courage to suggest anything likely to displease him. Flora paused beside his chair a moment, and noticing this, her father presently looked up.

"What is it?" he asked; "what do you want, Flora?"

"Can I speak to you for a few minutes, papa?"

"Well, yes, my dear, I can spare a little time," he said, laying down his pen; "what is it?" then observing her more narrowly; "why, how agitated you look! Don't be afraid, my dear; do you want some money to buy a new ball-dress?"

"No, oh no! I have plenty of those." Flora hesitated a moment, and then said desperately, "Couldn't I help you about those papers?"

"You! no, my child," with an amused smile; "it's very amiable of you to offer, but you couldn't understand them."

Flora had taken the plunge now, and was resolved to go on. "Suppose you had a son, papa; would you let him study law?"

A shade crossed Mr. Livingston's face; the great disappointment of his life was, that he had no son. "Yes, Flora, I presume I should."

"Then," said the young lady, mustering all her conrage, and raising her sweet blue eyes; "why shouldn't you teach me?"

"You, Flora! what an extraordinary idea!"

"Yes, papa," she went on quickly; "I don't mean to take me in court with you, but teach me so that I could help you with your cases at home; I should like it so much!"

"Mr. Livingston turned his chair around, and looked at his daughter very gravely. "If you make this strange proposition because you would like to help me, I am very grateful; if you make it because you have any foolish woman's rights notions in your head, I am exceedingly displeased."

Flora flushed scarlet. "Are you willing to teach me so that I may help you?" she asked.

"No, certainly not."

"Oh, why not, papa? Don't you think I have sense enough?"

"You have very good sense, Flora," replied her father; "enough sense, I should have thought, not to make such an absurd proposition."

"Why absurd?" demanded Flora, rather excitedly.

"Because of your sex. I am very sorry, Flora, that such a pernicious idea should ever have entered your head. I have endeavored to have your education so conducted, as to make you what a refined gentlewoman should be. Such a proposition as this, shows that you have, somehow, imbibed some of the injurious theories of the day."

Flora was like some of the quieter animals, she was no warrior by nature, but driven to bay, she could fight fiercely. "Injurious theories!" she repeated, indignantly; "I do not admit them to be injurious. You say that if I were a boy you would allow me to study law, but you refuse me, because I am a girl. Yet I have a desire for independence and an aspiration for something more than frivolity, if I am a woman!" Then softening to sudden pleading, she said, "Oh, papa, please let me learn something useful; I believe it will make me better and happier than I am now."

Mr. Livingston regarded his daughter in astonishment, as much surprised as one would be, who should see a humming-bird, that was sporting in apparent contentment among the flowers, on a sudden ask to be transformed into an eagle, and aspire to reach the sun.

"Flora, you amaze me! he said, in extreme displeasure; "where is your womanliness, that you are not content with your lot in life, that you wish to give up your place in society and your prospects in the future, for a plan so preposterous as this?"

"What are my prospects in the future?" asked Flora, keenly.

"The prospect of being a good wife to some suitable man. Your ambition should be for his success; I have no patience with this talk about a career for women! A true woman is willing to lose her own identity in her husband's."

Flora listened, a look of suppressed wrath blazing in her blue eyes, that suddenly burst forth into words. "I protest against that theory, utterly!" she cried; "I have an immortal soul, as truly as any man, and I believe that in the eyes of God, men and women are equal, and that I have the same right to an independent career as if I were a man."

"Flora! Flora! where have you learned such monstrous notions?" exclaimed her father, sternly.

"They are eternal truths," she said earnestly; "but of course, I cannot change your views. Once for all, papa, do you refuse to teach me your profession?"

"Absolutely and emphatically."

"That is all, papa," and she turned to leave the room; her courage was all gone now, and her lovely eyes were full of tears.

Mr. Livingston looked after her with a really troubled air. "Flora," he said, "I don't want to be harsh with you. You are young, you don't look at these things in their true light. You need not despair because you cannot be a lawyer; a brilliant social career is open to you, and that is what you are really fitted for. Why, little girl, you can marry the richest man in New York before spring if you like," he added, with a smile.

"I don't know that I care to do that," replied Flora, coldly, though her color rose a little; "even if I should have the opportunity," she added.

"You will have that, I don't doubt," Mr. Livingston said. "Here, child; wait a moment." He unlocked a drawer that Flora knew very well, as the mine from which, ever since she could remember, the source of various pleasures had been drawn, and took from it a hundred dollar bill, which he handed to his daughter. "There," he said, "take that for your dress, for Mrs. Duncan's ball. You must be the best dressed, as well as the prettiest girl there. And now leave me to plod over my papers, while you plan with mamma what the dress shall be; that is much the most suitable occupation for you."

Flora took the money, and thanked her father; but as she left the room, she felt as if he had bartered away her birthright for a mess of pottage.

That night when Mr. Livingston and his wife were alone in their own room, he related to her, with many expressions of regret, Flora's extraordinary proposition. Mrs. Livingston heard him, the shade deepening on her always anxious face.

"What a shocking idea!" she said.

"Very, where do suppose she could have taken it up?"

"I think I can tell you," replied the lady, after a moment's thought. "She has imbibed this fancy from her drawing-teacher, Miss Stanley. I distrusted her from the first; she was educated at Essex College and is a great friend of Mrs. D'Arcy's—you know, the woman-doctor. I was sorry that you allowed Flora to take lessons from her; we must put a stop to this at once."

"Oh certainly," assented Mr. Livingston; "if that is the sort of teaching she gives, the young woman must be dismissed immediately."

"Yes, we cannot too strongly show her how entirely we disapprove of these horrible doctrines regarding woman's position that have recently crept into so much prominence."

Mrs. Livingston had at one period of her life protested against her destiny as bitterly as did ever any revolted slave ; but having for years past been contented with her chains, she could endure no thought of revolt in others.

"Flora has such a fine chance of settling in life, too, just now ; " said Mr. Livingston, presently. " Mr. Le Roy is, I think, really in earnest."

" I believe that he is," replied Mrs. Livingston, with a look of triumph. " It would be a grand match, but Flora is so strange to him, that sometimes I am afraid she will lose him entirely. I assure you, Mr. Livingston, I have many misgivings about her."

" I know you do, my dear ; I know you have a great many anxious hours ; " then after a moment, he said : " Le Roy will be at the Duncan's ball, I suppose ; I gave Flora one hundred dollars just now to buy a new dress with. If we dismiss this foolish teacher, who puts such mischievous notions in Flora's head, and throw her as much with Le Roy as possible, I think a match will be sure to result."

So these good parents laid their plans, and yet if they had read an account of how certain savages deck out their young daughters with beads and feathers, and then offer them to some great chief for sale, they would probably have been much shocked at such unchristian and barbarous practices.

CHAPTER XIII.

MR. GLITTER'S VIEWS.

LAURA STANLEY's early impressions of her new home had been by no means favorable, and she at first felt as if she could on no terms remain in it, but a few days' residence there awakened so strongly her interest in Mrs. Moulder, that she soon became reluctant to leave her ; the more so, as she saw that the gentle lady seemed to find consolation and comfort in her companionship. Mrs. Moulder was a woman of fine education, which she had kept up so far as her limited means would allow ; spoke French very

well and had taught it to her children, that is, to her girls ;
Master Aleck having refused to learn it on the ground that
it was not manly ; a theory in which he was sustained by
his father.   Daily Laura's wonder increased that such a
woman as Mrs. Moulder could ever have married such a
man as Mr. Moulder, the contrast between them was in all
respects so striking.

Laura's pleasantest hours with her new friend were
passed in the little sitting-room, where she would bring her
drawing-materials sometimes of an afternoon when the
children were out ; and on one of these occasions, she had
an opportunity of asking the question that so puzzled her.
The conversation had turned on early marriages, and Mrs.
Moulder said :

" I believe they are generally a mistake ; neither a man
nor a woman can know what their real needs in a life-com-
panion are, until they are fully matured.   Now I was a
mere child when I was married ; only seventeen."

" Do you mind telling me about it ? " asked Laura.

Mrs. Moulder hesitated a moment ; her sweet face clouding, then she said : " I was a very romantic girl, and at six-
teen imagined myself desperately in love with a dark-eyed
school-boy, the son of a neighbor.   My parents opposed
any engagement, and to break off the affair I was sent away
to boarding-school.   While my heart was yet sore with
this disappointment I met Mr. Moulder, who was the
brother of one of my schoolmates.   He made himself very
pleasant to me ; I liked his fatherly manners and could not
endure the thought of a return to my home, never a very
happy one—recollect I was only a weak and foolish young
creature, and yielding to Mr. Moulder's persuasions, in a fit
of recklessness and defiance, I ran away with him."

" Oh, Mrs. Moulder ! why, I should never have thought
of your doing such a thing ! "

Mrs. Moulder smiled, sadly.   " That was a great while
ago, Laura ; you cannot imagine what a change twelve years
have made in me.   I was very young and ignorant, then.

Why, I had not the slightest idea till I came to New York with him, what Mr. Moulder's occupation was; I was just so silly as never to have thought to ask him. I had known him indeed only a short time; he had made himself very agreeable; and when so matter-of-fact a man could propose an elopement, you can fancy that his feelings were very deeply stirred."

"I can readily imagine it," replied Laura; "you must have been very lovely then."

A faint color rose to Mrs. Moulder's soft cheeks. "He thought so, perhaps, and I know he meant to be kind to me. He is, too, after his own fashion," she added loyally. "He has strict ideas as to wifely duty and submission, but he does not intend to be harsh."

"And do you agree in these ideas?" asked Laura. "Now, tell me; you are as devoted a wife and mother as I ever saw; but are you contented?"

"Oh, Laura, don't ask me!" Mrs. Moulder cried, waving her hands, as if to push away the thought. "For years after I married I was rebellious; I loved my children and my home devotedly, and yet, sometimes, it seemed to me as if I had capacity for something else beyond domestic drudgery. But I have done my best to silence these ideas. I have endeavored to become reconciled to whatever might seem hard in my lot in life, and by God's help I hope I have succeeded."

Laura did not urge the subject; she had no wish to startle her new friend too suddenly with her pet theories, and was heartily glad that the deep religious feeling which was part of this sweet woman's nature, could help her to endure what, to the high-spirited girl, seemed intolerable trials.

On the morning after this conversation, when Laura came down to breakfast, she found a note waiting for her. It was written on delicate paper, stamped with a monogram and crest, and contained these words:

5*

"*Mrs. Livingston regrets to be obliged to request Miss
Stanley to discontinue her lessons to Miss Flora Livingston.
Herewith is enclosed the sum of eight dollars ($8.00), due
for lessons already given.*"

Laura read these words thrice, utterly unable to account
for her sudden dismissal. Then a surmise of the true reason came to her, and her cheeks flushed with indignation at
the insult given her, because she had dared to encourage
her friend to strive for independence. The morning was
dark and gloomy, threatening snow, all her surroundings
seemed sad and depressing, and Laura, feeling keenly the
blow she had just received, set off on her round of duties
with a heavy heart.

When she reached Mr. Glitter's, she found that she was
a few moments early for her class, and thought that she
would go into the reception-room to wait. Here she discovered Mr. Glitter, and a pleasant-looking lady holding
some tickets in her hand. The school-principal's manner
was more than usually pompous and important.

"What do you say these tickets are?" he was asking,
as Laura came in.

"Tickets for a lecture on Oriental Customs by Mrs. Jo-
sephine Reisender; she has lived for some years in the East
and has made many observations of interest; she desired me
to present you with a few, for the use of the school."

"No, madam, no; I cannot take them," said Mr. Glitter;
waving his hand majestically. "I disapprove wholly of
females as public speakers. It is wrong, it is unwomanly;
I may even say it is demoralizing."

The lady smiled and said, "Did I not hear that your scholars were at Madam Ristori's *matinée* on Saturday last?"

"Yes, certainly; but that is different, very different," he
repeated positively, as if he felt his ground to be a little
untenable and must strengthen it by reiteration. "Women
of unexceptionable character as actresses in standard plays
I admire, and to a certain degree respect; but women
aping men as lecturers I entirely disapprove of."

"Then you think it quite right for women to earn their living by repeating other people's words to an audience, and quite wrong for them to earn their living by repeating their own words?" the lady asked, with a slightly mischievous twinkle in her eyes.

"Women as public speakers are unsexed," Mr. Glitter replied severely; "a woman's place is home."

At this moment, Mrs. Glitter, a small thin woman, very plainly dressed and looking harassed and overworked, appeared at the door.

"Alfred," she said, "can you go down to the bank for me, to draw some money? I am very busy this morning."

Mr. Glitter walked to the window and looked out. "It is beginning to snow," he replied; "no, I don't think I can venture out this morning; you will have to go."

The wife hurried away with a weary look, and Mr. Glitter went on with his remarks: "Yes, madam, a woman's place is home; these women-lecturers had far better be darning their husbands' stockings and taking care of their babies."

"As Mrs. Reisender has neither husband nor children, she can scarcely follow either of these occupations," replied the lady with an amused smile; "but I'll not trespass on your valuable time any longer, sir; good morning."

She passed out with a slight bow of recognition to Laura, who remembered that she had seen her at Mrs. D'Arcy's; and the two exchanged a glance of comical significance, as the little man walked majestically up stairs, apparently thinking that he had annihilated all women-speakers.

The absurd aspects of this scene struck Laura so forcibly, that the current of her thoughts was quite changed by it, and she went up to her lessons in a more cheerful frame of mind. They were gotten through pleasantly, for Laura was a favorite with her scholars; but she was glad, as she was always, when the twelve o'clock bell released her. As she left the house, wrapped in her waterproof, she

met Mrs. Glitter coming in, wet and worn-looking; giving
her a brief greeting, Laura went out to get a frugal luncheon, and so to the Academy of Design for an afternoon's
work.

This was a Saturday, one of the days, therefore, on which
Laura gave a lesson to Bessie Bradford; and as the Brad-
fords lived quite up-town, on Forty-ninth street, when
Laura left the Academy, a little before four, she took a
Madison-avenue car.

It had been snowing now for some hours, so that the
track was very heavy, and in consequence of the storm,
the car was crowded ; as Laura made her way through the
throng inside, some one touched her arm, and she found
Mrs. Bradford sitting by her. The old lady greeted her
with a bright smile, and cordial shake of the hand.

"You are going to our house, aren't you, my dear?"

"Yes," replied Laura. "You know this is my day."

"I know it is ; but you have good courage to be out in
such weather."

"Oh, I don't mind that in the least ; and for that matter,
it is no worse for me than for you."

The lady laughed. "I am a relic of the old school,
when girls had some strength and health," she said ; "and
I am glad that you are an exception to the modern young
ladies, who are so many of them ailing."

"My health is perfect," rejoined Laura ; "I am always
unromantically well."

"I am glad of it ; I am heartily glad of it, my dear ;
but aren't you tired standing up so long?"

"Not in the least ; I have been sitting all day."

"That is one of the rights that men have lately given
women," observed Mrs. Bradford. "The right of standing
up in the cars."

"Oh, that's all fair," said Laura. "I have no objection
to that—I believe in equality in all things—but there is one
thing I do object to ; we women are not recognized in the
state, of course, but I really think our existence might be

remembered in the arrangement of vehicles we use as much as we do these."

"How, my dear? I don't understand."

"In the length of these straps, one would think no woman ever used them, they are so short as evidently to have been constructed only for the accommodation of men. My arm fairly aches with reaching up to this one."

Mrs. Bradford laughed at this fancy of Laura's, and then a fresh crowd of people coming in, they were separated and the thread of their talk broken.

The car was going up Madison-avenue, and on the rise of ground the clogged track began to tell heavily on the poor horses; they tugged and pulled, but the progress was very slow; the driver struck them cruelly with his whip, and they staggered on, the steam rising in a cloud from their reeking bodies into the cold air.

Laura, who was near the front and could see all this plainly, felt the tenderest compassion for the poor patient brutes working so thanklessly. The men in the car looked out curiously or speculatively.

"Ought to have doubled up," said one.

"They pull pretty well!" remarked another.

"Ah, here we are!" cried a third, as, coming to a steeper rise, the horses stopped short.

The driver raised his heavy whip and lashed the helpless creatures furiously; they strained hard, their hoofs beating the ground, their mouths open, their sides heaving with the struggle. One heroic effort, and the car moved again; Laura glanced at Mrs. Bradford, seeking sympathy; the good lady's eyes were full of tears, the men continued their rough jests.

"The next hill 'll fetch 'em," said one.

"Can't stand this much longer, you know," predicted another.

"What'll you bet, Bob, we don't get to Eighty-sixth street till seven o'clock to-night?" said one handsomely-dressed youth to another ; and the two proceeded to lay a bet with much interest in the result.

It was sickening to Laura to see the dumb animals toiling and suffering, and to be unable to help them; and she was heartily glad when Forty-ninth street was reached, and she and Mrs. Bradford could leave the car.

"It was a cruel shame to overload those horses so ! " Laura exclaimed, as the two crossed to the sidewalk.

"It is very hard ! " replied Mrs. Bradford; " and I hope that some day we shall be sufficiently advanced in civilization to be able to correct some of these abuses."

The Bradfords' house stood about midway of the block on Forty-ninth street, and the two ladies made their way towards it, in the face of an almost blinding snow-storm ; their footfalls were unheard as they sank into the soft white flakes which had fallen over the earth, the wheels of passing carriages made no sound, and it seemed as if a great hush had come over the busy city. Laura was a little startled, then, when she heard her name called quite close to her; and turning she saw that a *coupé* was drawn up near the sidewalk, and Flora Livingston's sweet face was looking out at her. She was very lovely; her black velvet hat was adorned with pink roses and a few stray snowflakes had floated on to them and into her golden curls, while the cold air had given her cheeks an unusual color.

"Get in, Laura, and drive a little way with me," she said, as her friend came up.

"Impossible," replied Laura ; "I have to give a lesson to Bessie Bradford at four, and it is after that now."

"Oh, I'm so sorry! I know that mamma has written you a terrible note, and I want to tell you, dear, that I had nothing to do with it."

"I never thought you had, Flora."

"No, indeed; and I must try to see you sometimes, though you can't come to the house any more. There, don't look so angry," she said, piteously ; "it was not my fault."

" I am not angry with you, Flora dear, though I am a little indignant at my dismissal."

" It was all because I asked papa to let me study law."

" Ah ! and he refused ? "

" Of course, I was sure he would. You know, it's no use to contend against fate, Laura. But I won't keep you here in the snow; good-bye, dear."

The two friends kissed each other; and as Flora drove away, Laura ran up the steps to the Bradfords' house, the door of which was standing open to receive her.

CHAPTER XIV.

THE BRADFORDS' HOME.

THE prevailing impression which the home of the Bradfords gave one was of comfort, from the warm tints of the square hall of entrance, where crimson and brown were the prevailing colors in walls, furniture, and carpets, to the cozy library, where in cold weather a cannel-coal fire was always burning,—everything about the place spoke of substantial wealth and home pleasures.

Bessie Bradford was a pretty and promising girl of fifteen, with considerable talent for drawing, and a profound admiration for her young teacher, so that the two got on admirably together. As Laura came into the library, where the lessons were always given, she glanced at the clock, in dismay.

" Half-past four," she exclaimed! " Oh, that is too bad! I'd no idea it was so late ! "

" Never mind, my dear," said Mrs. Bradford; " come up stairs and take off your wet wraps, and then you must stay to dinner. Guy will see you home."

Laura gladly accepted this invitation, half conscious that part of its charm lay in Mrs. Bradford's last words. She went with the kind old lady to her room, where, in arranging her dress for the evening, she perhaps took more than usual pains to see that her hair and ribbons were becomingly arranged.

Going back to the library again, the next hour was passed in the lesson, which Laura gave faithfully and well. Just before it was over, Mr. Bradford came in, and shortly after the front door was again opened with a latch-key, and Laura felt that the only son had come home, even before Mrs. Bradford said so.

"There is Guy; now Miss Stanley, put up those drawing-materials; you have had quite enough lessons for to-day. And Bessie, will you ring for dinner?"

A few moments later, Guy came into the room, fresh from the toilette, with which he had removed the traces of the day's toil; certainly a very fine-looking gentleman, with such a stalwart figure, and such an honest face. He had no expectation of finding Laura with his family, and as he saw her, a quick flush rose to his cheek, responsive to the sudden blush that swept even to Laura's brow. The two shook hands, but their words of greeting were merely murmured phrases.

Mrs. Bradford watched them with a smile. "I've kept Miss Stanley to dinner," she explained; "I thought it was too bad to let her go away through the storm, and I promised that you would see her home, by and bye."

"I shall be very happy to do so," responded Guy heartily; and seating himself by his sister, the three were presently engaged in an animated conversation.

Mr. Bradford sat watching them for a few moments, and then he said to his wife: "Annie, my dear, that seems a very nice young lady."

"Very nice, indeed," responded Mrs. Bradford; then dropping her voice to a mysterious undertone, "and I think Guy likes her."

"Of course he does," said Mr. Bradford, innocently; "he always likes nice young ladies."

"But I mean very particularly—"

"Ah, Annie, are you trying match-making again?" her husband asked, with a smile.

"It's time Guy was married," replied the old lady, a little aggressively; "he is nearly twenty-eight years old, you know."

"I'm afraid you'll have no better luck than you did with the Boston girl we met last summer," suggested Mr. Bradford; "I don't think Guy is much inclined to matrimony; you have been trying to get him a wife, ever since he was twenty, but without result so far."

"He never has fancied any one, I know," admitted Mrs. Bradford ; "but I like Miss Stanley better than any one I've seen yet, and I think Guy does too."

Mr. Bradford smiled. "That's an odd way of putting it," he said; "I'm afraid sons don't always choose the women their mothers most fancy ; but you may be right; she seems a sensible, as well as a handsome girl, and I shall be satisfied if Guy is; he must suit himself. We believe in old-fashioned honest love; don't we, Annie ?"

The old lady did not reply in words, but her hand went out to meet her husband's, while their eyes met with a glance of affection, unchanged in forty years.

Presently after this, the summons to dinner called all the party to the charming dining-room—crimson-curtained and glowing with the warm reflections from a glorious fire sent back in ruby sparkles from cut-glass and polished silver.

It was a thoroughly charming meal, well-cooked and daintily served. In contrast with her recent plain and unpleasant surroundings the change was very agreeable to Laura, and then Guy was placed opposite to her and all the time she was conscious of his earnest eyes and the subtle intoxication of their influence.

When dinner was over, the party went into the drawing-room, in order that they might have some music. This room, although large and handsomely furnished, had none of the dreary grandeur which afflicts so many of our state parlors. Its walls were tinted, and adorned with some choice pictures, its furniture was well-chosen, and there were flowers and books in it, as if it really were an inhabited region. Mr. Bradford disposed himself comfortably on the sofa ; Mrs. Bradford sat with her knitting, near the shaded lamp on the center-table, and Laura took her place at the piano. It was a very fine instrument and she revelled in its rich notes after her long deprivation of music, for the Moulders had no piano. She played for some time, Guy sitting near her in silent appreciation of the music, and then sang a few simple ballads. She had a good contralto voice, and while making no pretence of extreme culture she executed with taste and feeling. Altogether the evening was a delightful one to Laura, endowed by nature with strong feelings and intense love of the beautiful, anything ugly or unartistic in her surroundings was a pain to her ; and she enjoyed keenly the beauty and comfort of this scene, and the harmony of the family with whom she was.

And then Guy was there, watching over her, talking to her, and later, taking her home. When they were out in the snowy streets, and she was leaning on his arm, Laura could not help saying somewhat of the thoughts that were in her heart.

"How happy you must be in such a home, Mr. Bradford ! "

"I am," replied Guy, heartily. "I thank God, daily, that I have so many blessings in my life."

"Your parents are so devoted to each other, so thoroughly kind."

"Yes, if I can but realize as much happiness in marriage as they have, my brightest dream will be embodied ; their's is the sort of union I believe in, equal confidence and affection on each side."

They had come to the corner of the street now, but no car was to be seen. "I'm afraid they're not running," said Bradford ; "I'm sorry I didn't send for a carriage."

"It doesn't snow at all," said Laura ; "and if you don't

mind, I should like to walk. You know I'm a country girl, and like a tramp; indeed, I feel as if I had not had enough exercise to-day."

Guy readily assented to this proposal, and the two crossed to the avenue. The storm had in fact ceased, and as the sidewalks were partially cleared, progress was easy down the wide way which was quite transformed by its fairy robes of snow. All the unsightliness of the street was covered with a soft white carpet ; the houses were decorated with fleecy draperies and ornaments, the railings sparkled with frosty incrustations, and glittering icicles hung from the lamp-posts, while the lights, flashing out on the scene, had their lustre·returned and multiplied by the brilliant reflections.

The two young people enjoyed their walk; Laura felt somewhat less embarrassed, than when Guy had been only sitting near her, and watching her. They talked on topics of practical interest, and the two miles of distance was passed over, only too quickly.

"I am sorry we are here," Guy exclaimed, as they ascended the steps of Laura's home; "I wish our walk had been at least a mile longer."

"I am very much obliged to you for your escort," Laura said, as the door was opened by Jane, who, seeing who it was, instantly disappeared with a grin.

"Don't thank me for what was such a pleasure to me," Guy replied in a low voice. "Good-night."

He held her hand with a firm grasp, but only for a moment, raised his hat, and as the door closed, turned away. Chateaubriand tells us of "*les échoes du sang*," which reveal the secret of unsuspected relationship to those who have the same blood in their veins, and the pressure, even of a gloved hand, has ere this awakened heart-echoes that proclaimed in tones that would not be stifled, the eternal consanguinity of souls.

CHAPTER XV.

THE CONCERT-SALOON.

On the morning after the sad night which Rhoda spent
in watching over her sick friend's restless sleep, when
Maggie woke to a new day, to the surprise of her faithful
companion, instead of seeming worse, as Rhoda had feared
she might, she was apparently better and stronger than
she had been for some time before. The subtle disease
which baffles the skill of the most patient observers, had
taken another turn, and in the course of a week, Maggie
was able to sit up all day and to occupy herself with some
light work which Rhoda had procured for her from a
collar-factory. This improvement in the sick girl's condition, made both friends more averse than ever to asking for
assistance ; they cherished their independence proudly,
and would both have suffered more than they had yet
endured, rather than be under obligations to any one.
Maggie still talked of going to her home, and cheered by
her friend began to build up a sort of hope that, when the
severity of the winter was over, she might be able to make
the journey to her native hills.

To pay the expenses of this trip, every penny was laid
by that could be saved. All day long the two girls sat
and sewed in their cold cheerless room ; lighting a little fire
in the grate only when driven to it by the utmost severity
of the weather. Rhoda procured what little food they had,
and under pretence of having eaten while she was out,
often fasted for hours, that she might be able to bring to
her companion some little comfort or delicacy. Patiently,
devotedly, did this girl, whom the world would call lost,
endure the trials and the hardships of her lot ; always
gentle to her friend, hard-working, self-denying, but holding in her heart a burning revolt against the position to

which misfortune and man's social laws had condemned
her.

One evening, Rhoda stood dressing for her night-work
at the saloon; a work which, much as she detested it, could
not be given up or neglected, now that money was so
doubly precious. Her long dark hair, clustering into
natural curls, was raised from her forehead over a roll, and
then fell into a shower of dusky ringlets, through which
a scarlet ribbon was passed. A black velvet bodice cut
low across the bust, displayed a neck which was well
formed, though it was somewhat thin. Her skirt was of
crimson stuff, quite short, while neat white stockings and
high boots set off the slender, well-shaped lower limbs.
The vivid colors of her dress, the showy style of her costume, were in singular contrast with the dingy dulness of
the room, nor was the expression of the girl's face in
harmony with the meretricious attire. She assumed her
garments rapidly, carelessly, scarcely glancing into the
little cracked mirror, seeming impatient of any attempt at
adornment. Maggie was in the bed, half-sitting, half-
reclining, and wrapped closely in a dark shawl. Her pale
face and bright hair, making a little spot of light under
the rays of the kerosene lamp, which was placed near her,
so that she might continue her work, a whole pile of linen
and lace which was heaped on the bed beside her, and with
which her thin white hands were busy. Presently they
rested from their toil and looking up at her friend, Maggie
said:

"Rhoda, won't you have the light on the dressing-table?
You are almost in the dark, there."

"It don't matter," replied Rhoda; "I believe I'm all
right, ain't I?"

As she spoke, she turned and came to the bed so that
the light fell full on her gay dress, her waving hair and
dark eyes. Maggie looked up at her, wistfully.

"Yes, you look real nice. Rhoda you are very pretty,
do you know? when your eyes are soft as they are now."

"Pretty!" exclaimed Rhoda, with a passionate gesture. "What is the use of my being pretty? Sometimes I look at myself in the glass at the saloon, and know that if I had half a chance, I could be as handsome as many of those fine ladies; but what's the use? The world says I am a creature of the dust, my youth and my good looks that ought to be my kingdom are my disgrace!"

"Why, Rhody, dear!" exclaimed Maggie, in surprise. "What makes you so fierce to-night? you haven't been that way this long time."

"I haven't been so to you, perhaps, Maggie, but I'm so all the time in my heart. However, I had a fresh reason to-day."

"What, something that happened when you were out?"

"Yes, I applied a week ago for a place in a store on Sixth avenue; a pretty good place too; I'd have had ten dollars a week, and wouldn't have had to go to the saloon any more. I didn't tell you, 'cause I meant to surprise you with some good news. As if there could be any good news for us!" she added, bitterly; "well, to-day I went for the place and was refused!"

"Why?"

"You can guess why, Maggie," a deep flush sweeping over her face; "the boss said he couldn't have any girls that weren't virtuous. Virtuous!" she repeated, with a savage emphasis, "the man himself keeps a girl on Twenty-second street, and he took a fellow in my place that I've seen in the saloon, and—well, he's not so *virtuous* as I am, yet he could have the place at fifteen dollars a week, because he is a man! It's a cruel, bitter shame, Maggie!—this damnation that waits for women, if they make one misstep. Because I have stumbled, I am a thousand times worse than the men who roll in the dust."

"But not really, Rhoda," said Maggie; "not in the sight of God."

"You can hold on a little to the old faith, Maggie,

and I'm glad you can," said Rhoda, in a softened voice.
"But it's too hard for me. I suppose God - is just, but
man is so cruel, and it is only men I see. There I must go,
or I shall be late at the saloon. How I hate that place ! "
she added, fiercely ; " I hoped to get away from it, but I'm
not *virtuous* enough to leave it, and so must go and take
my nightly dose of insult ! "

Maggie's hazel eyes had filled with tears at the force of
Rhoda's words. " It's too bad, Rhoda ! " she said, plaintively. It's so hard ! I wish I was away, so you wouldn't
have to go to that horrid saloon ! "

Rhoda was down on her knees by the bed in a moment,
" My darling, don't say that ! I love so to have you here
with me ! why, Maggie, you are all that keeps me from despair ! "

" And in the spring we'll go away together, won't
we ? "

" Yes, dear, yes ! " then jumping up, Rhoda affected to
be very busy finding her hat and cloak, and putting them
on rapidly. Just as she was leaving, she came to the bed
and tossed an orange upon it. " Oh, by the way," she said,
with an assumption of great carelessness ; " here's something I got very cheap; now eat it up, don't let me find
anything but the peel when I get home ; good bye."

Without waiting for a reply, she hurried from the room
and out into the streets ; but as she went on, she felt heart-
sick. The fruit had been bought with the few cents that
should have purchased her own supper ; she was tired and
hungry and cold, almost despairing ; she had spoken
cheerful words to her friend, leading her to think that the
two would some day go away together, but she had really
no such hope. To her, the future was all black and grim,
she would work and earn money enough to send Maggie
home ; and after that, she would be left to wrestle alone
with her fate—a fate that she realized only too plainly,
seeing by the lurid light of experience, the hideous doom
that awaits the outcasts of society when their youth is past.

She detested the life she was leading, and yet her very
devotion to her friend forced her every day to drink the
bitter cup to its dregs, for society and the world offered her
no hope of escape from it. If she had been a man, her early
errors would have been forgotten or unheeded, and with
the resolution and industry she had, a dozen remunerative
occupations would have been open to her ; as a woman,there
was no hope, the curse must follow her wherever she went,
and the only means of sustaining life was to toil all day at
such work as she could get from shops where no questions
were asked, and in the evening to be at the beck and call
of the frequenters of a concert-saloon.

Yet, the girl had a certain spirit of her own, which made
her respected, even among these rude men ; she had a sharp
tongue and a sort of ready wit, that was at once fascinating and repellent, so that she held her own bravely, like
some bright flower that keeps its petals unsullied, though
it spring from a muck heap.

The saloon where Rhoda waited was in a cellar, a short
flight of steps leading down to it; but this uninviting entrance was rendered attractive by a transparency over the
door, representing two young women of extreme robustness
of figure and scantiness of drapery, reclining in an impossible attitude on a green bank adorned with startling red
flowers. Within, discreetly veiled by the ground glass
which was set in the doors, was a scene of showy brilliancy.
A large room, rather low of ceiling, with many tables and
chairs arranged in rows through it, the walls hung with
pictures, equivocal in design and brilliant in coloring. On
one side was a bar, fancifully arranged, where two men
were engaged in "mixing drinks." At the upper end was
a small platform on which a band of four men sat, who
perpetually discoursed loud, but inharmonious sound ; it
could not be called music.

When Rhoda entered, there were but a few customers
in the place; a dozen other girls dressed like herself,lounged
at the tables or chatted in groups. They were all hollow-

eyed and haggard, most of them having a hard defiant look about the mouth, though there were some who had in their sad eyes only an expression of hopeless appeal. They were all painted, the rouge and powder giving their complexions an appearance of false brilliancy. In this respect Rhoda presented a marked contrast to the rest; her pale dark face was entirely colorless, except when some quick emotion sent the blood to her cheeks. As she came in, one or two of the girls nodded to her, but the rest took no notice of her ; she was evidently not a favorite here. She went and hung up her cloak and hat, and a moment after there was a rush of customers into the saloon—a party of Yale students in the city on a " lark," who were " seeing the sights."

They came in, filling the place with noise and merriment, joking with the girls and keeping them all busy. Rhoda waited on them with the rest, but as she looked on these young gentlemen, who were none the worse for saying and doing what stamped her companions with infamy, she felt fiercely wrathful against the unjust inequality ; and when one of the laughing youths ventured to touch her hair, with a gay compliment on its beauty, she turned upon him with such a bitter jest that he drew back dismayed, and she was presently left to herself.

Other customers came and went, and Rhoda kept on with her regular duties, doing her work well, even while she loathed the whole false scene of hollow laughter and ribald jest. The evening wore away, and it grew to be late ; the customers had thinned out, the tired band made long pauses between its discordant waltzes and polkas. Rhoda was sitting at the upper end of the room, resting her head wearily on her hand, when the door opened and a tall and handsome man appeared ; he hesitated a moment, looking about a little apprehensively, then seeming to be reassured, came in. As Rhoda saw him, she started to her feet, and hurried to a table, where two men were seated, turning her back to the new comer. It did not avail her, for he came directly towards her.

"Rhoda," he said, "won't you wait on an old friend?"

She turned upon him, and gave him a look, her black eyes blazing with suppressed rage. "No," she said, "I will not."

"Ah, ha!" retorted the gentleman, "we'll see if you won't."

He walked directly to the bar, where the head man hastened to wait on him, with every appearance of deference. There was a short conversation between them, and then one of the girls came to Rhoda, who had stood all this time with her back to the counter.

"The boss wants you," she said, in a frightened voice.

Rhoda turned and walked to the bar; the gentleman had gone up the room, and seated himself at a table in the corner furthest from the door. The saloon-keeper met Rhoda with an oath:

"What do you mean?" he asked, angrily, "by giving yourself such d—d stuck-up airs? Go and wait on Judge Swinton this instant!"

Rhoda flushed crimson; an indignant refusal rose to her lips. Was she to be forever an utter and abject slave! Then Maggie's hazel eyes seemed to look at her appealingly, she thought what the loss of this situation would be to her friend, and stifling back her anger, she walked to the table, where the judge sat, smilingly awaiting her.

"Come, Rhoda," he said, as she stood before him, "there's no use quarreling with an old friend—why I came here on purpose to see you! What'll you take to drink?"

"Anything you please," she said, in a hard, dry voice.

"Well then, we'll have a bottle of champagne for old acquaintance."

If he could have known what stinging pain it was to

her to have their association recalled! But to his dull
apprehension, he really fancied that their former connection
gave him a claim of friendship upon his victim.

Rhoda turned away, and going to the bar, gave the
order; the saloon-keeper, when he heard how handsome it
was, became all smiles, and she presently returned to her
customer carrying a waiter, containing a bottle and two
glasses.

"There! that's right! Now, sit down, and we'll have
a nice chat," urged the judge, amiably.

Rhoda sat down, mechanically, as if she had resolved
to go through the task, however abhorrent it might be.
She took the bottle, and drew the cork dexterously, afterwards filling the two glasses. The judge raised his with a
smile.

"Here's to your future good-luck!" Then, as Rhoda
neither responded nor touched the wine, he added: "Why
you don't drink anything! How's that?"

"I never drink," replied Rhoda, slowly.

"Never drink! Why how do you get along here?"

"The boss understands," she said; "I let the men order
what they please, but I never touch it. It does just as
well, though; they have to pay for it," she added, with a
sneer.

"You always were a very queer girl, Rhoda," the judge
said, looking at her curiously. "But I really wish you
would take just a taste of this champagne. You know you
ought not to treat me like a stranger," moving a little
nearer to her.

She turned her eyes on him again. "No, you are not a
stranger," she said.

The look seemed to make the judge a little uneasy.
"No, indeed!" he urged; "and I've come here to-night on
a real friendly errand. I suppose now you'd like to earn a
hundred dollars?"

"If I can, honestly."

A smile rose to his lips, but he checked it; something

in the girl's face cutting off the sarcasm. " Of course," he nodded; " what I want is very easily done, or rather not done, for I've only come to ask you not to do something."

" What, for instance ? "

" How devilish cool you are, Rhoda ! " he exclaimed, a little impatiently. " Don't you care for a hundred dollars ? "

" Very much," she replied. " One hundred dollars would give me many things I need. How am I to earn it ? "

The judge hesitated in singular embarrassment ; Rhoda waited quietly. After two or three beginnings, he said, abruptly, " You know Miss Laura Stanley, I believe ? "

" Yes."

" Well, it's about her."

" Indeed ! what about her ? "

" Nothing much, only I don't want you to tell her that you ever knew me."

" Why not ? Surely, when a poor girl has the honor of the acquaintance of such a distinguished swell as Judge Swinton, she might be allowed to mention it."

The Judge colored at the sneering emphasis of the words, but he affected to laugh off the matter as a joke. " You don't really care for that, Rhoda, and one hundred dollars is better any day than boasting of any man's acquaintance. Come, promise me you won't say anything to her about me."

" If I promise, how do you know I'll keep my word ? "

" Oh, I'll trust you Rhoda. I know you well enough for that," and he drew out his wallet. " You shall have the one hundred right down, if you'll say you won't tell Miss Stanley any tales about me."

" But why do you care so much about this ? "

" I didn't mind telling you," said the judge, leaning over with a confidential air; " I've taken a fancy to the young lady."

" Ah ! For what ? " the dark eyes questioning closely.

" Well, I think I shall marry her," the judge said, with a sudden assumption of frankness.

"Indeed!"

"Yes. You see it's about time I settled down. I've sown wild oats enough;" and he laughed carelessly, showing all his white teeth. "I don't care to have her know about the wild oats, though."

"Of course not," replied Rhoda, speaking always with a singular reserve and quietness.

"And you will help me, eh?"

"No."

The word was said so calmly, that he seemed hardly to comprehend its meaning. "What!" he exclaimed; "you won't take a hundred dollars, just to hold your tongue a few weeks, about that old freak of mine?"

"No."

"Why not?"

"Perhaps because I'm not on the Bench; I don't take bribes, Judge."

The man winced, as if she had struck him a blow, and flushed angrily. "You refuse, utterly?"

"Yes."

He frowned darkly, then with an effort he forced a smile. "You might, for old friendship, Rhoda; come, I'll make it a hundred and fifty. Do this just to please an old sweetheart; you know I was always clever to you."

She turned upon him the suppressed wrath that had been smouldering all this time, breaking forth suddenly into fierce words. "Clever to me!" she cried; "you can come to me with such cant as that! Do you think I have forgotten the coward blow that has disfigured me for life?" pointing quickly to her mutilated mouth. "Do you think I have forgotten the vile drugs and the lying plot you used, to ruin me? No, they are burnt into my memory like fire! I would not touch your money, if it would save me from death by torture, or from such a life as I lead, which is worse," she added darkly. "I have talked to you, to-night, only because I was forced to; but I am not so utterly low as to be willing to help you to bring another woman into your power."

The judge rose while she was speaking, and there was a cruel light in his blue eyes, as he answered, " You won't have my friendship or my money, Rhoda; well, you must take the consequences."

He threw a five dollar bill on the table to pay for the wine, and walked out of the saloon.

CHAPTER XVI.

MRS. DUNCAN'S BALL.

IT was the night of Mrs. Duncan's ball—one of the events of the fashionable season. The great parlors of her house, one of the largest in New York, were crowded with well-dressed people. Music from a fine band filled the air, which was heavy with the perfume of the flowers that decorated every room, while many wax lights shed their soft brilliancy over the gay scene.

In this throng of fair women and elegant men, the arrival of Mr. and Mrs. Livingston and their daughters created a sensation—even where there was so much grace— the extraordinary beauty of the two girls excited a murmur of admiration wherever they moved. The toilette which a fashionable *modiste* had constructed for Flora, was of her favorite color, blue—a silk of exquisite lustre, trimmed with soft blonde lace; her fair hair floated over her shoulders in many ringlets, a wreath of forget-me-nots confining the clustering curls above her pure forehead.

Maud was dressed as became a *débutante*, in white, with wild roses in her shining hair, and there were those who found more to admire in her haughty handsome face and flashing eyes, than in her sister's dainty loveliness.

Mr. Ferdinand Le Roy was in attendance, faultlessly costumed as usual, his hair and attire arranged with such

absolute precision as to be almost painfully exact. As
soon as the young ladies had made their greetings to their
hostess, he joined them, approaching with a certain air of
proprietorship.

"Twin rosebuds," he said, as he turned his steady yet
critical glance from one sister to the other, as if carefully
weighing their relative charms.

As Flora caught the look, Laura's words recurred to her;
there *was* a certain air of the Grand Seigneur about this
man. She felt an angry revolt against it, and when, a moment later, a gentleman came to claim her for a dance, she
walked off with a slight indifferent nod to Mr. Le Roy,
which perhaps conveyed somewhat of her thoughts. He
looked after her keenly, and then turned to Maud, who
bowed her stately head and took his arm, with a very evident desire to please.

The night went on ; but Flora, even while surrounded
by other admirers, was conscious, always, that this man was
watching her, with a gaze which never relented. She was
gay with her gay companions, she laughed with the rest ;
but there was with her all the time, a feeling of oppression,
a sense that she was not one moment free from that cold,
yet devouring regard. Wherever she went, whoever was
with her, she could see those steel blue eyes, compelling her
again and again to meet their look; and when at last he approached to claim her for a dance which she had promised
him, it seemed to her as if there were slowly overwhelming
her a stern power which she detested, and yet which she
was helpless to resist.

"Miss Flora," Mr. Le Roy said, as he drew her hand
through his arm, "you have been less kind to me this
evening than usual."

"Have I?" she asked, with an attempt at a smile. "I
have not intended it."

"I hope not ; come, let us go into the conservatory.
You do not care to dance?"

The words were spoken as an assertion, rather than as a question, and Flora acquiesced with a faint " No."

" Well, then, let us find a quiet place; I have something to say to you."

Flora did not reply, but at these significant words, her heart stood still for a moment, and then beat with heavy throbs that almost suffocated her.

They walked on in silence till they were in the shadowy aisles of the conservatory, away from the tumult of the ball, and where the music was softened to a faint sweet strain. Mr. Le Roy led the way to a rustic seat under the broad leaves of an overarching palm-tree, and motioned Flora to sit there. There was something imperious in the gesture ; but after one second of hesitation, Flora obeyed it.

Mr. Le Roy placed himself beside her and bent over her, his searching eyes reading her downcast blushing face. Then, after a moment of almost intolerable silence, he put out his hand and laid it on hers with a firm grasp.

" Flora," he said, " will you give yourself to me ? Will you be my wife ? "

She started with one quick impulse of recoil from that compelling touch, and glanced up at him hurriedly.

Mr. Le Roy smiled, in those blue eyes he had seen for the first time a look of fear, and he drew his grasp closer about her, as he said, " Flora, I have been aware of your preference for months past ; I have your parent's consent ; come, my sweet trembling little prisoner, you are fairly caught. Give me your promise."

She drew away, making a half attempt to rise. " Oh, let me go," she faltered.

" No," he said; " never again; you are fairly mine Flora; you won't give me any promise ? Nay, then, I must take a pledge."

The forceful eyes were close to hers ; the strong detaining hands held her fast, and the man pressed his lips to her cheek, while she remained passive, unable to escape. In her heart, there was a passionate revolt ; but it seemed

wholly impossible to put it into words, or to avoid submission to this irresistible will.

"Now, darling," he murmured, as he released her,
"you are my bride elect ; and before spring, I hope you will
be my bride in truth."

"Oh, no, no !" she exclaimed, with an irrepressible
shudder.

"Yes," he said, firmly ; "it must be so. You are startled now; this seems sudden ; but you must grow accustomed
to the thought. Shall we go back to the ball-room ? "

Flora assented eagerly, starting hurriedly to her feet;
but Mr. Le Roy laid his hand on her again. " Not so fast,
sweet one," he said ; and before he would let her go, he
forced her to let him touch her lips with his.

It was over then, as it seemed to Flora; a horrible degradation had come upon her ; she was no longer free, no
longer belonged to herself, she had received a master, and
been compelled to submit to the symbol of his power. As
she walked out of the Conservatory, she remembered with
sudden vividness, the old story of the Caudine Forks, and
the bitter humiliation of the Roman army. " I have passed
under the yoke," she thought, " I am a slave."

Her one strongest impulse, was to escape from her companion ; and when at the threshold of the ball-room, she
met a young man, who claimed her for the dance ; she left
her lover's arm, with an eagerness that was hardly disguised. Mr. Le Roy noticed it with a slight frown, but a moment after, a faint smile of triumph followed, as he caught
one timid backward look, that Flora stole towards him.

She went with her partner into the ball-room, moving
mechanically, not speaking, hardly conscious where she
was. The young man first broke the silence.

" Do you care to dance, Miss Livingston ? "

Flora started, and looked up at him. Until this moment, she had scarcely thought who her companion was; the
voice, the foreign accent, recalled him. He was a young
German, who had been presented to her early in the even-

6*

ing, and with whom she had made an engagement to dance. His name she remembered was Rudolph Ernstein, and she recollected that he had been spoken of as a scion of a noble family, who was travelling in this country for amusement and instruction.

As she glanced at him, she saw a pair of dreamy eyes, lighting up a delicate sensitive face, with broad intellectual brow, and fair hair and moustache. The look that met hers soothed her, she scarcely knew how; there was in it a sort of unspoken sympathy.

"If you are weary," he said, "we will not dance. Pray let it be as you wish."

"I am not tired," replied Flora. "This is a waltz, too; my favorite dance."

He took her hand, and in a moment they were whirling about the room. Flora discovered at once that her partner was a most accomplished waltzer, graceful in movement, supporting her respectfully, yet firmly. The music was one of Strauss' most exquisite creations; and the swaying motion, the harmonious strains, lulled her, till her sore heart grew somewhat quiet. Ernstein bent over her, watching with wistful eyes every expression of the beautiful face beside him. On a sudden Flora started and paused; Mr. Le Roy had approached the circle of dancers, and was watching her. She felt in a moment that her freedom was gone, and her first impulse was to escape again.

"What is it?" asked Ernstein.

"Let us go away!" she said; "I feel stifled here."

The young man offered her his arm, and they left the ball-room. "Will you go to the conservatory?" he asked.

"No; oh no!" she answered quickly. "Can't we find the air somewhere?"

"There is a window open in the library," replied Ernstein.

"Let us go there."

They went to the room, which was off the main suite of apartments; there were a good many persons in it, chatting

together, or looking over the engravings, but there was no
crowd. The two young people made their way to a
French window, which was ajar, letting the cool night air
into the heated house. As they approached it, they saw
that it looked on to a balcony.

"Oh, let us go outside!" exclaimed Flora. "The
moonlight is lovely."

"Don't you fear taking cold?"

"No, no!" she repeated, impatiently; "only let us get
out of this warm room."

Ernstein raised his hand to open the window wider,
and Flora drew back the curtain; but before they could
step out, a calm voice arrested them.

"Miss Livingston, you are to come with me; your people
are going."

Flora turned and met Mr. Le Roy's cold, disapproving
regard. "They won't mind waiting a few moments," she
said, defiantly.

"Will you go out, then? Ernstein asked with eagerness.

"No; Miss Livingston will not go out," said Mr. Le
Roy, sternly. "Flora, come with me."

She hesitated, and looked from one to the other, with a
glance that neither of them ever forgot. The young German held out his hand, entreatingly; his deep eyes mutely
seconding the appeal. But Mr. Le Roy put his fingers on
her wrist, with an unmistakeable air of proprietorship:

"Come at once!" he said, imperatively. And he drew
her hand through his arm, and led her away. "You forget, Flora," he added, as they went out of the room, "your
flirting days are over; you belong to me now."

CHAPTER XVII.

LAURA'S VISITORS.

To Laura the weeks of winter went by monotonously, in some respects sadly. Her residence at the Moulders' was not, in all respects, a happy one; to be a frequent witness of Mr. Moulder's overbearing conduct, and Mrs. Moulder's patient submission, was a constant trial to her, but she had become much attached to the gentle lady, who seemed to find comfort in her sympathy and affection; and this alone reconciled her to remaining in a home that would otherwise have been wholly distasteful to her. Sometimes Laura was quite out of patience with her friend, for her unfailing meekness and entire yielding to her captious and unkind husband—even when his demands were unreasonable; once she ventured to suggest an open rebellion.

Mr. Moulder had come home tired and cross; he found fault with the children, scolded about the singing of the canary, and made himself obtrusively disagreeable. Mrs. Moulder was as gentle as usual; she quieted the children, hung a cloth over the poor bird, and was ready to do anything to please her husband. All this was before dinner; but his wife's efforts failed to soothe him, and at that meal he was unusually surly. The turkey, he said, was underdone. Mrs. Moulder, though looking tired and pale, went herself to the kitchen and broiled a leg for him; when this was brought, he declared it was scorched to a crisp. She quietly laid it aside, and took the other leg to cook in the same manner. When she returned, flushed and weary, with this, she found him eating heartily of the breast, and his only comment, as she placed the joint before him, was that he " couldn't wait all night for his dinner."

Laura looked on with waxing indignation; she saw the

tears in Mrs. Moulder's mild eyes, and noticed that her plate was pushed away, almost untouched. It seemed to the impetuous young lady, that it would be wrong to keep silent any longer, and when, at last, the children were disposed of, and Mr. Moulder had gone to his club, Laura ventured a remonstrance.

"Agnes," she said, for she had already learned to call her friend by her pretty Christian name, "Agnes, I am so indignant that I feel as if I must say a word to you, may I?"

"I don't know, dear; perhaps you had better not."

"This much I must tell you," protested Laura, vehemently, "I don't believe you make Mr. Moulder any happier by yielding to him so utterly."

"Don't you think I do?" in gentle surprise.

"No. I believe he would really be better off with a wife who asserted herself a little. Now, you see, to-day, if you had not troubled to please him with his dinner, he would have eaten just what he did at last, and been better satisfied."

"Perhaps so; but I feel as if I must do all I can to suit him."

"I only wish you would try a change for awhile, and make a sort of declaration of independence!"

Mrs. Moulder shook her head. "I could not do it, Laura; it's not in my nature; and indeed, I don't mind what I do for him, if he will only be a little tender to me." And the soft eyes were full of a sad yearning, that was very pathetic.

It was not very often, however, that Laura was a witness of Mr. Moulder's most trying exactions, as she rarely saw him except at meals, which he generally ate in surly silence. Her own time was now very fully occupied. She had her drawing-lessons to give, and when she was at home, she spent every spare moment in practicing her art. She was struggling hard for the annual prize, given at the academy, to the best drawing; and was devoting her energies to a study from a cast which she designed to be her competitive picture.

Occasionally her evenings were intruded upon by visitors. Frank Heywood came very often, Guy Bradford about once a week, and Judge Swinton made some excuse for calling quite frequently. Laura treated the three visitors very differently.

With Frank Heywood she had long confidential conversations, which she keenly enjoyed, so that they came after a time to be on terms of the closest intimacy. Sometimes he would read aloud, while she went on with her drawing; sometimes she went with him to some place of public amusement, for which he had always an unlimited amount of tickets; and it was to him that she owed a constant supply of papers and new books.

When Laura was told that Mr. Bradford was in the parlor, she would take a sly peep in the glass, perhaps put on a bright ribbon, or another collar, and then going down to the sitting-room door, would knock softly. When Mrs. Moulder came to see what she wanted, she would tell her, with a face which she strove in vain to make indifferent, that she had a visitor, and could Minnie come down with her? "Presently," Mrs. Moulder would say, with a smile; and so Laura would go down to the parlor to meet Guy's hearty greeting and earnest eyes.

After a few moments, Minnie, who had delayed to put on a clean apron, would come in with her work and sit down demurely in a corner. Guy always greeted the little girl kindly, though experience soon taught him that the young chaperon would stay as long as he did, even if she dropped asleep at her post, as sometimes happened. Minnie was never sent for when Frank Heywood came; Laura herself could scarcely tell why; he was so like a brother, she said to herself; but Guy Bradford was different.

As for Judge Swinton, he rarely came, except under pretence of political business with Moulder, and Laura would be sent for, as the daughter of an old friend. Knowing as she did, that this man could at any time communicate her whereabouts to her father, she always obeyed the summons; but on these occasions, she never so much as entered the room without Minnie, who was strictly enjoined never on any account to go to sleep, or to quit the room, while the judge was in it.

Laura knew very well that he looked on the little girl with anything rather than favor; he would frown blackly at her sometimes, and rarely acknowledged her entrance by more than a condescending nod. Laura held these visits of his in utter abhorrence; her manner was always cold, though strictly polite, but nothing sufficed to check the bold admiration of the man's look, or the broad compliments with which he would bring a blush to her cheeks; and she was conscious, always, that only the presence of her little companion prevented some avowal from which she instinctively shrank.

There was another visitor whom Laura sometimes saw, though he was rather a friend of the whole family than of herself in particular. One evening when she came down to dinner a little late, she found a stranger at the table. A young man of perhaps five or six and twenty, thick-set, with square shoulders and heavy limbs; his hair was of a tawny red, and he evidently regarded it as very ornamental, for he wore it unusually long, and had a thick moustache and side-whiskers of the same brilliant color. His dress was showy, a brown coat with broad velvet collar, a large blue cravat, and very much of shirt bosom, on which blazed a diamond pin. As Laura came to her place, Mr. Moulder looked up importantly.

"My nephew, Mr. Fitlas, Miss Stanley; Miss Stanley, Mr. Fitlas, Mr. Jerry Fitlas;" he added, as if the name conveyed some great distinction. "Mr. Fitlas has just got back from a western trip for the firm of Star and Flash," he explained; "you know Star and Flash, of course."

Laura could not remember to have heard of the firm,

but she bowed to Mr. Fitlas, politely, who returned the salutation with an obliging nod.

"Yes," he said, "I've had a goodish trip this time; been away six weeks."

"How far west did you go?" asked Mrs. Moulder, who was always expected to carry on the conversation at the table ; Mr. Moulder eating steadily, but rarely speaking.

"As far as Kansas city," replied Mr. Fitlas. "Didn't get beyond the Rockies this time," he explained airily, speaking of the solemn mountains, as if they were children's playthings.

"And had you a successful journey?"

"Tolerable," answered Mr. Fitlas; "it didn't pan out very heavy. It was a kind of an unordinary trip, you know." Mr. Fitlas had rather a faculty for misusing or mispronouncing words.

"A what?" asked Mrs. Moulder, looking a little puzzled.

"Out-of-the-way-ish, you see; went to the smallish places. Drummed up the big places last fall."

"Oh yes, I remember."

"Yes, I've done a tall lot of travelling in the last six months, and I compliment myself I've done it pretty well."

The air of complacency with which he said this, was almost too much for Laura; a smile twitched at the corners of her mouth, and she glanced at Mrs. Moulder, who seemed carefully to avoid her eye, asking Mr. Fitlas, somewhat hastily, "Are you glad to be back in New York again?"

"Well, yes," replied Mr. Fitlas, with an air as if he were conferring the highest honors on the city by this declaration. "In New York I find the best oysters and the handsomest ladies I see anywhere;" and he looked at Laura, as if desirous of having her understand that she was included in this gracious declaration.

"I'm sure the ladies will be very much obliged to you for your appreciation and the rank to which you assign them," said Laura.

Utterly impervious to the sarcasm, Mr. Fitlas continued: "Yes, that is an assertment I've made hundreds of times. In Kentuck I was asked if the girls weren't tiptop. 'They're very nice,' says I; stunning, indeed; for they're all big, there," he explained. "But, says I, the New York girls beats the world; smaller you know, and for my part I don't like 'em so big."

"You've had an opportunity of seeing a great variety of places and people," remarked Mrs. Moulder.

"Well, yes, I have; there ain't many places but what knows Jerry Fitlas," he admitted. "Been in twenty-seven different States, and travelled ten thousand miles this last year. How is that for high?"

Mr. Moulder evidently regarded this as a witticism of the first order, for he suddenly burst into a guffaw of delight and exhibited for a time unusual animation. When the meal was over and the party left the table, Mr. Moulder called Mr. Fitlas into the parlor, where they were alone together.

"Jerry," he said, "I thought I'd just tell you about Miss Stanley."

"All right. What's up, now?"

"She's boarding here, you know, and teaching drawing."

"So Agnes said."

"But she ain't poor at all, though it seems like it. Her father's one of the richest men in Dutchess county."

"That's a poser! What makes her teach, then?"

"Just a notion she's took up. She's sort of inclined to go for woman's rights, and be independent, and all that sort of nonsense."

"That's the way they do it," said Mr. Fitlas, shaking his head mournfully. "There's a great deal of such ideas about, out west I met lots of girls who went for woman's rights, some of 'em real pretty too."

"It's all wrong," declared Mr. Moulder, testily; "women ought to stay at home, and do as their husbands tell 'em.

They ain't up to men, any way, and they're fools to try to be."

"Oh, of course," assented Mr. Fitlas, with his most superior smile. "We men run the machine. It's well enough to have women around, though," he added, thoughtfully.

"Certainly," concluded Mr. Moulder; "they're all right in their place, but not trying to take ours. It's preposterous!"

"But about this girl," said Mr. Fitlas, bringing the conversation back to its original subject, "I found her quite handsome."

"She's well enough looking," admitted Mr. Moulder, "and I thought I'd just tell you who she was; it might be worth thinking of, you know."

"I twig," replied Mr. Fitlas, shutting one eye, knowingly. "I hadn't thought of settling yet, but if there's money, I might look into the thing a little."

And with a view to prosecuting his acquaintance with the young lady whom he condescended to admire, Mr. Fitlas ascended to the sitting-room. But quite in vain; Laura had gone to her room, and did not again appear during the evening. However, Mr. Fitlas was not discouraged, as he continued from time to time to take a meal at the Moulders', and he made various attempts to play the agreeable to Miss Stanley.

CHAPTER XVIII.

SOME LEGAL ITEMS.

So the time passed on until the holiday season came. Two days before Christmas, Mr. Glitter's school closed for a fortnight, and as most of his pupils were away, or not taking lessons, Laura had a little leisure. She employed it in obtaining some trifling toys for the children and in executing two pictures, designed as presents for her kind friends, Mrs. Moulder and Mrs. D'Arcy. When the day of the great festival came, there was a noisy scene over the presents which came to the young Moulders, and so many violent quarrels between Aleck and poor little Agnes, who was always his especial victim, that Laura was glad to leave the house for the refreshment of the services in church.

Mrs. D'Arcy had invited her young friend to dine with her on that day, to meet the Bradfords and Frank Heywood; and as it was a long time since Laura had seen the doctor, she went a little early to her house, that she might have a chat with her before the other guests came.

She found the lady alone in her library, with a pile of papers by her side. The greeting between the two was most hearty; Laura presented the picture she had painted, and which Mrs. D'Arcy received with great pleasure, returning the present with a handsome box of water-color paints. When Laura had exhausted her admiration of this really most valuable gift, the doctor, who had listened with a pleased smile, said :

" I am heartily glad, my dear, that you like the box so well. But it won't melt away, if you take your eyes off from it for a moment, and tell me what you have been doing this long time."

" Working hard," replied Laura. " There's not much else to tell."

" That is a good report," replied Mrs. D'Arcy ; " I have heard of you sometimes from Frank Heywood; do you see him very often ? " looking at her keenly.

" Oh, yes ! " answered Laura, unconsciously, " very often; I like him so much ! "

" An excellent friend for you," the doctor said, again with a slight accent on friend; "and how is Mrs. Moulder ? "

" Only tolerably well; oh, Mrs. D'Arcy, I do grow so indignant at the way her husband treats her, and she so lovely and patient, and so delicate in health just now."

"It's a shame!" said the doctor; "I have more than half suspected it all along; in attending her, I have seen that there was some trouble on her mind that no medicine could reach."

"And can nothing be done to change this state of affairs?" asked Laura.

"Nothing, my dear, that I can suggest; the man has by law the right to treat his wife almost as he pleases."

"With no redress for her?"

"Only in case of actual brutal violence; and then, you see, how lenient the punishments are! When people prate against giving the ballot to women, they do not realize that it is needed at this moment, to protect them in life and limb; that the laws, as they stand to-day, actually sanction a certain amount of tyranny on the part of the husband; that bodily injury to a wife is scarcely noticed, while the same harm to a stranger would be severely dealt with. If a man take a purse from another man, and lay his hand on his arm while committing the theft, it is highway robbery, punishable with at least five years' imprisonment. If he beat his wife almost to death, it is a mere misdemeanor, to be condoned by a few weeks in the penitentiary, or a light fine; while if he take from her all her earnings, it is not even robbery!"

"Then there is legal authority for a man's abuse and ill-treatment of his wife?"

"Certainly; here are a few instances of man's brutality and its reward, taken from various papers, and which 1 have preserved."

The doctor opened a drawer in a table and took from it a book containing slips. From these she read:

"John W. Smith, who beat his wife on the head with a crowbar, was lately sentenced to six months' imprisonment! The woman's life was at one time despaired of; but she did not die, and so he escaped any serious punishment."

"Thomas Fitzpatrick, who beat and kicked his wife to death a few days ago, at their residence in Van Brunt street, was yesterday in dicted by the Grand Jury for murder in the first degree. He was arraigned, and his trial set down for the October term of the Court of Oyer and Terminer. The District-Attorney expressed a doubt whether the prisoner could be tried for anything but manslaughter, and he was admitted to bail in one thousand dollars."

" Now just contrast the amount of bail in this last case with that charged for offences against the property of other men."

" W. H. Weigel, indicted for perjury in giving false testimony in the Tilden Butler suit, and who had given five thousand dollars bail to appear, was arraigned and required to give the same amount of bail, with two sureties, justifying in ten thousand dollars each in real estate in this city, and was given until this morning to find bondsmen."

" Arthur Salisbury, painter, of No. 247 Eighteenth street, South Brooklyn, was yesterday held to bail in the sum of one thousand five hundred dollars, by Judge Ledwith, for attempting on Thursday night to pick the pocket of Charles Klein, of No. 102 Flatbush avenue, Brooklyn, while the latter was standing in Greene street."

" Thus we see that if a man kills his wife, it is so trifling an offence that he can be bailed for one thousand dollars ! while if he commit perjury, he must pledge four times that sum ; and a mere attempt to pick the pocket of a stranger requires half as much again security as was needed for the wife-murderer ! "

" It is horrible injustice ! " exclaimed Laura, her gray eyes glowing with excitement.

" Horrible, indeed ! " repeated Mrs. D'Arcy; " but it is no wonder that such atrocities are lightly punished, when we realize what is the general tone of our laws with regard to women. In most States the statutes declare that letters of administration shall not be granted to ' persons guilty of infamous crimes, or to married women;' and again, that wills can be made by all persons except ' idiots, persons of unsound mind, and married women;' an association so degrading, that it is no wonder that wives are regarded as household chattels, or inferior to their lords and masters.

Indeed the whole dicta of the law indicate that the wife is considered as the property of the husband, subject to him, and ever amenable to his correction. I have made a study of this," the doctor went on, " and here are some memoranda I have jotted down." Turning over the leaves of her book, she read:

" Bishop, in his work ' Husband and Wife,' a recognized legal authority, says, ' the relation resembles that of parent and child, guardian and ward ;' and again, ' the wife should conform to the tastes and habits of the husband.'

" The Supreme Court of Mississippi declared, 1834, Bradley *versus* the State : ' A husband should confine himself within proper bounds when he sees fit to correct his wife.' "

" Justifying the correction, however," said Laura.

" Certainly ; and Pennsylvania recently confirmed this decision ; in Richards *versus* Richards, the court declared, ' It is a sickly sentimentality, which holds that a man may not lay his hands rudely, if necessary, on his wife.' I could multiply these instances indefinitely, but these will suffice to show what the whole tone of our laws is. Laws which women have not helped to make, to which they have not even consented, yet which they must obey."

" What flagrant injustice ! " cried Laura. " It seems amazing that men do not hasten at once to do away with such oppression."

" They do not realize it, my dear," said Mrs. D'Arcy, mildly. " A change will take place in time, let us hope. But there is a ring at the door," she added, more lightly. " I think some of our friends must have come, and we had better go to the parlor."

The dinner passed off delightfully ; the company was genial and lively ; the conversation heartily gay. Laura for the day threw aside the care which often oppressed her, and even Frank Heywood caught the spirit of merriment and was unusually gay ; devoting himself part of the time to the entertainment of Bessie Bradford so assiduously, that Laura declared that he was carrying on quite a flirtation with her ; an idea which seemed vastly to amuse him.

It had been settled that Frank should wait on Laura home; but when, rather early, she rose to go, Guy Bradford started forward as if it were his privilege, of course, to be in attendance. Heywood had also risen, but Guy, scarcely noticing him, said :

"I may see you home, may not I, Miss Stanley ? "

Laura looked at him and then at Frank. "Mr. Heywood had offered to take care of me," she rejoined.

Frank regarded them both with his melancholy eyes. "If Mr. Bradford will take my place, I shall be obliged to him," he said ; "it is late, and I ought to go directly to the office."

Laura turned to him, eagerly. "You are not angry, Frank ? "

"No ; oh no ! " he exclaimed; "it is better so ;" and turned away.

Laura was half glad of the exchange, and yet the sad hungry look of those mysterious eyes haunted her for hours afterwards.

CHAPTER XIX.

FLORA'S CONFESSION.

THE days that followed were rather dreary to Laura. The cessation of her pupils and school brought with it a cessation of her money ; she began to feel keenly the pressure of a poverty heretofore unknown. The nine dollars a week she had been earning had barely sufficed, with the closest economy, for the absolute wants of the week, paying, as she did, seven dollars for her board, and a dollar a week to Bridget for her services ; so that, when the supply was cut off, she saw no means of even meeting her current

expenses. Then, too, the young teacher was very lonely
in this great city, at this holiday time, and had a home-
sick longing to see her mother. Hearing from her infrequently, she felt as if she only half knew how she was;
and now that every one else seemed to be with their
people, it was very hard that she did not dare to go to
hers. As she walked through the streets, and saw the
happy groups of mothers and children buying their holiday toys, or passed houses at night, and glanced in, through
half-open windows, at pleasant family scenes, there was an
intense yearning in her heart for a home—for a life that
had in it some of the softness and the beauty that was so
utterly lacking in her bleak surroundings.

The only refuge and comfort she had was in constant
occupation. She toiled early and late at her paintings,
and after some weary endeavors, was enabled to obtain a
little money by the sale of some pictures. Only a sum so
small, however, as to offer poor hope of earning anything
reliable.

Laura was troubled, too, at what she heard of Flora
Livingston. She had not seen her since the snowy day
when she met her on the street ; but Guy Bradford, who
was at Mrs. Duncan's ball, told her that it was reported
that Flora was engaged to Mr. Le Roy.

Laura was very reluctant to believe this, which seemed
to her most evil tidings, and was more anxious to see her
friend than ever. How to contrive a meeting she could
not tell ; but, in a possible chance of seeing Flora, she took
to haunting Fifth-avenue of afternoons.

She was walking slowly up the gay thoroughfare one
bright day, when a voice at her elbow pronounced her
name, and turning, she beheld Mr. Fitlas; gorgeous in an
overcoat of most showy construction, ornamented with
collar and cuffs of sable fur, which, together with a bright
plaid neck-tie and yellow gloves, made up an appearance
so astounding, that Laura had a cold shiver when she perceived that it was evidently his fell intention to join her.

"Fine day, Miss Stanley," he said. "Out for a promenade?"

"Yes," replied Laura, coldly; "I am taking a walk."

"Uncommon jolly this afternoon; lots of swells out," he commenced, as he walked on at her side, puffing out his chest, and making every effort to look tall and commanding. Laura was silent, and he asked, presently, "Much of a walker, Miss Stanley?"

"Yes; I take a good deal of exercise."

"Not so much as I do, by a long shot, I'll bet. When I'm off on business I walk to that degree it would amaze you! I've often said, I ought to have two pair of men's limbs to do what I do."

An irrepressible smile curled Laura's lips. "It must be fatiguing to be so industrious," she said.

"It would be to some fellows; but it ain't to me. I'm tough; hard as a nut," he added, proudly.

At this moment Laura saw Flora Livingston; she was walking slowly down a cross-street, and was alone. Here was an opportunity not to be lost, and the young lady hastened to avail herself of it. "You must excuse me," she said, hurriedly, to Mr. Fitlas. "I see a friend whom I would like to speak with. Good-morning;" and she turned away, leaving Mr. Fitlas to pursue his conquering way alone.

A few rapid steps brought Laura to her friend's side. "Flora!" she cried, eagerly, "Flora, dear!"

At the sound of her name, Flora started, and looked around; then, seeing who it was, a smile of pleasure broke over her face. "Laura!" she exclaimed; "oh, I'm so glad to see you!"

"And why haven't you been to me?" asked Laura; "I've wanted to see you so much!"

"I couldn't come before; I've been so busy, and so—— so guarded," she added. "To-day I am only out because—— well, because I suppose they think I'm safe, now!" A strange bitter smile crossed her lips, a smile

7

singularly out of keeping with the amiable expression natural to her sweet face.

"Can't you come home with me now?" urged Laura;
"we can talk so much better there, and it isn't far."

"Yes, I can go with you, a little while," answered
Flora; "I'm supposed to be at the dress-maker's; but I can
go there, just as well, later."

The two friends were soon at Mr. Moulder's, where
Minnie, who opened the door, was quite overwhelmed with
admiration of the beautiful lady. Laura lead the way into
the stuffy parlor, and as she drew up the window-shade to
let in a little light that might make it less gloomy said,
"This is a forlorn place, compared to yours, Flora; my
fingers often ache to try, at least, to improve the arrangement of the furniture a little!"

The young lady glanced around the small room with
sad eyes. "You are happier here than I am in our grand
parlor," she said; "for here you are free!"

Now that the two were face to face, Laura noticed a
subtle change which had passed over her friend. She was
paler than when she had last seen her; the fair complexion
was almost transparent in its extreme delicacy; there was
a faint droop in the corners of the mouth, and the lovely
blue eyes had a look of weariness in them.

"And are you not free?" asked Laura.

"No," replied Flora, abruptly; "have you not heard?
I am engaged to marry Mr. Le Roy!" The last words
were uttered with an irrepressible quiver of the lips.

"I had heard something of it," answered Laura gravely,
"but I waited to hear the truth from yourself. You have
my best wishes, dear."

"Thank you!" murmured Flora, without looking up.

"Will the wedding take place soon?"

"In the spring."

There was a moment of silence. Flora, sitting with her
eyes always fixed upon the floor; then Laura said, gently,
"And are you happy?"

"Happy!" exclaimed Flora, looking up; "happy!" And Laura saw that the blue eyes were full of tears.

"My darling!" she murmured, holding out her arms; and in a moment, Flora was sobbing on her friend's shoulder.

For some time no connected conversation was possible; then Flora told her story, in somewhat broken fashion; but so that Laura gathered a good deal of it. Mr. Le Roy had offered himself to her at Mrs. Duncan's ball, and though she had not actually accepted him, she yet felt herself, in a measure, bound to him, by what had passed between them. She scarcely gave a hint of what that had been; it seemed quite impossible to allude to it, though it lay in her memory always as a mark of servitude, almost as an indelible stain.

It is very difficult to describe the state of mind of such a girl as Flora Livingston. Brought up in absolute ignorance of the vices and passions of the world, carefully guarded in all her association with the opposite sex, nothing but a love, intense and absorbing, could ever have fully reconciled her to a familiarity. To her, a kiss was the symbol of surrender, so compromising that marriage must follow as an inevitable consequence. The gay men who go through life catching the perfume of every flower, and culling recklessly the roses of pleasure, cannot understand the feeling of a virgin heart like this; a pure white lily, whose petals could not be touched, without marring their beauty, and who would yield to the first strong hand that was put forth to pluck it from the parent stem.

And yet Flora had not given up, without some struggle. On the night after the ball, Mr. Le Roy had called at her father's, and been formally accepted by him as his daughter's suitor; but for days Flora had refused to see him.

"At first I felt as if I could not meet him again," she said to Laura. "It frightened me only to think of it. But he was very kind; sent me some beautiful presents and flowers, and then mamma came and talked to me; told me

how much he loved me, and how much it would please her
to have me marry him. Poor mamma ! I never before knew
how many anxieties she had—and so at last I saw him
again, and now we are engaged."

"But, Flora, you ought not to have yielded, if you do
not love him."

"Perhaps not, Laura ; but I am not like you. I could
not resist so many entreaties. I like Mr. Le Roy well
enough, only I am afraid of him sometimes. However,
mamma says I shall get used to him and learn to love him.
But the worst thing about it is, I don't feel free any more,"
she said, with a passionate outburst. "The thought that
I am bound worries me perpetually, and I have lately
found it in my heart to envy some forlorn old maids of our
acquaintance, because they, at least, are free."

"Then why don't you break it off, Flora ? "

"Sometimes I wish I could ! But it has gone too far
now ! There is to be an announcement-party at his sister
Mrs. Courtenay's, next week. No ! I must go on to the
end now ; but I wish—oh, how I wish, that I was back at
college, in the old happy days, with you ! "

Some further talk took place between the two, but without result; and Laura saw Flora go away with many misgivings as to her future.

CHAPTER XX.

NEW YEAR'S DAY.

A FEW days later came the great annual *fête* of New
York—the wonderful saturnalia of the western metropolis
—New Year's Day. Laura was invited to pass it with
Mrs. D'Arcy, and was with her hostess in good season.
As all-important on such an occasion, it may be mentioned
that the doctor's dress was a rich purple silk, trimmed
with handsome lace, while Laura wore a white muslin,

which had been made for commencement-day at Essex. This filmy stuff was looped over black silk, in the then prevailing fashion; and with scarlet ribbons in her hair, and at her throat, she looked, as the doctor told her, like some bright wholesome winter berry.

The early morning had brought to Laura two bouquets. A large and handsome one, with "Mr. Bradford's compliments," and a mere knot of choice flowers, "From your friend, F. H." Laura left these last in a vase at home; they were a valuable present, as a study for some small water-color pictures. The bouquet she carried in her hand.

The doctor's drawing-room began to fill early, and Laura enjoyed keenly meeting the many well-known men who called to pay their respects to the distinguished lady. Of course, among the throng of visitors, there came some of her old friends also. Frank Heywood looked in for a few moments, and Guy Bradford dropped in late in the afternoon, when, as he honestly averred, he thought there would be a possible cessation of callers. At the first opportunity Laura thanked him for his flowers.

"They are such a pleasure to me," she said.

"It is delight enough to me to see them in your hands," replied Guy, with a look that deepened the color in Laura's already glowing cheeks.

"And where have you been to-day, Guy?" asked Mrs. D'Arcy, who was just released from other visitors.

"I have not made many calls," replied Bradford, "but I last came from the Livingston's." Then turning to Laura: "I saw Miss Flora, who inquired after you, Miss Stanley."

"Did she?" asked Laura, eagerly. "How did she look?"

"Shall I tell you just how she impressed me?"

"Yes."

"Well, then, she was dressed in white, with a great many blue ribbons, and round her neck there was a splendid gold chain.   Mr. Le Roy was there, and I don't know why, but I constantly thought of some pretty white dove prepared for a sacrifice."

"I hope that won't turn out to be a warning fancy," said Laura, with a sigh.   "Who else was there?"

"Mrs. Livingston, in a gray dress, like an anxious presiding fairy; Miss Maud, very handsome, with a little crowd of adorers trying to win her smiles; and an indefinite quantity of young Livingston girls, all in white muslin, all pretty, and, seemingly, all inclined to flirt!"

Laura laughed at this description, and some other guests coming in at the moment, the conversation turned to the commonplace platitudes which are the staple of New Years' calls.

Guy presently went away, and as the evening advanced, quite a throng of callers filled the doctor's parlors; these all dropped away, after a time, and at last Laura took her departure at a late hour, Mrs. D'Arcy sending her home in her carriage.

When she reached the house the door was opened for her by Mr. Moulder, who was in an unusually amiable frame of mind, and looked quite beaming; attired in his very best clothes, and with his red face redder than usual, from the frequent potations of his New Year's calls.

"Ah, Miss Stanley," he said, in a very impressive manner, "I am glad you have come; there is a visitor waiting for you."

"Indeed! who?"

"Judge Swinton."

Laura walked into the parlor, where she expected to find Mrs. Moulder, who had said she should see a few of her old friends; to her dismay there was no one there but the judge.   He came forward to meet her with effusion, his sensual face flushed, his bold eyes bright with excitement; he had evidently been doing his part in drinking to the day; his voice was thick, and the atmosphere about him impregnated with the odor of wine.

"My dear Miss Stanley, Happy New Year, and many returns!"

"Thank you," replied Laura, coldly, withdrawing her hand from his quickly, and seating herself at a distance from him.

Mr. Moulder took a chair, an expression of satisfaction irradiating his rubicund countenance. "I suppose you've been very busy to-day, Judge."

"Rather so. I received at home for three hours this morning, and since then have made about twenty calls."

"Ah, official?"

"Some of them," answered the judge, shortly. He scarcely took his gaze from Laura as he spoke. She was looking unusually handsome; the glow of the fresh air still on her cheeks; her gray eyes sparkling with animation; her dress setting off her full round form. The visitor was evidently impatient of any words except from her.

"You have not been at the ward meetings for some time, Judge," Moulder went on slowly, evidently fully persuaded that he was the principal attraction to his guest.

"No, but I'm coming soon." Then rousing himself, "And by the way, Moulder, that last mass-meeting pulled on us pretty strong. We are thinking of another assessment."

"All right, Judge, all right. I shall be ready," replied Mr. Moulder, importantly.

"Yes, I know we can always rely on you," said the judge, with a bland smile; "I'll be at headquarters next Thursday evening, and, Mr. Moulder, I have a word for Miss Stanley alone; a message from her father."

"All right, Judge, all right; I'm proud to have seen you. Good-night."

Mr. Moulder got himself out of the room, after a hearty grip of his honor's hand, and Laura was alone with this man, whom she had so long dreaded. It seemed as if now that he was thus unrestrained with her, he could hardly control himself; he approached her with an expression in his eyes that made his mere look an insult, and bent towards her, till she could perceive the thick odor of wine and tobacco that hung about him.

If it had been possible for him to be aware of the utter loathing with which he inspired this young lady, he would perhaps have gone out from her presence hastily; but such a nature as his can no more comprehend such a nature as hers, than the black beetle that crawls on the ground can understand the emotion of the bright bird that floats in the sunshine.

A man of this stamp imagines that every woman is at heart like himself, sensual, mercenary, false; that the apparent difference is one of manner only, and that he can easily find a responsive chord, which must vibrate to the touch of a being so charming as he believes himself to be. Full of some such thought, this ornament of the New York Bench bent down, and strove to take Laura's hand. She sprang to her feet on the instant.

"You said you had a message from my father!" she said, as she drew back a step.

"That was only a blind," explained the judge, with a knowing wink; "I haven't heard from your father at all; I only wanted to get Moulder out of the way; you'll forgive me, won't you? all's fair in love and war, you know."

He attempted to draw near her as he spoke, but Laura retreated as he advanced, till she reached the limits of the small room, and stood with her back to the mantle-piece.

"If you have no message for me, I'll bid you good-night," she said coldly; and she attempted to go towards the door.

The judge interposed himself, hastily. "No, don't run away," he urged; "I have something to say to you, Laura, you little beauty! you must know how I love you!" And he put out his hand to seize her.

"Stand back!" exclaimed Laura, imperiously; "you are forgetting yourself, Judge Swinton!"

"No, I ain't! you little wretch! I mean every word I

7*

say !" drawing still nearer; "say you'll be mine; I'll
marry you !" he whispered, with an irrepressible tremor
in his voice. "That's square, now; come, you beauty, give
me a kiss ! "

He was quite close to her ; an unctuous smile on his lips,
a leer of triumph in his eyes ; his arms outstretched, almost
clasping her. An irrepressible angry disgust seized Laura;
she felt that the contamination of his touch was not to be
endured, and as he would have caught her, she drew back,
her gray eyes flashing fire, her fine face set in resolute
defiance, and pushing away his hand, passed him suddenly.

At college, Laura had been a practiced gymnast, and
there was a strength one would not suspect in that shapely
hand and slender wrist. The judge drew back a pace in
utter astonishment, and before he could get over his surprise, she had escaped from the room.

He recovered in a moment, and hurried in pursuit; but
there was no one in the entry, and when he reached the
foot of the stairs, there was only the sound of light footsteps
ascending, and the faint rustle of silk, which ceased a moment after, as a door closed sharply.

The man went back to the parlor, but the flush had faded
from his face, and his eyes had grown hard and cruel. He
took up his hat, put on his overcoat, and went out, walking
quickly, like one who has a fixed purpose; he soon reached
an avenue, where he entered a car, and so made his way to
the dingy street in which the Bludgetts lived. It was
quite late now, and, after a moment's hesitation, the judge
went up the steps of the small brown house. Before he
could knock, however, a man opened the door to go out;
and, taking advantage of this, the judge went in and up
stairs to the little parlor. The door of this was ajar, and
he saw Mrs. Bludgett sitting near the fire, reading by the
light of a shaded lamp. At his tap, she started like a
guilty creature, and hastily concealed the book she had
under her shawl ; then she opened the door timidly.

"Good-evening, Mrs. Bludgett," the judge said, graciously. "Is Bludgett in?"

"No, he ain't home yet," replied the woman.

"Is he at the sample-room, think you?"

"Yes sir, I guess he is."

"But it's after twelve," objected the judge.

"I know it is; but these nights he do stay out awful late. Will you come in, and I'll go around and fetch him?"

"No, thank you, no; I'll go there myself," and Judge Swinton went once more out into the night.

It was quite late now; the air was cold with the intense chill of midnight; the stars shone overhead with a remote frigid glitter; the wheels of the few passing vehicles rang with a metallic chime against the pavement. But though the narrow streets seemed somewhat deserted, when he turned into a wider thoroughfare, there was enough of noise and tumult. Groups of men, unsteady on their feet, were staggering along, filling the night with discordant songs, shouted words, and coarse laughter; and a few women, evil-eyed and hollow-cheeked, were among them. The disorder seemed to culminate at a corner, where was a brilliantly-lighted shop; a place with many bottles and casks, piled high in the window, and with the words "Sample-room," gold-lettered, on a blue ground, over the door.

Within there was a score of men, leaning over the bar, sitting at tables, or sprawling over seats, all more or less intoxicated, all disreputable-looking, heavy-browed, noisy. The judge passed in, and made his way to Bludgett, who was engaged in a loud conversation with two men; bullet-headed, ugly-looking fellows, with flat noses, small eyes, and square shoulders.

"Ah! here's the boss, now!" exclaimed Bludgett; a smile of pride expanding his swarthy features, and relaxing his thick black eyebrows.

The men looked round, and bowed respectfully.

"How are you, boys?" said the judge, shaking hands

with each, in great apparent cordiality; "what'll you take?"

"Whiskey straight, for me," replied the taller of the two.

"And you, Bangs?"

"I'll have a tom-and-jerry."

"All right; and you may give me a hot-scotch, Bludgett."

As that worthy turned away to fill the order, the judge asked, "How's biz. boys?"

"Pretty well," replied Bangs.   "We was at the Seventh Ward 'sociation, Monday night."

"Ah! and what happened there?"

"They appointed Fuller to go to Albany, and see about the Avenue K railroad."

"I know," nodded the judge; "that was all right."

"'Twouldn't 'a' bin, if it hadn't 'a' bin for us," growled the latter man.

"How's that, Snuggers?"

"Some on 'em wanted to put in Turner; he's a nice party, he is; regular bolter; wants to go in for reform!" with an expression of profound contempt.

"I know," said the judge, impatiently.   "Well?"

"We jest went, and got a lot of our fellows from the Sixth, and brought 'em in. Some of the 'sociation wanted to make a row; said they wasn't residents of the ward; but we swore 'em in, and, well,"—with a low chuckle— "I guess they thought it wouldn't be healthy to fight us."

"Well done! well done!" cried the judge, laughing, till all his white teeth gleamed.   "You know how to manage a meeting; you're well worth your salary. Let me see, what places do you hold now?"

"I'm an assistant-clerk to the comptroller," said Snuggers, whose large knotted hands looked quite incapable of holding a pen.

"And you, Bangs?"

"I'm in the Department of Charities and Corrections."

" What salary ? "

" A beggarly eighteen-hundred a year apiece," answered Bangs.

" Is that all ? It ought to be more ; I must attend to that." Then, as they took up their glasses, which now stood ready to their hands, he added: " Here's to your better luck, boys ! "

" Thank you, your honor," exclaimed both the men in a breath, and they drank to the toast, heartily.

" How's the list, Bludgett ? " inquired the judge, turning to that valuable man, who had now returned to his post.

" Foots up pretty well, your honor; think the majority next time will be heavier than ever," and he presented a book, in which long lists of names and residences appeared.

" Looks very well, Bludgett," commented the judge, after glancing at it for a moment. Then putting down his now empty glass, and leaning on the counter, he said : " I'd like to see you about a little business. Can you spare time ? "

" Certainly, Judge, certainly," replied Bludgett, with alacrity. " Here, Bangs, you take my place a moment."

Bangs, seeming to think this a great honor, readily accepted the trust, and Bludgett led Judge Swinton into a small room in the rear of the shop. Here there stood a table, much stained with suggestive rings, and several chairs in great disorder.

" Some of the boys been in here," said Bludgett; " and things ain't been put to rights."

The judge accepted the apology graciously, and drawing a chair, the two men were soon engaged in earnest conversation. It did not last long, and as the judge rose to go he said :

" I may depend upon you, then, Bludgett? for mind you, I'm resolved upon this ! " his eyes flashing vindictively.

"It's a dangerous game," Bludgett replied; "but I'll stand by you, Judge; you make your plan, and I'll find the men to carry it out."

CHAPTER XXI.

A VISIT FROM BRIDGET.

A DAY or two later, Mrs. Moulder and Laura stood together in the sitting-room, dressed for a walk. Laura had persuaded her friend, whose habits were very recluse, to go out with her, to see some pictures. The expedition had been planned for some time, but her household cares, or illness, had kept the poor lady at home. On this day, however, the weather was warm and bright; the children were arranged for, and all things were propitious. Mrs. Moulder looked very lovely, plain as her dress was. It consisted of a well-worn black silk, a cloth saque, evidently not of this year's design, and a simple bonnet, with brown ribbons. As she tied this on, Laura said :

"That's a pretty hat, Agnes, and very becoming."

"Do you think so ? It's quite plain. I made it myself. There! does my hair look nicely ?"

"Very," replied Laura ; "but there ought to be a bow here, at the back of the hat; don't you think so ?"

"Yes, I know that very well ; but I had not ribbon enough. It seems to me, sometimes, as if I never had enough of anything," she added, with a sigh. "I am always piecing, and patching, and contriving, and it takes twice as long to make anything in that way."

"Certainly it does," assented Laura; "and I often wonder how you accomplish what you do, and you have no sewing-machine either ?"

"No."

"Mr. Moulder ought to buy you one."

"Perhaps some day he will ; but he does not feel as if he could afford it now."

Laura thought of the assessments which Mr. Moulder had so readily promised to pay the other evening, and the constant expenses of his club, and political meetings, which were, no doubt, readily met ; but before she could speak again there was a knock at the door, and as it was opened the portly form of Bridget Malone appeared.

Generally, Laura quite enjoyed a few moments' chat with the good washerwoman, when she brought home the clothes ; but to-day a quick scarlet flushed her face as she saw her.

"Ah, Biddy," she said; "you're early this week."

"Well, Miss, I am, thin; and its hurried I've bin to git the things home."

"Are they up stairs ? "

"Yis, Miss; I put thim on the bed."

"Very well; " then coming a little nearer, Laura said, with a painful blush, "I can't pay you to-day, Biddy; you'll have to wait till next week." It was the first time in her life that she had ever been unable to pay a debt, and she keenly felt the humiliation.

"Shure and that's not what I come about at all ! " exclaimed Biddy, very loudly and indignantly. "It's not Bridget Malone that wad be comin' afther yes for money, but I'd like to spake till ye's both, if ye's have the toime."

"Certainly we have," responded Mrs. Moulder, readily. "Sit down Biddy. What is it ? "

"Well, thin, it's about a young gurl as lives in my house ; two young gurls as I may say. One on 'em says she's seen you, Miss Stanley ; her name's Rhoda Dayton."

"Oh yes, I remember her, very well," replied Laura. "I liked her when I met her; she seemed quite superior to her life," she explained to Mrs. Moulder.

"She is thin, intirely," replied Bridget; "she's a good gurl, is Rhody, and if ye's could see how kind she is to her friend, the poor sick lamb ! "

In her own language, Bridget then sketched the history of the two girls, their struggles, their sorrows, their pride.

"Whin Maggie was very bad, three wakes ago," she concluded, "Rhody said she'd have to try to get help. But afther Maggie was betther, and thin they wouldn't have ony help from onybody, the proud things! but now, Rhody's been turned out of the place she worked at nights," —good Bridget did not like to shock the ladies by speaking of the concert-saloon—"and last night Maggie was waur again, lyin' on the bed with the big blue eyes of her stairin', and red spots in her poor thin cheeks, the crayther! and talkin', talkin' all the time about her home: callin' 'Mother! Mother!' till ye'd crip all to hear her."

"Poor thing! Poor thing! But how can I help her, Biddy?"

"I was thinkin', perhaps, ye'd tell the docther about her, the saints presarve her noble heart! She might come and see the poor lamb."

"I'll do that, surely," replied Laura, promptly; "I'll go to Mrs. D'Arcy this very afternoon."

"Thank ye, Miss; I knew ye'd help thim if ye could; the Vargin bless yer swate face!"

Laura smiled. "It's little enough I can do," she said; "I only wish it were more;" then, as Bridget rose to go, she asked, "And how's Pat now?"

"Shure he's very bad, agin," replied Bridget, with a gloomy face. "He was off New Year's, at Bludgett's, (bad cess to him for a murtherin' scamp! sellin' pisen to the min, till they're crazy like!) and niver came home at all the night; he was sick the marnin' and I was not sorry," she added, as hard-heartedly as was possible for her. "It might be a warnin' to him, but I don't know what I'll do wid him."

"I am sorry you have so much trouble," said Laura; and then, with a gleam of mischief in her eyes, she asked: "Don't you wish we women could vote, Biddy, so as to shut up all these abominable dram-shops?"

"Indade I do, Miss!" said Biddy, in all earnestness; "I'm thinkin' there'd not be many of 'em in our ward if the poor wives and mothers had a hand in givin' licenses. Sorrer a one would any man get from me!" she added, resolutely.

"That's right, Biddy."

"But, I'll not be kapin' ye's ony longer, wid you're things on. Good day to ye's both," and the worthy woman went away.

As she disappeared, Mrs. Moulder said, "I never feel so bitterly the want of money as when I hear of a case like this. I should so like to be able to help the brave girl!"

Laura thought again of the various expenses in which Mr. Moulder indulged himself and said, as the two went out, "But Agnes, your husband must be quite well off."

"He is, I presume, though I don't really know anything about it."

"That does not seem quite right. I should think you ought to understand his affairs fully; in case of sickness or death it might be very important that you should know them, and under all circumstances, it must be better."

"Perhaps so, but he has never told me anything, and only gives me money when I ask for it, almost as if it were a charity on his part"—with a faint sigh.

"You have no allowance, then?"

"No, though I do wish I had! no words can tell you how I dread and dislike asking for money!"

"Do you mean for the ordinary expenses of housekeeping?"

"Yes, for everything. Mr. Moulder always seems to think I spend so much! and yet I try hard to be economical."

"And you are, Agnes; you are too economical by half! I have seen your self-denial, your sacrifices, your anxieties, you dear patient woman!" Laura exclaimed, warmly. "It's an outrage, that you ever have to ask for money!"

Mrs. Moulder smiled faintly. "There, there, Laura, don't get too much excited over this, and don't let us spoil our pleasant afternoon by thinking of disagreeable subjects. I want to forget care for a little while."

Laura was silenced, and after a moment made an effort to lay aside all that was annoying in her own position and her friend's, and devote herself to the entertainment of her companion. The two ladies made the tour of the free picture-galleries, that are ever open to the lover of art in New York, and Laura, leaving Mrs. Moulder to go home alone, made her way to Mrs. D'Arcy's.

By good fortune she found the doctor at home, and soon interested her in the story of the two girls.

"I will go there at once," said the good lady. "The carriage is at the door; shall I take you home on the way?"

Laura thanked her, and the two were presently driving through the now darkening streets. On their way, Laura spoke of Flora Livingston's engagement.

"To my mind it is a very sad affair," commented the doctor. "That man will never make any woman happy. I know something of him, I was once in the same hotel with him at Newport for two weeks, and saw him constantly. He is cold, selfish, and tyrannical in his nature, and regards women as created only for the amusement of men. A delicate flower, like your friend Flora, will pine beside him, as a violet would pine in the shadow of an iceberg."

"I dread the marriage very much," said Laura; "I only wish I could persuade her, even now, to break it off!"

Mrs. D'Arcy shook her head. "There is not much hope of that, I fear. A girl brought up as she has been, is rendered almost incapable of independence. A fashionable training so hampers a woman's body and mind, that one can no more expect freedom of action, in any of its victims, than one can expect the Chinese ladies with their distorted feet to walk like the bright warrior Hippolyte."

As Mrs. D'Arcy closed her somewhat forcible comparison, the carriage stopped at Mr. Moulder's door, and Laura bade her good-night. After parting with her young friend the doctor ordered her coachman to drive to a neighboring green-house. Going in there for a few moments, she presently came out with a small bunch of violets and roses in her hand, not tied up in a stiff bouquet, but loose on their stalks. She was carrying them when, a short time later, she ascended the rickety stairs of the tenement house, and knocked at the door of the room where Rhoda and her friend lived.

It was opened by Bridget, who uttered a cry of delight. " Shure here's the docther herself, the Vargin be praised ! Come in, my leddy, come in ! "

The doctor entered the humble room, the perfume of the flowers floating out and seeming to purify the close air.

Maggie lay in the bed, her golden hair floating in disorder over the pillow, her eyes closed, her cheeks lighted with a fever flush ; Rhoda knelt beside her, watching over her friend, with hollow anxious eyes. As Mrs. D'Arcy approached, she rose and greeted her with a half defiant look on her face. The doctor held out her hand.

" How do you do, my dear ? " she said. " Bridget sent me word how ill your friend is, and I have come to see her."

The words and tone seemed absolutely to overcome Rhoda ; she took the offered hand, her face softened, her proud eyes filled with tears, and as if unable to speak, she turned away silently.

It seemed as if the fragrance of the flowers spoke to Maggie, in some mute tender language. As it reached her she opened her eyes and put out her thin white hand.

" Violets ! " she said, faintly; " has spring come already, mother ? "

The doctor placed the blossoms in the fragile fingers, and it was as if they were an irresistible introduction for the stranger who gave them ; the sick girl suffered quietly the gentle touch of the physician as she felt her pulse, and even answered quite rationally one or two questions; but presently, again her thoughts wandered away.

"Ferdinand gave me these," she said, holding up the flowers; "they are very sweet, and he was kind to-day; not so cold as he is sometimes, like an icy day, like one of his own northern winter days, when it is cold—so bitter cold!" and she shivered; "but why is it cold now, mother, if it is spring, and the violets are come?" then suddenly she looked wildly about the room. "Where is Ferdinand? it is so long, so long, since I saw him," she cried: "Ferdinand! Ferdinand!"

"Who is it that she asks for?" inquired the doctor of Rhoda; "any one that can be brought to her?"

"No," replied Rhoda, darkly. "The man never will come here again. It is Mr. Ferdinand Le Roy."

CHAPTER XXII.

A WARNING.

FROM the time of this first visit of Mrs. D'Arcy, the condition of the two girls was improved. Maggie grew better, under the action of certain judicious remedies; but more than all, perhaps, from the influence of the kind lady's gentle presence, and words of hope. Mrs. D'Arcy spoke of it now as quite a settled thing, that Maggie should go to her home during the first mild days in February.

"We always have some really warm days in the latter part of the month," the doctor said. "You shall be all ready to start; and the first bright, soft morning, you shall be away. In twenty-four hours you will be at home, and the spring will already have begun."

Such words as these would bring a look of delight to Maggie's eyes; and in order to be well enough for the journey she was ready to follow every direction the physician gave. The definite hope was such a comfort! There was no longer any uncertainty in it ; she was to go, and Rhoda was to go with her. Mrs. D'Arcy had arranged all that ; she had promised to get passes over the road for both girls; and the rest of the expenses, they were going to earn money to meet.

As Bridget had said, Rhoda had been turned out of her place at the concert-saloon. Going in there, a night or two after the visit of Judge Swinton, the keeper of the place had called her sharply to him :

"You may jest not take off your duds at all to-night, Miss Dayton," he said; "I don't want you any more."

"Why not ?" asked Rhoda, in surprise.

"You're entirely too uppish to suit me. I've put up with your tricks long enough, and you may jest get out of this."

"Very well," replied Rhoda, very quietly, though her pale face was paler than ever. "You'll pay me what you owe me, I suppose ? "

"Yes, I'll do that, and I'll give you a piece of advice into the bargain ; if you go to any other saloon, better be a little meeker. It don't become you to be puttin' on airs like a decent woman."

Rhoda's face was glowing now, her dark eyes blazing. "It don't become you to insult me !" she retorted; "your life is worse than mine, and you know it; I don't give girls drugged drinks, and cheat drunken men out of their money ! "

The man winced at this home-thrust, and muttered an oath, as Rhoda took her money and turned away.

She was glad to be free from the detested place ; and yet the loss of her wages would be something serious to her. She more than suspected Judge Swinton's agency in her dismissal, and her heart was very bitter, as she went back to her wretched home only to find Maggie worse, raving in an attack of fever that was more alarming than

any she had yet had. For a day or two her lot seemed
darker and more hopeless than ever; then, like a good
angel, Mrs. D'Arcy came.

After her first visit, Rhoda's life took on a color that
it had not known for years before. The doctor procured
for her plenty of sewing that was really remunerative, and
she could earn more, by working at this all the evening,
than she had earned at the concert-saloon. Then, too, the
manner in which the good lady treated her, during her
daily visits, was balm to Rhoda's poor sore heart. Mrs.
D'Arcy was as kind to her as if she had been the cherished
daughter of a friend; spoke with her so tenderly of the
past, so encouragingly of the future, that to the forlorn
girl a new hope sprang up.

One Saturday afternoon Maggie and Rhoda were sitting together as usual. Their room showed several little
tokens of greater comfort. A bright fire was burning in a
tiny stove, which heated the room and cooked their food
much better than the old rusty grate had done. The window was shielded by a neat white curtain, which was
drawn back so that the sunshine could fall upon a pot of
mignionette and one of roses, both in bloom; their sweet
blossoms and pure perfume seeming to give the once
dreary apartment an air of refinement. Maggie was slowly
executing some delicate embroidery, which she worked
upon, according to the doctor's orders, "only when she
felt like it," and which was to bring her a nice sum when
finished. Rhoda was employed upon some of those small
dainty garments which must be made by hand, as no
machine can give them the delicate finish they require.
The silence was interrupted by a knock at the door, and
at Rhoda's reply, Mrs. Bludgett came in.

Her dress was of the poorest description, a dingy black
alpaca, with a rent on one side of it, which was pinned
together; a coarse shawl was wrapped around her, and on
her head she wore a bonnet, rising very high over her
forehead in some absurd past fashion, making her pale

face look paler in contrast with the yellow and red roses which filled the space above her scanty hair. She was shivering with cold when she came in, and her poor lips were blue, her poor nose red.

Rhoda made her welcome, and gave her a seat by the fire; she cowered near it for a few moments, and then loosening her shawl, as she felt the heat, the girls noticed that her left arm was in a sling.

"What's the matter with your arm, Molly?" asked Rhoda, looking at it, sharply.

"I sprained my wrist," replied Mrs. Bludgett, without looking up. "I ain't been very well, and wouldn't have come out to-day, only I wanted to see you quite particular."

"Anything private?" asked Maggie.

"Well, yes," replied Mrs. Bludgett; "'tain't anythin' about Rhoda; only about some folks she knows. I don't want to worry you with it."

"All right," said Rhoda; "when you're ready I'll walk a little way with you. I must go out to get something for supper, anyhow."

"Let's go then," said Mrs. Bludgett, jumping up.

"Why you havn't been here a minute," said Maggie; "not long enough to rest yourself."

"I want to get home as soon as I can," replied Mrs. Bludgett. "Bludgett might come in, and he don't like me to go out."

Rhoda put on her hat and cloak, and the two presently went away together. As soon as they were in the entry, Mrs. Bludgett said, in a mysterious whisper:

"I'll tell you here, Rhody; I don't darst to be seen talkin' with you outside."

"What is it?"

"Judge Swinton was at our house last night; I knew he and Bludgett was up to some sort of mischief, and I listened at the door. He'd a' killed me if he'd found me out," she shivered; "but he didn't, and I heard part of what they said."

" Well—'

" They're a-goin' to carry Miss Stanley off ! "

" To carry her off ! "

" Yes. I don't jist know how ; but I heard something about a carriage, and that Bangs and Snuggers was a goin' to help. They're dreadful men," she said with a mysterious look ; " wouldn't stop at anything ! There was Tom Allen, was murdered down by our house, last winter ; it was called a mysterious murder ; no one ever know'd who done it ;- but I know ; *they* done it ; Allen was the boss of a gang of voters on the other side, and they wanted him out of the way, before 'lection. They'd as soon murder a man, any day, as not, and they'll carry her off, where no one 'll ever find her ! "

" No, they shan't," cried Rhoda. " I think I can stop that."

" I thought you could do something, may be ; but you'll have to be quick," said Mrs. Bludgett ; " for I think they're goin' to carry her off to-day."

" To-day ! " Rhoda exclaimed, in horror ; and it's after four o'clock now ! "

Without waiting to hear Mrs. Bludgett's words of good-bye, she hurried into the room again.

" I've got to go quite a ways, Maggie," she explained, hastily, " and may not be back for a good while ; you won't mind waiting, dear ? "

" No, oh no, don't hurry home for me ; I feel so well to-day, I shan't mind being alone."

Rhoda kissed her friend, and went out again. Mrs. Bludgett was already gone, and hurrying swiftly down the stairs, Rhoda made her way as rapidly as possible to the avenue and entered a car. There were not many people in it, and it seemed to her, that never had a vehicle moved so slowly before, as it went on gliding down town in the now rapidly-increasing darkness. With many stoppages, and one or two delays, the journey was over at last ; but when Rhoda got out at the City-hall Park, the lamps were lighted, and night had already settled over the city, and there was a terrible apprehension tugging at her heart, as she made her way through the throng of people that jostled each other in their hurry to secure seats in the cars, that were starting for different localities up town.

Reaching the sidewalk presently, she entered a side door in a large, white, marble building, and ascended a winding flight of stairs, to the editorial rooms of the New York Trumpeter.

"Is Mr. Heywood in?" she asked, breathlessly, of the man in waiting.

"I think he is; who shall I say wants to see him?"

"I don't think he knows my name; but my business is very important; please let me go to him?"

Something in her manner seemed to impress the man with her anxiety. "Come this way, then," he said; and he led her through a narrow entry, to one of many small offices.

As he knocked at the door, a fresh sweet voice called, "Come in," and, a moment after, Rhoda entered.

The room was very small, almost filled up by a large table, covered with papers. Above this burned a shaded lamp, the light of which fell on the fair handsome face of the young journalist. He looked up in surprise at Rhoda's entrance, but rose, politely.

"You don't remember me," said Rhoda, eagerly; "but I have seen you several times before; it don't matter where, for my errand is one of more than life and death! I come to you as a friend of Miss Laura Stanley. Judge Swinton has some horrible plan on foot to carry her off!"

"Where? When?" demanded Frank, growing suddenly pale.

"To-day—this evening, perhaps—I don't know how, but you will see there is no time to be lost."

Heywood had already seized his hat. "Come," he said; "we will go together, and you shall tell me everything as we drive up town."

Only stopping for a word of explanation regarding his absence to his chief, Frank hurried down stairs, followed by the young girl. At the door he gave her his arm, and the two crossed the street to a carriage-stand, where Heywood promptly engaged a coach.

"Where shall I tell him to drive?" he asked, as he helped her into it.

"To her house, I think, first," said Rhoda.

Frank gave the man Mr. Moulder's address, and then sprang in beside his companion.

During all this time Rhoda had scarcely taken her eyes from her escort; she watched with a most singular look the slender figure, the resolute delicate face, and the small strong hands that were so firm in their motions. There is a great deal of character in a hand, and the movements of Frank's slender fingers, as he tossed his papers into some sort of order, as he held open the door for her to pass out, as he helped her into the coach, seemed to fascinate her strangely. He was entirely unconscious of her observation; wholly occupied by his own thoughts, and the necessity for prompt action, he never glanced at his companion till they were seated side by side; then he turned towards her.

At this moment the light from a lamp fell strongly on both faces. Rhoda's, pale, sad, with a strange wistfulness in her intense gaze. Frank's, handsome, careworn, and with a deep mysterious light in the eyes. As their glances met, the young journalist started visibly, and a flush colored his sensitive complexion. Rhoda did not turn away, her regard lingered a moment, and there was in its eloquent earnestness a mute question.

8

CHAPTER XXIII.

AS BOOK-AGENT.

On that same Saturday, Laura Stanley made a new experiment in trying to earn money. The vacation was over, and she had resumed her work; but the pressure of want of resources was heavy upon her; a little relief had come to her in a letter from her mother, full of kind expressions and warm affection; and enclosing a ten dollar bill. With this she had been able to pay one week's board, and what was due to Bridget; but there was the other holiday week, with its outlays unmet. She never had, even when earning her nine dollars a week, more than a dollar for contingent expenses; and the cost of her drawing-materials alone made considerable inroad on this. Then there were the ever-recurring needs for gloves and shoes, and the many items which are almost indispensable in the toilette of a lady. Laura had been well fitted out in the essentials of a wardrobe when she came to town for the winter; but small wants arose, from time to time, which she could not meet out of her present salary; and she was often obliged to do without comforts that had heretofore seemed necessary to her. She no longer dared to indulge herself in riding in the cars; but no matter what the distance might be which she had to traverse, or however bad the weather might chance to be, she would walk; protecting herself, if it stormed, as well as she could, with a water-proof and umbrella; but being often very wet and cold and weary. A girl of less strong constitution would probably have been injured by these exposures; but Laura never took cold, and a good night's rest would refresh her completely after almost any fatigue.

Situated as she was, it is not, therefore, surprising, that Laura grasped at any means of earning a little addition to her slender income. One day her attention was attracted by one of those advertisements which meet the eye almost every day, in the newspapers. This one ran thus :

"Agents wanted. Good agents can earn from $3.00 to $5.00 a day by selling a popular new book. Apply at 501 Nassau Street. Room 24."

This looked very attractive. From three to five dollars a day ! Why, that would be riches to her ! Of course, she could give only a part of her time to this new occupation ; that is, at first ; but if she could earn only one dollar a day, in addition to her present income, what a relief and happiness it would be to her ! Then she could in one week, secure enough to pay the board bill she was still owing. It is true, Mrs. Moulder never asked her for the money, but then Laura knew that she needed it, and the thought weighed upon her all the time. Now, however, she would no doubt soon be able to pay off this debt ; and so the enthusiastic girl went on weaving quite a golden dream.

The first afternoon that she had leisure, Laura went to the place named in the advertisement. She found a large building containing many offices, and was forced to mount three flights of stairs, before she discovered room 24. Knocking at the door, which bore a sign, having on it the words "RITT & HIGGINS, PUBLISHERS ;" she was bidden to come in, and found herself presently in a good-sized apartment, with shelves around it, filled with books, and with a sort of counter at one end, behind which two men were seated, busily employed in writing. One of these came forward to meet her.

He was a tall, low-browed person, with light hair, and shrewd light eyes.

"Good-day, ma'am, good-day," he said, with great appearance of cordiality.

"I came in answer to an advertisement ;" explained Laura.

" Yes, ma'am, yes, all right ; Ritt is my name ; I'm the man to talk to. I should say, you'd be a first-rate hand at the business," he added ; looking at her glowing hand-some face, with a glance which expressed a financial esti-mate, rather than admiration.

" Will you please to explain it to me ? " asked Laura.

" Certainly, certainly. It's a very popular new book you are to sell;" and he picked up a large volume, showily bound. " It is called 'The Accordeon,' and contains a description of the homes of our poets, together with ex-tracts from their works ; six hundred and seventy-one pages of printed matter, and ten fine copper-plate engravings;" he repeated, glibly ; turning over the leaves as he spoke. " We have it in two bindings, Turkey morocco, price five dollars, commission to agent, eighty cents ; muslin, three dollars, commission, fifty cents. You might be able to sell, say, six books a day; profit, three to five dollars, as per advertisement."

" I'm afraid I couldn't sell so many as that," said Laura, her heart sinking at the receding prospect of money-making.

" Oh yes, you could," replied Mr. Ritt, positively ; " you'll have plenty of customers ; good looking ones always do;" with a wink that was intended to inspire con-fidence.

" I don't think I had better try," and Laura drew back, somewhat coldly.

But Mr. Ritt would not let such a promising agent escape thus easily. He persuaded Laura to sit down, and then was so eloquent in his description of the merits of the work ; so profuse in stories illustrative of the money that had been made by other "ladies" who had undertaken the business, that Laura at last yielded, and consented to see what she could do.

" The way we fix it," explained Mr. Ritt, "is, you take two books with you, one in each binding, as samples ; and then when you've made a sale you come back here and get other books to supply customers. We generally have a deposit from agents, as security; but I'll trust you without any, if you'll just give me your name and references," he said, looking shrewdly at her.

Laura gave these as desired; mentioning Mrs. D'Arcy as her reference, and went away with two books, each enclosed in a neat paper cover. The detail of the matter, now that she was close to it, seemed to her rather disagreeable; but perhaps she might make some money, since others had done so well.

When she was at home, Laura looked over her new wares. The book was evidently a device to make money; but the pictures were pretty; and as the poetry, though partly made up of the productions of rhymesters heretofore unknown to fame, contained also selections from our really deserving poets, she concluded that she could honestly recommend it as a pleasant parlor-table ornament.

Two or three days intervened before she was able to begin her labors as agent, and then came Saturday, her most leisure day. This morning was bright and clear, and as Bessie Bradford was out of town, so that she would have no lesson to her in the afternoon, Laura resolved to set out on her expedition.

She wore her dark dress, and fur-trimmed sacque, carrying her books in a neat, twine satchel, and despite this evidence of her trade, her whole appearance was so lady-like, and pleasing, that her occupation was not likely to be at once suspected. Mr. Ritt had advised her to go to the wholesale establishments down town, and to lawyers' offices on Wall street; and with no misgivings, Laura proceeded to follow his advice. The first place that she entered, was a large importing house on Broadway. As she stepped into the handsome store, a young man advanced to meet her, from behind a pile of boxes and bales.

" What is it, Miss ? " he asked, politely.

" Can I see the owner of the store ? " stammered Laura.

Now that she had fairly begun, the business did not seem so easy as she had thought it would be before she started.

"You mean Mr. Hall?"

"Yes," she faltered. The other young men had turned from their work, and were looking at her, with a stare of somewhat bold admiration.

"This way, Miss;" and the young man who had first addressed her, led her through a narrow path among the boxes to the rear of the store. ". A bad place for dresses;" he said, as Laura's frock caught on a projecting nail; "but we don't have many ladies here. There is Mr. Hall;" and he showed her into a handsome private office.

A gray-haired, hard-faced man was seated at a desk; he glanced up with a look of annoyance at her entrance: "What's your business?" he asked, gruffly.

"I have here a book, sir," Laura began; but no sooner had she uttered the words, than Mr. Hall interrupted her rudely:

"No, ma'am no; we want no books here;" and he called angrily after the young man who had not had time to go far away: "Here, Clark, show this young woman out; how often have I told you not to let any book-agents in, eh? There, take her away!"

Laura was ready to sink with anger and mortification; hot tears rose to her eyes, which she forced back only by an effort of pride; and she hurried out of the store, catching, before she escaped, a titter which ran among the young men, at the manner of her dismissal.

After this she walked a block down a cross-street before she could make up her mind to a second attempt; she was already so sick of her new occupation; then she recalled some of Mr. Ritt glowing descriptions of the money that had been made in this way and thought, as many books certainly were sold by agents every year, she surely ought to be able to succeed, if others had; and so fortified herself to a resolution to go on with her experiment. Coming presently to a large dingy-looking building, which appeared to be a wholesale iron establishment, she made bold to enter it. Thinking from her experience that it was well to ask for some one by name, Laura inquired if Mr. Bland was in; having read that title on the sign at the door.

"I am Mr. Bland," said a merry-faced old gentleman, who was standing near a pile of iron rods. "Want to see me?"

"If you please."

"Load on the rest of these rods, John," he said, to a stout porter who stood by; "Mr. Strong will tell you where to take them. Now, Miss, will you walk this way?"

He led Laura into a small cosey-looking office, where a heap of coals was burning in an open grate. "Take a seat by the fire," he said, cheerfully; "and warm yourself, you must be cold."

"No," replied Laura, "I am very comfortable; I have come to ask you to buy a book."

"A book! oh, that's it, is it? and pray what kind of a book may it be?"

"It is called 'The Accordeon,' and is about our poets."

"The Accordeon!" repeated Mr. Bland; "what a funny name! Sounds like an instrument of music;" and he laughed at his own wit. "Makes me think of summer evenings, when the fellow over the way always plays on an accordeon;" and he chuckled, merrily.

Laura felt quite encouraged and produced her prettiest copy of the book; "Will you look at it?" she said.

"Well, yes; I'll look at it;" and Mr. Bland took the volume in a fat pudgy hand; "Very pretty, very pretty, indeed. How much does it cost to occupy this, now?"

"To buy it do you mean?" asked Laura, a little puzzled—"Five dollars."

"Five dollars, eh! That's a good deal of money;" then laying the volume down, as if he had no further interest in the matter, he asked; "and how many of these books have you sold to-day?"

"I haven't sold any yet," admitted Laura.

"Haven't, eh? I thought so; let me see; eleven o'clock now; that ain't a very brisk business, is it?"

"No;" Laura confessed.

"What do you do it for, then?"

He had been so pleasant heretofore, that Laura could not quite resent this question; "That is my affair, not yours, isn't it?" she retorted, smiling.

"Well, I suppose it is," Mr. Bland assented; "but you ought not to be going out as a book-agent."

"I must earn my own living."

"No, you mustn't; and I hope you haven't got any such foolish idea. Women can't earn their living, and don't, we men take care of them."

"Not very good care; to judge from some of the poor creatures one sees."

"Oh, well; they are only the exceptions and prove the rule; it's all nonsense for women to try to support themselves; even those who pretend to are all helped by some man; all of them," he repeated dogmatically; "and you ought to be getting married. If you had a good husband to take care of you, you wouldn't be doing this sort of thing."

Laura rose. "Well, Mr. Bland, are you going to buy my book?" she asked, coldly.

"No, Miss no, I can't; dear me, what should I buy an Accordeon for? I ain't a sentimental young man to want an accordeon, either musical or poetical;" chuckling again.

Laura took up the volume. "Good-morning sir," she said.

"Good-morning, Miss, good-morning; and my best wishes to you! Hope you'll get a good husband; that's my best wish;" he called after her; as she hurried from the store.

This was perhaps a little better than her last experience; at least, she had not been directly insulted; and yet Laura felt hurt and vexed. She had been treated so entirely as if she were an inferior being; played with,

patted on the head, as it were ; encouraged to hope that if
she were very good, she might be rewarded—not by independence, not by earning an honest living—but by a husband !

Now Laura did not object to the thought of a husband,
abstractly considered ; and when the possibility of such a
possession presented itself to her, a certain pair of earnest
eyes seemed to look into hers ; but she protested with her
whole heart, against having such a gift come to her, as a
mere means of support. " Why cannot men realize that
women are rational beings, with the same wants, impulses
and ambitions that they have ! " she thought. " Why must
we forever be treated like dolls, as if beauty were our
greatest possession, and the securing a husband, our noblest
achievement ! "

On the whole, however, her interview with Mr. Bland
had somewhat encouraged Laura, and she ventured to try
her fortune again. Three times in as many stores, she was
repulsed sharply, though politely ; but at last, she came to
a broker's office, in which her arrival seemed quite opportune.

" Here's some one to see you, Mr. Duncan," the young
man outside said ; as Laura came into a handsome neatly
furnished office, and asked her usual question.

" All right," responded a cheery voice ; " bring him
in."

The young man glanced at his fellow clerk with a
smile of amusement, at the masculine pronoun ; and there
was in his smile, a something that Laura resented, especially as it was accompanied by a whisper, which broad-
ened the smile into a laugh.

She entered the inner room and found herself face to
face with a bluff, red-cheeked man, about forty, who started
in a little surprise as he saw her. " A young lady ! " he
said ; " Books to sell, eh ? "

" Yes, sir."

" As a rule I don't see book-agents," he explained,
8*

looking at her boldly; " but I'll make an exception to-day.
I've just made ten thousand dollars, and I feel disposed to
be jolly."

" That's a good deal of money," said Laura ; seeing
something was expected of her.

" Yes, pretty well ; was in a corner on Erie and cleared
my little pile. But young ladies don't understand. Come,
my dear, let me see the books."

Laura started at the familiar address, and drew herself
up.   Mr. Duncan observed this with a laugh.

" Don't mind me," he said ; " I'm an old married man
and feel privileged to say sweet things to pretty girls.
Ah ! the Accordeon," he went on, taking up one of the
volumes ; " that's neat now, really quite tasty ; " surveying
the binding with his head on one side.   " What's the
damages ? "

" The price of this one is three dollars ; of the other,
five," replied Laura ; who was beginning to get an insight
into the mysteries of New York slang.

" Well, my dear—there I go again ; you really must
excuse me—but I feel so uncommonly jolly to-day ! I'll
take both.   I'm going out of town to night to spend
Sunday with my wife ; and I'll take these with me as a
present to her and my aunt."

Laura was quite pleased with the bargain and resolved
to let him have the books and go back to Mr. Ritt's for
other samples.

" I hope the ladies will like them," she said.

" Of course they'll like them.   They're poetry, and
my wife dotes on poetry.   There," as he handed her the
bills for the books ; " now you can go and buy yourself a
new bonnet ! "

" Thank you," replied Laura ; and she rose to go.
" Good-morning."

" Good-morning, good-morning, my dear; and I say,
whenever you have books to sell, be sure and come here ;
I'd pay a dollar any day to look at such a pretty face ! "

This conversation had been conducted on the part of the gentleman in a very loud voice, and the clerks outside had evidently overheard a part of it. As Laura passed out, one nudged the other and she heard him say :

"She's one of 'em ! "

CHAPTER XXIV.

FURTHER EXPERIENCES.

WEARY, rather from mental emotion than from bodily fatigue, as it was now past noon, Laura went to a cheap restaurant, and took a cup of tea and a cracker. The few moments of quiet thought thus obtained, together with the refreshment of the food, revived her spirits, and she felt equal to a fresh effort; she was indeed gifted with one of those elastic temperaments that throws off care easily ; and is never morbidly depressed ; and when she reached the establishment of Messrs. Ritt & Higgins again, she was resolved to continue her efforts, and make a fair trial of what she could earn as a book-agent.

Mr. Ritt met her with great manifestations of delight at her success. "Sold 'em both, eh ? Well, that is good ! I told you how it would be ! I knew you'd make a first-rate hand at it."

"A great many people refused to see me, though ; " objected Laura.

"Of course, of course ; some'll do that, you must expect it ; but when you learn the trade better, you'll find you can sell 'em off like hot-cakes, just like hot-cakes ; " he repeated, encouragingly.

"I wish I could ! "

"Well, you will, you will ; you see you must flatter 'em a little ; sometimes tell the men they look so kind, you're sure they'll buy something. Lord bless you! some of 'em would be tickled to pieces at a few pretty words from such a handsome lady as you ! "

"I don't think I could do that," said Laura; "but if you will give me some more books, I'll try what I can sell this afternoon."

Mr. Ritt put up two more volumes, and thus supplied, Laura went out to try her fortune again.

She had the usual luck in several offices which she entered; the men were evidently very busy; declining mostly even to look at her wares. The afternoon wore on, and Laura was once more growing discouraged when she came to a large seed-store. On the outside there were tasteful wire-baskets, and rustic flower-holders; within there was a large shop, neatly arranged with pictures of flowers on the walls, and so many articles suggestive of the country and the summer, that for a moment, Laura seemed to be transported from the dull city, to some pleasant rural scene. A very pleasant old gentleman appeared as the presiding genius of the place; to him she applied.

"A book to sell, Miss?" he repeated, and he turned upon her a pair of mild, yet searching blue eyes. Something questioning in their gaze, made Laura feel more keenly than anything had yet done, that her position was a cruelly trying one.

"Yes sir," she replied; "I am endeavoring to dispose of a volume of poetical selections."

The old gentleman took the book and looked it over carefully. "It is neatly gotten up, and some of these pictures are quite interesting," he said; "what is the price of this one in simple binding?"

"Three dollars."

"I will take it," he said; "and now may I ask you a question or two?"

The face was very earnestly kind, and she answered; "Yes sir, certainly."

"How long have you been doing this sort of thing?"

"This is my first day."

"I am glad of it; I hope it will be your last, too."

"Why?"

"Because, a young woman like you, ought not to be going about in this way, into strange offices among all sorts of men."

"But you do not seem to remember, sir, that I must earn money in some way," Laura said, quickly.

"And is this the only way which you can find?"

"This is one of the very few occupations which are open to my sex. I was refused a clerkship in a wholesale store, because I am a woman; I am teaching drawing at half the salary paid to my predecessor, because I am a woman; and now you tell me I ought not to earn money in this way, because I am a woman! What am I to do? Even if I am a woman, I am hungry and thirsty, and cold, like a man; I have to pay the same board as a man; I must wear warm clothes as well as a man; in short, I need money to spend as much as if I were a man; and yet, because I am a woman, I am not allowed to earn it!"

Laura spoke with a sudden eloquent earnestness; the wrath and trouble of the day seeming to find vent in words. The old gentleman shook his head as she paused:

"You are very earnest, young lady; I see that you are honestly trying to support yourself; but take an old man's advice: go home, have a little patience, and by and bye, you will get a good husband to take care of you!"

Laura was so provoked at this close of what she hoped would be some words of sympathy, with her overwrought feelings, that she could scarcely restrain a bitter reply. By an effort, however, she choked back any answer, and with a cold salutation, left the place.

Another book was sold, however; that at least comforted her a little, and she went on with the weary work. At several other stores she was repulsed; the evening was beginning to approach, and Laura felt that she must soon turn her steps homeward, when, as she walked slowly on, jostled and stared at, by the now increasing crowds of men, she came to a large Insurance Office, in which the lamps were already lighted. Resolved to try just once more, she went up the steps and opened the door.

"Can I see Mr. Boardman?" she asked; for she had read that name on the door.

"I am Mr. Boardman," said a man, who was standing with his hat and overcoat on as if just ready to go out.

"Can I speak to you a moment?" asked Laura; but even as she uttered the words she was sorry she had made the request.

The man was about thirty-five years old, with thick black hair, and a heavy black moustache. His features were good; he would have been called handsome; but there was in his sensual mouth, his clouded eyes, an expression that Laura distrusted.

"Certainly, Miss," he replied, with alacrity; "come into my private office."

He led the way back to a small room, that was lighted only by the glow of the fire in a grate, motioned Laura to a seat on a comfortable lounge, and turned on the gas.

"And now, what is it?" he asked; seating himself beside her with easy familiarity, and looking at her with undisguised admiration.

"I have some books to sell," replied Laura, in the usual formula.

"Books to sell, eh? let me see them."

Laura drew one out of the case. "It is poetry," she explained.

"Will you show it to me?" he said; "you know where all the pretty places are better than I do."

Unsuspectingly Laura opened the book and turned over the pages. "Here are pictures of the homes of the poets: this is Mrs. Sigourney's house at Hartford."

"Very nice, very nice," replied Mr. Boardman, bending nearer to her, his eyes turned on her fresh handsome face, and not on the book at all.

Unconscious of this, Laura went on. "Here are some other pretty pictures,"—here she started in horror—the man had passed his arm around her waist, and was clasping her tightly.

"You are the prettiest picture of all; you are as sweet as a rose;" he said, excitedly.

Overwhelmed with anger and amazement, Laura struggled to escape. "Let me go!" she cried; "how dare you touch me! let me go!"

Her gray eyes flamed with excitement, and something in her face made even his dull senses understand that she was in earnest.

"A wild-cat, eh!" he said, sullenly, as she escaped from his grasp. "What business have you coming into a fellow's office, if you ain't willing to be agreeable?"

Laura hardly heard the words; as soon as she was free she fled from the room, going out so precipitately that she was well aware that one or two loungers in the office looked after her with amusement, as if they guessed what had happened. Into the gathering darkness outside she fled; her face burning, her heart beating with its load of outraged thought.

The shadows were deepening; the streets were very full of men, and Laura's first anger changed slowly to a feeling of utter loneliness and sadness. The surging throng around her seemed so many enemies, any one of whom would wound her or hunt her. Among all these strong, pushing, busy men, there seemed no place, and no hope for a woman to expect justice or mercy. These resolute-browed, swift-going, strong-limbed animals, who represented the great brute force of nature, its resistless power, its relentless will, could crush out so easily the gentler, more spiritual being, who represented the beauty, the grace, the harmony of creation! Among these tough-fibred, hard-headed creatures, pressing onward in the eager chase for wealth and place, would there ever be any way made for the delicate ones, who yet were entitled equally with them to a fair chance in the battle of life?

Oppressed with the burden of her own reflections she en-

tered a car, and took a seat at the extreme upper end.
Pulling her veil down, and leaning her head back, she paid
no heed to the crowd around her. Now that she had a
partial rest, she was conscious how very weary she was, and
yet she remembered that before she went home she must
stop in a store where she was in the habit of buying
drawing-materials, and get some crayons that she would
need for the work she intended to do that evening.

It was nearly six o'clock now, and Laura was faint and
hungry from her long fast; but she left the car a block
before it reached Twentieth street, and made her purchases.
She was very fearless about being out in the early evening,
and indeed frequently in these short winter days did not
reach home until after dark. Coming along armed with
her bundle, she never noticed a man lounging on the corner, who gave a quick start as he caught sight of her, and
signalled to another man, who was on the box of a carriage,
that was drawn up near the sidewalk. This person at once
became alert, and gathered up his reins and whip; while
the first man climbed to a seat beside him, and the vehicle
moved on quickly in front of the young lady.

When Laura reached Mr. Moulder's house, she was surprised to see a carriage standing before it, and a man on the
steps talking with Minnie, who held the door open.

"Here is Miss Stanley, now!" exclaimed the little maid,
as Laura came up the walk.

"What is it?" asked Laura.

The man, who was an ill-looking person, answered: "A
note from Mrs. D'Arcy;" holding out a letter.

"From Mrs. D'Arcy!" exclaimed Laura, in surprise;
and she took the proffered missive, and stepped into the
hall to read it. Opening it near the gaslight, she found
it contained these words:

"I am requested by Mrs. D'Arcy to inform Miss Stanley that Mrs.
D'Arcy is very ill, and would like to see Miss Stanley at once.
"MARY COLTON, M. D."

The name was that of a lady-physician, whom Laura had met at the doctor's, and she never doubted the genuineness of the letter.

"When was Mrs. D'Arcy taken ill ?" she asked, coming back to the door.

"I don't know ma'am ; all I know is we was sent to fetch you."

"I am to go in the carriage then !"

"Yes, ma'am."

It must be very urgent, reflected Laura ; then to the little girl: "Minnie, tell your mamma that I have been obliged to go to Mrs. D'Arcy, who is very ill."

"Won't you wait for dinner ?" suggested Minnie.

"No, oh no ; I must go at once. Good-bye, dear; I don't know when I shall be at home."

And Laura hurried out and entered the carriage; the man shut the door with a bang, and climbed up beside his companion.

"She was easy caught," he said, as they drove away; "I never did see anybody walk into a trap with their eyes open quite so slick !"

CHAPTER XXV.

AN ABDUCTION, AND ITS CONSEQUENCES.

ABOUT ten minutes after Laura went away, Frank Heywood pulled the door-bell at Mr. Moulder's. He was alone now. Rhoda, after recalling herself to his memory, and putting him in possession of all the facts with regard to Judge Swinton's pursuit of Laura, had left the carriage at a point near her home, as she could be of no further use, and dreaded leaving Maggie too long alone.

It seemed to Frank, in his anxious impatience, a terribly long time before Minnie opened the door, though really only a few moments passed until she appeared.

"Is Miss Stanley in?"

"No."

"Hasn't she come home yet?"

"Yes; she came home a little while ago, but went right off again."

"Alone?"

"No ; in a carriage that Mrs. D'Arcy sent for her."

"Mrs. D'Arcy's own carriage?" he questioned, breathlessly.

"No, a hack, I think. But what is it, Mr. Heywood? What is the matter?" for Frank's manner alarmed Minnie.

"Something very wrong, I'm afraid, Minnie : but I can't stop now to explain it to you. Who came for Miss Stanley? any of Mrs. D'Arcy's people?"

"Well, no," replied Minnie; "two men came, and they weren't nice men, either ; rough and horrid-looking, I thought."

This confirmed the worst suspicions, and Heywood said, quickly : "I am afraid that Miss Stanley has been deceived in some way, I have no time to tell you how ; but, Minnie, try to remember all you can about this carriage ; what sort of an one it was, and what color the horses were, so that I could recognize it again."

Minnie, who was a quick-witted little creature, seemed to catch his meaning at once. "It was a dark close carriage; there were two men on the box, and it had one white and one brown horse."

"And which way did it go?"

"Towards Ninth-avenue : I noticed that because I thought it wasn't the right way to go to Mrs. D'Arcy's."

"Thank you, Minnie, thank you ; I will try to bring Miss Stanley home ; " and hurrying back to his own conveyance, Frank jumped up beside the driver, and started on what seemed an almost hopeless quest.

Meantime Laura, who had at first been so absorbed in anxious thought that she did not notice in which direction she was being taken, began presently to think that she must be near her friend's house, and looked out eagerly. To her surprise, she was in a part of the town which she did not know. She could see through the darkness that there were low ugly-looking houses on each side of her, and just beyond these, on the one hand, she could dimly catch a glimpse of shipping, towering masts, and black smoke-stacks, coming into view at the street-crossings. Amazed at so stupid a blunder, which had brought her so far out of her way, when every moment was precious, she knocked on the front window to attract the attention of her driver, and tell him to change his course.

The man paid no manner of heed to this, except that he seemed to be urging his horses forward. Finding it useless to try to attract his attention in this way, Laura leaned out of the window, and called:

"Driver! Driver!"

"See here, Bangs; this ain't a-going to do;" said the man who held the reins; " she's got to be quieted somehow."

Laura resolved not to be carried out of the way in this high-handed fashion, and, still without a suspicion of any-thing beyond stupidity on the part of her conductor, shouted again:

"Driver! Stop! Driver!"

This time her words appeared to produce an effect; the carriage came to a stand-still, and one of the men got down and came to the door. Laura turned to speak to him; but before she could utter a word, he drew up the glass on that side, and then came quickly around to the other door.

"Thought it might be cold," he muttered; "Now then, ma'am, what is it as you wants?"

"You are taking me the wrong way—" Laura began, leaning towards him; but before she could finish her sen-tence, a cloth was flung over her head; she was conscious of a strong sickly odor; there was a rushing sound in her ears, as of a thousand hammers pounding heavily; she could feel the blood beating in her brain; she struggled for a moment, groping in the air blindly with her hands; then her head sank back, and total insensibility overwhelmed her.

The man drew up the other glass of the carriage, and climbed up again beside his companion.

"She won't make no fuss for awhile," he said, grimly, and the driver whipping up his horses, the vehicle proceeded more rapidly up the river-side avenue.

It was just at this moment that Frank Heywood caught sight of the carriage. The direction which the coach containing Laura had taken, together with a knowledge of where some of the evil resorts of the city were, had led the young journalist to think that she might be carried off to this quarter of the town, and here he came in pursuit. He had explained his object to the coachman, a warm-hearted son of Erin, who, with the chivalry of a true Irishman, was fired with a desire to aid in securing the young lady.

"And do ye think that's the coach?" he asked, with much interest, as they came in sight of the vehicle.

"I do, Mike," replied Frank; "it looks like it to me. Drive as near as you can to the side of the avenue, so that we can get a good view of it."

"I'll do that," answered Mike, suiting the action to the word.

"There! don't you see?" cried Heywood. There are two men on the box; there is a light and a dark horse; a close carriage too, and both windows shut!" he added, under his breath; a new horror coming over him.

"The bloody scamps!" exclaimed the coachman, in great excitement; "Shure, I'll stand by you, captain, to put an ind to their divil's game!"

"Thank you, Mike," said Frank cordially; "I may need your help."

"And ye'll get it shure," protested the coachman heartily, and dropping his voice, he added: "If you want one of thim raskils knocked over, captain, say the word, and I'm your man."

Heywood smiled a little. "I hope it won't come to that,

Mike ; but I'll tell you what we will do ; put your horses to
their speed, and drive right across in front of the carriage ;
then when the men speak to you, as they probably will,
answer them back ; you can give as good as you get, I
suppose ? "

" I can that," replied Mike.

" Well, keep their attention occupied with what you
have to say, and leave the rest to me; only be ready to
follow the carriage again, if I give the signal."

" I'll do that, thin, captain; will I go at onst ? "

" Yes."

In a moment Mike had whipped up his horses and was
running a race with the closed carriage. It lasted only a
brief time; he turned his horses' heads suddenly, directly
across the avenue, and both vehicles came to a stop, amid
a storm of oaths from the two men, and rejoinders from
Mike, so ingeniously and scientifically aggravating as to
keep the full attention of his enemies concentrated for
some minutes on himself.

Frank watched the collision with set teeth and braced
sinews. His face was unusually pale, as it always was
under circumstances of violent emotion, and his eyes shone
with a glitter of excitement. As the two conveyances
became entangled, he swung himself down with wonderful
dexterity from his place, and quick as thought glided to
the carriage where Laura lay, and unperceived by any one
in the darkness and confusion, opened the door and sprang
in beside her.

In another second the closed coach had swung ahead
and was going on with increased speed. Indeed, all this
had passed so rapidly that Mike stared in amazement to
see what had become of his late companion. A white
hand suddenly appearing and beckoning from the rear
window of the other coach appeared to reassure him, however, and he followed it at a short distance.

Meantime the rush of cold air which Heywood admitted into the carriage revived Laura, who slowly shook

off the effects of the drug and sat upright, supported by
Frank, who raised her head so that she could inhale the
freshness. As she recovered, a few words explained to her
the deadly danger in which she had been, and rapidly
regaining her self-command, she was quite ready, presently, to second the plans of her preserver.

None too soon, the vehicle going on swiftly, turned
suddenly up a cross-street and drew up before a gloomy
looking house, standing by itself, and surrounded by a
waste of jagged rocks that had been blasted into all sorts
of ugly shapes.

As the carriage stopped, the door of the house opened,
and Judge Swinton appeared, a dim light following out
from the hall, his large figure and square head, on which a
wide hat was slouched.

"All right, Bangs?" he asked, anxiously, as he approached the door.

"All right," replied that worthy, who had sprung
down from the box, and stepped to the carriage-door.
"I've got her safe; had to chloroform her, though, judge,
but you'll find her quiet as a lamb—"

He stopped short; a sudden change came over him; his
jaw fell, his eyes started, till, small as they were, they seemed
likely to leave their sockets; while Judge Swinton, partak-
ing of his consternation, stood staring as if paralyzed.

Before Bangs could touch the door, it was opened from
the inside, and they saw, not a pale and swooning girl,
but Frank Heywood's alert figure and sparkling eyes.

"Who the devil are you?" demanded Judge Swinton;
recovering after a moment from his first stupor.

"I am a reporter for the New York Trumpeter," replied Frank, as he sprang out. "And I'll make an item of
this for the paper if you like, Judge," he added, with a
mocking smile.

His honor's only reply was the utterance of a very ugly
word, which he gave under his breath, but with great
force as he turned on his heel and reëntered the house.

"Now, Miss Stanley, if you'll take my carriage, I'll see you home," said Heywood, as he assisted Laura to alight.

Mike was close by with his coach, and a few moments later the two young people were seated in it. Neither Bangs nor his companion, who had been watching the judge for instructions, appearing to think it wise to interfere.

This seemed almost a matter of regret to the worthy Irishman ; "I wish I had a crack at thim bloody villains," he muttered to himself, as he drove away.

CHAPTER XXVI.

JUDGE SWINTON APOLOGIZES.

On Mr. Moulder's steps, Frank parted with Laura. "I can't come in," he said ; "I have already left my work longer than I would for any other reason."

"I can never thank you enough for what you have done for me this evening," Laura declared, clasping both his hands in an effusion of gratitude.

"It was not much to do," replied Heywood ; "and I enjoyed it ; positively I have not enjoyed anything so much for a long time !" and in truth his eyes shone with a lustre that Laura had not seen in them before, and as he spoke he looked really happy.

Minnie presently opened the door with an exclamation of delight at seeing Miss Stanley safely back ; and so Frank bade her good-bye, and reëntering the coach was driven back to the office where he rewarded Mike munificently for his evening's work.

Laura, when the excitement was a little over, felt herself so weak and languid from the effects of the drug, and the many fatigues of the day, that she was glad to go at once to her room, where some tea and toast refreshed her body, and a long chat with Mrs. Moulder soothed her spirit. A good night's rest, and the quiet Sunday which followed, restoring her completely to her usual strength and cheerfulness.

Monday morning's first mail brought Laura a note from Judge Swinton. It contained an apology for his attempted abduction, which he endeavored to excuse on the ground of his extreme attachment to her, and wound up with a formal offer of his hand, and a request to be allowed to call upon her.

Laura read this with rising color; she could not find it in her heart to excuse the insult she had received, even when forgiveness was claimed on this ground, and the framing of a severe reply was a partial relief to her feelings of indignation. Her answer ran thus:

"Miss Laura Stanley cannot accept Judge Swinton's proposal, and declines to receive his visits."

As she came down stairs with this missive in her hand, she stopped for a moment in the sitting-room to shew it to Mrs. Moulder.

"There, Agnes," she said; there is some satisfaction in being able to write that!"

"Isn't it almost too hard?" asked Mrs. Moulder, gently.

"Not a bit. There is one privilege that men have left us; the privilege of refusing them. This, you know, is the only revenge society permits to us women."

"He is a dangerous man, though," reflected Mrs. Moulder.

"He is," replied Laura; "but I think he has done his worst. I shall take care to keep out of his way in the future. I have seen him until now only because I feared he might tell some of my people where I am; but not even to prevent that will I ever see him again."

"I think you should be careful about being out after dark, hereafter."

" Yes, I will do that ; I have no fancy for being carried off again."

And that much of caution Laura strictly adhered to. She made it a rule to be at home every day before twilight fell, and avoided going out, except on the ordinary round of her duties. Peremptory as was her reply to Judge Swinton, however, it did not apparently have the effect of entirely discouraging his suit. Not many days after her note was sent, as Laura sat in her room one evening, Minnie knocked at the door, with the message that a gentleman wanted to see her.

" A gentleman! who is it, Minnie ? " asked Laura sharply.

" I don't know. Pa told me to tell you to come down."

The mention of Mr. Moulder aroused Laura's suspicions. " I am very busy this evening," she said ; " and I cannot see any one. You may tell your father so, Minnie."

The little girl went away, and Laura returned to her work, glad that she had had the presence of mind not to fall into so shallow a snare. She had been drawing some little time, and was completely absorbed in her labors, when there was a heavy footstep in the entry, and, a moment after, a knock at the door.

" Come in ! " called Laura.

Some one fumbled at the lock for a moment; then the door opened, and Laura was amazed to see the portly form of Mr. Moulder. She started up and came to meet him.

" Miss Stanley," he said; " Judge Swinton is in the parlor and would like to see you."

" I cannot go down," replied Laura, with a quick angry flush.

" He is a very distinguished man," said Mr. Moulder, severely ; " a man whose visits any young lady might be proud of."

" I have already declined to receive them," answered Laura, somewhat imperatively; " and it is quite useless for him, or any one else, to ask me to do so."

9

"You won't go down then?" demanded Mr. Moulder, roughly.

"No."

"You are a very foolish young woman," he said, rudely. "It's preposterous not to see him."

"I think I am the best judge of my own actions," replied Laura, stiffly. "I consider Judge Swinton a man whose courtesy is an insult, and you may tell him so, if you please."

Mr. Moulder stared at her in utter amazement at her audacity. "I certainly shan't do that," he said. "But of course you will do as you choose."

"Decidedly," and Laura closed the door on the retreating figure with a somewhat peremptory action.

This seemed likely to be final, and for some time after this, no event occurred to disturb the even tenor of her life. Her daily tasks at the school, at the academy, and at her drawing-lessons, occupied her time with a monotony that would have been wearisome, had it not been that she fought her way on bravely, with a hope that hard work now, might help her in the future. Mrs. D'Arcy procured for Laura after a time another pupil, and she had succeeded in finding a market for some of her small flower-paintings, which brought her in from week to week a trifling sum.

She made no second attempt to act as a book-agent. Her one day's experience had been sufficient for her. She went down to Mr. Ritt's office soon after that eventful Saturday, and closed her account with him; but no persuasions on his part could induce her to subject herself a second time to the insults she had already encountered.

So the weeks drifted slowly by until February had come, and was drawing to a close. Laura did not see Flora Livingston again, though she heard of her through Guy Bradford. One evening, shortly after Mrs. Courteney's ball, he came to see Laura. She was very busy, but not liking to miss the visit, came down into the stiff little parlor with some of her drawing-materials, and spread them out on the table, pursuing her labor at intervals while the conversation went on. As a first topic of interest, he described the grand entertainment to announce Flora's engagement, at which he had been present; told how majestic Mrs. Courteney was; how stately Mr. Le Roy was; and gave a tolerably good description of Flora's elegant dress.

"She used to be such a spirited looking girl," he said; "but that evening she walked through the rooms, leaning on Mr. Le Roy's arm, with her eyelids drooped, her face pale, her whole appearance like that of some fair Grecian captive led in chains to adorn the triumph of a victor."

"Poor girl! There is no prospect of escape, I am afraid; and yet it does not seem possible that her whole independence can be crushed out so easily."

"Probably not," replied Guy. "She looks now like one subdued, rather than conquered. Some day perhaps she will revolt."

"I hope she will!" exclaimed Laura; "I hope with all my heart she will, before it is too late!"

It chanced that while this chat was proceeding, Minnie was out of the room, and as Laura uttered these last words, Guy left his seat, and came and stood near her chair.

"Marriage without love is an intolerable thought," he said.

Laura felt his approach with some blind sense, that was not of sight and hearing, and bent a little lower over her work. "Yes," she replied.

"But marriage with love is the crown and triumph of life."

There was a strange thrill in his voice as he spoke, and she knew that those dark eyes were reading eagerly her downcast face. With an effort she answered:

"Such a marriage as that of your parents, for instance."

"Yes, and such a marriage as I sometimes dream of for myself."

It seemed absolutely impossible for Laura to reply to this, and an eloquent silence fell between these two. Guy bent so near Laura that she could feel his breath stirring her hair; almost hear the beating of that honest heart, that was fluttering in a tumult of timidity and longing—then there was a touch on the handle of the door, and Minnie reëntered the room.

For once, Laura was not glad to have her little chaperon return so promptly to her post of duty ; but, as usual under such circumstances, the young woman was the first to recover herself, and Laura held up one of her drawings for Guy to look at with so quiet an air, that the poor fellow fancied she had not in the least shared the emotion that swayed him, and that she was perfectly indifferent to all that absorbed him so entirely. He resumed his seat with some short, almost crusty, reply, and sat for a few moments staring at her with earnest troubled eyes. It was nearly hopeless to try to carry on any conversation with him, and when, a few moments later, Frank Heywood came in, it was almost a relief to Laura. Not so to Guy, however, he shook Frank's hand with somewhat less than his usual cordiality, and, after glowering at the intruder for a few moments, took his leave.

Laura was amused and yet annoyed. She could read this big honest fellow like an open book ; while to him she was a wonderful being, whose smile was happiness, but whose favor he knew not how to win, he was to her a transparent soul. She more than half guessed the secret of his heart ; she realized fully the jealous suspicions with which he regarded Frank, and she regretted that he went away, as she knew he did, puzzled and unhappy.

Heywood, too, seemed to divine the situation ; he looked after Guy with an amused smile, and when Minnie had run away to bed, as she was always allowed to do when Frank came, he said :

"Laura, Bradford didn't like my coming in."

"Perhaps not ; but I am very glad to see you."

"Well, I shan't trouble him often after this, for I am going away."

"Going away!" repeated Laura, in consternation.

"Yes, I am going on a tour through the Southern States for the paper."

"Oh, I'm so sorry; that is, for my sake. Will you be gone long?"

"Six weeks, two months, perhaps longer; it depends upon how much I succeed in doing."

"Oh, dear me, Frank; I shall miss you dreadfully!"

"I think you will, Laura; but I shall have all sorts of things to tell when I come back, and I'll write to you, of course."

"Oh, yes, and I shall see your letters in the paper, which will be almost as good as talking with you. How soon do you go?"

"I don't know exactly; to tell the truth, Laura, I am going to do rather a quixotic thing; I wouldn't have any of the fellows in the office know it; but I don't mind telling you."

"What is it?"

"You remember Rhoda Dayton's friend, Maggie?"

"Of course I do, I have heard from them often through Mrs. D'Arcy; I wanted to go down and see them, but the doctor advised me against it."

"She was right," said Heywood; "a visit there would do them no good, and might compromise you. If you have heard from Maggie lately, you will know that she is much better, and ready to make her journey home. Only waiting for a pleasant day, indeed, to start with Rhoda. Now I propose to be their escort."

"You, Frank!" exclaimed Laura, opening her eyes.

"Yes, of course some people might think it odd, but I believe it can be arranged so as not to attract any notice. Mrs. D'Arcy is to see them off, and I will meet them at the cars. It is only a twenty-four hours' journey, and they are going directly to the same part of the country that I wish to visit, so that I can accompany them, and perhaps make their trip more comfortable."

" What a good fellow you are ! " exclaimed Laura.

"Perhaps not quite so much so as you think," said Frank, with that inscrutable smile that sometimes crossed his lips.

CHAPTER XXVII.

MR. FITLAS SPEAKS.

THE week that followed this evening was rather a dreary one to Laura ; she did not see Frank again, as he was doubtless busy with his preparations for departure; nor did Guy Bradford visit her. This last absence troubled her more than she was willing to allow even to herself. She had grown to depend so much on seeing him frequently, and had so hoped that he would call soon again, that as the evenings went by without bringing him, she became quite worried and anxious.

But in the absence of these two friends, another admirer did his very best to console and entertain the young teacher. Mr. Fitlas suddenly became very pointed in his attentions ; sending up his card to call on Laura several times, and bringing to her on each occasion a monstrous bouquet, which he presented with many pompous expressions of regard.

It had for some time past been quite a settled thing, when Laura went to the Bradfords' on Saturday afternoon, to give her drawing-lessons to Bessie, that Guy should come in before the hour was quite over, and under pretence of the growing darkness, wait upon her to her home. But when the Saturday following his last visit came round, and found the teacher at her post, Guy did not appear, although Laura lingered as late as possible, hardly confessing to herself, how much a desire to see her brother had to do with the minuteness with which she was inspecting her young pupil's work.

"Don't trouble yourself so much about my stupid picture, Miss Stanley," Bessie said, at last; "I think I can finish it now."

At this moment the door opened, and Laura looked up with a start and a blush; but it was only Mrs. Bradford, who after greeting her with her usual kindness, said:

"My dear, hadn't you better stay to dinner? It is beginning to grow dark. Guy is away; but Mr. Bradford will see you home."

"Oh no!" exclaimed Laura, very quickly; I have work to do to-night, and must go directly;" and she hurried away.

He was not in town then, there was some little comfort in that thought; perhaps he had not neglected her intentionally; but there was a sort of oppressive loneliness in Laura's heart as she took a car, not daring to walk alone through the darkening streets.

When she reached the Moulders', Minnie informed her that "dinner was most over, and she'd better hurry right down.'' As it was so late, Laura took off her hat and sacque in the parlor, instead of going up stairs, and went at once to the dining-room. As she came in with a feeling only of weariness, and a desire for rest, she was annoyed to find Mr. Fitlas with Mrs. Moulder at the disordered table, which had been deserted by all the rest of the family. The gentleman greeted her with effusion:

"Good-evening, Miss Stanley, I'm in luck to-night, surely. I came down here to get a snack, and now it seems I am to have the pleasure of your company."

"How tired you look, Laura!" exclaimed Mrs. Moulder, anxiously, as the young lady took her seat.

"I am rather tired," replied Laura; "I have had a fatiguing day."

"Take this, dear; it will do you good," urged Mrs. Moulder, handing her a cup of tea.

"And here is some turkey; garbled turkey, I think they call it," said Mr. Fitlas, helping her from a dish before him.

Laura took the proffered edibles, at first with a feeling as if she could not swallow anything; but a draught of tea helped to restore her, and she presently began to realize that she was very hungry. In so healthy an organization as hers, something more than a light trouble of the heart is needed to destroy the appetite, and Laura presently did full justice to her dinner.

"Uncommon pleasant day for the season," remarked Mr. Fitlas. "I've been in the Park this afternoon; very lively there; lots of genteel people out!"

"Were you walking?" asked Mrs. Moulder.

"Not muchly," replied Mr. Fitlas, severely; "I never walk there—was in Bill Flash's drag."

"That must have been pleasant," said Laura; "though in fine weather I think one enjoys the Park more in a walk than in any other way."

"It's well enough to take a stroll in the Ramble," remarked Mr. Fitlas, as if he were making a judicial decision; "but I've observed that one never sees the real swells anywhere else."

"That settles it then," said Laura, with a twinkle of amusement.

"Here are some canned peaches, Laura. Will you try some?" asked Mrs. Moulder, presently, producing a dish of inviting looking golden fruit.

"Did you put them up yourself?" asked Laura, as she accepted some.

"Yes; I put up fourteen cans last summer;" with a faint sigh, as if the memory of the labor were a weariness.

"There is some danger that these sort of fixins will fumigate, isn't there?" inquired Mr. Fitlas, solemnly.

"They will what?" asked Mrs. Moulder, puzzled.

"Fumigate," repeated Mr. Fitlas.

"Oh, you mean ferment; yes, unless the proper cans are used there is sometimes trouble with them."

The conversation continued in a not very exalted strain, maintained principally by Mr. Fitlas, and consisting in a considerable degree of boasts of his own adroitness and prowess, during which he glanced frequently at Laura, as if to mark the effect of what he said, upon her. As she was rather bored than otherwise by all this, she was glad to have finished her meal and to be able to leave the table. To her annoyance, as she rose, Mr. Fitlas rose also, and followed her up stairs.

As she had left her hat in the parlor, Laura went in there after it, and there again she found Mr. Fitlas close beside her.

"Miss Stanley," he said, in a tone of unusual importance; "if you could sit down a moment, I should like to speak to you."

"Certainly," replied Laura, in considerable surprise; "what is it, Mr. Fitlas?"

She took a chair and looked steadily at the young man, perceiving now that he was arrayed with extreme gorgeousness. His cravat was of the most brilliant crimson; his shirt front was curiously embroidered; and a tuberose adorned his buttonhole.

Mr. Fitlas, with his color heightened, cleared his voice with a hem, and placed himself in a chair near Laura. The clear gaze of her gray eyes seemed to disconcert him strangely; he drew out a handkerchief, wiping his brow nervously; the powerful odor with which the cambric was saturated, combined with the perfume of the flower, quite filling the room with its sweetness.

"Miss Stanley," he began at last; "it's a pretty important thing when a fellow makes up his mind to—to—you know, to—to—"

"Well?" asked Laura, surprised at his confusion.

"I was a going to say something very particular about myself," he began again, moving uneasily on his chair.

9*

"You see the fact is, you've done for me. I'm smashed; upon my word I am now! I never did see any young lady that was quite so stunning every way as you are," he said, desperately.

"I am much obliged to you for the compliment," replied Laura, catching his meaning with a sudden half-amused annoyance; "but, really, Mr. Fitlas, it is quite a waste of time to tell me so."

"Don't say that, now, Miss Stanley," he protested with an earnestness she had never before seen in him. "I don't ask you to pile right in, you know; but I'm going away to-morrow, and I just thought I'd like to say a word to you before I go. I'd like to have you think over the matter," bending a little nearer; "and just remember, if you do think of trotting in double harness, I'm your man."

"You are very kind, Mr. Fitlas," replied Laura, seeing that the young man really intended to pay her the highest compliment; "but I have no such thought, I assure you, and you had far better look elsewhere."

"Don't see it," replied Mr. Fitlas, resolutely. "You suit me, and if I suit you, why shouldn't we make a double team?"

"Oh no; I must decline the honor," Laura persisted.

"Why, Miss Stanley, why? Now you'd better think twice of it," he urged; "I'm in good business; Moulder will post you up about that. I don't mind telling you that I get two thousand a year and travelling expenses; that ain't bad now, is it?"

"No, very good, but—"

"Don't say no," he interrupted, quickly; "you mayn't understand all about me. I dare say now you think me fast, but I'm a pretty steady man, I am, honestly; I've sowed some wild oats," he admitted, with an air of modest merit; "but as fellows go, I'm about as good as they make 'em, and if I was really married, you know, why I'd settle down."

"I've no doubt, Mr. Fitlas; but you must find some

other wife. I cannot entertain your proposal for a moment," Laura declared, positively.

" You don't mean it now ? " he queried, despondently, his red face growing deeper-hued; then brightening a little; " you ain't mad at me, because I said some things against Women's Rights are you ? Really, now, I'm willing to let women vote, I am."

" They will doubtless be much obliged for your gracious permission," replied Laura, rising.

Unconscious of any sarcasm, Mr. Fitlas went on, following up what seemed to him an advantage : " Perhaps you think I ain't much of a literary man, but I do read some, it's a fact I do; not old books, to be sure, Shakespeare and Tristerum's Shanty and those ; but I've read all Orlando Bobb's works, and I take the Day Book regular."

Laura with difficulty curbed in an almost irresistible laugh into a smile. " It is no use, Mr. Fitlas," she said ; " I don't want to wound you, but don't you see that we should never really suit each other, in the least ? We had far better be good friends, than try to be anything else. Good-bye ; I hope you'll have a pleasant journey," and she escaped from the room.

CHAPTER XXVIII.

A STROLL IN THE PARK.

On the next day, which was Sunday, Laura went to church in the morning, and in the afternoon, feeling a vague unrest, started for a stroll in the Park. The day was unusually mild for the season; a week of sunshine had melted the snow from the streets, so that the walking was excellent, and the air had in it a softness suggestive of the yet far distant spring. Laura took her way up town through one of the side avenues, and reached the great pleasure-ground, without meeting any one whom she knew.

As she passed through the gateway, her heart gave a bound of delight. She felt for a moment like a prisoner let loose, a child of the country, an intense lover of nature, the escape from the endless brick and mortar, the wearisome straight lines of the city, was such a pleasure to her! The trees were bare of leaves, to be sure, but there was infinite grace in the outlines of their branches, as they rose in delicate pencillings against the sky. The grass, though faded and brown, was danced over by a net-work of fairy shadows that fell from the slender boughs as they swayed in the wintry breeze, and in every hollow were piled heaps of snow that flashed in the pale sunlight, while the lake was a sheet of gray water bordered by broken ice, and shaded by sombre evergreens.

Laura walked on briskly, enjoying the spring of the damp earth under her feet, the sweep of the fresh wind, the scent of the moist ground, and the aromatic odor of the cedar trees.

The exercise brought an unusual glow to the round cheeks, and a sparkle to her gray eyes, while her abundant hair tossed by the air, fell into tiny ringlets about her face; and as she pressed on with light elastic step, she was as fair an embodiment of healthy handsome womanhood as one might wish to see.

Her way at first lay along the margin of the lake, on a path that was quite deserted; but as she came round a turn, she perceived a gentleman advancing towards her, and her heart gave an involuntary bound as she recognized Guy Bradford.

His face changed with a flush that seemed to reflect the blush on hers, as he advanced to meet her with a smile of unmixed delight.

"Miss Stanley, this is delightful!" as his hand closed over hers with a firm clasp. "I am so surprised, and so pleased!" he went on, honestly, as if his heart were so full

that it must find relief in words. "May I walk with you?
I was only out for a stroll ; do let me be your escort," he
added, as Laura seemed to hesitate.

"I shall be very glad to have some one pilot me about,"
she admitted. "I have been so little in the Park that it
seems to me a sort of labyrinth, of which one might easily
lose the clue."

"I know it by heart, so that I shall be a safe guide,"
Guy said, as he fell into line with her. "Do you mind
taking my arm?" offering it.

Laura glanced up at him ; the brown eyes were looking
into hers, wistfully, eagerly. "I think not," she began ;
then seeing the hurt look that crossed his face ; "yes, I
will," she said, putting her fingers on his arm ; "it is
surely more sensible here, and I don't think I shall outrage
conventionalities very much."

"Indeed, no," said Guy, looking intensely happy.
"Surely, Miss Laura, you put me at least on the footing
of an old friend."

"Of course I do," replied Laura, heartily ; "and do
you know, I rather like taking your arm, if I please, as a
symbol that for once, I am free to do as I like."

"Aren't you always?"

"No, indeed, Mr. Bradford ; I feel nearly all the time
like a prisoner, and the thought that was uppermost in my
mind when I met you this afternoon, was of delight at
the few hours of liberty I could have here. For a little
while I resolved to forget everything unpleasant, and only
enjoy this lovely day and this charming scene."

"It is delightful," said Guy ; "at least it is now; the
day seemed rather gloomy before I met you."

The tone was significant, and in a little embarrassment
Laura said, "I thought you were out of town, when I was
at your house last evening, your mother said you were
away."

"I was ; I have been off on business for nearly a week ;
but I got back late last night ; I thought of staying away

over Sunday, but I am heartily glad that I did not now," he added; pressing her hand a little closer to his side.

There was a moment of silence. They had been walking on at a good pace since they met, and had now reached a point where the path approached the carriage-road. A good many vehicles were sweeping by; the crunch, crunch, of the horses' feet, and the roll of the wheels sounding steadily. The occupants of the conveyances were mostly of the stronger sex; many of them flashily dressed, round-shouldered, sitting well braced on skeleton-wagons, behind fast horses; their whole souls seeming to be given up to interest in the quadrupeds which drew them; but occasionally an open coach with a half-tipsy party of red-faced men went by; men with loud voices, who stared rudely at every woman they passed.

"Let us hurry on," said Guy; "I can't bear to have those rowdies glaring at you so;" and he looked down at Laura's fair face tenderly, yet with true masculine jealousy of even a glance at the woman he admired.

Laura laughed. "It is rather annoying," she said; "do you know, sometimes I feel as if I would like to go veiled like the Turkish women; some of your sex are so rude."

"I only wish you could," said Guy, heartily; "I only wish you could wear a veil; that is, provided you took it off for me!"

At this moment a handsome four-in-hand was driven past; a showy turnout, with horses decked out in gold-mounted harness, drawing an open clarence, fitted up with crimson linings, and having a liveried coachman and footman. On the back seat was a large fair man, with a blonde moustache; and beside him sat a darker and less heavily built person, with black beard and bold blue eyes. As this last caught sight of Guy and Laura, his regard which had been running lightly over the loungers, suddenly concentrated itself into an angry gleam.

By one of those subtle influences of which we are all

conscious, but which no one can explain, this concentrated
gaze seemed to draw the attention of both the young people. As they looked up, Guy raised his hat with a cold
bow, and the gentleman returned it with a sweeping salutation that was evidently intended to include the lady.
Guy glanced quickly at Laura; she did not return the
bow, but a quick flush rose to her face.

" Do you know Judge Swinton ? " he asked, in jealous
surprise.

" I have met him at Mr. Moulder's," replied Laura;
" but I have dropped his acquaintance."

" I am glad of that," said Guy, with a look of relief.
" He is a bad unprincipled man; not fit for the society of
any respectable woman."

" Yet he is one of those whom you men have intrusted
with the administration of justice ! "

" Yes," admitted Guy; " and it is all wrong; utterly
and horribly wrong ! Indeed, our political system is in
many respects so corrupt, that I am sometimes almost
hopeless of a cure for the many evils."

" I don't think we women could do much worse," retorted Laura, smiling.

" Hardly, if you tried; and I for one believe that we
shall never have any improvement in our politics till we
have women taking their just part in them."

" Of course, you need women in government as much as
in the family. It has always seemed to me as absurd to
exclude women from politics as it would be to banish them
from the home. Government is only family management
on a large scale; and is administered now very much as a
household would be which should be ruled by men alone."

" I should like to see my good mother and half-a-dozen
ladies like her, acting as city mothers," said Guy, laughing
lightly. " The city fathers certainly make a poor hand at
city housekeeping."

" There is one point then on which we should agree, if

your mother were running for alderman; I should do my
best to electioneer for her."

"I am not quite clear that I should like to have you,"
said Guy, again with a telltale pressure of the gloved hand;
then, catching sight of Laura's face, he added: "You are
thinking what right have I to say what I would wish to
have you do; I have none now; but sometimes I dare to
dream and to hope!" his voice dropping to a tremulous
passionate undertone.

They had turned out of the wide path now, and were
strolling along a narrow winding way. On the one side
the rocks rose gray and snow-decked above them; on
the other, they could catch glimpses of the dark waters of
the lake; while overhead the pale sky dropped flecks of sunlight through the tangled branches on to their path.

Laura's head was drooped, and they walked on for some
distance in silence; meeting every little way other couples,
strolling like themselves. At last Bradford said: "Miss
Laura, may I come to see you this evening?" his dark
eyes supplementing the request with a deeper significance.

The color mounted to Laura's cheek, and it was a moment before she could frame the simple answer "Yes."

"I have something to say to you; something that I
cannot tell you here where there are so many strange eyes
upon us. If I come this evening will you let Minnie go to
bed early?"

"I don't know as to that; I can't banish the poor child,"
replied Laura.

The words seemed to Guy lightly spoken; he could not
guess that they were the result of a playfulness assumed
in a sort of desperation to hide a deeper feeling.

They had reached the broad path leading to the Park-
gate now, and a few moments more brought them to the
entrance, where Laura said she must take a car, or she
would not be at home in time for the evening meal at Mr.
Moulder's.

"And I, too, must hurry home," said Guy; "I have

promised to wait on mother and Bessie to evening service, but when that is over I shall come to you. Will you be expecting me ? " his eyes scanning her face eagerly.

" Certainly, since you have said you will come," answered Laura, with a blush; avoiding the clear gaze that seemed to dazzle her. " Good-bye."

She sprang on to the platform of one of those clumsy vehicles that see very much of the tragedy and comedy of New York life, and so was lost to view.

Seated in a corner, with eyes that were fixed on some imaginary distance, Laura fell into a reverie; but how different was this, from the sombre thought that absorbed her on her ride down town the night before ! Then, life seemed all dulness and gloom, dreary as the bleak night around her. Now, her reflections were as golden as the bright rays that the setting sun was casting over the city. She scarcely ventured to define her thoughts; but the blood in her veins was dancing to some happy tune, and the future rose before her fair with the enchanted " light that never was on sea or land."

CHAPTER XXIX.

CROSS PURPOSES.

IT was to Laura like a harsh discord after some strain of sweet, soft music, to go down to the dull dining-room at Mr. Moulder's and descend from the fairy realms in which she had been dreaming, to the prosaic realities of common life. The place seemed more than usually dingy ; she was a little late, and the table was in that ugly half disorder that one sees when the members of a hungry family have helped themselves as they please, and put down their dishes wherever it chanced to be convenient, without any regard to order. Mrs. Moulder was daintily exact in her habits ; but Mr. Moulder thought it was " all nonsense to be too particular," and she had long ago given up the attempt to have the table served as she would wish; so the dish of chopped beef stood at an acute angle to Mr. Moulder's plate, a bread board was on one corner of the table, and a preserve bowl appeared to have wandered aimlessly out of its moorings and to be stranded, stern foremost, against the tea-tray.

It was "Sunday out" for Jane, Mrs. Moulder's solitary maid-of-all-work, and the day had been anything but one of rest to the poor lady. She looked worn and hollow-eyed, and there was a listless, almost despairing weariness in all her motions. Mr. Moulder's face was more than usually glum, as if his duties at church had tended rather to sour, than to sweeten his disposition, and the children, weary of a long day in doors, were restive and quarrelsome. Minnie, who had been helping her mother, looked tired and cross, and Master Aleck who appeared to have finished his meal, was amusing himself by going about the room and tapping with his fork on every object that was capable of producing a noise.

At Laura's entrance, Mrs. Moulder looked up with a faint smile. "Oh, here you are, Laura; I'm afraid your supper is rather cold; you are so late!"

Something of the radiant look was still on Laura's face, and she answered brightly, "I have been walking in the Park, and it was so lovely that I lingered longer than I ought."

"Never mind about that, dear; if you can only make a comfortable meal. Aleck, run to the kitchen and get Miss Stanley some warm toast; it is all ready on the dresser."

"I don't want to go," said Aleck, sulkily; "send Minnie."

"You have finished your tea and she has been working very hard," remonstrated Mrs. Moulder; "I had rather you would go, Aleck."

For reply the boy beat a loud tattoo on the grate-pan with his fork, shrugging his shoulders defiantly.

"Send Minnie," ordered Mr. Moulder, gruffly ; "it ain't boy's work to wait on the table."

"I will go myself," said Mrs. Moulder ; a faint pink coloring her delicate face.

"No, no, let me go ! " exclaimed Laura, starting up.

But Minnie was too quick for them. She was watching her mother with anxious eyes, and as the two ladies rose, sprang from her place and was away before either of them could reach the door.

"She has been working like a good child all day," Mrs. Moulder said, looking after her affectionately ; "I don't know what I should have done without her ; she has helped me so much about both dinner and tea."

"It's no more'n she ought to do," growled Mr. Moulder ; "girls ought to learn to keep house ; it's all they're fit for ; " with a vicious glance at Laura, against whom he seemed to have an especial grudge, ever since her refusal to see Judge Swinton.

The young lady felt the telltale color rise, and a sharp reply was on her lips, but she caught a pleading look from Mrs. Moulder and restrained herself.

At this moment a slight diversion was made by Master Aleck, who having exhausted the noise-producing capacities of every available inanimate object in the room, varied his programme by thrusting his fork into his youngest sister's back. The child set up a shrill cry.

"What is it, dear ? " exclaimed Mrs. Moulder, in consternation.

"Aleck stuck a fork into me," moaned the little one.

"Oh, Aleck ! how can you be so naughty ! " Mrs. Moulder exclaimed, despairingly. "Come here, Aggie dear ! "

The little girl fled to her mother's arms, while the boy drew back to his father, glaring at her defiantly.

"He was only in play," said Mr. Moulder ; then seeming to comprehend dully, some of the indignation which shone in Laura's eyes, he went on: "boys will be boys."

"And girls must learn the lesson of patience, early," retorted Laura, with a glance at the drooping form of the gentle wife.

"Certainly," said Mr. Moulder, testily; "women ought to be brought up to be wives and mothers; that's what God intended them for."

"And men ought to be brought up to be good husbands and fathers."

"Oh, that comes of course," Mr. Moulder replied, uncomfortably. "But women ought to feel that home is the place for them. I've no patience with these new-fangled notions about women's voting and such stuff; it's preposterous," he added, roughly.

Laura, never over patient, was fast waxing wroth: "And I believe thoroughly, in giving the ballot to every woman, as well as to every man;" she said, firmly.

"Pretty figure they'd cut in time of war!" sneeringly; "If women vote they must fight."

"And, logically, the men who can't fight must not vote!" retorted Laura, with a glance at Mr. Moulder's heavy figure and face, lined with wrinkles.

"That's different," growled Mr. Moulder, flushing angrily.

"My dear, I'm sure you would give women what is justly their due," remonstrated Mrs. Moulder, gently.

"Women ought not to talk about what they don't understand," said Mr. Moulder gruffly, and Laura escaped from the room.

This sort of thing was intolerable. Laura felt jarred and out of tune, and yet was repentantly conscious that, as on many another occasion, she had been too hasty. The happy afternoon in the Park, the happier evening that was coming, ought not to have had so discordant an interlude. She longed to escape to some place of calmness and peace, and going to her room resumed her hat and sacque.

"I am going to church, Agnes," she said to Mrs. Moulder, whom she met in the hall; "only around the

corner to St. Gabrielle's. If—if Mr. Bradford comes to
see me before I am at home, please have him asked to
wait."

"Certainly, dear," said Mrs. Moulder, with a smile.
"You are not afraid?"

"Oh, no, it is such a little way, and the streets are full
of people."

The church to which Laura bent her steps, was one of
the finest in the city; a grand building, rising in solid walls
of gray stone without and within; softly illumined by
many gas-lights, that lit up the gorgeous colors of the great
screen behind the altar, and the magnificent adornments of
the chancel, shedding a fainter radiance down the aisles,
and on the band of worshippers. The vaulted roof rose
deep and blue in lofty mysterious height; the walls were
rich with heavy carvings, and the deep mullioned windows
sombre with shadows. The feet of belated people echoed
on the tessellated pavement of the aisles, and the swell of
the great organ rolled out in solemn music.

A blessed calm stole over Laura's spirit as she entered
this spot, from whence the cares and sorrows of the world
seemed banished. Above all the storms and strifes of earth
there stretched the eternal heavens, and the petty trials of
life vanished in the thought of eternity.

After awhile the Te Deum was sung; the grand strains
swelling in a triumphant pæan; the voices of the choir
rising and mingling in exultant harmony. As Laura listened, she seemed to see the dwellers of the past, who had
been inspired by these thrilling chords. Long lines of
knights with fierce eyes flashing under plumed helmets, and
bearing stained banners, the bloody relics of hard-fought
fields, came filing into a grand old cathedral to kneel and
join in the chorus that celebrated a battle won. A king,
fair-haired and handsome, trailed his purple robes up the
broad aisles of a solemn fane; beautiful women and gaily-
dressed cavaliers thronging after him to rejoice over his
release from prison. A queen, pale-browed and sad-eyed,

led her stalwart soldiers into a dim old church, to give thanks for a victory that had cost her the life of a husband. All gone now; faint shades of the past, sporting their little hour on the world's stage; fighting, loving, dying, forever departed, vanished like the forgotten sunshine of the days in which they lived. A fleeting life, passing away like the clouds of a summer morning; but sometimes, ah, how full of sweetness! For to Laura, sitting in the quiet church, through all the service, through all the sermon, though she listened reverently, a voice was saying in her heart, "Guy is coming! Guy is coming!"

Presently the discourse was over; there was a brief pause, and the last hymn was sung:

> "Glory to thee, my God, this night,
> For all the blessings of the light."

Laura's heart repeated the words earnestly, and as she bent her head for the final benediction, she included Guy's name in her prayers. A momentary hush, and then the rustle of silks and the clatter of many feet on the pavement, as the congregation passed out. Laura, to whom the past hour had been one of ecstacy, felt a sudden chill as she left the warm church for the dark cold night. Outside, there were many persons waiting for friends; she expected no one, but as she came down the steps, some one left the crowd and joined her. It was Frank Heywood.

"Good-evening," Laura said, with a bright smile; "how came you here?"

"I went to the house and they told me you were at church, so I came over. I have only a moment to spare; I am going away to morrow."

"So soon?"

"Yes, the weather is mild, Maggie is much better, and all things are arranged to start by an early train in the morning. I only ran up for a moment to bid you good-bye."

"How sorry I am that you are going; that is, for my sake; I've no doubt you will enjoy the trip."

"I think I shall," replied Frank. "I have a longing to see the South once more; you know I was born there, and it will be delightful to me to breathe again that soft air, and see the hills and the pine forests."

"Shall you go to your home?" asked Laura.

"No," said Heywood, sadly; "I have no home to go to; that is, I have no parents or brothers or sisters. As for the rest of my people, I shall avoid them rather than seek them."

While they were speaking, the two young people had been walking towards Mr. Moulder's, and as the distance was short they were presently almost there.

"You will come in a moment," said Laura, as they approached the house.

"No, I cannot, I have too much to do; but, Laura, before I go I have one word to say to you."

"Well, what is it?"

"You have never told any one about your first night here, have you?" hesitating.

Laura's face flushed quickly. "No one but Mrs. Moulder."

"She's trustworthy, no doubt; but don't tell any one else."

"Why not?"

"The knowledge might be used to your disadvantage. There, dear; I feared I should wound you," he said, looking into her face, tenderly. "I have wanted to say this for a long time, but I have put it off, for fear that you might feel hurt. I would not have spoken now, only that I did not like to go away without giving you the warning."

They were standing on Mr. Moulder's steps now, and as Heywood spoke, Laura reading his heart in his honest gaze, put out her hand, impulsively. "And I thank you for saying it," she exclaimed; "Frank, you are just the best and truest friend that ever a girl had!"

The young journalist's eyes sparkled. "I believe that you understand me, Laura," he said; "and your memory will be one of the pleasantest things that I shall take with me."

At this moment the door was opened by Jane, who had just come in, and was very smart in her "Sunday clothes." Seeing who it was, she grinned knowingly, and went away again, leaving the two on the steps.

"And you can't come in a moment?" asked Laura.

"No; I must bid you good-bye now." He had both her hands in his as he spoke, and he drew her gently towards him.

Laura's eyes grew humid. "I shall miss you so much, Frank! Write to me very soon. Good-bye."

"Good-bye, dear," and he bent towards her and touched his lips to her cheek.

Laura never thought of resenting the action; indeed she was half-minded to return the caress; Frank seemed so different from other men. "Good-bye! good-bye!" she cried, as he ran down the steps, following with moist gaze the retreating figure. Then, as he waved his hand for a last farewell, she turned to go into the house.

At this moment she caught sight of Guy Bradford. He stood at the foot of the steps, looking up at her with eyes that seemed burning with a sombre light, and with a face that she could see even through the dimness, was desperately pale.

Her first impulse was to greet him with a smile; but the smile died away utterly as he raised his hat to her with a cold salutation, and turned away.

Then it came to her that he had witnessed the parting between her and Heywood, and that he had interpreted it by the dictates of his own jealous heart. For an instant she was tempted to run after him, and force him to listen to an explanation; then the conventional impropriety of such an action occurred to her, and she went slowly into the house ; but as she closed the door, it seemed as if the darkness of the night was not shut out, but went gloomily up stairs with her.

CHAPTER XXX.

MAGGIE GOES HOME.

THE next morning very early, a little group of friends were assembled in the Jersey ferry-house, to see Maggie and Rhoda off. The sun was just coming up, shedding a pale light from the eastward over the city ; the air was chill and damp, for there were piles of half-melted snow lying beside the street, and a mist was rising from the river. Outside, there was a perpetual tramp of vehicles, as wagons, carriages and trucks, passed across the wooden way, and rumbled down to the boats. Within there was a hurrying rush of eager people, crowding to the ticket-office, and then passing in single file through the narrow gateway : a human tide that ebbed all day, that never flowed, and yet that never ceased.

Maggie and Rhoda had come down in Mrs. D'Arcy's carriage, and now the sick girl was seated on one of the narrow, hard benches, waiting a moment to bid her friends good-bye. She looked very pale ; but there was the light of a happy excitement in her great blue eyes. Rhoda, neatly dressed, stood by her, seeming to have no thought but for her companion, whose every motion she watched with anxious care. Mrs. D'Arcy hovered near the two girls, her fine face soft with motherly tenderness.

Good Bridget Malone, who had come in, panting and puffing, had just hurried up to the group. Her broad visage was quite red with the nip of the frosty air, and a smile was struggling around her mouth, though her kind eyes had a suspicious dampness about them.

10

"Here ye are, the crayther!" she cried, coming up to Maggie. "Sarvice to ye's, me leddy," to the doctor; "shure it's glad I am that I'm in toime."

"Why Biddy!" exclaimed Maggie, with a faint smile; "did you come way down here to see me off?"

"I did, me lamb, I did," bending near the sick girl; "and I thought I'd niver git across the strate, at the last," she went on, to the company generally. "What iver way I wint, thim 'fellers was a hollerin' at me: 'Out the way, now!' and, 'Move on, will ye?' and swearin' 'till ye'd crip to hear thim. Shure they're an awful lot, thim min!"

"I'm glad you got here, Biddy," said Rhoda.

"And here's somethin' for ye's," Bridget whispered to Rhoda, drawing her aside, and presenting a basket neatly covered with paper. "Jist some doughnuts and cookies I made up for ye's; they'll be nice to ate in the cars maybe."

"Oh, thank you!" cried Rhoda, warmly; her dark eyes filling with tears. "How good you all are!"

"There's Mr. Heywood!" exclaimed Mrs. D'Arcy, as the young journalist came in, his delicate face looking blue with the chill of the early morning.

At the mention of his name, Rhoda glanced towards him, and a quick flush swept over her features. Frank turned to them all with a bow and a smile, and then went to the office to buy his ticket.

"I think we had better go on, now," said Mrs. D'Arcy, who was going over the ferry with the girls; "this is a poor place for Maggie to be waiting."

At this moment a woman, shabbily-dressed and forlorn-looking, made her way through the crowd, and came hurrying up to them. It was Mrs. Bludgett. Her wonderful bonnet was on one side; her shawl was dragged up over one shoulder; her dress, which was quite long, showed traces of the street mud. In her hands she carried six huge oranges, which, as soon as she came near enough, she poured clumsily into Maggie's lap.

"I couldn't get here before," she gasped; "Bludgett was late this morning ; but there, I brought you these."

"Oh, thank you, Molly; thank you!" said Maggie; "you're very kind."

"It ain't much," responded Mrs. Bludgett; "and I can't stay a minute ; I don't know what he'd do if he should find me here," glancing apprehensively over her shoulder.

"We will put some of these in your bag, I think," said Mrs. D'Arcy, gently taking the fruit out of Maggie's lap; and with Rhoda's help she disposed of it in a neat travelling satchel, that already showed signs of being well provided with eatables. "Now, my dear, we really must go ; Mr. Heywood is waiting at the gate for us, come, my dear."

With the assistance of Mrs. D'Arcy and Rhoda, Maggie rose, and thus supported, walked feebly across the wide room; Biddy, who scarcely attempted to conceal her tears, following with her basket, and Mrs. Bludgett stealing after them, with every now and then a timid backward look.

At the gate, Maggie and Rhoda turned to bid their faithful friends farewell.

"Good-bye, and God bless ye, my lamb," sobbed Bridget, kissing Maggie's thin cheek. "The Vargin purtect her !" she murmured, as she drew a little back to give a parting kiss to Rhoda.

"Good-bye, Maggie, good-bye," said Mrs. Bludgett; then motioning Rhoda aside a step—"Here, Rhody, here's something I thought you'd like to have," producing from under her shawl a gaily-covered book. "It's the 'Boundless Blunderbuss, or Cunning Crucified,'" she whispered, mysteriously; "and it's awful exciting."

"Thank you, Molly," Rhoda said, with a smile; "good-bye ; take care of yourself ;" she added, significantly.

So the little group passed through the gateway, Maggie turning once, her blue eyes looking back with a strange wistful sadness, in a gaze that seemed to pass beyond the waiting women, and seek out some form, imagined rather than seen.

A moment after, the cold damp air of the river struck
the sick girl with a sudden chill, and she drew her shawl
around her mouth, as a violent fit of coughing shook her
meagre frame. Rhoda and Mrs. D'Arcy hurried her into
the ferry-boat, and there presently Frank Heywood joined
them. Only for a short time, however. After greeting
them, he passed on to the front of the boat, so as to be
among the first to leave it and secure a good seat in the
cars. Thanks to this, when Maggie at last, with feeble
steps, reached the train, an excellent place was provided
for her; and Mrs. D'Arcy saw her seated by Rhoda, with
her basket and shawls at her side, and every arrangement
possible for her comfort on the long journey. Then the
good lady bade her friends good-bye, and a moment after
she left the car, the engine gave a final snort, and started
away on its swift rush through the country.

All that day and all the next night the travellers jour-
neyed, borne on almost without pause; sliding past quiet
villages; halting a moment at busy cities; then away in a
swift race, waking the echoes in the still open country, as
the train sped through leafless forests, or dashed across
wide fields, stretching brown or snow-clad on either side.
The iron wheels rung out their monotonous chime; soft
over the sandy road, loud at every bridge and causeway,
through all the long hours of daylight and the still longer
hours of night. The sun came up at first dim and watery,
rising higher and flinging a warmer glow over the wintry landscape; then sinking down to the west and
hiding among low-lying clouds that veiled the horizon.
The stars came out one by one in the deep heavens, glowing
brighter as the shadows gathered, until they shone a myriad diamonds on the black vault overhead.

Towards morning a ghostly old moon hung her horned
crescent above the hills, showing wan and weird through
the skeleton branches of the trees, illumining to silvery
beauty the smoke-wreaths as they floated off in fantastic
curls along the track.

Another day dawned and still the travellers were on their way. Maggie was beginning to look very pale and tired now; but there were many miles yet to be traversed. The sick girl had passed but a restless night; and after awhile on this second morning, fell into a sleep which lasted some hours. When she awoke, the sun, which still smiled upon them, was declining once more; but at the first glance she gave from the window, her eyes flashed with delight.

"There are the hills!" she cried; "open the window, please! Oh, I am almost home!"

Frank, who had been as tenderly devoted as any brother to the two girls, drew up the sash, admitting the air that was soft with a peculiar balminess unknown to more frigid climes.

The scene around them had indeed changed; the snow and the ice had vanished entirely, the grass was waving green on every sunny slope, the low hills were covered with pine trees, and away in the horizon, high piled against the sky, were the forest-clothed heights of the Blue Ridge.

A new animation came to Maggie. "See how the water runs in the cricks!" she said, giving the southern pronunciation to the word, and pointing to the mad mountain-streams that were dashing down the hill-sides, gullying deep the yellow soil, their bright waves flashing in the sunshine. "There must have been a big 'fresh,' this season! and oh, Rhoda, look! quick now, under the pine trees there! the eye-brights are all in flower!"

"The eye-brights," repeated Rhoda, bewildered.

"Yes, that is what they call them here. Look now at the foot of the trees, don't you see? Great beds of little white flowers?" and she pointed with her thin hand eagerly at the white blossoms of the anemone that lifted their starry eyes to the spring sunshine.

"I see, dear," said Rhoda; "and there are violets, too; I saw a tuft just now, close to an old stump"

"How delicious the air is!" Maggie ran on, leaning her head out to catch the soft southern breeze. "And look at that tumble-down house, with the gourds hanging on a pole in front of it, and the little darkies rolling in the sand; and see, yonder, that old cracker wagon on the cross-road. Oh, Rhoda! it will give me new life to be among the scenes and the people that I belong to."

"I hope it will, darling; but don't exert yourself too much; you know we have a long way to make yet."

"I will be quiet, dear," said Maggie; "for it does hurt me to talk against this noise;" and she leaned back, looking out in rapt enjoyment of the familiar scenes.

Heywood, too, seemed to be strongly affected by the landscape that recalled so vividly the home of his childhood. His strange eyes had a deep yearning in their gaze, and there was a nameless shade on his delicate features. Rhoda, who had watched him whenever he had been with them during the journey, watched him now, with a singular intentness in her gaze.

All the afternoon the train was moving at a very different rate of speed from that at which they had been going further north; stopping every now and then at solitary houses, or what seemed to be an utter wilderness, but which turned out to be a station from which people came and went. And at one of these lonely halting-places Maggie and Rhoda's journey came to an end. This place was as forlorn as any of the others; a clapboard building, with a rude unpainted platform running along one side of it. No dwellings to be seen, only a bit of scrubby forest on the one side, and a field of broom-grass waving yellow on the other side of a red clay road, heavy and hopeless looking. To Maggie, however, the spot was very welcome.

"Here we are!" she cried, as the train halted; starting up in her excitement and going forward almost without help from Rhoda.

Frank Heywood followed with the wraps and baskets

to the door, but he was not to leave the cars here, and the moment for bidding his travelling companions farewell had come. They both shook his hand very cordially. Maggie thanking him with tears in her eyes for his tender care and kindness; Rhoda holding his fingers for a few seconds, hesitatingly, almost as if she would say a word to him beyond those of farewell; but there was no time for delay, and after a brief instant she passed him with some murmured expressions of adieu. For a little they saw his slender figure as he stood on the platform waving his hat to them; then the rumbling train disappeared into a pine forest.

Beside the station-house there stood drawn up a tumble-down old carryall with a sleepy-looking black driver, and into this conveyance the two girls presently got; Maggie still feverishly excited as she looked with childish eagerness at every object they passed: the russet-colored scrub oak to whose branches last year's leaves still clung, the grass and flowers by the wayside, and most of all, the distant blue hills. A brooding stillness seemed to reign over the scene, and there was a spicy freshness in the silent air. As they drove slowly on they could hear the wild carol of some unseen bird's song; the perpetual chirp of the frogs in the low-lying swamps, the hum of the summer insects that were already abroad.

They had not very far to drive, for which Rhoda was thankful; as the road was of the worst description, and the pounding and plunging must certainly be bad for her feeble companion. After going about a mile the way made a turn, and they came in sight of a little house standing by itself under the shade of a great willow tree. A house so small, so poor, so shabby, that even Rhoda was a little shocked when Maggie cried, joyfully:

"There is our place!"

There was a broken fence about the tiny cabin; a well, with a swinging "sweep," in one corner of the yard; and some bright tins shining on a bench at one side. There

was no path leading to the door, for the earth about the
house was all beaten hard; but beyond it, at the back,
there was a small garden-patch where vegetables were
planted and a few early flowers were in bloom.

As the rattling vehicle drew up before the house there
was a sound of one moving within, and a very old colored
woman came hurrying out. She was tall and gaunt; a
dark calico, faded to dinginess with many washings, hung
about her bony figure, and a turban of bright cloth was
wound around her head. As she caught sight of the sick
girl she hastened to her with a cry of delight:

"De Lord bress my precious honey, pickaninny! is you
done come back to ole mammy?"

Maggie, her eyes full of tears, sprang out of the carriage into her old nurse's arms. "Aunt Phœbe, aunt
Phœbe," she sobbed; "I'm so glad to be home!" kissing
the wrinkled black face again and again. And mamma?"

"You're mamma is in de house, honey, she ain't been
bery smart dese here days; but she 'specs you, she'll be
powerful glad to see you and de young missus;" she added,
politely.

Maggie ran on with her nurse, while Rhoda waited to
look after the baggage and pay the driver; going then to
the house to join her friend.

The door of the cottage opened directly into a small
room, carpetless and bare. On one side was a high dresser,
or "chest of drawers," with a cheap picture above; there
were some straw-bottomed chairs standing about, a lounge
was drawn up near the fire, and before it was spread a bit
of rug. In the deep chimney a pile of light-wood was
burning with a cheerful blaze, and on the lounge lay a
little pale woman, almost as pale as Maggie herself; a
shrivelled bit of humanity, dressed in a very old white
wrapper. Beside her, Maggie was kneeling, weeping in
her arms, and Rhoda knew that at last the sick girl's prayer
was granted and she had found her mother.

CHAPTER XXXI.

A GRAND DINNER-PARTY.

THERE came to Laura Stanley after Frank Heywood's departure, a weary time. She heard from him occasionally, and his letters to her or in the papers, were almost the pleasantest things in her life. Her other friends were almost lost to her. Mrs. D'Arcy had one of her daughters and her family with her, on a visit, and was so much absorbed with them, that Laura scarcely saw her at all. Guy Bradford she did not meet after that unfortunate evening; he never called on her; she never saw him at his house, nor did she again linger there in hopes of meeting him; for there was something in Mrs. Bradford's manner, that made her feel as if the kind lady had heard from her son his version of what had passed, and when the two met, she had a way of looking at Laura, in a gently grieved manner, as if the young teacher had done her some injury which was very bad, and yet for which she could not be blamed. As for Mr. Fitlas, he had disappeared entirely from the scene; having departed on another of those immense trips which were the principal occupation of his life.

The days and weeks passed on, and Laura struggled to meet cheerfully the duties of her monotonous life. Her round of teaching was distasteful to her; her home was not comfortable; almost everything that to her made up the charm of life, was denied to her. But still she toiled on, never giving way to the melancholy that would have overwhelmed her if she had yielded to it. Working hard every day in the tread-mill round; displaying a quiet heroism that was better than the rash bravery that has won renown to men on cruel battle-fields.

In one direction she had her reward; her untiring in-

10*

dustry made her life easier to her than it would have been without it ; and loving her art as she ever did, its exercise when she could choose its subjects was a pleasure. Still existence seemed to the young teacher very sad-colored; she would walk sometimes of an afternoon on Fifth avenue and see other girls, no older than herself, driving by in elegant carriages, or strolling past her with their friends; and a sigh, hard to repress, would rise to her lips, not of regret for the mere luxuries, but for the friendliness, the companionship, the happiness, that was denied to her !

Once when she was out walking thus, she met Flora Livingston. Her sister Maud was with her. Maud, handsomer than ever, her rare dazzling beauty set off by the paleness, the subdued look that had stolen over Flora's once bright face. Laura passed the two with a ceremonious bow; but a moment after was surprised to hear her name called, and to find Flora close beside her. Laura turned with a glad smile of greeting, and Flora, as she shook her friend's hand, said, hurriedly:

"I can't stay a moment, only tell me if you are at the same place yet?"

"Yes."

"And will be for some time?"

"I think so."

"If you do move, please send me word at once, and Laura," very earnestly; "don't think that because I don't come to see you I don't think of you often; I do, and I believe you are the best friend I have."

"I will always try to be, dear."

"I know you will, but I must go now, Maud is waiting."

"Stop one moment, Flora; is the wedding-day fixed?"

"Yes," replied Flora, with a faint blush ; "haven't you heard ? It is to be immediately after Lent, on the thirteenth of April."

"So soon !" for it was late in March, now.

"Yes, good-bye; " and Flora turned back to rejoin her

sister, who had stood all this time with a look of contemptuous disapproval on her curling lip.

As Flora rejoined her she said, crossly : " I don't see
what you wanted to speak to that girl for, Flora; she is
entirely out of our set."

" She is an old friend of mine, and I shall always speak
to her when I meet her," replied Flora, with a flush that
showed that the old spirit was not wholly dead yet.

" Well, we must hurry home, now ; we shan't have any
more than time to dress, as it is."

Maud spoke the truth in this ; there was to be a grand
dinner-party at the Livingstons' that evening, the last before
the wedding, the invitations to which were to go out on
the morrow, and when the two girls reached the house,
Mrs. Livingston met them with some anxious hurrying
words:

" You must make haste, girls; half-past four, now, and
all these people coming at seven ! "

" There," said Maud to Flora; "I told you we ought
not to have stopped for anything."

" And for my part I would have been glad to be out so
late that I should have missed the whole evening," replied
Flora, as she went to her room.

At seven o'clock, Maud and Mrs. Livingston were down
stairs, ready to receive their guests; but Flora was still in
her room. She was sitting in her boudoir, ready dressed.
A heavy lilac silk, with point-lace frills, giving her a sort
of matronly appearance, which accorded well with the
pensive style of her loveliness. She was in a chair, drawn
up before the fire, which burned in a tiny grate; her small
feet raised to the fender ; her fair head supported on her
ungloved hand. A knock at the door startled her from her
reverie, which seemed anything but a cheerful one.

" Come in," she said, languidly, and a very pretty and
elegantly-dressed lady entered the room. A dark-haired
lady, with brilliant black eyes, sparkling white teeth, and
a glowing complexion; a lady, whose every movement was

full of a vivacity that was attractive, though perhaps not always quite natural.

This was Mrs. De Lancy Winthrop, formerly Miss Henrietta Lennox, and one of Flora's intimate friends. A year ago she had made a so-called excellent match with a millionaire, old enough to be her father. As Flora saw her she put out her hand to greet her cordially, and Mrs. Winthrop cried :

" You naughty puss, I am sent for you. Your mamma is in quite a fret that you are not down yet, and was going to send Clarisse up with some cross message, when I interceded, and asked to be allowed to go for you, as I wanted to see some of the pretty things that have come since I was here last."

" I am very glad you came," said Flora; " for that will give me an excuse for being late."

" And now, what have you got to show me ? "

" There are the presents on the table," resumed Flora, indifferently ; pointing to a litter of opened boxes, and tissue-paper, and cotton, from among which shone the gleam of silver and gold.

" Oh, how lovely ! how sweet!" cried Mrs. Winthrop, going into ecstasies over the various pretty objects, while Flora looked on with an amused smile. " You don't seem to care much for them," said the lively lady, at last.

" No," replied Flora, " I don't. One gets bored even with presents after awhile, and I have had so many."

" What a queer girl you are, Flora ! Why, when I was married, I thought the bridal gifts were the best thing about it," with a shrug ; " but there, we must go down or I shall be scolded as well as you."

" Stop a moment," said Flora ; " who has come ? "

" Oh, nearly everybody, I fancy. Mrs. Courteney is there ; she has on the heaviest mauve silk I've seen this season, and such lovely duchess lace ! Aunt Murray is there. Isn't she prim, though ! I always fancy she is watching me with those gimlet eyes ; and the Thorntons

are there, and that fascinating young German, Ernstein.
I mean to have a flirtation with him this evening ; he has
the prettiest eyes I've seen this season," she added, with
the air of a connoisseur.

"Oh, Etta ! How can you talk so."

"*Que voulez-vous, chérie?* One must have some excitement ; in another year, you will be amusing yourself in
the same way."

"I think not," said Flora. "It isn't my style ; but—
but Etta, are these all the people that are down stairs ? "

"No ; oh, how stupid I am ! *He* is there, my dear, of
course you only care for that information. Mr. Le Roy
is there, looking as handsome and cold as ever. By the
way, Flora, perhaps it will be just as well if you don't
care for flirting ; he doesn't look like a man that would be
very patient with anything of that sort ; " she added, significantly.

The two ladies presently descended to the large drawing-
room, reaching it only in time to take their places in the
procession to the dinner-table. Mr. Le Roy led Flora in,
of course, and on the way took occasion to say a word of
disapprobation :

"Flora, you were late down."

"Yes," she replied, shortly.

"I trust that this is not a habit of yours ; punctuality
is one of the virtues that I prize most highly. I am never
behindhand myself, and I don't like those who are with me
to be so."

Flora made no answer ; her face colored a little, but as
they reached the dining-room at this instant, an answer
was not necessary.

At the table Flora sat between Mr. Le Roy and Mr.
Ernstein. The young German several times made an attempt to talk with her, but as his next neighbor on the
other side was Mrs. Winthrop, who appeared resolved to
be as good as her word and open a flirtation with him, he
was kept so much occupied that he had little opportunity

for more than a few words to Flora, who was thus left for entertainment, to the solemn commonplaces of Mr. Le Roy.

The dinner was a very stately one, served *à la Russe*, and occupying several hours in its discussion. The table was brilliant with silver and gold plate; dressed with flowers, and sparkling with elegant glass; but as the moments went by, Flora's face grew more and more weary, and in her lovely eyes there was a look of settled sadness.

It came to an end at last, the long meal, as does everything earthly, and the company moved back to the drawing-room. Mrs. Winthrop, who appeared to have arranged her evening's work to her satisfaction, retired to the shadows of a bow-window with Ernstein, where a very animated conversation appeared to be progressing between them; though every now and then the young German's dark eyes would follow Flora's graceful figure with a gaze so intense, as sadly to interfere with the proper replies to his companion's airy nothings.

Flora was for a little while left at leisure to move about among the guests; but presently Mr. Le Roy came up to her, and in his usual imperious manner drew her away to a seat on a sofa.

"You don't look very well this evening, Flora," he said; "you are pale, or is it your dress? I should have thought lilac would suit you;" looking at her as one might at a doll one was attiring. "I'm afraid it is too trying. Why don't you wear pink, like Maud?" and he glanced at that young lady, who was standing near, brilliantly handsome in a rose-hued silk.

Flora changed color a little. "She is quite a different style from me, you know," she said, gently; then added with more spirit, "I have sometimes thought she would suit you best;" watching his face closely.

Mr. Le Roy's cold eyes turned with a slow deliberation from one sister to the other. "No," he said, calmly; "she is too *prononceé;* you are more the sort of a woman I admire; quiet and gentle."

" You think I shall be a sort of patient Grisell ! "

" I hope so," he replied, gravely. "She always seemed to me quite the model for a wife."

" I am afraid I should hardly have been so meek under the trials to which she submitted," Flora said; and there was a little spark of defiance in her eyes.

" You will be put to no such tests, of course," replied Mr. Le Roy; "but I have no fear, pretty one. I can see that your nature is quietness itself !" his gaze resting upon her with a look of lordly approbation.

Flora's head drooped a little. " Perhaps not always," she said.

"I will trust you," Mr. Le Roy affirmed, graciously. "I have watched you very closely for the past two seasons. You are always amiable, though perhaps a trifle too excitable, but that you will overcome, doubtless ;"—with a magnanimous wave of the hand—"I have very strict ideas of what women should be; I wholly disapprove of anything in the least fast; now look at Henrietta Winthrop," pointing to where that lady, always in the prosecution of her flirtation, had seated herself beside Ernstein on a low couch, and was looking over a book of photographs with him, their heads in singularly close proximity; " I consider such conduct perfectly disgraceful ! " Mr. Le Roy went on, severely; " and I shall wish you to discontinue your intimacy with her in the future. I have a horror of anything that even suggests an impropriety."

Did no remembrance of his own conduct to Maggie occur to him? no thought of her ruined life? no fear of the solemn words, " Judge not, that ye be not judged ? "

CHAPTER XXXII.

FLORA SEEKS FREEDOM.

ONE afternoon, Laura Stanley was at work in the gallery of the Academy of Design. She was engaged upon a study of the head of Clytie, which was the subject she had chosen for her competitive drawing, and which she was executing with great pains in the hope of winning the prize. In the long room there were several other pupils, all working like herself in silence; around them stood the pale forms of many statues. Here the graceful Apollo, immortal in his majestic beauty, there the horrible group of the Laocoon, forever writhing in deathless agony, beyond the exquisite beauty of the Venus of Milo, lovelier even in mutilation than the most elaborate efforts of modern sculpture.

The light came into the room through the high windows but dimly, for it was raining heavily outside, and the thick clouds of a long storm hung low. Once or twice, Laura glanced up a little anxiously; she was much interested in her work, and feared that the gathering gloom would force her to leave it.

The door leading into the gallery opened, and a gentleman came down the steps, the tap of his boot-heels on the bare floor striking out sharply in the silence. Laura never noticed his entrance, and was somewhat startled when he came close to her and called her by name. She turned quickly, and recognized Rudolph Ernstein, whom she had met at Mrs. D'Arcy's on New Year's day.

"Miss Stanley," he said; "excuse me for disturbing you; but I have a note for you from your friend Miss Livingston."

"From Flora!" exclaimed Laura, putting down her pencils quickly, and taking the little missive.

"Yes; I think it is somewhat important, as she gave it

to me this morning, and asked me to take it to you as soon as I could; that must be my apology for venturing here."

"You are quite right, and very kind," Laura said, briefly, and she opened the envelope, the young German looking at her with intense interest as she read the note, which ran as follows:

" DEAR LAURA,
"Meet me this evening in Madison square at half-past five. Don't fail me.
"Your wretched
" FLORA."
" *April* 12*th.*"

The writing was scrawled as if written in a desperate hurry, and there were two deep lines under the date. As Laura noticed this, she looked up at the young man with a questioning trouble in her eyes.

"April twelfth," she repeated; " why to-morrow will be her wedding-day ! "

"I suppose so," Ernstein answered, with a slow color rising in his face.

Laura regarded him keenly. "Do you know the contents of this note, Mr. Ernstein ? " she asked.

"No," he said. "But pray command me, if I can be of assistance in any way," very eagerly.

"Thank you," Laura said, a little coldly ; "I don't see how you can aid us ; but I am very much obliged to you for bringing the note," more kindly; "it is but just in time."

"Miss Flora said you must have it by five o'clock," he explained. "I went to your house with it, and they told me you were here. So I followed you as quickly as I could."

"That was very good of you, I'm sure." Then putting up her drawing materials rapidly, she added : " I must go at once, so I will beg you to excuse me. Good-evening."

Thus dismissed the young man had no choice but to go; he lingered a moment, but there was no encouragement in Laura's face, and he went slowly away.

The young lady put on her hat and long waterproof, and, taking her umbrella, went out into the storm. Her watch told her that it was twenty minutes past five, as she left the great white building and went down the street. She had but a short distance to go, and was presently in the Square.

The rain swept with a monotonous rush across the open space, flattening the fresh-springing grass, scourging the gray pavements, running off in streams on either side of the path. The trees, still leafless, dripped moisture from every swollen bud; the benches beside the way were deserted and forlorn-looking; only here and there a drenched woman or hurrying man passed rapidly across the walks.

It was an uncomfortable spot in which to wait, and as Laura had no especial point of rendezvous to which to turn, she could only stroll slowly about, peering at every passer-by.

The sun was just about setting, and low in the western horizon there was a lurid gleam; but the clouds were so heavy, and the rain fell in such blinding torrents, that it was difficult to see far through the dimness. Twice Laura had crossed the length of the Park, and was beginning to feel uncomfortably wet, when some one came hurrying towards her, down a cross-path. Even when she saw the slight figure, Laura was not certain it was her friend; she was like herself wrapped in a waterproof, and on her head was pinned a thick blue veil, so that it was only when her own name was pronounced with a sort of gasping cry, that she was sure that it was Flora Livingston.

"I hope I haven't kept you waiting long, Laura," she said, catching hold of her arm. "Come, let us hurry."

"Where?" demanded Laura, in amazement.

"To the depot; I can tell you all there."

Checking her curiosity, Laura hastened on, with Flora clinging to her arm, and saying nervously, now and then; "You don't see any one following, do you?"

It was but a few moments' walk to the big ugly brick

building, from which travellers then took their way over
the Harlem Railroad, and presently the two girls stood
dripping in the long bare room, supposed to be adapted to
the wants of "The Ladies," a hopelessly dreary apartment, with ragged oil-cloth on the floor, worn-out sofas
and chairs scattered about, stained walls and dirty windows, on which the rain was beating heavily. Some time
would elapse before the departure of the next train, and there
were no other occupants of the room, but a tired woman
caressing a baby, and a stout Irish girl asleep in a corner.

Laura and Flora seated themselves on one of the sofas,
their wet garments making a little lake of moisture about
them, and then Flora lifted her veil, showing a white and
frightened face.

"How cold it is!" she shivered. "Do you think any
one can see in here?" apprehensively.

"No, oh no, the windows are too high from the
ground."

"Change seats with me, so that no one can see me from
the door," Flora went on, and Laura complied with the
request.

"Now, dear, what does all this mean?" she asked.

"I am going to run away," said Flora, with a sudden
resolution in her lovely eyes; "and you are the only person
I could think of to help me."

"To run away!" repeated Laura, blankly.

"Yes, Laura, I can't marry Mr. Le Roy; I cannot do
it!" piteously. "I tried to avoid it at the first, as you
know, but they persuaded me into the engagement. Since
then, a hundred times I have thought I would break it off,
but I had not the courage; now, I am desperate!" she
went on, almost wildly, "I would rather do anything,
submit to anything, than be his wife!" with a shudder of
strong disgust.

"You are right," said Laura, eagerly; "it is a pity
that you put it off so long; but it is far better to escape now
than to wreck your happiness for life."

"Yes, it will be an escape," Flora repeated; "an escape like that from a dungeon; like that from death! Laura you don't know what I have suffered in these last three months; I have tried to like him, I have, honestly." The blue eyes looking out appealingly from under the damp hair that hung in disordered curls low on her forehead.

"I believe you have, dear."

"Yes, I have said to myself, he is handsome and distinguished and wealthy, and I shall be happy; but I knew in my heart all the time, that I should not be happy! If he had been kind to me, a little gentle, I think I could have gone on," plaintively; "but he is a born tyrant! I must submit to his wishes with unquestioning obedience. I must dress and act, as it suits him; I must endure his caresses as it pleases him to have me," with an indignant flush; "I should be a slave bound hand and foot, if I married him, and I cannot! I cannot!"

"No, darling, no," said Laura soothingly; "you shall not marry him if I can help you to prevent it; but tell me what you propose to do?"

"I hardly know," responded Flora; "except that I am going to take the next train out of town. I never made up my mind to run away until last night. He was alone with me all the evening; and—and—I felt that I could never go through another such interview. It degrades me even to think of it!" she exclaimed, hotly.

Laura patted her hand gently: "Well, dear, you need not now."

"No, I will forget it if I can," Flora said more calmly; "when I went to my room last night, I resolved to run away, and to get you to help me. How to send you a note I could not think. I dared not trust the mail, and I could not send one of the servants. I was in the hall this morning when Mr. Ernstein rang the bell. I saw who it was and thought I could confide in him; he looks very kind!" with a faint sigh. "He only asked for mamma. It seems he is going away and called to bid good-bye. He was shown into the drawing-room, I ran to the library and scrawled that note, then to the drawing-room before mamma was down. How startled he was when I came in! He said I looked like a ghost; and I suppose I did. When I gave him the note, he cried out in his eager foreign fashion, that he would deliver it for me if it cost him his life, and then he took both my hands so eagerly!" with a faint smile. "I had only just time to say all I wanted and bid him good-bye, when I heard the rustle of mamma's dress. You don't think any one could come here?" she broke off suddenly, catching Laura's hand as the door opened.

"No one for you, I should think, dear. There, you see it is only another passenger;" as a stout old lady waddled in, went to the register, from which no heat proceeded, and turned away with a look of disgust. "Try to be as quiet as you can," Laura urged, "and tell me what you intend to do, Flora, for I do not yet understand."

"I scarcely know myself," replied Flora; "I have left that partly to you. I found out there was a train north on this road at half-past six, and I thought perhaps I could go to some of your people. I must hide a little while, you know; and you can tell me somewhere to go, can't you?" with a look of anxious appeal.

Laura was fairly puzzled, and was silent a moment; but she was resolved not to add to Flora's troubles, and recovering her presence of mind, with a quick intuition, she rapidly arranged what seemed best to do under the circumstances. Even this brief delay troubled Flora, however she was watching her companion eagerly, and presently said, fretfully :

"Can't you help me, Laura? Oh dear! how cold and wet I am! If you can't do anything for me I will just go away and kill myself! I'd sooner a thousand times do that, than go home to be married!"

"My dear girl!" Laura remonstrated, gently; "don't be so impatient; remember you have taken me completely by surprise; but I think I can tell you what you had better do. You can't go to my house, it would not be pleasant for you; nor can I go there at present; but I have an uncle who lives near Dover Plains, and that you know is on this road. This uncle of mine is a kind man and will receive us gladly, no doubt. I say 'us,' for I shall go too."

"You, Laura!"

"Yes, dear, I could not let you go away alone through the storm to a strange place; and then, too, you know your flight must be well guarded, so that no ugly stories can attach to your name. If you go with me, you will be protected from anything of that sort."

"Oh, Laura! how good you are!" the blue eyes soft with grateful tears.

"You are glad to have me go, aren't you, poor dear?"

"Glad! oh yes, it will give me new life and courage! I have been so miserable! You think I am right to go, don't you?" anxiously.

"Yes, if this is the only way in which you can avoid a distasteful marriage, you are entirely right."

"It is the only way," said Flora; "I could never have had the courage to break off anything at home; but away, I can be firmer, especially if you are with me; you are so brave and strong." Then presently she said: "I had such a time getting away! I was so afraid some one would see me as I came down stairs; I crept out on tiptoe, and could only bring these few things with me in this little bag. In my hurry I forgot my overshoes, and my feet are very wet. I think that is what makes me so cold." And indeed her poor lips looked blue with the chill.

"My dear child! and there is no fire here! You are hungry too, perhaps; you have had no dinner, let me go and get you a cup of tea."

But Flora would not allow Laura to leave her. "No, no," she cried, "don't go away; besides, I could not swallow anything."

Laura tried to make the poor trembling creature some-what comfortable; but as the passengers began to come in rapidly, she grew constantly more nervous, till at last, Laura suggested that they should go outside and walk up and down. " I think it will really be better than sitting here," she said ; " and safer from observation."

Flora seized the idea, eagerly. Laura bought the tick-ets, and the two passed out of the room on to the platform beyond. Here they were under cover of a wide roof, but the water was sweeping in torrents into the enclosed court on which they looked. There were no cars yet on the nearest track, and those at a distance looked black and dismal, like miniature prison-houses. Two lanterns at either end of the long walk, sent out into the darkness a red ray which gleamed here and there on the round surface of the wet cobble-stones of the pavement, or shone along the iron rail. Above their heads there was the roar of the con-stantly-falling drops on the roof ; near them the rush of the wind as it swept across the city in gusts, driving the restless rain before it.

Up and down, up and down in the gloom, the two girls paced slowly. Flora seemed very tired, her feet moved but languidly, and she shivered almost constantly with the cold. Laura became so alarmed about her at last, that she would have had her go back into the passenger-room, which was at least warmer than outside, but Flora would not listen to this.

" No, no, " she cried ; " there are so many people in there that some one might easily come in that I know. Let us stay out here, I can walk a good while longer." Then in a moment : " Oh, if the cars would only come so that we could go away ! I should feel better, I know, if we were once off ! "

Laura tried to while away the weary moments by tell-ing her companion about the pleasant farm-house to which they were going ; but the poor thing's thoughts were constantly with the people she was leaving, and the trouble her flight would cause.

"Do you think it will be a pleasant day to-morrow, Laura?" she asked.

"I don't know, dear; very likely; there was a little light at sunset."

"What a rush there will be at the church if it is; and what will people say of me!"

"Don't think of that now, dear; see, they are bringing the cars down; I think we can get in presently."

As she spoke, four horses appeared through the darkness; their hoofs clattering and slipping on the drenched pavement; the bells on their collars jingling. The two girls paused to watch them. They saw them led across the yard into a sort of well of obscurity on the other side from which the faint glow of a lantern presently shone. There was a moment of silence, except for the noise of the storm, and then there was a quick tramping, as the horses pulled at the load; the rumble of wheels, and two cars were drawn slowly forward, showing long lines of lighted windows, which cast faint gleams across the blackness of the night.

"Now dear, I think we can go," Laura said, cheerfully.

"Yes, let us be quick! See, people are coming out!" Flora whispered, agitatedly.

They walked rapidly forward towards the end of the car nearest them. As Flora said, a good many people had come out on to the platform, and there was some confusion. She had pulled down her veil again, and Laura felt her trembling as she drew her forward; but escape was almost at hand.

The entrance was reached, Laura had raised her hand to the iron rail to help Flora; but just as the fugitive girl would have stepped up, a heavy grasp was laid on her shoulder. A cry of utter anguish rang from her lips, for there beside her in the gloom, stood Mr. Le Roy!

His face was unusually pale, and there was an angry light in his eyes that made them shine like polished steel.

"Flora," he said in a low, stern voice; "come with me!"

Laura kept tight hold of the hand that was clutching hers convulsively now. "Miss Livingston is going with me," she declared, firmly.

"I beg your pardon, Miss!" Mr. Le Roy said, haughtily; "I allow no one to interfere here. Flora, I have a carriage waiting on Madison avenue. Come!"

They could not see the poor girl's face for the thick veil that shrouded it; but they could hear that she was moaning piteously. Mr. Le Roy had passed his arm around her waist, though Laura still kept hold of her hand; she felt it shiver a moment longer in her grasp; then the hold relaxed and she saw that the slender figure was drooping and would have fallen but for its support.

"She has fainted," Mr. Le Roy said, calmly; "stand back, Miss; I can take care of her."

With a motion that in any one but so elegant a gentleman would have been called rude, he pushed Laura aside and bore the fainting captive away.

Laura followed at a little distance, heart-sick with indignant scorn. But Mr. Le Roy had taken his measures well; two men were waiting his orders at the Madison avenue entrance, and with their aid, he lifted his helpless burden into the carriage, which was presently driven away and vanished in the darkness, followed by the rush of the dreary rain, and the cry of the wild night wind.

11

CHAPTER XXXIII.

A FASHIONABLE WEDDING.

THE next morning dawned bright and beautiful; the very perfection of an early Spring day. The heavens were of that exquisite blue that seems fairly to sparkle with light, and only here and there floated lazily a graceful white cloud. The city streets, washed by the storm, were fresh and clean; the grass in the squares waved green; the lilacs and willows hung out thin delicate leaves, and the hyacinths and tulips flamed their gay blossoms in the sunshine.

Two o'clock was the hour appointed for Flora Livingston's wedding, and Trinity chapel, where the ceremony was to take place, had put on a gala appearance. All around the chancel there was a wreath of flowers; the altar was dressed with the choicest exotics; half-way up the broad aisle, two young gentlemen with bridal favors in their button-holes, held a white satin ribbon, allowing no one to pass this airy barrier, unless entitled to the privilege by cards of invitation. Owing to this precaution there were still some empty pews reserved for the bridal-party; but the rest of the building was thronged with a fashionable crowd. Outside, a carpet was spread for dainty feet to tread on, and on either hand a stout policeman kept back from too close encroachment the throng of nursery-maids, small boys and gaping idlers, who had collected to see the bride go in.

Laura Stanley was in the church, seated near the front on the side-aisle, watching with breathless interest for the entrance of those whom she could regard only as captor and captive. The Bradfords were there among the invited guests; Mrs. Bradford, as pleasant-looking an old lady as one would wish to see, in her rich purple silk and black-lace

hat; Bessie, a sweet little creature in white muslin, and Mr.
Bradford and Guy in the regulation-dress of the gentleman
of the period.

When he had first caught sight of Laura's earnest face,
Guy had changed color perceptibly, and now was studying
her with wistful eager eyes; while she, in her absorbed
watch wholly unconscious of the scrutiny, never once
glanced towards him. Mrs. De Lancy Winthrop was there
among the particular friends, brilliant in an imported costume of cameo shades, and in the absence of her last victim,
prosecuting a vigorous whispered flirtation with a dark-
haired stylish-looking young man, Mrs. Courteny's eldest
son.

. The moments passed slowly on; the organist played
one selection after another, the gay crowd whispered and
laughed, but the bride did not come. After two—now
people are consulting their watches all over the church;
the organist begins another opera, always so arranged that
he can leave off at any moment, and play the more appropriate tune. A quarter-past two—the organist begins to
look impatient; he has another wedding to play for at
three. The stout sexton walks about impatiently; the
ushers go a little way down the aisle, and young men on
the steps take an observation up and down the street.
Half-past two—people are growing anxious; mammas
shake their heads; some one, no one can say who, says
Miss Livingston was ill last night, and this rumor flies, one
knows not how, over the church. Laura has grown very
pale; Guy, who is watching her, notices this, and wonders
the cause. The hands on the watches point past the half
hour, and are turning towards three—suddenly there is a
bustle outside; the sexton hurries to the door; the ushers
take their places; the organist begins to play a wedding-
march; every one looks towards the entrance; the bride is
coming!

First up the aisle there swept slowly some of the nearest relatives· Mr. and Mrs. Courteny, Miss Murray, and

certain other aunts with their families. Then appeared Mr. Le Roy's tall figure and calm resolute face, advancing slowly with Mrs. Livingston on his arm. Mrs. Livingston in heavy gray silk and Brussels-lace shawl, her anxious face more troubled and worried than usual.

Immediately following came the bridesmaids and groomsmen, six of each; so that for awhile, the aisle seemed full of floating tulle and pink roses, the men appearing as mere insignificant appendages, only tolerated as a means of showing off the beauty they accompanied. Maud had the place of honor as first bridesmaid, and there was a smile on her haughty lips as if she rejoiced that at last she had come into her kingdom.

These all passed on and took their places at the chancel-rail, and then slowly, slowly, there came up the way through the staring crowd, the central figure of this pageant, the bride. Leaning on her father's arm; clinging to it as if, as it seemed to Laura, without that support she would have fallen, Flora walked forward with the faltering step of one condemned and led out to doom. Her dress was of white silk covered with point-lace, the costly gift of the bridegroom's sister; far over the crimson carpet the elegant draperies trailed behind her; and as she passed on, one could catch the gleam of the diamonds that hung in her ears and around her throat. The veil fell over her face, and only a shadowy outline of fair hair and drooping head, could be distinguished under its heavy folds.

As she reached the steps of the altar she paused for a moment, and gave one sudden look backwards, but in an instant Mr. Le Roy, who stood awaiting her, put out his hand and took hers, as if to help her up, never after that relaxing his hold.

The service began; three white-robed priests being in attendance to give *éclât* to the ceremony. The words fell steadily on the now quiet air:

"If any man can show just cause why they may not lawfully be joined together, let him now speak—"

A pause; the bride shook with a sudden convulsive struggle, like one trying to draw away ; but the iron clasp held her fast, and the clergyman's voice rose again.

"I know a just cause," Laura thought, desperately; but she realized full well that it was of no use to protest, and in her sorrow and regret she turned away from a sight that only pained her.

At that moment, for the first time her glance met Guy Bradford's; he was not far from her, and he was watching her with those faithful eyes, so full of the unspoken sympathy of pent-up passion, that, spite of all the troubled thought that had just now oppressed her, Laura's heart gave a sudden great bound of happiness, and the color came flashing back to her cheeks.

The service proceeded ; the solemn vows were repeated; Mr. Le Roy's voice could be heard distinctly pronouncing the words that bind a man with so much tenderness, " to love and to cherish." Flora's response was wholly inaudible. Had she sworn "to love, honor and obey" this man ? Then came the last awful declaration :

" Those whom God hath joined together, let no man put asunder."

Laura's eyes as if spell-bound by an attraction beyond her own volition, turned again to Guy Bradford. Still that same devouring regard. A sort of audacity in it now, as one who would ask a question. Laura's cheeks were burning with a bright carnation, and her gray eyes were so eloquent of a response, that she turned them quickly away, lest too much of her heart should be revealed.

Presently the ceremony was complete, and the bridegroom, with masterful hand, raised the veil that covered the brow of the bride. Then she turned so that the crowd could see her as she came slowly down the aisle, leaning on the arm of the man who was now her husband.

Her fair face was blanched to a shade of blueness around the mouth, her lips were parted as if in some mute entreaty, her eyes were full of a sort of timid horror; but on either cheek there was a bright scarlet spot, and curious people staring at her, declared that she looked uncommonly well ; young Courtenay, who considered himself a judge of female loveliness, stating authoritatively, that she was "out and away the handsomest bride of the season."

CHAPTER XXXIV.

LAURA HEADS A DEPUTATION.

THE week after the wedding passed to Laura very much like the weeks that had preceded it. She hoped for several days that she might have a visit from Guy Bradford, but he never came, and the time passed on in the steady routine of teaching and study. One morning she went as usual to her duties at the school, where for two hours every day she was busy in correcting crooked lines, pointing out defective spaces, and all the drudgery of watching over girls, who were as yet not beyond outline-drawing of the simplest sort. As one set of scholars went, and another came during the time, there was little to vary the monotony of the occupation, and the young teacher always welcomed the sound of the twelve o'clock bell which released her.

To her surprise on this day, after the tinkle had died away, her pupils instead of making a stampede for the door as they generally did, lingered in the room, falling into groups, all evidently excited over some topic. As the minutes went on, the crowd instead of diminishing, increased, older girls from other classes coming in, until it was evident that the room had been made a rendezvous for some consultation.

Laura, who was delayed a moment while finding her hat and sacque, presently became the centre of a group of young ladies.

"Let's ask Miss Stanley; she's one of the teachers,"

said a bright-looking dark-haired girl, whom Laura knew
as Elvira Leighton, one of the leaders of the school.

"Well, what is it?" asked Laura, pleasantly.

"You are a graduate of Essex, are you not?" demanded Eloise Dickinson, a pretty blonde, pressing forward eagerly.

"Yes."

"The girls all speak pieces there at Commencement,
don't they?" inquired several voices.

"Certainly."

"Then I don't see why we can't!"

"Nor I, nor I!" exclaimed a dozen scholars.

"Do keep still, girls," cried Elvira, imperatively;
"how can Miss Stanley understand anything, if we all talk
at once?"

"You tell her about it, then," suggested Eloise.

"I will if you'll be a little quiet," said the young lady,
looking about at her flock of followers, and for a moment
awing them into silence. "You see, Miss Stanley, Maria
Mordaunt has written a valedictory address, and we want
to get leave to have her read it the last day."

"Miss Thornton, the composition-teacher, asked her to
write it," put in Eloise.

"Yes, and she says it's beautiful; now don't you think
it would be nice for her to read it to us?"

"Of course," said Laura, who had thus far not been
able to put in a word. "Don't you have addresses from
some of the graduating girls?"

"No indeed, we don't!" exclaimed Elvira, scornfully.
"We have some stupid old professor from the college, or
some high and mighty horrid old honorable, to give us the
prizes, and we must all sit meekly in rows, while he talks
and Mr. Glitter talks, and then after that we have a dance;
that's all the exercises we ever have!"

"I'm sure," chimed in Eloise, "I don't see why we
can't have a Commencement like Essex. I know some of

us could make as good speeches as the Columbia students
do."

There was a murmur of assent to this, and then several
voices cried, "Go on! Go on!" and Eloise returned to
the point by saying:

"Now, Miss Stanley, we want you to help us to get
Mr. Glitter to let Maria read the valedictory."

"I! how can I help you?" asked Laura, in surprise.

"Well, we would like to have you go with us when we
ask his permission," explained Eloise. "We think you
would know what to say."

"Then you haven't tried yet?" inquired Laura.

"No—that is—we all got around Mrs. Glitter the other
day in the school-room, and asked her. She told us she
had nothing to say about it; Mr. Glitter must decide."

"Oh, she's so good!" Elvira said, contemptuously;
"she is as meek as Moses, with that conceited little man."

"Young ladies!" Laura said, reprovingly, though there
was a smile twitching at the corners of her mouth; "You
must be a little careful how you speak of your teacher."

"Oh well, you know, Miss Stanley, he is a stuck-up
thing," Elvira declared; "but then, of course we've got
to be very polite to him."

"Certainly;" several girls admitted, solemnly.

"And when do you propose to send your deputation to
wait on him?" asked Laura.

"I suppose we shall have to put it off till to-morrow,
it's so late now," Eloise said, consulting a tiny watch.

"I should think it would be best, and send up to let
him know beforehand," Elvira suggested.

"And you'll go with us, Miss Stanley?" asked several.

"Yes, I will go with you."

"All right, it shall be to-morrow then."

"That's settled, now let's go," said Elvira; "we shall
be late to luncheon, as it is. Thank you, Miss Stanley,"
with a backward glance at the young teacher as the whole
gay crowd hurried away.

Laura followed at a little distance, and as she went down stairs, caught such expressions as, "Won't it be jolly?" "Isn't she lovely?" and other phrases indicating that her promised assistance was regarded, as of great value.

The following morning, when she again met her class, Laura detected, at once, without any previous knowledge, that something unusual was astir. One of the oldest of her scholars approached her with an air of responsibility and said, "Miss Elvira Leighton asked me to tell you that Mr. Glitter sent word that he will meet you in the reception-room, in the recreation hour."

A dozen other girls were listening to the message, and Laura's reply: "Very well, now we will begin our lesson," only sent them off reluctantly to their places.

It was more than usually difficult for the teacher to keep the attention of her classes during the next two hours. The girls were whispering and writing messages to each other constantly, and, sensitive as a field of flowers to the touch of the summer breeze, were all shivering and swaying with the unusual excitement.

Never was the note of the twelve o'clock bell more welcome, and as it sounded, the scholars started from their places, sending pencils and india-rubbers rolling on the floor in their eagerness, while Eloise Dickinson and Elvira Leighton were in the room almost in a moment. As if to do a little special honor to the occasion, they were both dressed with unusual care, and there was a flush on their bright young faces that betrayed the nervous flutter of their hearts.

Laura led the way down stairs, followed closely by the young ladies, and at a short distance, by a picket of little girls, who were flung out as skirmishers, in advance of the main body of the school, deployed in the upper entry to await the commencement of hostilities.

When the three reached the reception-room, there was no one there, and they were kept waiting some minutes

11*

before the majestic tread of the small man was heard approaching.

"You tell him, Miss Stanley," Elvira whispered, nervously.

"Yes, and we will help," said Eloise, encouragingly.

Mr. Glitter came in with an important air, and saluted the three condescendingly. "You asked for a conference with me, young ladies," he said; "I can spare a few moments."

"We came to speak with you, in regard to the closing exercises of the school," Laura replied, stepping forward. "Some of the pupils have requested me to ask your permission to allow Miss Mordaunt, the valedictorian of her class, to read an address on the last day."

"To read it herself?" demanded Mr. Glitter, sternly.

"Yes; it seems she has already written it, and it meets with the approbation of the composition-teacher."

"I have heard something of this," said Mr. Glitter; "and I think it exceedingly strange, that Miss Mordaunt should even have written it without asking me."

"Miss Thornton said she might," put in Elvira.

"Miss Thornton had no right to allow it, without my permission," Mr. Glitter declared, peremptorily.

"But since she has written it, and it is of a character to do credit to the school, you will allow her to read it to her young friends on the last day, will you not?" Laura asked.

Mr. Glitter slowly turned his light eyes towards her: "No, Miss Stanley, certainly not. And I must add, that I am exceedingly surprised, and I may say displeased," very severely, "that you have made so strange a request."

Laura flushed wrathfully; the two girls reflecting the glow in their faces, and Elvira said: "All the girls want to hear it."

"Yes indeed," echoed Eloise.

"Then I am sorry that the young ladies of my school, have so unwomanly, so improper a wish."

"Will you be kind enough," asked Laura, speaking slowly, in her effort at self-command ; "to explain to us, why it is unwomanly, and improper to wish to hear this composition read ? "

Mr. Glitter cleared his voice with a dignified ahem! "Because it is putting forward a young lady, in a way of which I cannot approve. Women should be shrinking and modest, avoiding the public gaze."

"Will you tell me who has laid down this rule for women's conduct ; women themselves, or men ? "

For some time past there had been an indistinct murmur outside the door, as if an excited crowd was with difficulty holding itself back, and now the murmur swelled to an actual muffled whisper. Mr. Glitter glared at Laura for a moment, as if in speechless amazement at the audacity of the question, then he said:

"A lady of proper instincts never wishes to appear in public."

"You can scarcely blame us for not being aware of this, till you graciously condescend to tell us," Laura replied, her eyes flashing, her quick temper hurrying her, as so often before into imprudent speech ; "when from the wife of our President, to the mothers of these very young ladies, women are accustomed to appearing in public at balls and entertainments, apparently quite unconscious that they are doing anything wrong."

At this, a faint titter became distinctly audible outside the door, and Mr. Glitter's insignificant countenance grew quite purple with anger. He stood before these three women, shorter by several inches than either one, and did his best to annihilate them and their upstart pretensions.

"That is very different," he said, arbitrarily ; "but I wholly decline to discuss this question. It has been my aim to instil into the young ladies under my care, modest views of their position and duties in life. I now hear with the strongest condemnation, theories advanced which I consider of a dangerous, I may even say of an alarming tendency; and I beg that this subject may never again be thrust on my attention;" waving his hand authoritatively. "For the approaching closing exercises of the school, I have secured the services of the Honorable Slowboy Dawdledums, who will deliver an address, and I wish him to see only such modest demeanor among the young ladies as befits the True Woman."

With these crushing sentences Mr. Glitter stalked from the room, the dignity of his exit being, however, seriously impaired by the fact, that his appearance caused the flight of a flock of little girls, who sped in various directions, with sounds of suppressed laughter.

"It's an outrageous shame!" Elvira exclaimed, hotly, as the little man disappeared.

"I think he's real mean!" cried Eloise, with her eyes full of tears.

"The idea of *his* undertaking to tell *us* what is womanly," said Elvira, with superb scorn.

"I remember old Dawdledums," Eloise added presently. "He made the address three years ago; he's as stupid as an owl, and preached to us an hour about woman's inferiority, and humble duties."

"It would certainly seem more suitable to have one of your own number make an address, than any man who knows nothing of your thoughts and feelings," said Laura. "However, Mr. Glitter is autocrat here, and has a right to arrange his school to suit himself."

"I suppose so," admitted Eloise; "all the same, I think it's real mean!" finding refuge once more in the school-girls' favorite formula to express indignation.

CHAPTER XXXV.

MRS. D'ARCY'S VIEWS.

As Laura walked away from the school and down the pleasant streets, gay with a throng of well-dressed people all abroad to enjoy the spring sunshine, she had an uncomfortable feeling that she had been very imprudent, and anticipated that some annoyance would result from her action that morning. Dissatisfied with herself, blaming herself, and feeling a longing for some confidence and sympathy, she resolved to go to Mrs. D'Arcy, whom she had not seen for some time, but who, she had heard, was now alone. She turned her steps towards the doctor's house, and was walking down Fifth-avenue, when among a crowd of young people she saw Guy Bradford. He had a very pretty and youthful lady beside him, and Laura's heart contracted with a spasm of agony that was a new revelation to her.

As Guy caught sight of her, he changed color, and half started from his companion as if he would speak with Laura; but she acknowledged his salutation with a bow so frigid as to be a perfect check to any such intention. She did not see the look of pain on his face, she only knew that she was more miserable than she had ever been in her life before, and hurried away at a pace that was most unconventionally rapid. She was angry and vexed with herself. Was she to allow any man to make her wretched? She declared again and again that she would not, and yet, all the time, the thought of the estrangement between herself and Bradford, the thought of his new-found friend, was an agony to her, worse than she had thought she could endure.

Laura reached Mrs. D'Arcy's at an opportune moment; the doctor was at home, and just going to luncheon. She

welcomed her young friend with her usual heartiness, and
brought her into the dining-room with her. As Laura took
off her hat, and the first flush of the exercise she had been
taking died from her face, the doctor, who was looking
at her earnestly, noticed that something was amiss.

"You look pale and troubled, my dear," she said;
"what is it? Come here, and let me feel of your hand. Ah,
hot, as I feared!" She went on, "feverish, something has
worried you; take a cup of tea, and tell me all about it."

Laura and the doctor sat down together at a table
spread with a substantial luncheon, and although Laura
could not eat much, it was pleasant to find herself once
more with her kind friend, and she opened her heart to her
on the subject of the morning's adventure.

"I was dreadfully imprudent," she wound up, ruefully;
"I got provoked at the insolence of that little man; but
of course I ought not to have spoken as I did."

"It was no more than he deserved," answered Mrs.
D'Arcy; "nor half what you might have said; however,
perhaps it was more than it was wise to say."

"Yes," said Laura; "I'm afraid my rashness this morning will cost me my situation."

"Not this term, I fancy, the year is so nearly out, and
next winter you must have a better place. I don't wonder
that you were provoked, it is amusing, and yet annoying, to
see how utterly competent some of these small men feel
themselves to mark out the limits of endeavor for women
who are their superiors in every way!"

"How long do you suppose we shall have to endure this
sort of thing?"

"We shall be called upon to exercise our patience for
some time longer, I fear. Just so long as all our literature
is pervaded with the thought that women are inferior, so
long will our sex be held in a low estimate. It is curious,"
the doctor went on, falling into one of those veins of
thought which Laura always liked to hear her pursue; "it
is curious to observe what a singularly contradictory idea

one would think men held of us from their writings. Indeed, a stranger to this planet would suppose from the way in which women are mentioned, that instead of forming one half of the human race, they were some especial class of beings who only occasionally came under the notice of the majority of the community.

"On the one hand we are spoken of as 'angels;' acknowledged as the embodiment of the refining influences of the world; toasted after dinner as 'lovely woman;' mentioned approvingly as 'the women, God bless 'em,' and flattered with choice nonsense. On the other hand, no phrases are hard enough with which to characterize the faults and follies of the sex. 'With the inconsistency of a woman,' writes one man, forgetting that Francis I. and Charles I. and a host of other men have come down to us through history as by-words of inconsistency; 'with womanly curiosity,' scribbles another; never remembering that the gaping loungers of the village-store, athirst for news are men, not women. 'With the cupidity of a true woman,' sneers another; blind to the fact that the Shylocks of the world are men! The amount of such trash that one finds is really aggravating!" the doctor wound up, her dark eyes glowing with unwonted fire.

Laura, who was ever responsive to a touch like this, quite forgot her own troubles, as she replied with animation, "Yes, I have noticed often this sort of fling. I was reading only the other day, a novel by a popular English writer, in which the story is written as if told by a woman, and she is made to slur her own sex perpetually. I recollect one phrase which ran somewhat thus: 'Does a woman ever know why she does anything? Did Eve know why she ate the apple? Not she!'"

"Had the man who penned that, no knowledge of history?" cried Mrs. D'Arcy. "Had he forgotten, or did he never hear of the calm reasoning of Hypatia; the astute policy of Elizabeth of England; the iron firmness of Catherine of Russia? If some of these scribblers could be put once more under their mother's tutelage, and smartly rapped for any fault or inaccuracy in their writings, it might teach them that women know what they are doing, and have good reasons for their actions."

Laura laughed quite merrily. "That book was full of insinuations of this kind," she said; "and the poor author would be quite belabored if he should have a knock for every false charge, and mischievous insinuation."

"Oh, I dare say," replied the doctor; "if you will come to my study, I will show you a quantity of slips which I have collected, and from which any stranger to our world would certainly form a most curious idea in regard to those 'weak,' 'strong,' 'kind,' 'cruel,' 'angelic,' 'wicked,' 'silly,' 'shrewd,' 'generous,' and 'mean' creatures; for all these phrases are applied to women by the flippant men-writers of the day."

The two ladies went up presently to the pleasant office, and the doctor opened her desk and took out her book of extracts. "Now here," she said, "are two expressions, in one of the most carefully-written journals of the city, which have especially annoyed me. In an article on a certain class of our sex whose existence must always be a sorrow and a shame to us, occurs this expression: 'It is an understood thing, that for a certain sort of dirty job you must get a woman. Every man knows that the only animal that will strike an enemy when it is down is a woman!' When I read that, my blood boiled with indignation. This was penned by one of that sex whose members kill their wives and destroy young girls, and I thought of the men who had struck helpless women unable to rise; of the husbands who have kicked their wives to death when they were in a situation that made them peculiarly powerless, and especially liable to injury; of murdered girls whom fiends in the form of men have rendered senseless by brutal violence and then deliberately killed, that they might not witness against them. Oh, my dear, the record of what our sex has suffered from the other is a long and bitter history, a history that centuries of freedom and happiness can never make us forget ! "

There was a moment of silence. " It is a cruel thing to remember," Laura said, softly.

" It is not well to think upon it," rejoined the doctor; " lest it make us unjust in our turn. We must remember that there are many good and kind men in the world, and that it is only the weak of their sex, that indulge in these foolish flings."

" Oh, I know that very well," admitted Laura ; " some of the bravest and strongest writers in defence of the equality of the sexes, are true-hearted, noble men."

" Yes, and in blaming their sex for whatever of injustice they have been guilty of, we must remember that from their superior strength, men have made the laws, written and unwritten, of the world, and these laws have been honored for so many centuries, that it is difficult now to understand how very cruel they are."

" You touched just now on one of the vital aspects of the question of woman's enfranchisement," said Laura. " Do you think that the unfortunate of our sex will be helped by the ballot ? "

" Unquestionably," replied Mrs. D'Arcy, earnestly ; " I consider that this is one of the most important arguments in favor of giving it to all. It is admitted that the worst feature in the position of so-called ' fallen women ' is, that in consequence of their fall, they lose all self-respect and all hope of reclamation. Now if these poor things had the ballot, they would have an individual power, which would in itself give them a certain sense of independence. Look, for instance, at poor Rhoda ; if she were a voter, with influence over voters, she would be treated very differently by men. She would feel that she had personal power and commanded respect, and the possession of this power would help her, as it has helped many a man, to earn money, and to a position of respectability."

" When I speak on this subject of giving suffrage to

women," said Laura ; " I very rarely hear any arguments
of value brought against giving us equality, but am met
constantly by the vaguely horrible statement that the ballot will unsex us ! "

" It makes one fairly out of patience to hear that absurd phrase," rejoined the doctor. "Does any one know
what it means ? Of course nobody supposes that women
will literally become men ; but really sensible people do
seem to think that if we can vote, we shall all grow loud-
voiced, hard-featured, coarse and masculine. Men are not
willing to admit that they are injured by the ballot, though
it is sure to demoralize us; nor will any man allow that his
own wife, mother, or sister, will be thus transformed ; but
imagines that in some mysterious way all other women will
be turned into atrocities, and this in the face of the fact that
women have voted in Wyoming for three years without
loss of their best qualities. One would think to hear this
talk, that women are gentler, purer and more religious
than men, simply because they cannot vote ! "

" You believe that the difference of character between
the sexes is a radical one, do you not ? "

" Certainly, radical and God-ordained. Man represents in the world, the element of strength and force ;
woman that of love and spirituality; the coöperation of
both is needed to form a perfect society or government.
But of all the foolish ideas advanced against giving us our
freedom, I think the fallacy that we shall destroy marriage is at once the weakest and the most insulting. To
hear this, one would suppose that it was man who most
sacredly kept his wedding-vows, most dearly loved his
home, most faithfully worshipped his God ; when the
exact reverse of this is true ! To our sex, marriage in its
highest sense, is a union for time and for eternity, is the
prize of life, and if we have increased power placed in our
hands, we shall assuredly strengthen, instead of weaken
the sacredness of this divine institution."

"How grandly you can put these thoughts into words,"

said Laura; "I am so apt, in arguments on these points, to lose my temper, and say sharp things, instead of really answering objections."

"Oh, well, my dear, when you have as many years over your head as I have, you will grow calmer; your impetuosity is only a fault of your youth. But come, you have not half told me all I want to know about your own life. Now that Frank is away, do you hear from him often?"

"About once a week," replied Laura. "You know he won't be home until the last of May; he has been gone much longer than he at first intended."

"Indeed! He has written to me only twice, so that I do not understand why his trip is to be prolonged."

"It seems the Trumpeter people want him to extend his journey further south; they are very much pleased with his letters to the paper."

"They are excellent; so spicy, and yet so well written. I see that they meet with the highest praise from all quarters, and are copied all over the country."

"I am so glad!" exclaimed Laura, heartily. "He is such a noble fellow, he deserves to succeed."

"He does, indeed. But now that he is away, do you see much of Guy Bradford?" with a look, which she endeavored to make indifferent.

Laura could not repress a vivid blush. "No," she said, "he has not called on me for a long while."

"Hasn't he? why not?" then sharply: "You have not refused him, have you, Laura?"

"Oh, no, indeed!"

"What is it then? Don't mind telling an old lady like me, my dear; what is the trouble between you?"

"There is nothing to tell," replied Laura; "he has not been to see me, that is all."

At this moment the doctor's tidy maid appeared at the door, to say that the carriage was ready.

"Then I must go," said Mrs. D'Arcy; "as I have a good deal to do this afternoon. Shall I drive you home, Laura?"

"No, I am going to the Academy," replied Laura; " and as that is so near, I will walk over."

"Very well, dear ; and, Laura, keep up your heart; I have a presentiment that all your troubles with Guy will come to an end some day ; " and with these mysterious words the doctor bade Laura good-bye.

CHAPTER XXXVI.

THE BRIDE'S RETURN.

At the end of three weeks from their marriage-day, Mr. and Mrs. Ferdinand Le Roy returned to New York. For their wedding tour they had gone to Washington, and made a short journey in Virginia ; but the season was yet early; there was no one at any of the summer resorts which they visited; there were many rainy days, and it was a relief to Flora when Mr. Le Roy proposed that they should go back to the city. It had been suggested when these two were first engaged, that they should make a bridal trip to Europe, and Mrs. Livingston hinted broadly to her proposed son-in-law that this was the correct thing to do ; but Mr. Le Roy had made several voyages across the ocean, had indeed spent the last summer on the continent, and declared he was tired of Europe, and should prefer going to housekeeping at once, and later, visiting the watering-places. Flora would have liked better the trip on the water, but, of course, her wishes were quite secondary, and, indeed, of no sort of consequence, in comparison with Mr. Le Roy's preference.

So one dull afternoon, when a heavy rain was beating the blossoms of the lilacs to pieces, and strewing the streets with the flowers of the alianthus trees, a carriage brought the newly-wedded pair to their home.

It was a stately house, standing on the corner of Fifth-avenue and one of the Fortieth-streets. A double four-story, mansard-roofed, brown-stone mansion, with drawing-rooms and library, reception-room, dining-room and many bed-chambers. Spacious, sumptuously furnished; but seeming to Flora on a drearily large scale for two people.

Mr. and Mrs. Le Roy were not expected back so soon, and as they passed into the wide hall which was cold as with the chill of a cellar, and so into the parlor, grand, gloomy and dark, a shiver passed over Flora and it seemed to her like entering a tomb; the sound of the great door shutting with a heavy clang adding strength to the fancy.

In one respect, however, the young bride was sure that she would be better off here, than she had been during her miserable wedding-tour. Here, she would certainly not always be under the cold eyes and critical observation of her husband; here she would at least have a little more liberty. And, in truth, on the following morning Mr. Le Roy went down town soon after breakfast, and Flora had a few hours of freedom. The first use that she made of it, was to send a note to Laura Stanley, asking her to come and see her in the morning, the time especially fixed, as that during which she would be most secure from interruption. This dispatched without her husband's permission, she was at leisure to order her carriage and go to see her, mother with his permission, graciously accorded that morning at breakfast.

It was Saturday, before Laura was able to answer her friend's summons, at the time of the day mentioned. But on that morning, which was warm and delightful with the freshness of May, the young teacher rang the bell of the palace in which Flora had the privilege of residence, in exchange for the gift of her youth, her beauty, and her freedom.

The visitor was shown into the reception-room by a most imposing and dignified man-servant; a sort of second or cheaper edition of Mr. Le Roy—Mr. Le Roy bound in calf, as it were—but was not left long in this lower resting-

place, being presently translated by the same flunkey to
an upper story and to Flora's own boudoir.

This room, like every other in the house, was large, too
large to be cosey; the furniture was too ponderous for perfect taste; but Flora had some of her own pictures and
ornaments in it, and in the grate there burned a bright
fire. The young mistress of the elegant establishment
rose from a low couch to meet her friend, and the two
were face to face, for the first time since that stormy night
at the railroad-station.

A strange subtle change, hard to define, but very evident, had passed over Flora; she looked not three weeks,
but three years older than before her marriage. Her face
was thinner than Laura had ever seen it; her cheeks
glowed with a scarlet spot that was not the hue of health;
and around her mouth there lurked a shade of disgust.
But in her eyes there was the most striking transformation;
their limpid loveliness was gone, and they had in their
blue depths an expression as if some haunting horror
lurked beneath them. So one may see a pure and placid
spring, which reflects on its calm waters the azure of the
heavens, changed by the presence of some slimy reptile
that crawls and riots in its beauty; the light and the color
are still there, but in place of a fair mirror there is a
turbulent pool.

Laura looked at her friend, earnestly a moment, holding her hand, and noting that it felt thin and feverish in
her grasp.

"My dear girl, why do you have a fire on this lovely
day?" she asked. "Your hand is hot now, and it is very
warm outside."

"Is it?" said Flora; "it seemed to me cold this morning. This house is so big and dreary, that I think it must
be always damp. But as you say it is warm, I will open a
window."

She walked hastily across the room, and pushed up
the heavy sash, which, perfectly adjusted, rose obedient to

her light touch. "Yes," she added; "it is very pleasant outside."

"Do you go out much?" Laura asked next; feeling that for the moment, commonplaces were the only phrases that could be ventured on with safety.

"Every day in a carriage. I don't know that I shall ever be allowed to walk again. Mr. Le Roy does not think it dignified for his wife to walk," with a little bitter laugh; "except perhaps to church on Sunday; I believe he thinks it proper to walk there."

"You have a magnificent house," Laura observed.

"Yes, I suppose so, but it's too big. I hate such large rooms; now look at this, one of the smallest in the house, as huge as a barn! I wish I could have a dear little den, like mine at home."

"Had you a pleasant journey?" Laura hazarded next.

"A pleasant journey!" repeated Flora, with an accent of intense irony. "Oh Laura, what is the use of our pretending that everything is all right in my life when we both know so well that it is all wrong? A pleasant journey! it was as pleasant as the journey of Francesca di Rimini in the Infernal Regions! No, not so pleasant," she added, hurriedly; "for she was at least with the man she loved."

"Flora, my poor, dear girl," said Laura; "can you find no comfort in your fate, now that it is decided?"

"Comfort? no, none! how can there be any hope in such a life as mine? I am bound to a man who —— well, he is my husband," she broke off abruptly; "that makes him sacred, I suppose?"

"It is perhaps better not to speak hardly of him," Laura said, quietly.

"I will try not, then; but it will only be guarding the secrets of the prison-house." She left her seat and walked up and down the room restlessly. Laura watched her face a moment in silence, then she said:

"Do you mind telling me, dear, what happened after we last parted?"

Flora started and came back to her place. "He took me home," she said; "I never recovered consciousness till I was in my own bed. There were people invited that night; the bridesmaids and groomsmen for a rehearsal of the ceremony; but I was too ill to go down stairs. They had the rehearsal though, with Maud in my place. I only wish she had been in my place on the next day!" with sudden vehemence; "I was very ill all night and the next morning I begged and implored them to put off the wedding. I think they were troubled; I saw tears in my mother's eyes when I appealed to her to save me; but they said matters had gone too far, I was only nervous, and would feel better when it was over. I was so weak, though, they thought they would never be able to dress me, and at the last they gave me a glass of strong spiced wine, or I could not have gone through the ceremony. As it was, I fainted during the reception afterwards, before it was half over, and when I left the house with Mr. Le Roy it was not to go to Philadelphia, as every one supposed, but only to a hotel in town. It was two days before I was able to leave the city."

"My poor, poor child!" Laura could only say this, very compassionately; what consolation or sympathy was possible!

"Poor indeed!" replied Flora, darkly; "lost to happiness, ruined in self-respect, bankrupt in hope;" and she rose again and resumed her aimless walk.

"No," said Laura; "there is no reason why you should take such an utterly gloomy view of your future life. You are young, Flora, and all is not lost, even if you have met with the terrible misfortune of an uncongenial marriage. You must rouse yourself to find new interests and objects of endeavor."

"How can I find them?" demanded Flora; "I have literally nothing on earth to do. Mr. Le Roy does not wish to have me sew; does not care to have me draw. I have no way of filling up the endless hours of the weary day, but lying here and eating my heart out in useless regrets."

"But, Flora, you ought not to yield to an unreasonable request from your husband; he has no right to dwarf your mind and mar your happiness. You can still mark out for yourself a line of study, or of labor, and he cannot justly interfere with it."

"I don't know," answered Flora; "he thinks he has a right to dictate all my actions. Oh, I see you look as if you thought I ought not to give up. I know I ought not to sometimes, and I don't always, I can tell you. We have had some bitter scenes already," her cheeks flushing deeper at the remembrance. "But in these he always conquers in the end; I am so miserably weak, you know, and he—you don't know how hard he is!"

"You must try to grow stronger, and you will in time learn how to live together," said Laura, encouragingly. "It is very hard for me to advise you, but this much I am sure must be right; you can certainly study if you choose, without his interference!"

"Why should I study?" asked Flora. "What would be the use?"

"I will tell you," said Laura; "I have thought of you often since you have been away, and it has seemed to me that in your talents as a writer you might find comfort."

"How?" but Flora had again stopped her restless walk, with a new interest in her eyes.

"I think those verses you read me last fall were almost, if not quite, good enough to print. Now, suppose you try your very best, and write a really fine poem, or article; I have a friend who knows all about the papers and magazines here; he would tell me where anything of yours had better be sent."

"Do you think I could write anything that a first-class periodical would accept?" asked Flora, coming a step nearer.

"I do; I know how good the verses are which you have

12

already shown to me, and I am sure, with a little care, you may produce something very meritorious."

" Oh, Laura ! you give me new hope in life ! "

" I am glad of it, dear, I think if you are a faithful worker, that literature may be to you what it has been to so many sad hearts, a consoler, a stimulant, a hope."

For a moment the old clear light came back to Flora's eyes. " What a glory it would be if I could make for myself a place among the poets of the land ! oh, Laura, if I could see my name in the list of our writers; that would be a happiness worth living for ! "

" You can at least try for the prize," said Laura.

"I can and I will," replied Flora. " Laura, you were always my good angel at school, you are my good angel again, now."

" Well, dear, then since I have given you something pleasant to think of, do sit down and let us talk of it tranquilly."

Flora came and sat down, but presently began to shiver, singularly; " I am cold," she said, and she took up a costly shawl, that was thrown over a sofa, and wrapped it around her, drawing her chair close to the fire.

" You are not well," Laura said, alarmed at the blue shade of pallor that was creeping over her friend's face.

" No," replied Flora, bending over the blaze ; " I have never been well since that night. You know how wet and cold I was then, and I have had that same chill come over me many times. I never fainted before in my life, but I have fainted often since; however that belongs to the secrets of the prison," making a gesture, as if to dismiss the theme, with a small hand that glittered with diamonds.

" Don't you take anything for these chills ? " Laura asked presently, seeing that her friend's form shook with the unnatural cold.

" No; it will pass off presently, and then I shall have the fever again. Sometimes lately I have thought I was going to die," she said, gloomily; " and I have been glad of it; but now, I will try to live to carve out a career for myself that shall yet give me, at least, fame."

The chill slowly left Flora, and a flush succeeded it; under its influence she grew excited, and talked eagerly, almost gaily, with Laura of her work in the future. She insisted that her adviser should stay to luncheon, and had it served in the boudoir; a dainty meal of delicate viands set out on rare china and costly silver. But, when Laura, at last, went away, though she had spoken so cheerfully, her own heart was full of forebodings over her friend's future.

CHAPTER XXXVII.

RHODA'S DEVOTION.

WHILE Mr. Le Roy was enjoying life to the utmost, in receiving and making bridal visits; in going to splendid entertainments gotten up in his honor; in displaying to all his friends his new house, his new carriages, and last, his new wife, who was a means for showing off certain appurtenances of his, which he could not himself use; such as diamonds, laces, silks, and satins; while he was floating on the very crest of the wave of success, and basking in the sunshine of prosperity—the victim of his caprice, poor Maggie Bertrand, lay dying in her miserable home; her last hours saddened by the cold touch of poverty, and darkened by the shadow of an ineffaceable disgrace.

After the first excitement and joy of her return had passed away, Maggie was, as might have been expected, much worse; lying for days tossing in feverish suffering, and never rallying enough to be able to leave her bed for more than an hour or two at a time. Rhoda had at first proposed to go back to New York at once; but she lingered from day to day, because she saw that her presence was absolutely essential to the comfort of the sick girl, and finally because she realized that the end was not far off, and resolved to remain till her last sad duties to her friend were over.

Mrs. Bertram had lost her husband and only son, in the war between North and South. They had never been people of any station or wealth, but before that catastrophe, had lived comfortably on the labors of some half-dozen slaves, and the produce of a small farm. When the men of the family were gone, however, and the negroes were free, there was little left for the support of the poor lonely woman, but the milk from a few cows, and the eggs from a flock of poultry.

The colored nurse, aunt Phœbe, remained faithful to her former mistress, and these two old women took such care of the poor place as their feebleness permitted ; barely keeping themselves alive on the little money that their humble industry procured. The farm was, indeed, nominally rented to a neighbor, but he paid a mere pittance for the use of the few worn-out acres, and the money came from him but uncertainly, and often, not at all.

Mrs. Bertram knew all Maggie's sad story, which had, in truth, at one time furnished a theme for the gossips of the neighborhood ; but in her widowed loneliness she was only too glad to welcome the wanderer back ; and to do honor to her arrival, a little feast was arranged that for a moment concealed from Rhoda the extent of the poverty of her friend's home. She was not long in finding it out, however, as day after day the slender stock of provisions grew smaller, and presently resolved to set herself about some work which should make her, at least, not a burden on these poor people. She found that formerly Mrs. Bertram had made butter when she had had the help of a couple of able-bodied women, but that now she was content to sell the milk from her cows at a miserably low rate to a man, who came for it every day, and peddled it out in an adjoining town. Rhoda who had been brought up on a farm changed all this; she brought out the disused churn, and under her vigorous management, soon had a dozen pounds of nice butter ready, which she took to the town herself and sold for a good price; continuing thereafter to supply a certain grocer with so much a week. She went out on to the hill-sides and picked the wild strawberries when they came to be ripe, and took them also to market, often walking many miles under the hot sun, and growing very brown with its burning. Then, too, she took care of the poultry which had never done so well before, producing so many eggs that aunt Phœbe said, "I 'clar to gracious, Miss Rhody's done got de gifts, she has sure 'nuff."

In all these various ways Rhoda added so much to the family income as more than compensated for what little she ate, and she felt that she thus earned the melancholy right to watch over and make comfortable the last hours of her poor dying friend. But despite her utmost exertions, it was not possible to do all that she wished, and again and again, Rhoda endured the pang of seeing Maggie suffering for luxuries, which she could by no means procure for her.

So, in toil and watching and sadness, the weeks passed slowly on, till May had come, the loveliest month in all the Southern calendar, and Maggie's life which had been for a week past a mere flutter, was fast flickering away. She lay, at the close of a long bright day, on the couch in the little sitting-room, to which Rhoda daily carried her in her strong arms, that the sick girl might have a change from the bed in her small room. The brief Southern twilight was over all the scene, the sun had set behind the Blue hills, and the azure of the heavens had changed to an opaline lustre, across which lines of fleecy clouds were floating. From the dark pine forests there came the long sigh of the night wind, breathing with that inexpressibly mournful cadence which is heard nowhere but in those evergreen groves, while the song of a distant mocking-bird mingled a thread of plaintive melody with the solemn diapason.

Just within the little cottage Mrs. Bertram leaned back in a rocking-chair, resting her weary head on a pillow, while Aunt Phœbe stood like a tall sentinel watching by Maggie's bed, and Rhoda sat on the door-step, looking now on the scene outside, and now on the sufferer within.

Maggie had lain for some time quiet, when she opened her eyes and said, feebly, "I wish I had some ice, my mouth hurts me so! Isn't there any ice?"

This had been the one craving it had been most difficult to satisfy. Ice was, in that region, very expensive, and it had only been possible to procure a little of it, and at rare intervals. At the sound of this plaint, Rhoda turned away her face with a look of anguish, while Aunt Phœbe bent down and said:

"No, honey, dere ain't no ice, dis here night, will you have a drink of water?

"No—no," fretfully. My tongue is hot as fire! If I only had a little ice to cool it!" with a sort of moaning cry.

So hard! so hard! That her dying hours should be rendered more suffering for the want of this simple luxury, while the man who had destroyed her, had not an ungratified wish!

The moans continued for a little while; Aunt Phœbe fanning the wasted face, out of which all the beauty had fled.

"The mocking-bird is singing"—Maggie said presently, speaking faintly; "it will be a beautiful night for a dance;" her poor mind was wandering now. "Where are Lucy and Susie?" then half starting up and speaking louder: "Why haven't Lucy and Susie been to see me?"

Mrs. Bertram covered her face. This was a question that Maggie had asked so often; the young girls that were her childhood friends, had never come to her since her return, and yet the man who was worse than she, could be the honored guest of the highest in the land!

Maggie turned her large eyes, which flamed deep in their hollow sockets, from one face to another.

"No one comes to see me," she said; "Why not?"
then putting up her hand with a feeble imploring gesture;
"Oh I know, I know, I am not fit to be their friend! I am
lost—lost—lost!"— With a gasping cry her head sank
back, the last faint rays of the day dropped from the hills,
and the light and the life were over together!

The time that followed, was, to Rhoda, dark as some
long horrible dream, during which she heard ever sounding like a mournful refrain, the sad whisper of the wind
in the pines. Her own agony over the loss of her friend
was terrible. She had loved this young girl with the
strength of a passionate nature, concentrating all its
affections on one object, and now that she was gone, she
thought of her loss, with piteous regret for her unalleviated
sufferings, with black despair of her own future.

Her first impulse was to leave at once the scene of so
much sorrow; but she was prevented from this by the
condition of Mrs. Bertram, who, long a victim to a subtle
disease, sank rapidly after Maggie's death. It seemed
cruel to leave the fading invalid with only the old negro
woman; and so Rhoda staid on till the feeble spirit had fled,
and then lingered till she saw mother and daughter sleeping
side by side, with the solemn hills shadowing their resting-
place, and the great pine forests sighing over their graves.

After this, her last duty was done, and the lonely girl
could turn her weary steps back to the great city, where
her few friends lived. Aunt Phœbe accompanied Rhoda
part of the way on her journey, for she was going to spend
the remnant of her days with a son who lived in Richmond. It was partly on her account, that Rhoda took this
way of returning home, and partly because in Richmond
she could take a boat for Washington, and thus make her
trip more cheaply than by land.

The two women reached the Virginia capital in the
noon of a beautiful summer day, and there sadly parted.
The poor black mamma seemed to feel that Rhoda was the
last link between her and those that were gone.

"You'se done been so kind, Miss Rhody," she said, "to de poor lamb and ole missis, I done breaks my heart dat you's gwine away."

"It's very bad, Phœbe; but you know I must go," Rhoda answered.

"I spose you must, Missis, dough it's mighty hard on ole Phœbe. But den please de Lord, it won't be long afore I goes too, to de bressed land where de tears is all wiped away!"

Rhoda answered by some kind words of farewell; but in her heart she thought, "If I could go too; oh, if I could only go too!"

The boat in which she was to make the trip was a small old affair; one of a line of second-class steamers, plying between Richmond and Washington. It was near the hour of starting when Rhoda went on board and, leaving her bag in the cabin, passed out on to the open deck. As she stood there she felt utterly heart-sick; around her there were only strangers, behind her was the grave of her friend, before her, what?

She had seated herself in a quiet corner and was watching the scene with dry eyes, which were feverish from long weeping, when she started with a little cry of joy. Among all those unknown people there was one friendly face. Frank Heywood was walking down the deck. In another moment he caught sight of her eager face, and came hurrying to her.

"Rhoda! How glad I am to see you! And Maggie?"

The sad story was soon told; Frank listening with deep interest to all the details, and then answering in turn Rhoda's questions as to how he came to be there.

"I wanted to ascertain some facts about this river that I could learn better by making this trip than in any other way," he explained; "I am ordered to Washington too, so that by taking this boat, I combine several advantages."

"It is a great good fortune to me that you are here,"

Rhoda said; "I was feeling so lonely, and dreaded so much the long journey alone."

"It is a pleasure to me, too," Heywood replied, kindly; "I know something of this part of the world, and I can point out to you some of the places of interest as we pass."

So the two sat together on the deck, while the boat dropped down the beautiful river; passing slowly the grass-grown earthworks, and crumbled forts, that were once the witnesses of so fearful a carnage. Looking out on the smiling landscape of valleys and hills and waving forests, it was difficult to realize that this fair scene had once been torn by cannon-shot; its peaceful quiet destroyed by the ceaseless roar of artillery, and that in every tranquil glade, and by every sparkling stream, there were soldier's graves.

As they steamed steadily on, the beautiful day declined to its close; the sunset faded slowly away over the low banks of the river, now widening to its mouth, and before the brief southern twilight had passed, the boat had made its last stop at the river towns, and swept out on to the blue waters of Chesapeake bay.

Away on either hand the banks lay dark and wild, shewing scarcely a sign of human habitation; forests clothing their sides almost as closely, in many places, as on that day three hundred years ago, when the first discoverer pushed his adventurous bark into these unknown waters.

As the red glow died away on the one side, the red moon rose on the other, lifting its broad and wrinkled face slowly above the horizon, shedding a faint lurid light across the rushing waves: then rising higher, and growing fairer and purer, as does some soul which elevates itself above the mists and sins of the world, until as it soars heavenward, it shines with the calm light of the perfect day.

As the night advanced, the wind grew fresher, a strong head-wind that retarded the progress of the boat, and drove the passengers to the shelter of the cabin.

Rhoda and Frank were still on the deck, when almost every one had gone away; but at last Heywood said:

12*

"I really think you should go below, Rhoda; it is growing very cold."

"I am sure I can stay here if you can," said Rhoda, looking at her companion quickly; "I dread going to my berth and being alone. If you will let me, I will stay as long as you do."

"Certainly," replied Frank, cordially. "If you are not afraid to stay, I like to have you here; but I think I shall go down myself soon."

They walked about a little longer, the white moon shedding a mild light upon the scene, making a long track across the waves, and flinging a myriad diamond sparkles into the foaming wake of the ship.

The wind was very fresh; as the night grew deeper it tossed the waters into billows, and beat against the prow of the boat, sending a triumphant whistle across the smoke-stacks and through the rigging.

At length, Heywood and Rhoda both decided to go below. As they passed across the deck for the last time, they met the captain, who seemed somewhat anxious; he stood looking at the shore for a moment, and then as he went to the engine-room they heard him say:

"Two hours behind time; tell Bob to put on more steam."

At the door of the ladies' cabin the two young people parted; Frank to as comfortable a state-room as the boat contained, Rhoda to a small close berth in the open cabin.

She threw herself into it without taking off her clothes, and drew her cloak over her. Lying there, she could perceive much more plainly, the strain and roll of the vessel, as it forged slowly ahead. Through the fixed slats of a small window, she could see how the waves ran past outside, and catch faint glimpses of the splashes of moonlight on their crests.

There were strange sounds in her ears, of creaking timbers and rattling chains; the glass articles on the centre-

table struck together with a perpetual jingle; the beat of
the machinery was like the panting of some great heart.
Sleep seemed an impossibility. Rhoda turned from the
contemplation of the night outside, to watch the lantern
that hung from the cabin roof, burning dimly as it swayed
slowly from side to side, keeping time with every plunge
of the ship. They seemed to be moving more swiftly now,
the turn of the paddle-wheels was more rapid, the spray
dashed in blinding sheets across the window outside.

Suddenly a terrific shock shook the boat from stem to
stern; there was a sound, deep, muffled, horrible; a sound
as of rendering and tearing ; then wild cries and the
tramp of many feet.

At the first alarm, Rhoda sprang from her berth, and
hurried, with a score of frightened pale-faced women, up to
the deck.

Here there was a scene of wild confusion ; one half the
boat a wreck ; men running about in mad terror, the cold
waters rising about them on every side.

In the uproar, the horror, the white darkness, Rhoda,
staggered on, groping with some blind instinct till she
found herself by Heywood's side.

The young journalist was pale, but his eyes shone with
the fire of an almost glad excitement, and his voice was very
firm as he said :

" The boiler has burst, the boat is going to sink, Rhoda,
we must leave it, and we must jump quickly in, or we shall
be sucked down with it."

In the water all around were floating fragments of the
dismembered vessel, and already a score of people were
hanging to these spars and boards.

" Can you swim ? " asked Rhoda.

" Oh yes, and you ? "

" No."

" Trust yourself to me, then, I will help you. Come, or
we shall be too late."

Under their feet the boat was sinking sinking; over

their heads the fierce wind was howling ; below them the black waters raved and swayed.

Frank took Rhoda's hand, and together they made the desperate leap.

There was an awful shock and chill, as the cold waters closed on them, a blind struggle, a horrible sense of suffocation, and then they came to the surface, and Rhoda found herself clinging to a plank by Heywood's side.

How swiftly the current carried them away ! They seemed to be caught in some eddy, for it was but a few moments before they had drifted far back from the boat, and were tossing almost alone, on the wide waste of waters.

Dimly they discerned for awhile the outline of the crippled boat ; but presently that disappeared; they could not see the other passengers that were floating like themselves; they seemed to be two lost lives hanging between the pitiless heavens and the unmerciful sea.

The board to which they were holding fast was a small one, always half submerged, sometimes almost sinking under their weight; a frail barrier between them and death.

Frank turned his head a little. " We are drifting towards the bank," he said; "if we only had a little larger support, I think I could swim enough to guide it to the shore."

"This plank is hardly large enough for two," Rhoda whispered, looking at her companion strangely.

"I wish it were larger," Frank admitted.

The two white faces were very near together, they were like two souls standing in the presence of God.

"Frank," said Rhoda, very softly ; "I shall not mind if this is the end. My life is a wreck and a ruin, and may as well end thus as any way."

"Don't say so," Heywood replied, gently ; "I hope some passing boat may pick us up soon."

Rhoda scanned with her dark eyes all the scene. Overhead the placid moon staring with untroubled calmness at the misery below ; close to the sea the wind rushing low, like a herd of furious animals tracking their prey ; around them the waves leaping up hungry for their lives ; no living thing, no prospect of a rescue.

The girl moved a little closer along the board ; her black hair dropping in wet masses beside her wan cheeks ; her eyes sombre with some dark thought.

" Frank," she said, " I know your secret. Will you give me a kiss ? "

Even in that danger the young journalist started and a look of terror crossed his face.

" No," she whispered ; " I shall never betray you. Only just once for friendship ; one kiss, it may be the last, you know."

Her companion seemed unable to frame a word, and there was a moisture in his eyes that was not of the sea as he bent towards her, and their cold lips met in a strange despairing embrace.

There was a moment of silence : Rhoda had drawn away a little ; she turned suddenly :

" Frank your life is better worth saving than mine, good-bye—good-bye ! "

The last words were uttered with a plaintive cry that betrayed the sharp anguish of the heart, and as they were spoken, the poor girl released her hold of the plank, and dropped out of sight beneath the ravening waters.

Heywood roused to horrified action, called her name again and again, and even swam a short distance from the board ; but all in vain.

An hour afterwards he was picked up by a boat sent out from a passing schooner, but no trace was seen of Rhoda Dayton; she had closed her brief life of sin and suffering by an heroic death, and found a resting-place for her sad heart, beneath the tranquil sea.

CHAPTER XXXVIII.

LAURA'S SUCCESS.

THE reward of Laura Stanley's industry had come at last in a tangible form. She had taken the first prize in her class at the Academy of Design. The picture on which she had spent so many hours of careful study, had been adjudged the best in the school, and the time had arrived in which she was to receive the public announcement of her good fortune.

It was a pleasant Spring evening in May, and Laura was in unusually good spirits as she drove with Mrs. D'Arcy to the white marble building, the scene of so many hours of labor, and now to be the scene of her triumph. Several causes combined to make the young artist lighter hearted than she had been in a long time. She had received that morning a letter from her mother, in which she told Laura that her father seemed to be at last reconciled to the thought of her independence, and had given his consent to her return home for a visit.

"He never says much, you know," said Mrs. Stanley; "but I think if you come to us for your vacation, he will be glad to see you, and oh, my child, I do so long to look on your dear face again!"

These tender loving words made Laura very happy; she would not be always an exile from her home; but presently when her last duties were done, she could go once more to those she loved, and breathe again the pure air of her native hills.

This had been almost gladness enough for one day; but the last pleasant touch was added, when Mrs. D'Arcy told her, on their way in the carriage, that all the Bradfords were to be at the exhibition.

"All of them?" Laura asked, quickly; "Yes, I know

Mr. and Mrs. Bradford and Bessie will be there; Bessie was so pleased to hear of my success, and said she should certainly come."

"Guy will be there, too," said Mrs. D'Arcy.

"How do you know?"

"I saw him this afternoon, and had a long talk with him, and he said he would not miss coming on any account."

The words were significant; Laura felt her face flushing even in the darkness; everything was like a happy dream to her that night.

Yes, Guy was there, waiting for them on the broad steps, coming down to meet them eagerly; his eyes sparkling, his hands extended, with words of proud, heart-felt congratulation.

As in duty bound, when they stood in the entrance, Bradford offered his arm to Mrs. D'Arcy; but Laura was quite contented to walk on the other side.

"Father and mother and Bessie are here," he said; "they came early to get front seats. Bessie is quite wild over the victory her teacher has achieved."

The rooms were already filled with a crowd of people as they went in; but among them all, Guy felt with a glow of admiration, that Laura was one of the handsomest women in the room. She had indeed taken unusual pains with her dress for this occasion. She had made, a week before, a successful sale of a set of flower-paintings, and with the money thus procured, had been able first, to settle her small debts, and then to purchase for the first time in nearly a year, a new dress. It was of simple gray stuff it is true, but was tastefully made, the dark blue trimmings with which it was ornamented, and the dark blue feather in her hat giving the costume a tint and character. Laura had now been in the city long enough to acquire that indescribable air of style which had once been wanting in her appearance, and as she came into the room the light of happiness in her gray eyes, and that healthful bloom on her cheeks, she was indeed as fair a lady as one might wish to see.

Her arrival created a little flutter of excitement among her fellow-students and their friends, to whom she was pointed out as the fortunate winner of the prize, and she was presently handed to a seat at the front.

The exercises were very simple. The President made a brief address, and then the names of the successful competitors for the various honors were read ; a burst of applause greeting each announcement. When this was over, the crowd rose from their chairs, which were pushed aside, and the inspection of the pictures commenced.

As soon as this movement took place, Laura was surrounded by a crowd of friends offering their congratulations, and when these had a little passed away, she found Guy Bradford again by her side. Of course he insisted she must take him to see her drawing, which they found with a group of admirers before it; of course he quite exhausted himself in complimenting the beauty of that fine head of Clytie which she had rendered with so much feeling ; but as they turned away at last, he changed the subject by saying :

"You scarcely spoke to me when I met you on the avenue the other day."

"Didn't I ?" asked Laura, uncomfortably conscious ;— "I think I bowed."

"Yes, you did ; but only just enough to avoid a cut. I would have deserted my cousin to go to you, if you had not been so very cold."

"Was that your cousin ? " asked Laura, quickly.

"Yes, and I fear you must have thought me a very lazy fellow to be away from work at that time of day."

"I was rather surprised to meet you."

"I'll tell you how it was. I was sent up town on business, and it chanced that my way lay for a short distance on the avenue. As I turned into it I met my cousin, Miss Clarkson, with a party of friends 'doing pictures' as she called it, and she coaxed me to walk a little way with her. But if I could have had my way, I would have deserted her for you, even though my reason told me then, that I should be only making myself wretched."

The last words were significant, and an eloquent silence followed; Laura feeling, rather than seeing, Guy's dark eyes studying her face.

At this moment Mrs. D'Arcy came to them with Mr. and Mrs. Bradford. "We are all going up stairs into the gallery," she said, " so you young people come too."

" You would like to go, Miss Stanley ? " asked Guy.

" Certainly," and the party presently went up the wide steps into the brilliantly lighted rooms, where the annual exhibition of Academy pictures was displayed.

There were a great many people here, and conversation, other than the most casual, was impossible. Guy and Laura followed the rest, admiring the many fine works of art which were scattered along the walls, and horrified at the atrocities in blue and green which disgraced the collection, wondering, as does every visitor at this place, how the Board of Examiners could have admitted that horrible daub, and why this really exquisite gem was not better hung.

"Next year I shall hope to have something here," Laura said ; "I trust I can do at least as well as that—" pointing to a monster painting of Mount Katahdin which rose, grand gloomy and peculiar ; a mountain of gray pudding above a green worsted plain.

"Fearful!" said Bradford; "Why was it ever permitted entrance here ? "

"That is a puzzling question to answer," replied Laura. "These good N. A's have very inscrutable rules; however, this wonderful performance is not in a very conspicuous position, it looks as if the Board was rather frightened at its own temerity in accepting it, and had it hung in this out-of-the-way corner, in hopes that no one would see it. Do let us go back and refresh ourselves by looking at that lovely Venetian scene again."

"But no," said Guy, "we have not seen the statuary yet." Sly fellow! He remembered that the little room where the sculpture is displayed, is often almost untenanted.

Laura, not thinking of this, readily agreed to his proposal, and they walked into the crimson-walled apartment, where were one or two ambitious colossal figures, and some really beautiful small heads.

"Shall we find a seat?" asked Guy; "I have something I want to say to you so much."

They sat down in a quiet corner; a few people came and went, but they were comparatively alone.

"I wonder if you know how long it is since I have been to see you?"

"It is a long time," Laura answered, in a low voice.

"It is almost three months; I could tell you the very number of the days. Do you care to know why I have not been?"

"Certainly I do."

"I thought until this afternoon that you were engaged to Frank Heywood;" Guy whispered.

"I fancied you had some such impression."

"And yet you never told me that I was mistaken?"

"You forget that I never had the opportunity."

"That is true; but if you had known how I was suffering, I think you would have sent me a letter explaining my error."

Laura smiled; it was a relief to her to try by a little pleasantry, to shake off the spell that was creeping over her —vague, delicious, but rendering her too conscious for the place and the scene. "That would have been a very extraordinary proceeding, certainly, Mr. Bradford; imagine my writing to you. 'I am not engaged to any one, please come and see me.'"

Guy looked hurt, man-like he thought of nothing, cared for nothing, but the passion that absorbed him. "You are laughing at me," he said; "You have no sympathy for the misery I have endured."

Laura was intensely happy and yet she was half provoked. "Why does he not say something definite ? " she
thought. "I cannot make all sorts of admissions in reply
to a few vague words." She was silent a moment; one
would have fancied that her burning cheeks, her downcast
eyes, her quick coming breath, would have revealed her
secret to any one; but Guy, uncertain and jealous, was
only puzzled and troubled.

"I don't believe you cared whether I came to see you
or not," he exclaimed.

"I did, very much," Laura said, quickly ; and the look
which she gave him, sent a throb of delight straight to the
honest heart beside her.

"Oh, Laura !" he cried, forgetting everything around
them, and bending near her till his arm almost clasped her.
"You do care for me a little, don't you ? "

Laura started up suddenly. "Mr. Bradford," she said,
"this is no place for us to talk so seriously; we are already
attracting attention. If you will come to see me to-morrow evening, I will answer as many questions as you
please."

Guy was half provoked and yet he realized that she
was right. He rose and offered her his arm. "I am a
stupid, blundering fellow," he said. "But I felt so happy
to-day when Mrs. D'Arcy told me that you were not
engaged, that I may be forgiven for being a little rash."

The whole bearing of the two was such as would, to
the most casual observer betray that they were lovers.
They stood before a group of statuary, but neither of
them looked at the marble forms. Guy's eyes were fixed
on Laura's face, and she was trembling, in conscious happiness, under his gaze. At this moment Judge Swinton
who had been idling through the galleries, came into this
room. He started when he saw the two young people,
and a black frown crossed his face. He gave them one
close shrewd look, and then turned away before either of
them had seen him.

Laura said presently: "I think we had better go out
and find our friends, don't you, Mr. Bradford?" glancing
up at him with a sort of sweet timidity that was an intoxication to Guy.

"You are right, I suppose," he replied with a sigh;
"if I could have my way, I would take you away from
every one for awhile, but I will try to be patient until
to-morrow evening."

They passed out of the room and joined the throng in
the larger galleries. It was rather difficult perhaps for
both of them to appear indifferent, but they did pretty
well, and resumed a sort of monosyllabic conversation
about the pictures; speaking some superficial words which
never betrayed the great flood of happiness that was beating deep down in their hearts.

As they were moving on thus, they noticed that people
were turning to gaze in a certain direction, and caught
whispered expressions of admiration. Following the crowd,
they looked to the other side of the room, and there stood
Mr. Le Roy and his beautiful bride.

Flora was dressed in a costume of green silk in several
shades; a French dress, wonderful in elaborate beauty of
design, and wore on her head a straw bonnet ornamented
by a wreath of moss roses. She was very lovely to look
upon, her fair hair elaborately dressed, her delicate complexion brilliant with that peculiar flush that Laura had
noticed before. There was, to her friend, always that same
unrest in her eyes, but to the casual observer, she was the
fortunate wife of a wealthy man; young, fair and happy,
and Mr. Le Roy had good reasons to feel complacently
satisfied with his choice.

Guy and Laura changed the direction of their walk so
as presently to meet the couple, and as the encounter took
place, cordial greetings were exchanged. Bradford had
long known both Mr. and Mrs. Le Roy, and under his
escort, even Laura received a condescending recognition
from the stately bridegroom. Flora was of course delight-

ed to see her friend, and as the two gentlemen exchanged
a word, she drew her a little aside.

" I have heard of your success, Laura," she said ; " and
I am so glad."

" Thanks, dear, and what have you been doing ? "

" Oh, I have written something ! " whispered Flora,
eagerly ; " Come and see me on Saturday again, will you ?
And tell me what you think of it."

It was a pleasure to Laura to see the light in her friend's
face as she spoke, and she at once agreed to visit her at the
time mentioned ; then, having exchanged farewells with
Mr. and Mrs. Le Roy, she and Guy passed on.

Presently, after this, the two found Mrs. D'Arcy, and
thé hour for closing the exhibition having come, they all
went to the doctor's carriage. As Guy took Laura's hand
to help her in, he pressed it with so fervent a grasp as to
be really painful, and whispered significantly—" To-morrow
evening."

CHAPTER XXXIX.

AN UNANSWERED QUESTION.

THE next morning when Laura reached school, she was
met in the hall by Mrs. Glitter, who informed her that Mr.
Glitter would like to see her after her classes were over.
Laura signified that she would be at his service at the time
specified, and went up to her duties. She more than half-
guessed why she was thus summoned ; but she was so happy
that no minor annoyance could trouble her. The next two
hours passed, she scarcely knew how ; she tried hard to
keep her thoughts on her occupation, but she found them
wandering away, again and again, into a dream. Once
when one of the little girls asked her, if that was correct
perspective ? she softly answered, " this evening," and
then blushed enormously at the child's look of surprise;

and try as hard as she might, nothing seemed real to her; there was a haze, an enchanted light over every object, and the fair vista of her thoughts closed always with Guy's coming.

After awhile the twelve-o'clock bell rang, and, the girls dismissed, Laura put on her hat and walked down to the reception-room where she found Mr. Glitter awaiting her. He fidgeted a little nervously at her entrance; he had grown to have a certain dread of the steady gaze of those gray eyes, but bowed with an assumption of dignity as Laura took her seat.

"Miss Stanley," he began, pompously : "we are approaching the close of our fiscal year, when it becomes proper for me to make my arrangements for the future. You are aware, perhaps, that school closes on the fifteenth of June."

Laura admitted that she was in possession of that fact, that she had indeed been for some time acquainted with it.

"Very good, you will not perhaps be wholly unprepared to hear that I have decided to dispense with your services for the ensuing year."

Laura colored slightly. "I am neither surprised nor disappointed," she said ; "as I should not, under any circumstances, have renewed my engagement here."

"You look perhaps to a more remunerative position elsewhere," Mr. Glitter asked, curiously.

"My plans are my own, sir," replied Laura, coldly.

"Undoubtedly," admitted Mr. Glitter, with a little angry flush. "But I will give you one word of advice at parting ; I have had a large experience, and I warn you that such sentiments as you have uttered in my presence are calculated to be injurious, I may even say, inimical, to your success as a teacher in any establishment."

"My sentiments are not likely to change," Laura said, as she rose ; "and I trust you may yet acknowledge their truth. I wish you good-morning, sir," and she left the room, before Mr. Gliter could recover from the surprise her last audacity had occasioned him.

As for Laura she pursued her way to her home, congratulating herself that she had curbed her temper and refrained from any saucy reply to her small antagonist, and then dismissing him from her thoughts, began again the delicious reverie that made life an enchantment.

For some hours that afternoon she sat in her room, painting a group of roses and lilies, that she was executing to order for the print-shops, where she now regularly disposed of her pictures. She put on the colors, pale pinks, deep greens, delicate whites, accurately, but mechanically; moving as one in a dream. So happy—so happy! Had existence ever before given to any one such an overflowing delight as it had now for her? Had ever such bliss enwrapped other human souls? She wondered no longer at the old-time stories of lovers' devotion; at Hero's long watches for Leander; at Juliet's death from despair of the crown of marriage; at Penelope's yearning fidelity to her wandering husband. No misery seemed so bad as loss of this new-found joy, no pleasure so great as its fruition. Her pulses were beating full and strong like new wine in her warm veins; her heart was full of a vague craving that was blissful pain.

At last, it seemed to Laura no longer possible to continue her occupation. As the hours of the day stole by, a strange unrest seized her, and she felt as if she must seek out some companionship. The thoughts that overwhelmed her were too absorbing, too intoxicating; they oppressed her by their intensity, and putting away her drawing-materials, she went down to the little sitting-room.

There she found, as usual, Mrs. Moulder with her children; Minnie sewing beside her mother, the little girl playing on the floor, the boy wandering about aimless except for mischief. The room was very pleasant, the afternoon sunshine was coming into it through the open window, the flowers on the stand were in bloom, the bird sang in its cage.

" Please may I help you twist the thread ? " Laura
asked, quoting the old nursery-rhyme as she looked in at
the door.

" Oh, yes; come in ! come in ! " Mrs. Moulder cried,
cordially ; " No one here will bite off your head."

" Then give me some work," Laura said, going to the
pile of stockings by Mrs. Moulder, and taking up a pair.

"Thank you my, dear, as much as you please to do ; "
then, regarding her carefully ; " How well you look this
afternoon, and how bright your eyes are ! and dear me, is
that a new ribbon ? "

" Yes," admitted Laura, with a blush and a smile ; " I
expect a visitor to-night."

" Ah ! a favored one too ! may I guess who ? The
gentleman who has not been in so long? Ah ! ah ! no
need to answer that question in words." Then with a
gleam of mild mischief, " Will you need Minnie's services ? "

" Well, no," answered Laura with down-cast eyes ; " not
this time, I think."

Mrs. Moulder laughed softly, the presence of the children prevented any especial words, and Laura rushed into
a description of the events of the previous evening at the
Academy. Mrs. Moulder was much interested in listening,
and for a while forgot to watch over the boy ; he was
unusually quiet for a time, and then little Agnes uttered a
sharp cry.

"The bird is out ! "

In a moment the tranquillity of the scene was broken
up ; they all started to their feet; Laura sprang to the
windows and closed them, the cause of all this tumult
flying from side to side of the room with short sharp notes
of alarm.

When quiet was somewhat restored, Mrs. Moulder
demanded how it had happened.

" Aleck did it," said Agnes ; " he opened the door of
the cage."

"Hold your tongue, tell-tale, til!" exclaimed the boy, angrily.

"It is very bad," said Mrs. Moulder; "I am afraid he will not go back to the cage, and it is so near dinner-time."

They all sat down again, leaving the door of the bird's house open, hoping that he would return to it; but he hopped about on the cornice, or flew high up near the ceiling, and showed not the slightest desire to return to his quarters.

Mrs. Moulder was evidently getting anxious. "Cherry! Cherry!" she called; "Come down little birdie, come down!"

No reply to these entreating words, but a few musical notes, and then a little song; the pretty creature evidently enjoyed his liberty.

"I wish he would come down!" Mrs. Moulder exclaimed; "It is very annoying to have him out just now!"

"Don't you think we could catch him?" asked Laura.

"No, the ceilings are so high we can't catch him, and I am afraid he won't fly down at all."

At this moment, what they had both been secretly dreading, happened; the front door closed heavily, they heard slow footsteps coming up stairs, and Mr. Moulder entered the room. He looked flushed with the heat of the day, and was, as usual, in his before-dinner humor.

"What's the matter? What's all this fuss about?" he demanded, looking from one to the other.

"The bird's out," explained Aleck.

"Bird out? well, what if he is? squalling little beast! He's always a plague."

"He'll go back to his cage by-and-bye, I think," said Mrs. Moulder, nervously.

Mr. Moulder gave a sort of grunt, and passed into the bedroom. As soon as he was gone, Mrs. Moulder turned to Laura.

"Do let us try to drive the bird down before he comes back."

13

The two ladies each seized a towel, and began to try to chase the little fugitive, who, however, only flew wildly about the room, keeping always above their reach. While they were thus engaged the dinner-bell rang, and Mr. Moulder reappeared.

"Well," he said, impatiently; "are we all to stand here waiting because of that screaming bird? Here give me something, I'll fetch him down."

"Oh, Alexander, don't be rough; remember he is only a frail little creature!" Mrs. Moulder entreated.

The words might as well have not been uttered. Mr. Moulder took a heavy towel and rushed after the now trembling and frightened warbler. He flapped at him once or twice, Mrs. Moulder crying piteously, "Oh, Alexander! don't, please, please don't strike so hard! oh, Alexander, don't, don't!"

Her words were of no effect; Mr. Moulder seeming to be enraged by the bird's escape, beat the cloth at him viciously, and presently with some effect, he hit the fluttering yellow wings; struck them again and again, and in a moment, brought a mere ruffled mass of feathers to the floor.

Mrs. Moulder picked up the tiny crushed object. "You have killed him, Alexander," she said, with intense mournfulness; "my little pet is dying! Little Cherry, dear little Cherry!" putting her cheek down against the soft yellow down. "His heart scarcely beats; poor little bird, poor dear little bird!" trying to smooth his broken plumage; "It is no use! he is dead!"

Mr. Moulder at first seemed half shocked at his own action; he stood looking at his wife in silence for a moment, then he said, roughly: "What a fuss over a silly bird! Come children, we'll go down to dinner," and he strode out of the room.

Mrs. Moulder laid the dead songster gently down on one of the flower-pots, and then, flinging herself on the sofa, burst into a passion of tears. "I have had him so many years!" she sobbed; "Poor little bird! He has been such a comfort to me, such a companion. Dear little Cherry! and now to have his poor life beaten out! oh, it is hard, cruelly hard!"

Laura was perfectly overcome at this display of grief from one usually so patient. "Agnes!" she cried, kneeling down by her; "Agnes, don't distress yourself so! Remember you ought to avoid agitation."

"I know, I know," Mrs. Moulder moaned; "I ought to control myself. I have feared I should give way this long time; this is only the last straw that has broken me down."

"Oh, do try to be more quiet," Laura urged, fairly alarmed at such a paroxysm of distress as shook her friend's frame.

"I will, I will try to be quiet," Mrs. Moulder said, bravely; "but life is all so hard, so hard! Work and endure and suffer, and no hope in the future," with a long sigh.

The first strength of the passion to which she had yielded was past, and Laura was able to soothe her friend with such gentle and hopeful words as she could think of; finally persuading her to seek her bed instead of attempting to go down stairs, and seeing her quiet there with Minnie by her side, before she went to her own dinner.

After all this excitement, Laura had not much appetite for such remnants of a meal as awaited her, and was sipping a cup of cold tea, as a sort of substitute for anything else, when the front door-bell sounded with a sharp clang. Her heart gave a sudden jump, a sense of suffocation overwhelmed her, and she was utterly unable to swallow another morsel, but sat trembling and almost panting, until Jane came in, and with a broad grin handed her a card containing the words, "Mr. Guy Bradford."

"A gentleman for you, Miss; he's in the parlor."

Laura went slowly up stairs, her heart beating with quick swelling pulsations, her cheeks burning with a tell-tale blush.

Guy was walking up and down the small room, restlessly; his face was very pale, his eyes shone with a strange inward light ; Laura paused inside the door, looking at him in surprise. He came towards her, and seized both her hands.·

"Laura," he said; "I went home last night as happy a man as there was in all the city, so happy that I could not sleep for joy. To-day I have heard something which has caused me intense pain; it is in your power to give me back that happiness, or to make me more wretched than I have ever been in my life before. Will you answer me one question ? "

Laura looked at him, surprised at the tone of agony that underlay the passion of his words. "What is your question ? " she asked.

"I suppose I ought to pick my words," he said ; "but between us two, who have so nearly looked on each other's hearts, there is no need of ceremony ; Laura where did you spend the first night in New York ? "

The demand was so entirely unexpected, so unaccountable, that Laura, for a moment stood perfectly speechless. She felt the blood rush to her face, and then recede, leaving her unusually pale.

"Won't you tell me ? " Guy urged, a dark frown settling on his brow.

"Why do you ask ? " Laura said, at last, drawing her hand away from his grasp.

"Why do I ask ? " he repeated ; "Why do you not answer ? "

Frank Heywood's warning words were in her ears ; under the sudden compulsion of this attack she did not feel as if it were possible to hurry into an explanation that ought to be careful and long.

"I wish you would tell me why you make this inquiry," she said.

"I will tell you," Guy replied. "Because to-day I have received a warning letter ; a letter which I have not allowed to influence me against you; a letter which shall have no weight with me now, if you will answer only this one question."

The tone was somewhat imperious, and Laura resented it instantly.

"You have no right," she said, quickly, "to ask me anything about my past life."

"No right!" exclaimed Guy, coming nearer to her, his eyes burning down into hers; "Laura, whether I have the right or not, can it be that there is any dark spot in your life that you are not willing to let all the world see?"

Laura flushed to righteous anger, and drew up her head haughtily—"You insult me by even a suspicion," she cried, hotly.

"God knows I would not insult, or wound you," replied Guy, hoarsely. "This explanation which I ask, is as life or death to me."

"And I declare that you have no right to ask it! Would you give me an equal right to question *your* life?"

Guy drew back a step, breathing hard. "That is a very different thing," he said. "Laura are you only seeking to avoid a question that you dare not answer?"

Laura was stung to intense indignation. "Mr. Bradford," she exclaimed; "your distrust, and your cross-examination are both an outrage. If after all these months of acquaintance, if after all that you know of me, you can still harbor, even for a moment, an injurious thought, you are unworthy of the regard I have given you."

He looked at her, growing slowly pale to the very lips. "It would be easy to remove my suspicions," he said; "do you utterly refuse to answer my question?"

"I do, absolutely."

"God forgive you, Laura," Guy whispered. "Good-bye." He moved as if to leave the room; took a step away, then turned suddenly and caught her in his arms. "I have loved you so much!" he gasped, and he pressed his hot lips with a sudden passion to hers, then almost cast her from him, and left the room.

CHAPTER XL.

OVER THE SEA.

AFTER the door closed on Guy, Laura sat for some time motionless in her chair, counting the passing moments by the quick beating of her heart. Her blood was on fire, her brain throbbed as if to bursting ; she seemed still to feel the touch of that strange embrace, still to hear the low intensity of that passionate whisper, and this remembrance overwhelmed all others ; wrath, indignation, resentment swelled in her breast, and then died out, suddenly quenched by the recollection of the despairing cadence of those words—" I have loved you so much ! "

If he had only said that at first ! If he would only have shown his confidence in her by offering her his heart, he might afterwards have asked her any question he pleased. But to come to her, with no right of affection, and make this peremptory demand was an outrage, and yet, how was it possible to be angry since he had uttered that piteous confession, with the sad light of his eyes, the mournful tone of his voice proving its truthfulness.

If he would only come back, she thought; if he would only come back ! Now that he had told his secret, she would gladly respond to it, and then tell him all of her life he might care to hear. For a time she hoped that he would return, and sat listening breathlessly to any passing foot-fall ; but the minutes went slowly by, and no one came up the steps again, until after awhile Mr. Moulder arrived from the club to which he had gone to spend the evening. This aroused Laura ; she started to her feet as she heard the latch-key placed in the lock, and fled to her room, getting herself into bed she scarcely knew how, only to toss in feverish restlessness through the long watches of the seemingly endless night, haunted by the recollection of Guy's words, his glances, the trembling clasp of his strong hands. Sleep was an impossibility for hours ; again and again she rose and went to her window, leaning her head out to catch the cool air ; looking up at the journeying stars and thinking that they too shone on him; straining her eyes in the direction in which she knew his house lay, with a longing to pierce the distance which separated them, and bring him back to her by force of her unconfessed love.

After awhile, however, youth and nature triumphed over this excitement and Laura fell into a deep sleep. It was troubled by strange dreams of Guy's appealing eyes ; but it lasted some time, and she did not wake until the morning was several hours old. With returning consciousness, there came the remembrance of the events of the past evening, smiting her like a blow, and she arose and dressed herself, feeling that one hope alone sustained her, the hope that Guy would come back to her.

Just as she had completed her toilet, her attention was attracted by unusual noises in the house. There was a bustle down stairs, and the sound of some one closing the front door. Going to the window she looked out and saw Mrs. D'Arcy just entering her carriage. Then the thought that Mrs. Moulder must be worse came to Laura, and reproaching herself for her selfishness in not remembering her friend sooner, she hurried out of the room. In the entry she met Minnie who stole to her side with a pale and terrified face, holding her finger on her lips.

" Mamma is very sick," she whispered ; " there came a little dead baby to her in the night, and she is so weak that no one can see her."

Laura was shocked and alarmed, she looked into the sitting-room and there found Bridget Malone, engaged in putting the place in order ; the neglected work-basket the dead bird on the flower-stand, everything speaking of the absent lady.

"Oh, Biddy, I'm so glad to see you here ! " Laura said, softly. " Do tell me all about poor Mrs. Moulder."

" Shure thin, she's very bad, intirely," Bridget murmured
in a low voice. " The master himsel' came for me two
hours ago, but the docther was wid her, and the poor dead
babby was born before I got here. It was not to come so
soon, you know," she went on mysteriously ; " but the poor
leddy was worritted yesterday evening wid de little bird
dyin' ; the docther says that was waur for her nor onything,
and so she was awful bad in the night, and the babby dead
when it came, as foine a b'ye as you'd wish to see, too."

" And how is she now ? " asked Laura.

" She's slaypin' quite paceful, the poor heart ! So I
jist a come out here to tidy up a bit."

" Where are the children ? "

" They're wid Jane, in the kitchen, barrin' Minnie ;
she's so quiet she's no harrm at all, and is watchin' by her
mother, the Vargin presarve her ! "

" Is there anything I can do, Biddy ? "

" No Miss, you'd better go and get yourself a bit of
breakfast ; shure you're lookin' all t'rough wid ye this
mornin'."

This obscure phrase evidently referred to the young
lady's unusual pallor, and the haggard lines under her eyes,
and as Laura did feel faint, though she was certainly not
hungry, she went down stairs and got a cup of coffee and
a bit of toast, in such comfort as was possible, with Aleck
and Agnes engaged in a perpetual skirmish behind her
chair.

Tired as she was, and anxious as she was, the day's
duties must be done, and Laura went away to the school
and to her pupils, going through with all the weary round
faithfully, but very sad-heartedly.

When she once more reached home late in the afternoon, she was told that the doctor had been twice, that
Mrs. Moulder was very feeble and that no one could see
her, as absolute quiet was indispensable. Laura ate her
dinner in silence, Mr. Moulder sitting gloomily in his
place, scarcely uttering a word; the children fretful ; every

one feeling the absence of the gentle being who was hovering between life and death up stairs.

The evening darkened down and Laura hoped with a sickening longing that Guy would come; but the moments crept by on leaden feet, each one seeming to be prolonged to agony, and then, when it was gone, to have passed too quickly; no one came, the house was strangely still, people stole about on tiptoe, the doors were closed with a muffled sound. Laura tried to draw; the lines danced before her eyes, tried to read; the words framed only nonsense; finally walked up and down her little room till she was entirely weary, and at last, at half-past ten, when all hope of a visitor was over, went to bed and fell into a dreamless sleep.

By some accident it chanced that although Mrs. D'Arcy visited Mrs Moulder twice a day, it was not until the third afternoon that Laura saw her. The doctor's visits on other days had been made when Laura was out; but on this afternoon, she waited a little for the young teacher to come in, and so met her in the parlor.

"My child, how wretchedly you look," were her first words. "You are as worn as if you had had a fit of sickness!"

"Never mind me," Laura said, quickly; "how is Mrs. Moulder this afternoon?"

"A little stronger, and I think with great care and absolute quiet, that she will recover. Her system has received a terrible shock, but I hope that she has sufficient constitution to rally."

"Do you think that the accident the night before she was taken ill, really injured her?"

"Undoubtedly it did, very seriously; Minnie told me all about it. I suspected as soon as I was called in that there had been some unusual agitation. I knew, of course, that she was never as well as she might be if her home were happy, and it was that long pent-up distress that added intensity to her grief when she gave way over her

13*

poor pet. Mr. Moulder little realized when he killed the bird, that he destroyed the life of his unborn son."

" He seems really troubled now," said Laura; " I notice that he is surlier than ever."

Mrs. D'Arcy smiled. " That is an odd way of putting it, but a perfectly correct one. He is cross because he is worried. He is not a deliberately cruel man; only selfish and inconsiderate;" then with a sudden change of tone: " But, my dear, you are putting me off from speaking of you and your affairs;" taking hold of her hand and bending her kind eyes steadily on her young companion's face. " What is the matter between you and Guy?"

" A—a cruel misunderstanding." Laura's lips trembled so that she could scarcely frame the words.

" You haven't refused him from some mistaken pride, have you, Laura?"

" No, oh no!"

" You know that he has gone away?"

" Gone! Where?" her eyes dilating with distress, her cheeks paling.

" To Europe, to England."

" Gone!"

Laura repeated the word with a sort of gasping groan, and hiding her face, sobbed convulsively; moaning in broken accents, " Guy! Guy!"

The doctor was distressed at her tumultuous grief. " My dear child," she said; " don't be so unhappy about it; he has only gone to England on business, he will not be away more than two or three months. My dear Laura, do try to control yourself, if you care for him. I know that he loves you, and all will certainly be made right between you."

" I'm a fool!" Laura exclaimed, trying to stifle her sobs. " I would not have given way so, only I have been so many days wretched and anxious."

" It will do you good then to tell me all about it. Come, my dear, let me hear the whole story."

Thus encouraged, Laura presently composed herself sufficiently to give a partial description of what had passed between Guy and herself, on that last unfortunate evening. Mrs. D'Arcy listened with profound interest.

"An anonymous letter," she said; "Laura, whom do you suspect?"

"Judge Swinton," replied Laura, unhesitatingly.

"I thought as much; he seems resolved to persecute you to the uttermost."

"Perhaps I was too haughty to Guy," Laura went on, "but it seemed to me that he had no right to make such a demand, and so roughly, too! If he had told me before he asked that question that he cared for me, it would have been different."

"Oh, then he did make an avowal?"

"Yes," replied Laura, her pulses tingling as they always did at that recollection; "it was just before he went away, as if it had been wrung from him."

"He was evidently made very wretched by what you said," the doctor answered; "it seems when he went down town the next morning, that he learned that Mr. Bolton, who was about going to England on important business, had been severely injured the night before on the railroad, and would be unable to start for some time. There was great consternation in the office over this, and on impulse, Guy offered to go in his place. The other partner, Mr. Clamp, was only too glad to have him go; the passage was already engaged, the steamer to start in a few hours. Guy had only time to pack his things, bid his people good-bye, and so sailed on Wednesday. Poor Mrs. Bradford feels very badly about it; she came to see me yesterday, and asked if I could explain Guy's conduct."

"And what did you say?" demanded Laura, eagerly.

"What could I say, but that I knew nothing?"

"Did she think I had anything to do with it?"

"Of course she did, my dear," the doctor laughed; "it seems Guy told her on Monday night, after the exhibition, that he was going to propose to you."

"Did he?" with breathless interest.

"Yes, and she was delighted to hear it."

"Dear old lady! I have always liked her so much!"

"She is as lovely as possible, and she admires you, my dear, as she told me, more than any girl she ever knew."

"How kind of her! But do tell me all," urged Laura.

"It seems that on Tuesday night after he left you, when Guy came home his mother was watching for him. He came in looking terribly pale; she called him to her in the library; but he would not come, he only said, 'It's all over between us, mother,' and so to his room, where she could hear him walking up and down half the night, and the next day he was off to England."

"If he had only come back!" Laura said, piteously.

"I dare say that by this time he is sorry he did not," Mrs. D'Arcy replied. "He was miserable, and with that impatience of suffering, which is characteristic of some men, his first thought was to get away. Very likely he is wishing himself back, now that it is too late, and I can promise him this, that so soon as he does return, he shall have a famous scolding from me."

The doctor's words soothed and comforted Laura very much. She, at least, knew the worst; her lover was gone to be sure, and it was a dreary thought, that the ocean rolled between them, but she had his friend's sympathy, and surely, surely, some day this cruel misunderstanding would pass away.

Hope, which for some days past had seemed dead in Laura's heart, sprang up again. Life no longer looked so utterly dreary; there was much to trouble her, no doubt; she must yet pass many hours of sadness, and have many anxious thoughts, but the black grief that had oppressed her was gone, and she could yet endure, and perhaps even enjoy, that existence, which had just now seemed a burden too great to be borne, and would once again face her duties with cheerfulness.

That evening as the young artist sat at her lately-neg-
lected drawing, Minnie stole up stairs on tiptoe, to tell
her that Mr. Heywood was in the parlor. Laura was delighted to hear this, and went down to greet him, with the
utmost frank cordiality of manner. He looked very well
and was quite brown with exposure to the sun; but his sad
eyes seemed to have a deeper shade in them, and they
filled with tears more than once, as he told Laura the
story of Maggie's death, of Rhoda's long devotion to her
friend, and of her noble sacrifice.

"She thought that the plank was not strong enough
for us both," he said, with a long sigh; "and she deliberately gave up her own chance of life to save mine!"

Laura listened with the deepest interest, and the two
talked a long time of the poor girl's many noble traits of
character, and the redeeming heroism of her fate.

At last the conversation came back to themselves, and
Laura told Frank of her triumph at the Academy, and her
intention soon to return to her home for the summer vacation; while Frank, in reply to her questions, informed her
of the absolute success of his journey, and the reward it
had brought to him.

"I am on the regular editorial staff now," he said;
"no more reporting for me, and I am so glad to be out
of it."

"What do you do, then?" asked Laura.

"Write editorials, news articles, and sometimes letters."

"And you have a good salary?"

"Excellent, more than that, I see my way to the ultimate achievement of my highest hopes."

"What are they?"

"I want to be editor-in-chief of some great journal, so
that I can conduct it according to my own views, and
make it the medium of my own thoughts."

"That will hardly be for a long time yet, will it?"

"No, oh no! I am too young yet; but I believe that it
will come in time."

"But now that you are so well off," said Laura, lightly; "you will be getting married."

Heywood smiled with that strange lightless smile that seemed to carry no joy, and regarded his companion with a singular questioning look. "No," he said, "I shall not marry; my work must be father and mother, wife and children to me. I believe that a great daily newspaper may be conducted only in the interest of truth, of justice, and of right. The experiment has never yet been tried as I hope to try it; but I trust that the day will come when I may shape, with my own hands, a paper which shall be a teacher of the people, a guide in the path of virtue, and reform, and this aim must for me take the place of all family ties. I feel myself more than ever consecrated and set apart for this work, since Rhoda's death," he added solemnly; "I must take care that her sacrifice to preserve me was not in vain. I must try to prove that my life was worth saving."

CHAPTER XLI.

MARITAL REPROOF.

The sunlight was coming into the room where Mr. and Mrs. Le Roy sat at breakfast, on the Saturday morning of the same week. The day was soft and warm, for it was early June now, and there were flowers on the table in the midst of the costly china, and heavy silver, with which it was set out, while in a deep bay-window there was a *jardinière* in full bloom. The place needed some such lightness to enliven it, for the walls were covered with crimson-velvet paper, the wood-work was of solid rose-wood, and the carpet was in rich shades of crimson and brown. Altogether it was such a room as would have seemed warm and pleasant on a winter's evening, but was oppressively heavy in tone on this bright summer morning.

Flora sat behind the richly chased coffee-urn, toying
with her breakfast indifferently, looking very pretty in a
white cambric robe trimmed with pink ribbons, and a
coquettish little cap resting on her fair hair. Mr. Le Roy
occasionally regarded her over his paper, with complacent
approval; but she never glanced towards him; her eyes
were dreaming and her thoughts were evidently far away.
Her gaze rested sometimes on the flowers before her, but
never once sought her husband's face. At last, the
starched man-servant who had been moving noiselessly
about the room, went out, the breakfast being served; and
Mr. Le Roy laid down his paper and addressed his wife.

"Flora," he said; "how much did those flowers
cost?"

She started, slightly, as he spoke to her, and looked
up, at first as if she scarcely understood the question; then
turned her eyes slowly to the bright blossoms.

"I really don't know," she said; "I told the florist to
put in what he liked."

Mr. Le Roy frowned. "And you never asked the
price?"

"No."

"Did you forget that I requested you to make a memorandum of what you spent," he asked, severely.

"I suppose I did forget," answered Flora, with assumed
indifference; "I don't think I thought of anything but en-
livening this dull room a little; at least, I did not ask how
much it would cost."

Mr. Le Roy bent his brows blackly, and was silent for
a moment, then he said: "Will you allow me to see your
account-book for the week?"

A faint color rose to Flora's cheeks. "It is up stairs,"
she replied; "but I fancy it will not do you much good to
look at it."

"I prefer to see it and judge for myself," replied Mr.
Le Roy, coldly.

"Very well." She swept out of the room without

glancing at her husband, whose eyes she indeed generally avoided, and Mr. Le Roy, after ringing the bell to inform the waiter that the meal was over, followed her. He found his wife in the boudoir ; experience had taught him that she never liked to have him come there, but he was resolved to have her understand that it was his house, and that he had the right of entrance to all parts of it, and he made it a rule to go into this room without knocking ; unless, indeed, the door were locked as it had been more than once.

On this occasion it was open, however, and as he came in, Flora was standing by her desk, holding a handsomely-bound account-book in her hand. She had a sort of naughty-child expression on her face, that might have disarmed a man capable of playfulness ; but Mr. Le Roy never noticed it.

" Well ? " he said.

" Well," replied Flora, holding out the book ; " you will see that I have put down scarcely anything."

Mr. Le Roy took it and turned over the leaves with an ugly scowl. " Is this a deliberate disobedience of my orders ? " he asked.

A kind word might have brought an explanation ; at this demand, Flora's delicate face flushed, painfully. " It is deliberate so far as this," she said ; " that I never did keep accounts, and I never will. It is useless for me to try to."

" You refuse then to render a statement of the money that passes through your hands ? "

" Yes," said Flora ; " I cannot do it and I wish you would not ask me."

" I have always kept a record of every dollar of my own expenditure— " Mr. Le Roy began.

" Oh, I dare say," Flora interrupted, with a glance that made the words almost contemptuous.

" And I expect my wife to do the same thing," he closed, sternly.

"I was never brought up to it, and I cannot begin it now," Flora answered.

"Not even if I give you explicit commands in the matter?" Mr. Le Roy asked, peremptorily.

"Not even at your commands," Flora retorted; "to be all day long putting down expenses in that book, is a slavery that I cannot and will not endure. Keep the accounts yourself, if you want to know how the money goes;" and she turned and walked to the window.

"I will," Mr. Le Roy replied, closing the book, his eyes shining with a cold glitter; "hereafter, until you come to me with proper submission to resume your neglected duties, I will take care of the expenditures."

"Very well," replied Flora, not turning her head; "then I will send the servants to you, every time they want ten cents to buy an extra loaf of bread."

A slow color came to her husband's face. "Yes," he replied; "and you will come to me yourself, every time you want five dollars to buy flowers."

Flora did not reply; he stood looking at the graceful figure outlined against the window, for a moment in silence, and then left the room.

When he was gone, almost before his footfall had ceased to sound in the entry, Flora closed and locked the door, her eyes were very bright, her cheeks were burning; she pressed her hand to her chest as if in pain.

"This life is horrible!" she murmured; "I think I would kill myself, if I had not one hope. I can earn money perhaps, and have my flowers in spite of him. My poor flowers! He knew he would wound me most by speaking of them. Cruel! cruel!"

She walked about the room, restlessly for awhile, but at last came and sat down by her desk, and it was here that Laura found her, when about an hour later she came to keep her appointment with her friend. Flora rose to greet her with delight, and the two were presently deep in a literary discussion.

"And now for the poetry," Laura said, after a little.

"I don't know what you will think of it," Flora replied, timidly. "It came to me the other day when I was in the country.

"Have you been away?' asked Laura.

"Yes, last week I went with Mr. Le Roy to see his aunt, Mrs. Stuyvesant, who has a country-seat near Rye. We drove out in the afternoon, and passed a very old church. They were speaking of its history, and how it had stood there before the Revolution, and then, while she and Mr. Le Roy were talking over family matters and people I did not know, I fell into a sort of dream and this poetry came to me. I finished it in a day or two of work at home."

"That is the best way to write poetry, I fancy," said Laura. "In a species of inspiration; I am impatient to hear it."

Flora took some sheets of delicate paper, and with a faint rosy flush suffusing her sweet face read :

"THE OLD CHURCH BELL."

"High in ancient church-tower swinging,
    Hangs the bell, whose sounding tide
Of sonorous music ringing
    Over all the country side,
      Of weal or dole,
      By peal or toll,
    Tells the story far and wide.

"Loud rang the bell when Revolution
    Shook our land from shore to shore,
Proclaiming high the resolution,
    A nation sworn to yield no more!
      Through weal and dole!
      By peal or toll!
    Till all was free from shore to shore!

" Turbulent, the vibrant chiming
  Rang for glorious news of peace,
From vale to hill the sounds up climbing,
  Sang the song that wars should cease,
    Now weal, and dole
    By peal, and toll,
  Mark how the tranquil years increase.

" Solemnly, in early morning
  Moan the notes that sadly tell,
A soul has gone beyond the dawning,
  A body needs a funeral knell,
    No weal, all dole,
    No peal, a toll,
  The years slow tolled with mournful swell.

" Silvery sweet the joyous swaying
  Of wedding-bells, that far out fling
Their melodious rapture, saying,
  ' For youth, and hope, and love we ring !
    For weal, not dole !
    We peal, not toll !
  The happy future life to sing ! '

" With liquid cadence, rising, falling,
  Mellow church-chimes fill the air
Of the peaceful Sabbath, calling
  All the village folk to prayer,
    From weal and dole,
    By peal or toll,
  Here is rest from earthly care."

As the reading ceased, Laura seized her friend's hands in both of hers and uttered some enthusiastic words of praise.

" You think it is really good enough to send to some Magazine ? "

" I do, indeed. Frank Heywood has returned and he will know just where it ought to go."

" And—and—if it is accepted, will I get paid for it ? "

" Certainly, but my dear girl, what can you want with money ? "

"I! exclaimed Flora ; " I need money as much as the poorest woman in the city; I have not yet a penny that I can call my own ; Mr. Le Roy expects me to keep an account of every dollar I spend and to show it to him ; even my own private expenses must come under his eye."

" You have no allowance then ? "

" No, none ; I think papa expected settlements, but Mr. Le Roy did not propose any, and of course papa could not insist. I have nothing of my own, I am only a steward of his money. The other day I went into Monel's; you know they have all sorts of fancy articles there, and I amused myself by buying some neck-ties and ribbons. I did not really need them to be sure, and bought them more to wile away the time, than for anything else ; however I put all down that I spent, in the account-book, and on Saturday, when Mr. Le Roy looked it over, he quite took me to task for wasting money ! This week I have only entered a few large sums that went for housekeeping, and he was so vexed at me this morning that I don't know that he will ever trust me with a dollar again." Then seeing that Laura looked pained, she added : " But I didn't mean to say anything about this, only you see that it would be glorious if I could earn money enough to make my private expenses, independent of him.

" I hope you can, my dear ; " replied Laura, cordially.

After this they talked for awhile of their plans and prospects for the summer. Laura told Flora how soon she would go to her home, and some of her intentions of labor and study, and Flora informed her that she and Mr. Le Roy were to leave the city soon ; but it was not yet decided in which direction they would go. It was settled that they were to be at Newport in August, and that was all that she knew definitely.

" I suppose we shall drift about with the fashionable current," she said ; " but where it will carry us I do not know. For my part, I had far rather go to some quiet place, where I could be rid of this perpetual wearisome

round of dress and gayety, and have some opportunity of
study; but of course, my wishes count for nothing. It
will be, as my lord decides."

"You must try and study a little every day wherever
you are," Laura said.

"I shall; if it were not for the hope that you have
given me, I believe that my life would be absolutely intolerable."

So the friends parted, Laura taking the precious manuscript away with her, and promising to give Flora the
earliest intelligence as to its fate.

That afternoon Laura went to give her last lesson to
Bessie Bradford. She had a sort of guilty feeling as she
came into the house, knowing that she was the indirect
cause of the absence of the dearly loved son and brother,
and her uneasy consciousness was not lessened when she
found Mrs. Bradford in the library. The old lady met her
very kindly; but Laura felt herself blushing furiously as
she took her by the hand.

Very few words were said, but all the while as the
young teacher was giving her lesson she was aware that
though Mrs. Bradford sat in her own corner, apparently
quite occupied with some fancy knitting, she was every
now and then looking shrewdly at her over her spectacles.
These steady, though kindly glances were very disconcert-
ing, and it was a relief to Laura when the hour was up
and she could bid both the ladies good-bye.

"Take good care of yourself, my dear," Mrs. Bradford
said, as she kissed her cheek. "We shall all be glad to
see you back in the fall."

The words and tone brought sudden tears to Laura's
eyes; she knew so well that the poor mother's heart was
with her son, and her own was so full of his image! The
old lady understood her by an instantaneous intuition
she pressed her hand again, and there was a moisture
clouding her own gentle gaze.

In a few days more the last of Laura's duties was done.

Her pupils were all gone, or going away, the school was about to close, there was nothing more to keep her in the hot and dusty city, and never did captive rejoice more at release from prison than she did in the thought of escape from its monotonous barriers.

During the last three weeks Mrs. Moulder had been slowly gaining strength; coming back bit by bit to life. She was still very weak, but all danger was past, and Laura was relieved from the most pressing anxiety on her account, when she bent down to kiss her wasted cheek in farewell. The sick lady looked a poor frail morsel of humanity as she lay in her darkened room, her soft brown eyes showing larger than ever as they gazed out from her white face; and seeing how helpless she was, how feeble her poor thin hands were, those hands that were so tireless in labor when she was well—Laura hoped that her husband would be moved to some greater tenderness and pity.

Mrs. D'Arcy was almost the last, as she had been almost the first, of Laura's friends whom she saw in the city; for she stopped at the doctor's to say good-bye on her way out of town; but at the station it was Frank Heywood who looked after her checks and handed her into the car, and it was his handsome, delicate face that gave her the last farewell smile.

CHAPTER XLII.

HOME.

THREE hours of swift gliding along the shores of the beautiful river; three hours of looking out on the water that flashed in the sunshine on the hills and valleys of the opposite bank, all clothed in their summer glory of greenness, brought Laura to a station in the highlands, where she left the cars. Among the people on the platform were

two young girls, younger than Laura, but resembling her
sufficiently to point out at once their relationship to her.
Pretty girls with rosy cheeks and bright eyes, very
plainly dressed in gray holland suits ; but looking healthy
and bright, with the brightness of their youth. As soon as
they saw their sister, they came running to meet her with
eager smiles.

"Kate ! Fanny ! How nice it is to see you again !"
cried Laura, and she kissed them both affectionately.

"Mother is here in the wagon." Kate said.

"Mother !" and Laura hurried to the rear of the station
where the carriages were drawn up.

There were the showy turn-outs of city people spending
the summer in the country, the forlorn old traps that could
be hired by passengers, and drawn back a little way from
the crowd, a substantial double-seated box-wagon with a
pair of heavily built bay horses before it. On the back
seat of this vehicle, sat a very little lady of perhaps fifty.
She wore over a dark calico dress, a long black silk sacque
of some past fashion, a plain bonnet and a green veil, which
she was holding on with her mouth. A fresh wind was
blowing, and the vehicle had no top to it, so that this bit
of *barège* and her ribbons, were flying about, giving her a
sort of distracted appearance. As she caught sight of
Laura she pulled the veil off, showing a pale care-worn and
prematurely wrinkled face, which lighted up now with a
smile of joy.

"My dear girl !" and Laura springing into the wagon
was clasped in her mother's arms. "How well you are
looking !" Mrs. Stanley said, presently, gazing with admiration at her daughter's handsome face.

"I am well ; and you, dear mother ?"

"I am about as usual ; very busy now, you know ; I
felt as if I could hardly spend the time to come for you
to-day, but Gertrude and Jeannie said they would do the
pies this morning, and I thought I would trust them for
once ; though I mistrust they will make the paste heavy."

"Oh, they'll do well enough," said Laura; "I'd rather have poor pies than miss riding with you!"

Kate and Fanny now joined them, having secured Laura's trunk, which was hoisted up behind by a stout porter, and then Kate taking the reins, they started on the drive.

Mrs. Stanley tried to put on her veil again; "My eyes ain't strong this summer," she said; "and I have to wear a veil out in the sun." It was but a forlorn old thing and she seemed not to know how to adjust it.

"Let me fasten it for you," said Laura; "and your collar is crooked too;" putting it to rights, tenderly.

"I came off in such a hurry," Mrs. Stanley said. "Your father sent the team around sooner than I expected, and I got all in a flurry."

Laura sighed, the words were so familiar. Her poor mother was always in a hurry, and she had for years been accustomed to hearing such expressions as these.

The drive was a beautiful one up the hills, seeming to be always climbing, passing beautiful country-seats; then going down long stretches of road, bordered on either hand by rows of feathery tufted locust trees; every now and then catching glimpses of the river and the opposite shore.

Over all the scene the sun was pouring his splendid beams; they glowed on the geraniums and verbenas that stood in elegant gardens; they danced on the grass of spreading lawns; they gleamed from the polished leaves of the trees, and flashed from the smooth blades of the young corn that grew in the fields of the open country.

It was a long drive, for Mr. Stanley's farm stood some ten miles back from the river; but it was a perpetual pleasure to Laura, she was so glad to be once more in the lovely country. She inhaled with so much gladness the fresh air and looked up in delight on the pure blue of the heavens, unstained by the smoke and dust of the city; watching the cloud-shadows as they crept softly over the

scene ; or following with an artist's eyes the track of the
wind as it swept across the fields of waving grain.

After awhile Mrs. Stanley began to grow very tired,
and Laura passed her strong arm around her waist to support her.

"My back hurts so, after I have ridden so long," the
old lady said, plaintively.

"It is a sad shame that we have no wagon with backs
to the seats," Laura replied ; "this is hard even on us
young folks, and it must be very weary for you."

"I wish we had a covered carriage, but your father
don't think it best ; " Mrs. Stanley said, meekly, as if that
settled the question.

By-and-bye, as the shadows were beginning to grow
long, a turn in the road brought the party in sight of a
substantial house, white-painted with green blinds, standing
under the shade of some maple and locust trees. Across
the road opposite to it were some spacious barns painted
red, at the back was a wide garden, and spreading away
from it on either side, were broad fields of oats, of rye, and
of corn.

"Here we are ! " cried Kate ; and as the wagon rattled
up to the gate, two other girls in faded calicoes, came
bounding out of the house.

"And there are Gertrude and Jeannie! " exclaimed
Laura.

"I wonder how they got along with the pies"—reflected
Mrs. Stanley, anxiously.

There was a joyful bustle as the party descended and
went into the house; but once there all was business
again. Kate and Fanny went to change their dresses for
calicoes like their sisters, while Mrs. Stanley, taking off her
hat and sacque hurriedly in the sitting-room, hastened to
the kitchen. Laura looked after her sadly. She knew that
with all these broad acres of productive land, her father
was amply able to give the girls leisure for improvement,
suitable clothing, and above all, to relieve her mother from

14

the care and anxiety that had worn her out prematurely, and yet she knew also, that it was useless to hope for any such change.

As she went slowly up stairs to her room she glanced at the well-known objects of furniture, all solid, sombre and grim, which had been almost unchanged since she could remember. Every thing was in good repair, scrupulously neat ; but all beauty, or ornament, or grace, was banished rigidly even from the parlor, which was so solemn and square in its arrangements, as to make it always seem a sort of sacred spot, not to be lightly approached by unhallowed footsteps.

While Laura was unpacking in her room, she heard a little panting breath, and Jeannie, the youngest girl, came into the room with a plate of cookies in her hand.

"Mother sent these up," she said ; "she thought you might be hungry, you know father don't like eating between meals, so we could'nt get you a dinner; but we'll have something good for your supper."

"Thank you, Jeannie," said Laura. "Stop a moment and help me unpack."

"Oh no, I can't ! " exclaimed Jeannie. "I'm in such a hurry ! I've got to hunt eggs and go for the turkeys yet, and you know we have four hired men this summer, and it is most time for their supper."

"Four hired men and no help ? " asked Laura.

"Well, Mrs. Clark comes to wash and iron ; but the rest of the week we get through ourselves, father does'nt think it worth while to hire any one all the time. But there, I must go, I'm in such a hurry ! "

The little creature disappeared, and Laura resumed her occupation with rather a heavy heart. The old home life seemed to come back to her with all its drudgery, oppressing her, and wearying her. No rest, no time for thought here ; a daily struggle with endless work, a breathless race from morning till night; this was the lot to which those whom she so dearly loved were condemned !

At tea-time the family reassembled in the long plainly-furnished dining-room. Mrs. Stanley came in with a coarse apron over her dress, and her thin gray hair somewhat disordered. A dim consciousness of this seemed to strike her, for she put her hand up to her head piteously.

"There! I haven't fixed my hair since I came in! I never thought of it till this minute!" she said, glancing at Laura; "I've been so busy I haven't had time to attend to it."

"Never mind, mother," replied Laura, smoothing back the locks for her; "do sit down and rest yourself."

Mrs. Stanley took her place at the middle of one side of the table, behind a waiter full of cups and saucers; the girls, who all looked tired and heated, placed themselves in their seats, and then there was a pause. The flies buzzed about; Mrs. Stanley flapped at them fitfully with a napkin; but no one touched any of the food, though the dish of potatoes was slowly losing its heat, and the tea must be growing cold. Presently there was the crunch of a footfall on the gravel walk, then the sound of some one washing in the back porch, and after some moments, a heavy tread along the entry, and at last the door opened and Mr. Stanley came in.

A man of medium height, squarely built, with long arms terminated by a pair of strong brown hands, and slightly bowed legs terminated by large feet encased in coarse boots. Above his powerful shoulders rose a muscular throat upholding a massive head, bald on the top and covered thinly on the sides with white hair. His face was lined and seamed in every direction with innumerable wrinkles; his bushy gray eye-brows overhung a pair of deep-set gray eyes; his nose was long, and his mouth thin-lipped, with a fringe of gray beard under the chin. His clothes, substantial in material, showed the effects of hard work.

As he came into the room, Laura rose to her feet; "How do you do, father?" she said.

Mrs. Stanley looked anxiously at her husband. "How do you do?" he repeated, scarcely glancing at Laura, and without noticing her extended hand, he went and took his place in the middle of the table opposite his wife. As soon as he was seated, he raised his right hand and then, while all heads were bowed, asked a blessing, solemnly closing with the words, "all which we ask through the love of Christ."

Laura had heard the old formula many times before, but it had never struck her till to-day, how strange it was to hear him ask any thing through love, who gave so little to love himself!

The meal proceeded, at first almost in silence; but it was difficult wholly to repress the eagerness of the girls to question Laura about New York, and presently a sort of suppressed conversation began. Mr. Stanley apparently paid no attention to what was going on, until it chanced that he asked for a cup of tea, and his wife who was listening to something that Laura was saying, did not at first notice him.

"Elizabeth!" he exclaimed, in a tone that at once arrested her attention.

"What is it Roger?" she cried, with a start.

"I asked for a cup of tea," repeated Mr. Stanley; "and I should like to have it, if you can take your attention away from these women's chatter long enough to give it to me." As he spoke his face grew into a net-work of wrinkles, the lines running up over his nose and down on his forehead, in a hard sneer.

Mrs. Stanley handed her husband the tea with some murmured apology; but after that, scarcely a word was spoken, and the meal proceeded almost in silence. When it was finished, there was a bustle to clear it away; Laura helped with the rest, but it was another hour before the cups and dishes were all in their places; the dining-room rearranged, and the great kitchen set in order for the night.

When the last duty was done, the mother and daughter went out on to the piazza for a chat, and the girls had at last, an opportunity to ask Laura some of the many questions they were curious to put. Before long, however, Mr. Stanley who had been ever since tea, reading the paper by a shaded lamp in the sitting-room, lit a candle, extinguished the lamp, and coming out into the entry, went up stairs. At this his wife started from the comfortable chair which Laura had brought out for her.

"I must go in, my dear," she said ; "I'd like to sit and hear you talk; but I'm very tired to-night. Your father has gone up, too, and as he has had a very hard day in the field, he'll be wanting me to rub him." So, good-night, it's so pleasant to have you back my dear child."

She kissed Laura's cheek affectionately, and then went away, in a hurry as usual, quite running up stairs, in her haste to be at her own post of duty.

For a little longer the elder girls lingered with Laura ; but presently they too went to bed, leaving her to sit alone and enjoy the charmed stillness of the summer night. It was pleasant to listen to the still small sounds that alone broke the quiet; the faint rustle of the leaves, the chirp of the crickets in the grass, the chant of distant frogs ; to inhale the dewy freshness of the air, to look up at the few stars that shed their tremulous light through the trees, and watch the glitter of the fireflies as they sported under the bushes ! In the tranquil loneliness she fell into a sort of dream, and her thoughts floated away from the scene around her, to the wanderer who was now beyond the ocean.

CHAPTER XLIII.

COUNTRY COUSINS.

THE days that followed, went by monotonously. Laura
assisted her mother and sisters somewhat about the house,
but spent most of her time at her drawings. She was exceedingly anxious to perfect herself in oil-painting the
next winter, and worked hard on some orders she had
secured before leaving the city, in hopes of earning money
to carry out her plans. Around her, were the materials
for endless studies of flowers and scenery, and she had
such a regular routine of employment laid out for each
day, that it helped the weeks of the summer to a rapid
flight.

For the rest of the family, the toil went on endlessly;
sweeping and dusting, baking and churning; the perpetual
duties of a farm. Mr. Stanley working hard himself at
the out-door labor, and holding the women relentlessly to
their in-door tasks, though making always this difference
in his own favor, that when he came in to his evening repast, his day was done, and he would spend an hour or
more in reading his paper, while they must still be busy
over the housework, and then very likely have sewing to
do. He was very little with his family, except at meals,
but his presence was always an oppression; chilling their
mirth, stopping their talk. At his approach, the ripple of
girlish laughter would die away, and frigid silence reign,
so that his coming was secretly dreaded by every one of
them, his departure always welcome.

In July the pressure of the harvest came, and there
were often eight or ten laborers to be looked after. Some
extra assistance was indeed hired at this time, but it was a
relief to every one when August came, and the harvest
part of the work was done. Now, too, there was a little

leisure for visiting; young people drove out in the evening sometimes, and there were picnics in the woods, and occasionally a dance at a neighbor's house.

The younger girls enjoyed these merry-makings keenly; but to Laura they had very little attraction. Her college education, and her city life, had given her a superior culture, and a polish of manner which set her apart as it were, from those around her, and, although she was glad to meet her old friends, she yet felt a certain isolation even in the gayest scenes.

One favorite cousin, Laura had; Caroline Lee, the daughter of Mr. Nathan Lee, the uncle of whom Laura had spoken to Flora, as living near Dover Plains, and late in August, Laura went to pass a few days with this young lady. Caroline was a rosy-faced, sensible-looking girl, with a rough wit of her own; an accomplished horsewoman, and well-known as driving the best animals in that part of the country. She met Laura at the station on the cross-road that ran near the place, and giving her a hearty welcome, the two were presently spinning across the country, in Caroline's neat light wagon, behind a fine roan roadster.

"That's a nice horse of yours, Carrie," said Laura, admiringly.

"It is that! Broke him myself; one of the best colts I ever raised; gets over his mile about as quick as any nag hereabouts."

"You like horses as well as ever, then?"

"Indeed I do! I'd rather have a horse than a beau any day!" with a laugh.

"Then you don't think of marrying?"

"Not I! Men are very well, some of them, but Lord! When I see what slaves most women get to be after marriage, I've no fancy for putting the halter over my head; no, thank you!"

"But you may find the right man some day."

"Perhaps, though I don't see any prospect of it at present."

They were going through a small village now, and drew up before a trough, conveniently placed, to water the horse. Not far off was a village-store : a low shabby building with a well-worn piazza before it, and on this were seated a dozen or more men, all without their coats, all showing the effects of the day's toil; all absolutely idle.

"Now look there," Caroline said, as they drove away, indicating this group faintly with her whip ; "look at those miserable loafers! I counted them, fifteen able-bodied men gossiping their time away! I should like to know where you will find fifteen idle women in all this village! They have been working all day as hard as the men, and they must work half the night too! Why don't some of those lazy fellows go home and help put the babies to bed or wipe the dishes. I've no patience with them!"

"Why Carrie, how fierce you are !"

"I am, I know; this is one of my standing grievances. Drive any evening through any of these villages hereabouts, and you will find just such a lot of men lounging at the store ; big hulking fellows who ought to be helping their tired wives at home, and when I think what they talk about too ! why the stories that are retailed by these village gossips are so disgraceful that when any of us women drive up, they are still in a moment ; they know their conversation is not fit for us to hear. When I have a vote, I'll pass a law that every man away from home in the evening, except on business, shall be fined."

"Then you believe that women ought to vote ? " asked Laura.

"Indeed I do !" replied Carrie, decidedly ; "the idea of those men making laws for us women !" with broad scorn, "what a farce it is ! It would be only amusing to think of these good, but very heavy farmers, fancying themselves competent to form a government without the help of the smart bright women hereabouts, if it were not so unjust. Why only think how wrong it is to exclude the mothers from the school-board ! They who feel the deepest interest in the education of the children must stand back, and let the men, who are apt to pass it by carelessly, decide everything ! It, is an actual fact that the last school-board we had here, consisted of farmers who knew so little, that they were obliged to send for a woman-teacher from the next County to come and examine the candidates for the District School ; these candidates being all women, of course. Now, how unjust to allow women to be teachers and examiners, and yet not allow them to be voters ! ”

“ It is absurd,” replied Laura, “ and you know, I am as strong an advocate of our rights as you are.”

“ I am glad to hear it ; you must talk with father when we get home; he is only half convinced.”

“ How does George stand ? ”

“ George ! oh, he’s all right ! ” with a merry laugh, “ you know it is ridiculous to give him the ballot and deny it to me ! ”

They had been bowling along at a good pace and soon arrived at a fine farm-house, which seemed to smile a welcome at them from all its broad white face, with the setting sun lighting it up. They drove up to the gate which stood inside the elms that shaded the place, and a tall young fellow wearing a stained shirt and soiled trowsers, and having an old straw hat on his light hair, came running towards them. He had a red and freckled face, and his body was so put together that as he ran, his legs and arms shook as if they would drop from their sockets.

“ There’s George,” said Caroline.

“ How do you do, George,” said Laura.

A broad grin irradiated the young man’s face as he came to meet the two ladies, and shook Laura’s hand. “ I’m real glad to see you, Laura,” he said ; “ I am now, real glad.”

“ And I’m glad to be here, George.”

“ How are the girls ? How’s Kate ? ” this last, with a sheepish blush.

14*

"All well," replied Laura, smiling ; for George's fancy for Kate was an open secret.

Caroline must look after the horse before she could join Laura, but a tidy maid-servant showed the visitor to her room. Every where in this house there were sunshine and flowers, and pretty things, and after the restrained atmosphere of her home, it was a rest to Laura to be where something was thought of beside toil, and where the influences were congenial.

Just before tea, Mr. Lee, or "Uncle Nathan," as all the country side called him, came in. He was a slow, quiet man, with an amiable face and a kindly heart, and Laura interested him very much by telling him how near she came to running away to his house with a reluctant bride, in the spring. She did not give Flora's name, but outlined the main facts of the story.

"I wish you had brought her up," he said ; "I guess if she'd once got here, we'd have taken good care of her!"

"I knew you would," said Laura ; "and that was why I thought of bringing her to you."

"And so she's married, now, dear heart!" shaking his head; "well, well, it's a world of trouble!"

After tea as they all sat comfortably on the piazza, Carrie attacked her father on her favorite theme.

"Father," she said ; "Laura believes in Woman Suffrage as much as I do.

"Does she?" asked Mr. Lee, looking at her in mild surprise. "Well now, I wouldn't have thought she did!"

"I do, indeed!" confessed Laura.

"I'll tell you just what troubles me about this Woman's Rights talk," Mr. Lee said, slowly ; "it seems right, accordin' to the Declaration of Independence, that all the women as well as the men should vote, since they have to pay taxes and obey the laws. But then to my mind their comin' for'ard is agin Scripter."

"Against Scripture!" cried Laura. "Oh no, you cannot find any place in the Bible where it says that women must not vote."

"Well, that's so! But then St. Paul, he says—'a woman must keep silence in the churches.'"

"He says in the next verse that women must not braid their hair or wear pearls," retorted Laura; "do you believe that, uncle?"

"Well, I suppose that ain't to be taken literal."

"Neither is the other," put in Caroline; "St. Paul did not want women to make fools of themselves by preaching out of season, or putting on too many fal-lals. For my part, I think women had a good sight better be writing and reading good sermons, than piling a bushel basket full of rats on their heads, or bunching up their skirts into wrinkles, and walking like camels!"

"That's so, now!" said George, with a sudden guffaw.

"No one asked you," exclaimed Caroline, suppressing him instantly. She was the elder, had boxed his ears in childhood, and kept a masterful hand over him ever since.

"If you take St. Paul literally, Uncle Nathan," said Laura, "I've been very wicked all winter myself; for he says, 'I suffer not a woman to teach,' and I've been teach ing for six months."

"Well," replied Mr. Lee, pensively; "it's main confusing; but if it was clear to my mind that the Scripters gave the women the right, I'd be for having 'em vote."

"The Bible says, in the first chapter of Genesis, that at the beginning God gave to men and women both, the ruling power. 'He gave them dominion,' and said unto 'them,' 'replenish the earth and possess it.' These are the words; the right of governing was not confined to men alone. And direct power was afterwards given to Miriam and Deborah as leaders, and to Anna and other New Testament women as preachers. But I think we may agree to this much, that God intended women and men to be united in their lives; that he created them to be helpmeets for each other; and that woman's influence as well as man's is needed in government."

"Yes," said practical Carrie; "do you suppose we should have such places on the roads as there are between here and the Plains if we had women commissioners of roads? No, indeed! They are a disgrace, and whether I can vote or not, I shall make a fuss about it if they are not mended before long. I only wish I was path-master!'

CHAPTER XLIV.

FLORA APPEARS IN LITERATURE.

THE same August sun that was shining over the hill-country of the Hudson, was lighting up also the quaint old town of Newport, all astir now with the gayety and life of its annual throng of pleasure-seekers. All day long, daintily-dressed women and men strolled under the elms which shade its quiet streets, lounged in the library, or stared at the round tower that still guards so dumbly, its secret of centuries. All the morning, crowds of grotesquely-costumed people plunged into the surf that sweeps up ceaselessly on the hard sands; all the afternoon, hundreds of carriages rolled along the beach or out to the fort; all the evening, there was dancing in brilliant ball-rooms, or dreamy sailing over a summer sea.

At the most select hotel in the place, were assembled distinguished and wealthy people from all parts of the country; inhabiting the detached cottages, lying under the shadow of the trees in its court-yard, or crowded into the large caravansera itself. Mr. and Mrs. Le Roy were there, occupying one of the little fancy villas, but taking their meals at the hotel. Mrs. De Lancy Winthrop was there, her parlor on the corner, a favorite lounging-place; Maud Livingston was there, the acknowledged belle of the season, queening it royally over a score of admirers, and Elvira

Leighton and Eloise Dickinson were there, enjoying the blushing honors of *débutantes.*

The sensation of the moment among this circle, was the appearance of Flora's poem in " The Constellation," a favorite Magazine. There it was in the September number, just out, with the signature at the end of the piece, " Flora Livingston Le Roy," so that every one knew who the fair author was. An extra supply of the Magazine had been called for, on account of this article, and " The Constellation" was to be seen lying on the table in every fashionable parlor.

Flora enjoyed keenly the early excitement of this success. The emotion of beholding one's own thoughts in print for the first time, is one of the most intoxicating that life brings, and for a day or so, she revelled unchecked in the delight of reading her words in dainty type, and the triumph of seeing her name, side by side with some of those most honored in the land. Maud had indeed, seemed a little startled, and even shocked on hearing of this new exploit of her sister's; but Mr. Le Roy had been away for several days, and other friends had only words of flattery for the young author.

One morning Flora sat on the balcony of the cottage, looking off dreamily at the glimpses of the sea which she could catch through the branches of the trees, when she heard footsteps below and some one calling her name. Looking down she saw Mrs. Winthrop, who was approaching. She was dressed in a Watteau costume, with a fancy hat on her dark hair, and beside her walked Rudolph Ernstein, whom Flora had not seen since the day before her marriage; while behind the two followed a girl with fancy baskets for sale.

At the door of the cottage the young German left Mrs. Winthrop, who was alone when Flora met her in the parlor. As the two exchanged greetings the hostess said :

" Wasn't that Mr. Ernstein with you, Etta ? "

" Yes, he arrived last night."

" Why didn't he come in ? "

" He had some sort of engagement, I believe; but he said he would call by-and-bye. I am very glad he has come," she went on gaily; " for I shall renew my flirtation of last winter with him. I'm getting awfully bored with young Courteney."

" I thought you liked him very much," said Flora.

" Oh, well, so I did at first, but I'm tired of him now; you know I never can like one man more than two months at the outside, and he has been on hand a terribly long time. I had a little flirtation with him last summer, and that alone is sufficient objection to him this year. I'd as soon think of wearing last season's dresses, as of renewing last season's flirtation."

" How you do run on, Etta ! "

" Why not ? One must amuse oneself. But here, I am forgetting all this time that I brought a woman with me who has fancy-baskets to sell. Won't you buy one? They are the prettiest I have seen; I'm sure you will like them."

A scarlet flush rushed to Flora's cheeks. " No," she stammered; " I don't care for any."

" Well, do let her come in, now that I have brought her here," Mrs. Winthrop said, impatiently; " I am ashamed to send her away. They don't cost much, either; she has some very pretty ones for fifty cents."

" It's no use," replied Flora; " I can't buy any."

" But why not ? " persisted Mrs. Winthrop.

" Well, if you must know," said Flora, desperately; " because I haven't any money. I shall have some next week, when I am paid for my poetry, but I haven't any now."

Mrs. Winthrop stared in amazement for a second, then seeing how pained and distressed her friend looked, her better feelings suggested the kindest course, and she left the room and dismissed the woman, returning in a moment with an effort to seem oblivious of any thing that had passed. Flora had recovered herself somewhat, but

her cheeks were glowing deep red, and Mrs. Winthrop's
first words were in allusion to this."

"Do you know, Flora," she said; "you have more
color this summer, than I ever knew you to have before?"

"Have I? Yes, I think I have; my cheeks burn almost
all the time."

"Oh, that's it?" questioning; "You know how disagreeable the Norrys always are; well, one of them said
the other day that you rouged. I denied it indignantly."

"You were right," replied Flora; "I don't need any
artificial color; I think I have a perpetual fever; put your
hand on my cheek."

"Why, it is burning hot!" Mrs. Winthrop cried, in dismay, as she touched her fingers to her friend's soft skin.

"And my hand, too;" and Flora put her small hot hand
into her guest's.

"Why Flora!" exclaimed Mrs. Winthrop, looking at
her with genuine anxiety; "you are ill in some way,"
then, as if catching a brilliant thought; "you are writing too much; it must be the poetry."

"No," replied Flora, with a smile; "it is not that; I
enjoy writing so well that I am sure it can't hurt me. It
is the only real pleasure I have."

"The idea of your saying that, Flora! However, I
think it must be rather nice to have some occupation."

"You make flirting your business," Flora replied.

"Well, yes, I do; I like to pursue it as a fine art; one
must have something to do."

"And do you expect always to flirt, Etta."

"As long as I can; after I am too old, I hope I shall
die."

"Oh, Etta!"

"Well, seriously, Flora, what *can* we women do? I
should like to have some active work, but society says No.
Wear fine clothes, make visits, amuse yourself, that is your
lot in life! When I was a little girl with my brothers,
and they talked of what they were going to be, I used to

say that I was going to be a lawyer; they would laugh,
but I believe I could really have made a good lawyer if I
had been trained to it. As it is, I have fulfilled my destiny, by marrying a rich man, and now must kill time as
well as I can."

Flora looked at her in surprise. "Why, Etta, I never
expected to hear you talk so earnestly ! "

"No; I know every one thinks I am only a frivolous
butterfly," replied Mrs. Winthrop; "but I do have some
serious thoughts, and some sad ones too, though no one
can understand it. The other day I told De Lancey I
wished I had something to do, and he looked at me in
amazement : 'Get some new fancy-work,' said he; 'I'll
order any thing for you from town that you want.' He
thought that I ought to be quite satisfied with that! When
he was sick last winter, and so restless because he could
not go down town, I wonder how he would have liked it
if I had told him to get a stick and whittle it into some
fancy pattern ! " and she laughed, somewhat bitterly.

"Of course," said Flora ; "women need an occupation
and an object in life, as much as men."

"And you mean to be a literary lady ? "

"I hope so; if I had not that hope I think life would
not be worth living."

"Oh well, we might as well make the best of it as it is,"
Mrs. Winthrop said, resuming her light manner; "take the
goods the gods provide, and enjoy as much as we can. There
is Mr. Ernstein, now," she added, catching sight of the approaching figure.

The young German stepped slowly, and half-timidly on
to the piazza, but Flora went forward to meet him with a
frankly cordial greeting, and so brought him into the parlor. A moment after, a gay party of callers dropped in,
and when they left, Mrs. Winthrop went away with them,
as they were going to make a visit at a house where she
wished to go.

When Flora and Mr. Ernstein were left alone together,

there was a moment of embarrassed silence. Flora sat playing with the ruffles of her white morning-dress; the young German watching her with intense, almost reverential admiration in his dark eyes. Looking up, Flora caught the glance, and colored faintly, as she said :

"I want to thank you for your kindness in taking that note to my friend."

"It was in time, then?"

"Yes," with a faint sigh; "it was in time."

"I only wish I could have done more for you," the young man said, earnestly; "I offered to help Miss Stanley, but she thought I could be of no further use."

"No," replied Flora; "you could not have helped us; but it was very good of you to offer—" then changing the subject—"Have you travelled far since I saw you?"

"Yes, as far as California; I thought to have returned to my home, by making the trip around the world; but when I looked at the Pacific, I felt as if I could not put its waves between me and all my friends here, and so I turned my steps back again, and here I am."

"Newport is very pleasant now."

"Very;" then earnestly, "but Mrs. Le Roy may I tell you? I have read your poem—it is so beautiful!"

"You like it?" Flora said, with a gratified smile.

"Like it! I have learned it by heart; it sings itself in my memory all day."

Flora was a little embarrassed. "It was a pleasure to me to write it," she said.

"And you have written others."

"Yes, several."

"Would you show me any?"

Flora hesitated a moment. "Yes," she said; "there is one little translation I have made of a minor poem of Goethe's, that I should like to show you."

Ernstein expressed his delight in earnest words, and Flora brought from her desk, the precious album in which she had collected her verses and stories.

"Do you remember," she asked, "some lines of Goethe's entitled ' *Das Bächlein ?* '"

"Indeed I do. I used to read them at school; I think I can recollect almost exactly the German words."

"Then you can judge the better of this," and Flora read in her soft sweet tones, her simple translation,

" THE BROOKLET."

" Thou brooklet, silver bright and clear,
  That wanders ever onward here,
  I pause and ask, in dream suspense,
  Whence comest thou here? Where goest thou hence?

" I come from darksome rocky caves,
  With flowers and moss I deck my waves,
  Upon the mirror of my breast,
  The calm blue heaven's reflected rest.

" Like happy children, free from care
  I wander forth, I know not where,
  He who has called me from the stone
  He, sure, will guide me safely on."

While she was reading, the young German watched her with all his soul in his eyes; looking at her as a worshipper in the old countries of Europe might look at a fair image of the Madonna.

As her voice died away he was silent a moment, then he did not break forth with extravagant admiration, but his few well-chosen phrases expressed greater homage than any she had yet received.

" I am not satisfied with the third line of the first verse," Flora said; " but I was so anxious to preserve the literal translation of the last line that I constructed the third with reference to that."

"It is admirable," Ernstein replied; " you have caught the spirit of the poem so entirely."

They talked a few moments longer, and Flora sat listening to him with a pleased light in her eyes and a faint color suffusing her whole face, when suddenly there was a quick step on the piazza, and Mr. Le Roy strode into the room.

Every particle of light faded from Flora's eyes, the rosy tint left her cheeks; she started up, dropping her book and trembling with an emotion she could not repress.

Mr. Le Roy was himself unusually pale; he had in his hand a copy of " the Constellation " which he threw on to the table, as he noticed there was a stranger in the room. He bowed slightly to his wife, greeted Ernstein courteously, and Flora resumed her seat with an effort at self-control.

The young German, who guessed that something was wrong, sat a few moments longer conversing with the ease of a man of the world on indifferent topics, then rose to take his leave. Mr. Le Roy politely urged him to call again, and Flora who had remained almost silent since her husband's coming, murmured some words of farewell. Ernstein responded appropriately, and so hurried himself out, and the husband and wife were alone.

Flora sank back into the chair; a tremor running through all her veins. Mr. Le Roy stood before her, his eyes blazing with a keen steely light.

"Flora," he said, " did you write the lines that bear your name in that Magazine?" pointing with intense scorn to " the Constellation."

" Yes."

"Then it is not a malicious forgery; but you have deliberately outraged me, by bringing yourself before the public."

Flora did not reply, but the blood swept back to cheeks and brow, and her lovely eyes grew dark with indignation

"I want words to express my displeasure!" Mr. Le Roy went on, violently: "During the last two days in New York, a dozen men have told me that they had read my wife's poem," with bitter emphasis; "and in half the evening papers I have seen, your name has greeted me in some conspicuous place."

Heart-sick as she was of the conflict that was to come, Flora's pulses beat with delight at these words. " Was it mentioned disrespectfully ? " she asked.

" No ; but it ought not to be mentioned at all," replied Mr. Le Roy ; " Good God ! Do you think I want you to be discussed in any way ? The idea of my wife's name being in the paper ! " with wrathful impatience.

" I cannot see anything wrong in it," said Flora, firmly ; " you do not withhold your own name from public meetings or movements in which you are interested."

" That is entirely different," asserted Mr. Le Roy ; " I am a man."

" And I believe that I have as much right to my individuality as you have to yours."

" You seem to forget that you are a woman and my wife ! " said Mr. Le Roy, with a sneer.

" I do not forget either," replied Flora, calmly ; " nor do I see why I should lose my liberty on account of either fact. You would not think that I had any right to interfere with your movements ; and I do not recognize that you have any greater right to coerce me."

" Then you intend to continue to print your trash in any paper that will take it ? "

" I intend to publish all that is considered by good authority, worth publishing."

" You will do nothing of the kind ! " he cried, angrily. " I absolutely forbid you ever again to print anything ! " Flora did not reply, and he went on, hotly. " *Flora Livingston Le Roy*, the idea of your being known in that way ; why you haven't really any right to any name but mine ! "

" Then you wish me hereafter to sign my letters, Mrs. Ferdinand Le Roy," with a faint twinkle of amusement.

" I forbid you ever again to print under any circumstances," he retorted ; then as she did not answer ; " do you hear ? "

"Yes, I hear."

"And will you obey?"

"No."

Mr. Le Roy looked at her, growing white with rage. Flora had become very pale again, but her eyes met his, resolutely. "You refuse to obey me?"

"I refuse to yield to what I consider an unreasonable and cruel request," she said.

"Have you forgotten your marriage-vows?" he demanded, furiously.

"No more than you have forgotten yours, Mr. Le Roy," very quietly; "I do not believe that under any circumstances you have the right to thwart my aspirations, to stifle my soul, to destroy my life. You swore 'to love and to cherish' me; for the love, I know what that means," with a gesture of infinite disgust; "for the kindness, the tenderness, the gentleness I had a right to expect, I have looked in vain. My vows, so far as I uttered them, were reluctant ones, as you know. In spite of that, I have done a wife's duty to you thus far; but I absolutely refuse to yield my hopes and objects in life."

"Then you intend to pursue the career of a blue-stocking, a literary woman;" uttering the words contemptuously.

"Yes, you do not give me any money, I will earn some for myself; you do not make my life happy, I will at least try to make it not an aimless one; and I decline to dispute with you further on this point."

As she spoke, she rose as if to leave the room, and took one step away. Mr. Le Roy sprang after her and caught her about the waist. "Flora," he said, hissing the words in her ear; "you *shall not* parade your name before the public; I *will* be obeyed; I am master here and you shall learn to know it."

She looked at him now, with a white and startled face, a cold fear in her blue eyes, and he let her go with a mocking laugh. As she staggered away, her eyes fell on her

book of manuscripts which lay open on the floor. She
turned as if to pick it up, but her husband was too quick
for her; he caught her look, saw what it meant, and
springing before her, picked up the book.

"More nonsense!" he cried; "no, you shall never see
this again."

With strong hands he tore it across, once, twice, and
tossed the fragments into the open fireplace, flinging a
lighted match upon them.

Flora uttered a cry as if he had been tearing her own
flesh, and as the flames curled up to devour the fruits of
her thought, she fell on the floor in a dead swoon.

CHAPTER XLV.

JUDGE SWINTON IS NOMINATED FOR CONGRESS.

AT another hotel in Newport on the same August
morning, there sat a group of men reading their papers and
smoking their cigars, and, according to their views of life,
enjoying themselves. This house was larger, more showy,
and more noisy, than the establishment where the Le Roys
were staying. Here on the broad piazzas and in the great
parlor might be seen gorgeously-dressed western women,
handsome and loud-voiced; returned Californians, quick-
eyed and eager, supposed to possess fabulous wealth, and
people from the eastern cities; people who liked fierce excitement and fast living. Here all day long there sounded
the click of billiard-balls and the roll of ten-pin bowls; and
here all night long there were music and dancing.

It was under the shade of the high roof of what was
called the gentlemen's piazza, that these men were lounging and reading the New York papers which had just come.
Among them was Judge Swinton, dressed in a light morning costume, looking fresh and handsome after a week of
what he called rest. It was in truth only a change of dis-
sipation; but the bracing air, the daily plunge into the surf,

had invigorated his strong frame, and he was in full and florid health. He turned over the pages of the New York Trumpeter, at first carelessly, then with sudden interest reading eagerly a narrative which was showily headed, "Murder in the Eighth Ward!" "Row in a drinking-saloon!" "The fatal shot!" "Several notorious roughs arrested!" etc.

He glanced quickly down the column, and then turned to a man who sat beside him. This last was a large person with a broad face and iron-gray hair, wearing a showy waistcoat, and having a great diamond blazing on his shirt-front.

"Tyne," said the judge; "this is a bad business in New York yesterday."

"What is it?" asked Mr. Tyne, laying down his own paper.

"There was a row at Bludgett's yesterday morning; a man named Potter went in to get a drink, and somehow he was killed. It don't appear to be clear who did it, but they've arrested Bludgett and Bangs and Snaggers, and two or three more of our best fellows. Here, just run your eye over this."

"I suppose it's in my own paper," said Mr. Tyne.

"Oh, you have the Planet; well, just see what that says about it."

"Here it is," replied Mr. Tyne, after turning his paper over a moment. "Hum—um—" as he read—"that's a bother! Do you know this Potter?"

"Yes, he's a very efficient man on the other side," with emphasis; "he's well rid of; but then we can't afford to have these fellows of ours all shut up till after election."

"No, no, of course not," Mr. Tyne assented, quickly; "they must be got off somehow."

"Yes, I'm afraid it will cost me a trip to the city, and that's a bore just now. I'll telegraph and see what can be done."

The judge left his seat and walked towards the office.

There was a heavy frown on his brow as he went; within
the last two weeks he had been introduced to Maud Livingston, and her haughty beauty had captured his errant
fancy. Laura was quite forgotten in this new pursuit, and
he was vexed at the possibility of its interruption. As he
approached the telegraph operator's desk, he was met by a
waiter.

"Judge Swinton?" asked the man.

"Yes."

"There's a woman who wants to see you."

"A woman," replied the judge, with a flush; "where is
she?"

"She's in the lower waiting-room; she's a—quite a plain
person," the man explained.

"Very well; show me to her."

The waiter led the way, the judge following to a side
room, used at some hours of the day as a sort of servants'
hall; there was no one in it now, but a shabbily-dressed,
frightened-looking woman.

"Mrs. Bludgett!" cried Swinton, as he caught sight of
the pale face and hollow eyes of the creature. "Your
husband sent you," he added, eagerly. "I have just seen
the paper. Tell me all about it."

She began to cry as soon as he spoke, looking indeed, as
if she had been crying almost all the time. "Oh dear," she
sobbed. "It is so dreadful! I only saw Bludgett for a
moment after he was took, and he said I was to find you,
sir."

"There, there, don't cry so," the judge said, impatiently;
"I'll get him out for you."

"Oh, I hope you will! I hope you will, sir! To think
that he should be in prison! I know I ought not to cry—"
struggling with her tears; "but I have had such a time!
I had to go to the boat alone, and after I got here, I thought
I should never find you!"

"Well, you have found me now, so try to tell me how
it all happened."

The woman put down the corner of the shawl with which she had been smearing her eyes, and looked at him with a kind of cold horror. "He done it," she whispered.

"Bludgett?" in a low tone.

"Yes."

"How do you know?"

"I was there—" with a shudder. "He hadn't been home all night. I was so worried, that I went out to the Sample-Room just to see what had become of him. He —he didn't like my coming," she said, putting her hand involuntarily to her side, where a deep bruise attested how he had shown his displeasure at her arrival. "I went behind the screen and just then these men come in; they was quarrelling when they come, and Potter, he presently tried to chaff Bludgett about the 'lection;' Bludgett was kinder —kinder—" casting about for a word, by which to express his state of mind, mildly—"he was put about you know, and tired, most likely, and so the man fretted him, and—and —there was pistols drawn; but it was Bludgett that fired the shot. Oh, I know it was! I seen it! I seen it! The man fell down all over blood," beginning to sob again.

"That's bad, very bad," said the judge, after a pause; "did any one else see it but you?"

"The other men must have seen it," faintly.

"Who were in the shop?"

"Only Bangs and Snuggers and Jones."

"Ah! all our men!" said the judge, brightening; "I think we can fix it; Mrs. Bludgett don't be so unhappy about it, I guess we can get your husband off."

"Oh, but how can you, when he done it?"

"What if he did? You won't tell that, I suppose."

"Will they ask me?" in a frightened whisper.

"Yes, very likely."

"Oh dear, oh dear, what shall I do?" and the poor creature rocked herself to and fro in agony.

The judge looked at her a moment with a puzzled face,

15

then he said : " I'll tell you what we will do, Mrs. Bludgett, I shall take the first train to New York and you
must go back with me."

" Yes sir."

" You can wait here till it is time to go ; " he turned to
leave the room, then said ;—" you can get some breakfast
if you like."

" Oh no, sir, I couldn't eat a morsel, I've tried to eat
and I've tried to read, but I can't do it. I'll just wait
here till you want me."

" Very well, make yourself as comfortable as you can,"
he said, not unkindly, " and try to cheer up, I'll get your
husband off, surely."

At this the poor woman only moaned feebly to herself,
" But he done it, I seen him ! " and presently, when alone,
laid her head down on a table that stood by her chair, and
so seemed to sob herself to sleep ; her hands fell nervelessly
by her side, and a book which had been hidden under her
shawl dropped on to the floor, displaying its showy cover
and amazing title: " The Haunted Behemoth, or the Hell-
hound of Andalusia ; a tale of Spain and the Alhambra."

Judge Swinton made good use of his time ; he found
among his Newport friends, some men who were familiar
with the net-work of New York politics, and three of them,
among whom was Mr. Tyne, together with Mrs. Bludgett
went back to the city with him. It was wholly detestable
now, with vile smells and foul airs reeking from every
narrow street and blind alley, and it was among these low
haunts that a great portion of these gentlemen's time was
passed for the next few days. Quite satisfactorily however to them, apparently, as when they met for refresh-
ments after their hard work, they drank each other's health
with many knowing winks and expressions of satisfaction.

The coroner's inquest over the body of the murdered
Potter, was conducted, during two long sultry mornings ;
the only witnesses were, of course, the people who had
been in the drinking-saloon. The men all swore that a

stranger who had accompanied Potter, had fired the fatal shot, and immediately after, in the confusion caused by his death, escaped from the shop. Mrs. Bludgett, who was put on the stand, kept her eyes fixed on her husband's with a piteous pleading look, all the time that she gave her testimony. It was, so far as could be gathered from her almost inaudible words, corroborative of the others, and so the four men were released with a verdict from the jury that "The deceased came to his death by a pistol-shot fired by some person to them unknown."

A night or two after this, a great political meeting was held in a large hall on the west side. Speeches were made by several prominent leaders of the party, and then Mr. Tyne nominated Judge Swinton as candidate for Congress, from the IVth district. The nomination was solemnly seconded by Mr. Moulder, and carried by acclamation; Bangs and Snuggers being foremost in demonstrations of approval. Afterwards the judge addressed his constituents on "the duties of the hour," and "the responsibilities of the high position to which he aspired," pledging himself to advocate "liberty, justice, and the principles for which our forefathers fought," and closing with a fervent declaration of his "entire devotion to the great party whose standard-bearer he hoped to be."

CHAPTER XLVI.

A LAST APPEAL.

WHILE these busy scenes were absorbing the energies of some of the rulers of New York City, while Laura was enjoying her few days of idleness with her cousins, taking endless drives over the country with Carrie, and playing croquet on the pleasant lawn at evening, her friend Flora Livingston lay ill, devoured by a fever that for days threatened to destroy her life.

It was hours before she recovered from the swoon into which she had fallen on that unhappy morning, and when she regained consciousness, it was not to come back to healthful life, but only to pass into the wild wilderness of delirium. She lay on the low bed in her cottage-room, looking by day at the splashes of sunlight that glittered in through the swaying branches of the trees, weaving strange fancies of fairy scenes, or listened at night to the solemn tones of the waves, dreaming of wide solitudes and infinite spaces, and babbling of a world of freedom beyond the stars.

In addition to the attendants who had accompanied Mr. and Mrs. Le Roy to Newport and who were the starched man-servant, and Clarisse, Flora's French maid, a competent nurse was hired to watch over the poor sick lady. Every morning Mr. Le Roy came to ask how his wife was, and every morning as Flora's glittering eyes encountered his, she shuddered and turned her face away with a cry of pain. Mrs. Livingston sat by her daughter's side many hours of each day ; and occasionally Maud swept in, radiant with the glory of fresh conquests, though somewhat annoyed at the temporary check to her gayeties which her sister's dangerous illness involved, and hosts of friends called to inquire after the invalid's health.

One afternoon as sunset was drawing on, after a long sleep, Flora opened her eyes and the light of reason had come back to them ; her mother who sat beside her, leaned forward to kiss her with some murmured words of joy that she was better.

"Am I better ? " asked Flora, softly.

" Yes, my dear, I hope so ; much better, and that you will soon be well ; but the doctor said you were not to talk much.

" What doctor have I had ? "

" Dr. Huntly ; it was so fortunate that he happened to have a cottage here this summer."

" When will he be here again ? "

"This evening; he generally comes about eight o'clock."

Flora said nothing more, but lay with half-closed eyes, looking very white and thin, now that the fever flush was gone. After a time she dozed again; but when the doctor came in, she was quite herself once more; was propped up in bed, and seemed anxious to talk with him.

The physician was a kindly, white-haired old gentleman, who had attended the family since Flora was a baby, and showed genuine pleasure at his patient's improvement.

"Better, decidedly better, my dear Mrs. Le Roy," he said, as he felt her pulse; "weak, of course, but we shall soon build you up, I hope."

"Then you think I shall get well?" she asked, fixing her large blue eyes on his face.

"Certainly, my dear young lady, certainly. You have had a severe illness, but you are young, not a very strong constitution, I remember, but I hope I shall soon see you about again."

"How soon shall I be well?"

The doctor shook his head. "I cannot promise; you must be patient for awhile, you may be a little slow in entirely recovering; I shall rather look for a rise of fever towards night for some time to come, but you will gain, no doubt, from this day. Any appetite, nurse?"

"Yes sir, Mrs. Le Roy ate a bit of toast to-night, it was not much, but more than she has taken before since she was ill."

"Good, very good."

And so the doctor went away, and had many expressions of encouragement regarding Flora's condition for her husband, her mother, and all inquiring friends.

For a few days more the invalid was very quiet, pale and feeble, but as the doctor had predicted, slowly gaining strength. Towards evening she sometimes had a return of fever, but at the end of a week she was certainly stronger, and often was able to rise from the bed for a

little while, and sit on the balcony that looked towards the
sea.   Here she would recline, watching the gorgeous
autumn sunsets fade over the waters, marking the slow
advance of the enfolding darkness, listening ever to the
appealing voice of the unresting ocean—calling sometimes
with a moan of yearning—whispering sometimes of the
peace and rest beneath its waves.

Gradually Flora was able to see a few friends; to talk
a little.   When Mr. Le Roy came in now, she received his
polite expressions of satisfaction at her recovery with some
suitable reply; but always avoiding his eyes, as if their
look hurt her, and invariably expressing fatigue when his
visits were prolonged, so that he was forced to withdraw,
the dictates of the invalid being on these points, as yet, impossible of contradiction.   Among the friends who came
to call on her was Mrs. Winthrop, who was admitted
despite some disapprobation on the part of Mr. Le Roy,
because her lively chat amused Flora.   Elvira Leighton
and Eloise Dickinson, too, were frequent visitors, their
light-hearted school-girl talk serving to enliven some of
the weary hours of convalescence.   Of course no gentlemen were received; but more than once as Flora leaned
over the balcony to inhale the refreshing breeze that blew
from the ocean, she caught a glimpse of young Ernstein,
who took his evening walk past her cottage, and had she
cared to watch, she might have noticed him lounging
sometimes near it, as an adorer will linger near the shrine
of a saint.

The days drew on and on, and September set his golden
seal on the year ; bright poppies, and flaming hollyhocks
glowed in the gardens ; a few autumn leaves hung themselves on the maple trees, and the golden-rod stood up tall
and graceful by the road-sides.   At morning, mists crept
up from the ocean and enwrapped all the village, and at
evening, heavy clouds hung low along the horizon, while
the storms out at sea, sent their echoes to the shore in the
louder wail of the clamoring breakers.

At the end of three weeks from the time when Flora was taken ill, she was much better, was able to walk about her room now, and even to go down stairs; but still, although so much stronger, having always some fever towards nightfall, which made her restless and often gave her sleep haunted by wild dreams.

"Do you really think I am better?" she said to the doctor one morning.

"Better my dear lady, certainly; not well yet, but I can see a great improvement since a week ago."

"Yes, I am stronger than I was then; but in the last few days I don't seem to have gained at all."

"There is a lack of vitality I will admit, Mrs. Le Roy; a want of elasticity in your constitution; but with care I hope you will convalesce more rapidly; perhaps a trip to the mountains may benefit you."

"Then I shall certainly be well some day?" looking at him, wistfully.

"Assuredly, my dear young lady," replied the doctor regarding her with a puzzled trouble; "are you very anxious to recover?"

"Oh no, I don't care much," and she turned away with a sigh.

The good physician looked at her earnestly; were there tears in her eyes? "Mrs. Le Roy needs cheering," he said, when he met her husband on the way to her room as he left it; "all the society that she can bear, music, flowers; not too much excitement, but amusement."

"Certainly," replied Mr. Le Roy; "I am quite willing to have her friends come to her. I will go out this evening and bring my sister to visit her."

Dr. Huntly remembered Mrs. Courteney's cold, stately demeanor, and thought that her society would scarcely be so cheerful as he could wish, however he had said what he could; he had done his duty.

When Mr. Le Roy entered his wife's room, she was wrapped in a crimson shawl, and seated in a wide arm-chair drawn up near the window; it was a cool evening, but the sash was open and Flora was looking out at the red light that flushed the sky and glowed over the sea. At the sound of her husband's step, she turned her head languidly.

"Flora you are very imprudent to be sitting in that open window," were his first words.

"I am warmly dressed," she replied; "and I like to feel the air, and listen to the sound of the waves."

Mr. Le Roy closed the sash with a firm hand; "I cannot permit such an exposure," he said.

His wife did not reply, but her thin cheeks flushed, the fever had come upon her and she threw back her shawl, showing the soft white wrapper that enveloped her slender frame. As Mr. Le Roy took his seat, the nurse who sat sewing at the window, put down her work and left the room.

"How do you feel this evening, Flora?" Mr. Le Roy asked.

"About the same."

"Dr. Huntly says you need more society; that you want cheering."

"I will tell you what I need more than that."

"Well, what.is it?"

She turned to him with sudden earnestness: "I need an object in life, Mr. Le Roy; when—when I was taken sick, you had said that I should never write any thing more. If you will unsay that, I shall get well."

A frown settled on Mr. Le Roy's face. "Flora," he replied; "I thought that this painful subject would never be reopened between us. I expressed my wishes then and hoped it would be sufficient.

"But I don't believe you thought about what you said," Flora rejoined, looking at him pleadingly; "that is, you know, it was just at first, and I don't think you realized all it would be to me to give up my writing. It came upon you so suddenly, and you were vexed, I know, but now, if

I tell you all, I'm sure you will not object to my doing what makes me so happy."

" You are only reopening a fruitless discussion," her husband said, coldly.

" Oh, I hope not, I hope you will not say so when I tell you all ; " her cheeks were burning now, her soft eyes full of piteous entreaty. " I have so longed to have an occupation, a pursuit, and it has given me so much pleasure to write my verses and stories."

" I have no objection to your *writing* them," Mr. Le Roy said, with significant emphasis.

" But it does not satisfy me to write them for my own eyes alone," she said; " I long to have others read my thoughts. I was so happy the other day when my piece came out. I felt as if I could be well and strong and—and enjoy life as I used. You will let me write again when I am able to, won't you ? " with intense longing in the voice.

Even Mr. Le Roy was in some dull way touched. "You are ill, now, Flora," he said ; " and you attach more importance to this fancy of yours than you would otherwise. When you are well, you will soon learn to forget it."

" I shall never be well if you take away my hope," she said, mournfully.

"Oh yes, you will ; you are only nervous and low-spirited, now."

"You are not answering my question," she said, feverishly; "Mr. Le Roy, I ask you, I entreat you, to give me permission to resume my writing."

" And publishing ? "

" Yes."

" I cannot do it," he said; " you do not understand. I have a horror of woman's rights, in every form. I think that women should be quiet and retired; I dislike more than I can tell you, to see any woman's name in print, and to have your name paraded before the public is something I cannot and will not endure ; " his cold autocratic manner returning.

15*

"Then you take away my one hope," very sadly.

"It is only your fancy to speak of it in that way," he said, impatiently; "you have everything to make life happy; this is only an invalid's fancy."

Flora did not reply. She leaned her head back in her chair wearily, and closed her eyes; her blood was throbbing in her veins; a tide was beating in her brain like the tide outside. The sunset had faded, night had fallen, and the voice of the waves sounded through the hollow darkness, hoarsely, threateningly.

Her husband sat a few moments longer, looking at her with a vague uneasiness, then he said; "I will tell Mary to bring in the lights, and then I will go over and get my sister to come and spend the evening with you. It will help to cheer you."

She still did not speak, and he slowly left the room. In a few moments the nurse returned with a candle and was about to light a shaded lamp.

"Don't light that," Flora said; "put the candle on the shelf, that will be enough; and now, Mary, I want you to go an errand for me."

"Directly, ma'am?"

"Yes."

"But I don't like leaving you alone, ma'am."

"Oh, never mind that," replied Flora, quickly; "I can ring for Clarisse if I need anything. I want you to go to the bookstore and buy me a new book, I don't care what, some novel or story."

"But it's quite a ways to the bookstore, ma'am. It will take me quite a time to go;" objected Mary.

"That is no matter; go as quickly as you can, we have an account there, so that you need not take any money."

"Yes ma'am."

The woman turned to put on her hat and shawl, and although she was not particularly slow in her movements, Flora presently called to her impatiently:

"Do hurry, Mary."

"Yes ma'am, I'm all ready now," and she came to the sick lady ; then looking at her anxiously, she said : "I don't really like to go."

"Oh yes, go ! go ! Do go ! and go quickly," Flora replied ; and the woman left the room.

CHAPTER XLVII.

THE END OF FLORA'S DREAM.

WHEN she was alone, Flora started up, and with trembling hands opened the window and went out on to the balcony. Night had fallen now, the branches of the trees swayed, the leaves rustled mournfully, the ceaseless voice of the ocean chimed monotonously, the breeze that blew across her fevered brow did not cool it.

"Go back to life," she cried, wildly ; " endure what I must endure ! Be his obedient slave ! Crush out every noble aspiration, sink down into a mere creature of his caprices ! No, no ! Better an endless rest ! "

She walked up and down the balcony, restlessly, her blue eyes glowing with a strange light ; then, suddenly turning, went into the house and passed down the stairs through a side door and so on into the darkness. She had wrapped her crimson shawl closely around her, and glided on with quick footsteps, taking the path to the sea.

The place was secluded ; the summer visitors had, many of them gone away ; the night was cold and moonless, and there were no groups of pleasure-seekers abroad. There was one person, however, who saw the fugitive. Rudolph Ernstein, who had been lounging near the cottage, saw Flora as she left it, and intensely startled and alarmed, ventured to follow her at a distance.

She hurried on, the sound of the in-coming tide ever louder in her ears ; the toss of the wind smiting her brow more sharply—a swift walk across the grass, down a road, over some waste fields, and she was on the rocks overhanging the ocean.

Running now, her white dress trailing behind her, her fair hair floating half-disordered on her shoulders, her breath coming in quick gasps, the light of a terrible resolution in her wide eyes.

To her brain-sick fancy, in the great arch of the heavens the stars swung and flamed, beckoning her to join in their mystic dance. Around her the rocks lay black, monstrous, cold, sliding under her feet, warning her away. Beneath her, the sea stretched ; vast, spectral, reaching away to the confines of the world, while the waves came leaping toward her, one over the other, hurrying, hurrying, always. Crowding and tearing in a mad struggle, till they flung themselves on the cold stones with an angry roar, and stretched up their white foam-tipped fingers, trying to seize her ; calling to her, calling to her, with their hollow voices.

In a moment she stood swaying and trembling on the edge of an overhanging cliff ; then she stretched her arms upwards, with a strange wild cry, and sprang into the clamorous sea.

Her cry was reëchoed by a startled shout. The young German had been watching her with constantly increasing terror ; he had not liked to appear to be pursuing her, and she had gone so swiftly that he could not come up with her, unless he ran. He was within two paces of her when she made her mad plunge, and an instant after her head disappeared under the waters, he sprang into the ocean to save her.

A moment and he had caught her in his arms, and was battling with the billows struggling for a foot-hold on the rocks. It was a rising tide and this helped him ; he had presently staggered with her to safety and was climbing slowly up the jagged face of the cliff. He reached the top, panting and exhausted, and paused a moment to take breath.

Flora lay in his arms utterly unconscious ; her face white as the face of the dead ; her fair hair fallen in a wet mass on his arm; her damp garments clinging around her slender figure.

So fair ! So fair ! in the pale starlight, the delicate features, the closed eyelids, were exquisite as some sculptured form, and the young man gazed down on her, his dark eyes full of the tenderest compassion and admiration. Then as he saw how utterly motionless she lay, a sudden horror came over him ; he bent his head low, but could perceive no breath through the parted lips.

" My God ! can she be dead, already ! "

He started up again, hastening on, his feet winged with terror. He was a strong man, and she but a light burden, and so half running, half walking, but hurrying always, he brought her, after a few moments to the cottage.

As he approached it, he saw that there was already an alarm ; lights were moving about, and as he came to the door, people hurried down the stairs to meet him. They were only the servants, however, but as he laid his inanimate burden on the sofa in the parlor, Mr. Le Roy and Mrs. Courteney entered it with the decorous propriety of evening visitors.

It seemed to Ernstein impossible to exchange words with them ; he had given a brief explanation to the nurse, and he now hurried out, merely returning the surprised and somewhat cold salutation of the brother and sister, with a bow as frigid as their own.

When they learned what had occurred, there was consternation, deep and overwhelming. To Mr. Le Roy it seemed so shocking, so improper, that his wife should have tried to drown herself, and been rescued by a stranger ! He could find it in his heart to be intensely angry with her, even while she lay utterly insensible to his approval or disapproval. Mrs. Courteney quite agreed with him that it was "very unfortunate."

" Very annoying; very unpleasant that Mrs. Le Roy

had done this," the lady said, as they conversed together
down stairs; while the physician and servants were above,
trying to bring back life to the poor pale frame. "But
she was always inclined to be unconventional; the publication of that poetry was quite, you know, quite out of the
way, and now this freak is extraordinary, deplorable!"

"It may be possible, however, to avoid the discussion
of it," Mr. Le Roy said; "so few persons are aware of the
occurrence that I think that by judicious management we
may be able to prevent gossip."

"Oh, by all means, if it is possible, let us have no gossip,"
replied Mrs. Courteney; "I have such a horror of gossip."

And so when the Newport world heard the next day
that Mrs. Le Roy was very much worse, hardly expected to
live, indeed, it was reported simply that she had had a
relapse.

No hope now, as the days dropped away into the eternity
of the past, Flora's life faded, fairer and paler her eyes
looking out dimly on the forms around her, among whom
she would soon be a shadow, she watched in a half conscious dream, the sunlight trail across the wall, and heard the
echo of the waves as if it had been the cry of her own soul.

One wild autumn night, when the moon was looking
through bits of jagged cloud, and a storm was dying away
over the sea, the end came.

Flora opened her eyes after an uneasy sleep; her mother
sat beside her; a night-lamp burned dimly on the table;
broad splashes of moonlight shone into the room through
the ragged branches of the trees.

"Mamma," she said, faintly.

"Yes, my dear," and Mrs. Livingston, looking worn
and sad, leaned forward to take her daughter's hand.

"Mamma, don't let any of the other girls marry men
they don't love."

"Oh, Flora!"

"No, mamma, don't urge them to marry any man,
however rich he may be, from any motive but affection."

"My dear, my dear! you break my heart!" said Mrs. Livingston, sobbing; "I did what I thought best for you."

"I know you did, mamma, there! don't cry so; I never blamed you, dear mamma;" feebly caressing the thin hand she held. "You thought I should be happy in my marriage, but it has killed me;" with a wailing sigh.

"Flora! Flora! my child; Don't say such wild words, and the doctor has forbidden your talking much."

"They are not wild words, and it will not hurt me to talk now," Flora replied; "if my fate can save any one else, it will not matter. There are the other girls, you know, and I want you to remember this," very solemnly; "that women as well as men need an occupation for their energies, and that marriage without love, is worse than death."

She paused, looking so white and exhausted that Mrs. Livingston started up in alarm. "Let me call Mr. Le Roy," she said; "he is only in the next room."

"No, no!" cried Flora, opening her eyes in sudden horror. "Don't let him come to me. Sit down by me, mamma, and hold my hand; I want no one but you." Then, after a moment, "Where is Maud?"

"She has gone back to New York."

"And all the girls are there, I suppose?"

"Yes; she has gone to look after them."

"And papa is there too?"

"Yes."

"Tell them all good-bye for me, I have loved them very dearly. I never knew how much till now; tell them to forget when I was cross to them, and think of me as kindly as they can; give them my love, and bid them good-bye."

"And Mr. Le Roy," Mrs. Livingston began once more.

"No, no! Don't let him come! Tell him I forgive him, if he ever asks you. But I don't suppose he will care;" very feebly. Then after a moment, "you are crying again mamma, don't, don't be so sorry! I am glad to die! oh, so glad ! " speaking ever with longer pauses—" God is very good ! I shall be happier there than here—the tide is rising—rising—how dark the water is ! There is light above —light and freedom ! "

Her eyes opened with a radiant smile in them, and after that there was silence in the room; silence except for the faint sigh of the wind, and the chant of the waves that was like a requiem !

CHAPTER XLVIII.

A VISITOR FROM THE CITY.

THE few days of Laura's visit to the Lees came to a close, and one late August afternoon she stood ready to return to her home, waiting on the piazza for Carrie, who was to drive her to the station. Presently her cousin appeared, but in a double-seated carryall, instead of in her own light wagon, in which they usually drove. Laura was a little surprised at this, and asked as she walked down the path :

"Am I to go in that ? "

" Well, yes," said Carrie, with a comical laugh; " we've got to take George, too, he is going home with you."

" Oh, is he? That will be very pleasant."

" He only made up his mind this morning ; or at least, so he says," explained Carrie ; " but he seems to think it will be a good chance to go and see Kate. He really is very spooney on her, you know."

Laura smiled ; " I think she likes him very well, too ; though how deeply, I don't know."

" Oh, I dare say she wouldn't have him," Carrie replied; " but he'll feel better satisfied to go."

Further conversation was cut short by the appearance of George, who came down the walk, arrayed in a stiff suit of black broadcloth, in which he seemed to have only a partial control over his limbs. On his head he wore a tall black hat, supernatural in its glossy shine, and his large feet were encased in a pair of highly-polished boots, so much too tight for him, that his ordinary shambling gait was changed into a sort of mincing prance. His usually red face grew crimson as he approached the carriage, and looking up with a sheepish smile, he said :

"You don't mind my going home with you Laura, do you?"

"Oh no! I am delighted to have your escort."

"I thought I'd jest run over for a day ; being as it's a slack time."

"Certainly ; the girls will be glad to see you."

He got in, and the three were presently rolling towards the station behind a powerful pair of horses, which Carrie drove herself, quite scorning the idea of George's assistance. As they passed through the village, the lively lady could not avoid a word or two on her favorite grievance.

"More lazy men at the store !" she said; "half of them smoking too, and yet they grudge their wives a few pennies for any little luxury or comfort. I will tell you something that I myself saw here last fall. I was in the store when a neighbor of ours came in, leading a child. It was a cold day, and the little creature had on a low-necked and short-sleeved frock. The woman's husband was loafing by the stove, and she went to him and asked him for twenty-five cents to buy some gingham to make high-necked and long-sleeved aprons for the little one. The man refused, though she begged hard. 'You can use some old thing at home,' he growled, crossly. She told him that she had nothing that would serve, and appealed to him almost in tears. Still he would not give her the money, and she went sadly away. As soon as she was out of sight, the man bought half-a-dozen cigars, paying for them more than double what he had refused to his wife."

"Oh, Carrie !" cried Laura, "don't tell me such dreadful stories! It makes me feel so helplessly indignant! Besides all men are not so cruel; now here is George, no one can imagine his being unkind to his wife."

"I hope not," said George fervently; "if I was married"—with a great blush—"I'd lie down on the ground and let my wife walk over me if she wanted to."

"I believe you would," laughed Carrie; "you're a pretty good old fellow, George."

The station was reached soon after this, and before long the train arrived; Carrie being one of those punctual persons who allow themselves only just so much and no more time than enough to reach the railroad, and have no fancy for hurrying away from home and then waiting half-an-hour on the platform. The cousins parted, with many kindly expressions, and after that Laura and George had a pleasant but uneventful trip through the hills, to the station near Mr. Stanley's farm.

When they left the cars, they found Kate waiting for them, to the great delight, no doubt, of the young farmer, who, however, only expressed it by shaking her hand so hard as to wring from her a little shriek of pain, and by a series of grins so sustained that one would have thought his cheeks must fairly have ached with the tension.

Kate not being so strong-minded or strong-handed as Carrie, allowed George to drive, and so the three presently arrived at the farm, which lay much nearer this railroad than to the other.

As they approached the house, they were surprised to see a smart-looking buggy, drawn up near the gate, with a neat horse pawing the ground before it.

"I wonder who is here!" Kate exclaimed, with country curiosity.

"Perhaps it's some of your beaus," George suggested, clumsily, looking apprehensively at the vehicle.

Kate laughed. "I don't have any such articles," she said.

At this moment Fanny came running out of the house.

She had on one of her best frocks, and her face was quite glowing with excitement. "Oh Laura!" she cried, "there's a gentleman waiting to see you."

"A gentleman!" Laura repeated, and her heart gave a great bound, a wild hope springing up and sending the color to her cheeks.

"Yes, from New York; but there he is now."

Laura looked, and on the piazza, fascinatingly attired in a light summer costume, stood Mr. Fitlas; as he caught sight of her, he came down the walk with a self-complacent smile on his face.

"Miss Stanley!" he said, extending his hand to assist her to alight from the wagon; "We meet again!" Then as he was introduced to the others, "Miss Kate, your servant! Mr. Lee, your most obedient."

They all walked towards the house, and as they went, Mr. Fitlas explained his presence. "Been beating up Dutchess County for the firm," he said. "But this time, in all the small villages. Got a team in Poughkeepsie, rather neat, don't you think so?" pointing back to it.

"Yes, very nice," replied Laura.

"Hire it by the week," Mr. Fitlas continued. "Heard you lived here, and thought I'd drop in."

"I am very happy to see you," replied Laura, thinking by the cordiality of her manner to remove any unpleasant feeling her visitor might have with regard to their last interview. "Will you come into the parlor?"

They went into the formal best room, and seated themselves on chairs that stood so decorously in their places that it seemed almost a sacrilege to move them. Kate and George did not follow them, but Fanny lingered near the door.

"When did you leave New York?" asked Laura.

"Two weeks ago," answered Mr. Fitlas. "Been having my vacation. Was to Long Branch. Very gay there; tip-top fun," with a knowing look. "Had to go to New York though, to get my orders from the boss before I came up here."

"Then you were at the Moulder's, of course."

"Yes, dined there one night."

"How is Mrs. Moulder?"

"Middling, only middling, I should say. Moulder's as hearty as a brick, and the young ones were all right; but Agnes looked rather slim."

"I hoped she would go away for awhile to the country."

"Didn't hear anything of it. Moulder was up on the Sound somewhere, at a clam-bake with some of his club; but I don't think Agnes was going anywhere."

After a little further chat, Laura excused herself and left her guest to be entertained by Fanny. She knew that country hospitality required that Mr. Fitlas should be asked to stay to tea; but she dared not invite him without her father's consent; and as she had not yet seen her mother, she went at once to find her.

Mrs. Stanley was sitting in the kitchen door, paring apples, she did not stop her work for Laura's coming, except to return her kiss.

"I'd like to get up, my dear, but I haven't the time, it's about six, and tea ain't near ready, so I'm in a terrible hurry."

"You know that George came back with me?"

"Yes, your father'll be glad to see him."

"And you know that a gentleman I met in New York is in the parlor?"

"So Fanny told me, who is he?" curiously.

Laura briefly explained Mr. Fitlas' state and condition, and then added: "I think I ought to invite him to tea."

"Well yes; I suppose so, I don't know how your father 'll like it, but then we can't send him away."

"Will you tell father, mamma?"

"Yes," replied Mrs. Stanley; "he'll be along presently, and I'll ask him."

Laura went up to her room to make some slight changes in her dress, and then returned to the parlor. She found that Fanny, who was young and rather in awe of the stranger, was entertaining him with a game of checkers. It appeared to be about drawing to a close as she came in, for at that moment Mr. Fitlas threw himself back in the chair so forcibly that it tipped up.

"Carry me out and write my epitaph," he cried; "I'm beaten."

This seemed very funny not only to Fanny, but to George and Kate who were now in the room, and the conversation was a merry one, until a heavy step sounded on the piazza and Mr. Stanley passed through to the back of the house.

In the kitchen he found his wife, who with the aid of the younger girls, had almost completed her preparation for tea. At his entrance, she looked up in a nervous flurry and went to him, timidly.

"Roger," she said, "George came back with Laura."

No answer, but her practiced eye taught her that her husband was not displeased.

"There is a young man here from New York, too," she added, hurriedly; "a friend of Laura's, we thought we'd ask him to tea."

"I don't want any of her city dandies coming here after her," Mr. Stanley said, with a frown. "Let him pay for his tea, if he's got the money to do it," with his habitual sarcastic curl of the lips.

"Then I'll ring the bell, and I suppose he'll go away," Mrs. Stanley replied, meekly.

For some reason her husband did not like this proposal either. "As long as he's here, you may go in and ask him to tea," he growled; "but I'll let her know I'll have none of her danglers coming round here after her."

Mrs. Stanley sighed faintly, but hastened to obey her husband's last orders; she laid aside her working apron, and went into the parlor to be introduced to the stranger and ask him out to tea; an invitation which Mr. Fitlas graciously accepted.

"Delighted ma'am," he said; "I feel myself rather hollow, and shall be happy to partake of your hospitality."

When the party went in to tea, Mr. Stanley somewhat unbent. The two new comers were men, and as belonging to his own ruling sex, to be treated like fellow sovereigns, with proper courtesy, he shook hands with both politely, and then they all took their seats.

After the blessing, Mr. Stanley turned to Mr. Fitlas, "Are you recently from New York, sir?"

"Yes, two weeks ago."

"And how are politics there? What do people say of the fall election?"

"Oh, we think it will go as it always does; straight out, you know."

"I see they have nominated some good men for Congress. Judge Swinton must be an able man."

At the sound of his name, Laura felt herself color. "He is a disgrace to the New York Bench," she cried, hotly.

Mr. Stanley turned his eyes upon her with cold disapproval. "You know all about it, no doubt," he said, with that wrinkled sneer that was so offensive.

"He is a man for whom I have no respect," replied Laura, firmly.

"Fortunately it is of no consequence what you think about it," retorted her father; "women are not expected to understand politics."

He then resumed his conversation with Mr. Fitlas, occasionally drawing George into it; but pursuing it evidently with no expectation whatever that his wife or daughters would either comprehend it, or take part in it.

Shortly after the meal was over Mr. Fitlas took his leave. "I must be flying," he said; "duty before pleasure."

"When do you expect to be back in New York?" asked Laura.

"Give it up," replied Mr. Fitlas airily; "two weeks, two months, can't say, all according to biz."

"Whenever you see Mrs. Moulder give her my best love."

"I will ; farewell Miss Stanley, it may be for years and it may be for ever," with an assumption of great careless-ness, " young ladies adoo, Mr. Stanley I shall hope to see you in New York, at my humble shebang ;" presenting a card to the old gentleman who took it politely, and so Mr. Fitlas departed in a blaze of glory.

George appeared to breathe more freely after he was gone. He had evidently felt that this city man, whose boots were smaller, whose hat was shinier, and whose hair was redder than his own, had in some measure eclipsed him. Now that he was gone, he could hang about Kate without fear of a rival; expressing his feelings, however, in looks rather than in words, for George was never much of a talker.

He was a very good-natured young fellow, however, and was so willing to wait on the girls, to run errands for them and to serve them individually and collectively in any way, that when, after a few days' visit he took his depar-ture, it was matter of regret to them all. And perchance more especially to Kate, who was secluded with him for an hour before he left, and who finally drove him to the sta-tion herself, the two going away with very red but very happy faces, and followed by the mirthful good wishes of the rest of the girls who stood laughing on the piazza.

CHAPTER XLIX.

FRANK'S STORY.

BEFORE the " sad September days " were over, Laura heard of the death of her sweet friend, Flora Livingston. Mrs. D'Arcy gave her the first news of it, sending her a gracefully-written obituary of " the gifted lady " which ap-peared in a fashionable journal. It was impossible for

Laura to more than guess at the real history of Flora's fatal illness; but as her tears fell fast to the memory of the fair young creature, she felt with a pang of passionate regret, that her life had been sacrificed to the dictates of the society in which she lived, and to the conventional ideas of "woman's sphere."

A letter from the doctor came with this paper, and in it she strongly urged Laura to visit her some time in October. This proposal suited very well with the young artist's own plans. She had filled her summer orders for paintings so satisfactorily, that she had received from the same employers a commission to prepare a series of sketches of autumn scenery and studies of autumn leaves. This work would necessitate her remaining in the country until it was executed, and would give her, when it should be completed, a handsome sum of money; indeed, Laura began now to see her way clear to earning a respectable income by her pictures, and to hope that she would never again be obliged to teach.

In her answer to Mrs. D'Arcy, she fixed the time for her visit, late in October, and to this the doctor replied, signifying her approval. The only means that Laura had of hearing from the one person, whose image was every day more or less in her thoughts, was through Mrs. D'Arcy's letters, and they possessed, therefore, an especial interest for her. In this way she had learned during the summer, that the traveller was well and had gone for a brief trip to the continent, and in this last note, the doctor said:

"I saw Mrs. Bradford yesterday; they have just returned to town. Guy is expected home early in November."

He would be in New York then, soon after Laura went to it; but in the months since they had parted might he not have forgotten her? He had been in gay Paris, he had passed over the routes where so many fair women are to be encountered; perhaps he had learned to fancy some one else. Laura's heart beat painfully, slowly, when she thought of these possibilities, but she resolved to face even this, bravely. If the only man she had ever cared for should be lost to her, she had still her art, and life should not be ruined to her, though she missed its best prize, a happy marriage.

So, while the days grew shorter and the nights wilder and longer, Laura toiled hard with brush and pencil. In the splendid mornings, she was in the woods, gorgeous now with all the flaming glories of autumn, enjoying with intense delight the beautiful scenes around her. The sunlight poured its radiant beams through the half-denuded branches of the trees; the fresh breeze rustled the fallen leaves that blazed on the russet ground like the scattered jewels of some conqueror's march, the fair spoils of the bygone summer, rifled by the daring hands of the flying scouts of winter's army of lawless winds. The trees uprose decked gorgeously in honor of the last festival of the dying year; the beech stretched its waving arms clothed with amber; the oak stood massive and sombre, wrapped in its purple mantle; the maple, bright harlequin of the grove, displayed its coat of many colors, crimson and gold, green and orange. Down the dim aisles of the forest the blue aster raised its head, and in swampy places the scarlet cardinal-flower kept its stately watch.

From these lavish beauties of the woodlands, Laura gathered the materials for a series of pictures that were unwritten poems. Keenly did she delight in thus embodying her favorite fancies; nor was it possible for her to be sad, while she had the constant stimulus of a congenial occupation.

During all these weeks of study and labor, while the young artist received the warmest sympathy from her mother and sisters, her father never proffered a question as to her work, never offered her one word of encouragement, and once, when his wife ventured timidly to ask him if he would not like to see some of Laura's pictures, he refused, saying, " They must be daubs; women can't paint anything worth looking at."

The task was done at last, and the laborer felt that she

needed a rest, before she began her winter's toil, and that she had earned a holiday. One late October day, with her pictures carefully packed in a portfolio, and a trunk containing a renovated wardrobe, for the cost of which she had earned every penny herself, Laura started for New York.

The leaves were nearly all gone, now; the woods lay brown and sere, awaiting their winter robe of snow; but the sunshine sparkled gayly as ever on the waters, and the heavens smiled a fair promise.

The trip down, reminded Laura vividly of her journey a year ago. That, too, had been made on a fall afternoon and by the same train, indeed, as this on which she now was. She recalled with a shudder, the horrors of her first night in New York, and thought with thankfulness, that even if to-day, she should reach the city alone and late, she would no longer be friendless.

The ride went on smoothly for perhaps two-thirds of the way, and then at a sudden turn of the road, there was the sound of the double whistle for down breaks, and the train came to an abrupt halt. "Another accident," thought Laura, as she looked out, anxiously. The scene was a lonely one; a forest on the land side, sombre and melancholy; the water on the other side coming up to the embankment whereon they were. No habitations near.

The passengers began to get out of the car, and to ask what had happened; so that there was presently quite a crowd on the spot that a moment before had been so desolate. Laura wished that she, too, could inquire what had occurred, and was looking for some face in the throng to whom she might appeal, when among the men she saw Frank Heywood. She immediately threw up the sash, and leaned out to attract his attention. He saw her in a moment, and came towards her with a smile of glad recognition.

"Why, Laura, how delightful this is!" putting up his hand to shake hers.

"What is the matter with the train?" asked Laura, after she had responded to his greeting.

"Nothing has happened to us," he answered; but some freight-cars are off the track below, and a great pile of iron is lying all over it."

"Then we shall be detained here some time."

"Yes, probably, several hours, I am afraid."

"How glad I am that you are here!"

"Thanks, and I am as glad to see you. I'll tell you what we will do," he went on; "you must come with me into the drawing-room-car where I have a small section to myself."

"Why, you are travelling in style!"

"Oh, we newspaper men have privileges, you know; I was sent to Albany on special business, and needed a quiet place in which I could write out my report."

Laura went forward with Frank to one of those miniature palaces, with which Americans are familiar, and into a tiny room panelled in many varieties of wood; padded with blue damask cushions, and having a mirror set on either side. There were doors to the little compartment, and by closing these they could be quite secluded. For a time, after they were established, Heywood was quite busy in writing an account of the disaster for the paper, while Laura amused herself by making a sketch of the view from the window. After awhile, however, the daylight faded, and it began to grow dark.

"Frank," asked Laura, laying down her pencils and glancing out apprehensively; "do you think we shall be able to start, soon?"

"I am afraid not. When I was out, just now, they said they had found that the track was injured by the crush of the iron, and they must replace some of the rails."

"And that will take a long time, won't it?"

"Yes, probably. They will have to work at a disadvantage in the dark. There was some talk of transferring the passengers, but there is a bridge just below at the break, which is so injured that it is almost impossible to cross it."

"You don't think we will be kept here all night, do you?"

"No, not so bad as that, I hope; I think we shall be in town before morning."

"Mrs. D'Arcy will hardly wait dinner for me as she proposed," Laura remarked.

"No; she will have heard at the depot what has happened, so that she will not be anxious."

Presently a man came through the car and lighted the lamp, closing the door of the section so that the two were shut in together. Laura grew uneasy.

"I think I will go back to my own car," she said.

"Why should you do that?" asked Frank, in great amazement.

Laura colored, faintly. "Well perhaps—perhaps it will be better;" hesitatingly.

A sudden light came into the young journalist's eyes— "I understand," he said; "it would be better—if—if—" he paused a moment, gazing out into the darkness, then he turned to his companion—"Laura," he said, "I am so much attached to you—I trust you so entirely, that I think I can confide in you."

"I hope so, Frank:" looking at him in surprise.

"Have you never guessed my secret?" he asked, turning upon her the full light of those strange eyes; "you have told me more than once that I was like a brother to you, if you had said a sister, it would have been nearer the truth."

Laura regarded her companion for a moment with an astonished gaze; then a hundred little circumstances rushed to her memory—"You are a woman!" she cried, clapping her hands in delight; "that is glorious!" and she caught Frank around the neck with a hearty kiss.

The young journalist looked really happy, and laughed light heartedly. "It is rather a large practical joke isn't it! Sometimes I keenly enjoy it."

"It's grand!" cried Laura; "Perfectly grand!' To
think of you being one of the editors of 'the Trumpeter!'
And going all over town as you please! And knocking
Bludgett down! And rescuing me from Judge Swinton!
And voting, I dare say!" As a grand climax—"Oh, it's
delicious!"

"And you never suspected me?"

"Never; I thought you were entirely different from
any man I ever knew; so gentle, so refined, seeming to understand my feelings so completely; I loved you, I have
often thought, as I might have loved a woman. But I
never dreamed of this!"

"Rhoda knew it," said Frank, "I don't know how; but
she discovered my secret, long ago."

"Now I understand her sacrifice to you," rejoined
Laura; "she was right in thinking your life worth
saving."

"I don't know as to that, but I hope I shall be able to
carry out my career as I have planned it. I think it involves some self-denial."

"Of course it does," replied Laura gravely; "very
great self-denial, you dear Frank! But do tell me how you
came to disguise yourself so; I have often wanted to know
more of your life than you have ever told me."

"You shall hear," replied Frank. "I was born at the
south, as you know. I was the only child and my mother
died in giving me birth. My father, who loved her passion-
ately, never remarried, but devoted himself to my education.
I lived with him on a lonely plantation and, less restrained
by conventionalities than most girls, was his companion
in his rides, his walks, and even in the athletic sports of
which he was unusually fond so that I grew up remarkably
strong and vigorous. The war came, and after a time my
father went away to fight, as he believed, for freedom. He
was killed; the negroes were free, our property was worth-
less, and I found myself at twenty, alone in the world, with
no protector and no home! I had an uncle, himself already

burdened with the care of a large family, and I determined
not to be dépendent on him. Full of a romantic belief in
my own possibilities of work, I took what little money I
could raise from the sale of the furniture of the house and
came to New York. I suppose I can say it now," the
young journalist went on with a smile ; " I was a very
good-looking girl."

" I can readily believe it," said Laura ; " you are a very
handsome young man."

" Thanks. Well, my beauty, such as it was, did me no
good ; " gloomily—" I had no friends, I was entirely un-
protected. I was insulted, refused work, unless I would
comply with the disgraceful propositions of my employers ;
in short, I had the experience which so many young women
have in the great city ; poverty, temptation, cruelty. I
was resolved not to sink where so many had fallen ; but it
was hard work sometimes. There was one man in particular who persecuted me so persistently, that at last I scarcely dared to go out, lest he should carry me off to some hopeless pit. Then I grew desperate, and as much to avoid him
as for any other purpose, I pawned my last article of value
—my father's watch—which I had kept securely till then,
and which, by the way, I have since redeemed ; and with
the money thus obtained, bought a suit of boy's clothes.
The change was delightful ! You can never imagine what it
was ! My limbs were free ; I could move untrammelled, and
my actions were free ; I could go about unquestioned. No
man insulted me, and when I asked for work, I was not
offered outrage."

" I know what that is," said Laura ; recalling her own
experiences as book-agent.

" At first, I thought I would only wear the dress for a
short time ; but one day I read in the papers an account
of that physician who recently died in Edinburgh, and who,
after a long life of honor, wide practice and the enjoyment
of many dignities, was discovered to be a woman, when
death had ended her career. Had her sex been known she

could not even have studied her profession—she began forty years ago—she would never have been acknowledged as capable, and would not have received a single one of the marks of distinction which were given to her. Her story moved me to attempt a like success; I resolved to carve out for myself a place in the world as a man, and let death alone reveal my secret and prove what a woman can do ; " with a resolute light in those deep eyes.

"You have set yourself a grand task ! " Laura said, enthusiastically.

" Yes, and thus far I have been able to carry it out according to my hopes. At first I had hard work, of course. I began as a news-seller ; studying at night to learn shorthand ; then I got employment on an evening paper, and at last on 'the Trumpeter.' Of course my dress enabled me to go to places and scenes which I could not have visited in the garb of my sex, and I have seen a great many odd and terrible things in that way. But thus far, no one but Rhoda, has ever suspected my secret."

" But I don't understand that dear little moustache," said Laura, who had been studying her companion closely.

"That is only a cunningly-devised fiction," laughed Frank.

" A very clever one, certainly," said Laura; " and do you vote at the election ? "

" Undoubtedly ; I have never missed one since I have been a man, and now you understand why I so thoroughly believe in woman suffrage."

This strange revelation of Frank's history offered food for a long conversation between the two, and they were both surprised and almost sorry, when the train at last started.

" It is just as well that we should go, however," Laura said, lightly; " since every one does not know the truth about you, and you really are such a very good-looking fellow that it might be quite compromising for me to be too much with you."

"I have longed to tell you my story for some time past," replied Frank; "I felt that we could be so much more at ease together."

"I thank you a thousand times for your confidence," Laura said, earnestly ; " and you will come to see me often, while I am at Mrs. D'Arcy's ?"

"I don't know as to that, I am afraid I shall be so busy for the next week, over the election, that I shall have very little time for visiting. By the way, the doctor has known my secret for three years; she attended me once in a severe illness, and I love the dear lady, like a mother."

At the depot in New York they found Mrs. D'Arcy's carriage waiting for Laura ; but Frank could only go with her to the door, where they parted, as the copy for the paper must be taken down as soon as possible, and Frank must hire a swift conveyance and go at once to the office.

Laura looked after the slight figure as it disappeared in the darkness, and thought that if there were some trials in the young journalist's life, there must surely be some compensations also.

CHAPTER L.

A NEW YORK ELECTION.

It was very pleasant to Laura to be once more with Mrs. D'Arcy, and to meet some of the friends whom she had seen a year ago ; to go out in the busy streets and to stroll through the art-galleries ; but again and again, as she moved about in the familiar scenes, the image of a graceful figure that had been there a year ago crossed her mind, and her eyes filled with tears, at the thought that the lovely young being who had so enjoyed the spring days of her youth, would never on this earth be with her again.

Laura's first visit was naturally made to the Moulders. She found the gentle lady looking much paler and feebler

than when she had first met her a year ago, with the same
patient light in her soft brown eyes, and apparently the
same infinite capacity for uncomplaining suffering. The
children were well, Aleck went to school this winter, which
was quite a relief, and Mr. Moulder was very busy just
now ; out a great deal about election matters.

This same election met Laura at every turn. As she
walked through the streets, she saw at eligible points,
great banners, bearing the names of various candidates for
office ; and every few blocks noticed large transparencies
over the headquarters of this or that political club. One
day when she was out with the doctor, their attention was
caught by a large bunting bearing, the inscription :

THE PEOPLE'S CHOICE

FOR CONGRESS.

HON. SILAS SWINTON.

and below these letters, a gigantic likeness of the judge.

"People's choice !" exclaimed Laura, indignantly !
"Women are not people then, since no woman, certainly,
has made this man their choice. Honorable, indeed ! "

" Brutus was an *honorable* man ! " quoted the doctor.

" But is it not terrible to think of poor Rhoda's wasted
life ; trampled into the dust because this man ruined
her, and then to think of his holding high office ! "

" It is only one of the many ways which we shall have
to suffer, until our sex is permitted a voice in these things,
my dear."

"When women have the right of suffrage, they will certainly not sanction such a state of affairs in politics as we
have now."

" No ; and assuredly the influence of good women is
needed as much in purifying the corruptions of government,

16*

as it ever was needed in charity or reform among the poor and needy."

"Of course, and it is no wonder that abuses exist, when such men as Moulder and Bludgett and the low creatures who haunt drinking-saloons, are allowed to vote, while the privilege is refused to women like you!"

"And you too, my dear," smiled the doctor; "but it is rather unreasonable to give the ballot to the worst men, and deny it to the best women. One would think that merit would be a more reasonable qualification than sex."

Another day when Laura was riding down town in a car, filled almost entirely with ladies, a quantity of hand-bills were thrown into the window. Taking up one of these she read :

"People of New York do your duty !"

"Is that addressed to me?" she queried, mentally. "I have been led to suppose myself a *person*, until lately ; let me see how I can do my duty ;" and she went on:

"If you love your country, register and vote ! If you desire an honest government, register and vote !"

"I love my country, and I desire an honest government," thought Laura ; "yet it seems these words are not addressed to me, after all ; since I am not allowed to register and not permitted to vote."

She folded the paper up and carried it home; showing it to the doctor and relating the incident.

"Now only think, there were in that car eight women and two men; I counted them; but according to this hand-bill, only two out of the ten human beings were worth addressing !" and she tossed the paper into the fire.

"It is rather hard," replied Mrs. D'Arcy ; "at every election, ballots for both parties are sent to this house. There is no one here who is permitted to use them, and yet the tax-collector never fails to hold me responsible to his claims. It would seem only reasonable that if my sex debars me from one duty, it should excuse me from the other."

A few mornings after this, when it wanted only three

days of the one appointed for the election, Laura was awakened quite early, by sounds of the firing of cannon and the ringing of bells. A good deal alarmed, she jumped out of bed. " It can't be a bombardment," she said to herself, reassuringly ; " we are not at war with any body."

However, as the portentous racket continued, she thought she would go and ask the doctor what it might signify. Accordingly throwing a dressing-gown over her shoulders, she hurried to Mrs. D'Arcy's room.

"My dear, what is it?" cried the doctor, who was easily awakened, and had the happy faculty of having all her senses about her at once.

" What is that noise ? " inquired Laura ; " don't you hear ? cannon firing and bells ringing ; do you think there is a great fire somewhere, or what is it ? "

The doctor threw herself back in the bed, laughing heartily. " It is only a contrivance to get voters out to register," she exclaimed. " Were you really frightened ? "

" I *was* a little startled," replied Laura; " but I am more provoked, now. It seems that these men think that women are deaf as well as ignorant. I protest that if they want to make such a hubbub to wake up only electors, they ought so to arrange matters that only electors shall hear it ; " and she departed to her room again.

The violent demonstrations were not over yet, however; that same afternoon as the doctor and Laura were driving up Fifth-avenue, a most mournful sound of a tolling bell was heard at a distance; the doctor looked really annoyed.

" I do hope that won't come this way," she said.

" What is it ? " asked Laura ; " A funeral ? "

Mrs. D'Arcy laughed again. " No, my dear, unless it may be considered as the annual funeral of the liberties of the women of New York. It is another invention to call out voters."

At this moment there appeared a huge cart with a high

white top, on which were inscriptions in large bright-col-
ored letters, entreating " the people " to " Stand up to the
duties of the hour," and to " Turn out in mass ; " together
with the names of certain candidates.   This frightful looking vehicle was drawn by four horses, and at every step of
its slow progress, a great bell under the cover, tolled with
a loud and portentous clang.

The effect of this horror upon the horses attached to
various private carriages which were abroad, may be imagined.   At its approach there was universal consternation.
Even the doctor's sober greys plunged with terror, as they
caught sight of it.

" This is a genuine outrage ! " exclaimed Mrs. D'Arcy.
" After each of the elections since this thing was contrived,
I have been called to see some lady who had been seriously
injured by her horses taking fright at it."

" It seems rather out of place here, too," said Laura,
looking out.   " There is scarcely a man in sight.   I see
plenty of pale and apparently terrified tax-payers, but
hardly any voters."

When the day of election finally came, the excitement
culminated.   In some parts of the city, it was not safe for
women to be abroad.   The nobler, the tenderer, the more
harmonious influences which " the gentler sex" are acknowledged to bring with them every where, were rigidly excluded from all weight in the choice of the rulers of a
city, of whose inhabitants more than one half are women ;
and brute force ruled everywhere.   In the upper wards of
the city, the polls were only the scene of heavy swearing,
hard betting and coarse excitement ; but the lower wards
were the theatres of fierce contests, drunkenness, rowdyism,
and in more than one instance, of actual violence.

Bangs and Snaggers were very busy, conveying certain
bands of men with suspicious haste from one polling-booth to
another, but discreetly refraining from casting more than
one vote apiece themselves, as being well-known public
characters.   They were also useful in several instances, in

challenging voters for the opposite party, and in actually deterring some timid souls from approaching the ballot-box where their alarming faces were to be seen.

At Bludgett's, business was very brisk all day; that worthy himself had "voted early," if he had not "voted often," and was at his post brewing strong drink for all comers; haranguing with a loud voice on the merits of his favorite candidate, and more than once mixing beverages so potent, that those who partook of them, and who were invariably of the opposite party, were unable after drinking, to deposit a vote, even with the most devoted assistance of their friends.

It was a hard day for many of the inhabitants of the city ; a hard day for those patriots who, on this occasion had half-a-dozen names and residences, and who were all so very enthusiastic for their cause that they had to vote its ticket at least once for each name. A hard day for the officers who had charge of the ballot-boxes, and whose dark and intricate duties involved a long and mysterious session after the polls were closed ; and a very hard day for the wives and mothers of those electors, who drank success to their party until far into the night, and went staggering home towards morning, to the women whom they legally "represented and protected."

Among these last was Mr. Bludgett. Utterly worn-out with nearly forty-eight hours of duty behind his bar, about five o'clock, while the night was yet dark, he came stumbling back to his house. As he groped his way up stairs, the door of the sitting-room was opened, letting out a little light by which he might the better see his way.

Instead of taking this as a kindly act, the man fell into a rage at sight of the trembling creature who stood, half behind the door, watching for him.

"What the devil are you here for ? " he demanded, fiercely ; "you ought to have been in bed hours ago ! "

"I did go to bed, I did, John ; but I couldn't sleep for

worrying, and I just thought I'd get up and read awhile," she replied, deprecatingly.

Her appearance indicated that she had indeed undressed for the night. She had on a ragged night-gown over which her shawl was wrapped, and her thin hair fell on her shoulders. As Bludgett came into the room, she closed the door and went quickly over to the table on which lay the book which she had evidently been reading ; but this time it was no showily-covered romance, but a poor, worn copy of the Bible. She took it up hurriedly and hid it under her shawl, then turned to her husband timidly :

"Has every thing gone right, John?" she asked.

"Yes, of course, the Judge is elected by a big majority. It's been hard work; but it's all O. K. now."

"I didn't mean that ; but—but," looking at him with an awful horror in her questioning eyes—"was there any row? any body hurt?"

The man drew his black brows together and turned on her fiercely—"There you go!" he cried ; "always afraid somebody'll be hurt. Haven't I told you to drop that? you've been a snivelling ever since—" he looked around with a shudder—"ever since, you know when. I told you t'other day I'd kill you if you didn't drop it."

"Oh, John, I didn't mean any harm ;" she sobbed.

"Didn't mean any harm!" he repeated, "aggravating a fellow when he comes in, all worn out! I'll teach you how to talk so to me. Blast you!"

The poor woman gave a wild shriek as her husband came towards her; but this seemed only to inflame his rage. He struck her a fearful blow with his clenched fist and she staggered and fell.

"There!" he said, with a horrible oath ; "will you go whining at me again?" menacing her fiercely.

The little book had dropped from her grasp as she fell ; she picked it up, and holding it clasped in her trembling hands, half raised herself from the floor. Her right eye was partly closed and the blood dropped over her pallid face from the gash beside it.

"John!" she moaned, "don't kill me! don't kill me!" swaying feebly and looking at him pitifully; "I love you John, and I—I pray for you, every day."

The words seemed to render the man absolutely savage. "You puling cat!" he cried; "you'll hang me yet with your fears, and your prayers, and your tell-tale white face! Blast you! you shan't say that again!"

He rushed upon her and beat her down; then setting his teeth hard, while his eyes glowed blood-red with fury, he seized her by her hair and pounded her head against the floor.

"John! John! dear John!"

The words were half a shriek and half an entreaty; but they availed her nothing; he only struck her more fiercely, his breath panting as he ground his teeth and fought her wildly. She writhed partly away from him, once half staggering to her feet, her garments torn, the blood spurting from several wounds.

"For God's sake, John! don't kill me—John, dear!"

At this moment he caught sight of the book which she still held. It seemed to stimulate his rage to madness; he snatched it from her and smote her down again, silencing that pleading voice by a stamp of his heavy boot-heel on the helpless mouth.

After this there were only moans, growing fainter and fainter; but the man, like one possessed by some fiend, struck and kicked the poor helpless body long after all motion had ceased, and until the crushed spirit had escaped from the tortures of this life through the terrible gateway of death!

CHAPTER LI.

CONCLUSION.

ONE evening when Laura had been in New York about a week, as she and the doctor were chatting over their dessert, a card was brought to Mrs. D'Arcy. As she looked at it a faint change crossed her face, and had her guest been observing her, she might have noted that the doctor looked at her with a curious expression for a moment before speaking.

" My dear, there is a gentleman in the parlor who wishes to see me ; do you mind going to the library until I send for you ? "

" Not at all," replied Laura ; " you know I am always entertained there ; pray don't trouble yourself about me."

The doctor preceded her guest up stairs and was at some pains to close the door of the parlor, which, however, Laura did not perceive, as she went at once to the library and ensconced herself before the fire with a book in which she was interested.

Meantime, Mrs. D'Arcy had gone into the other room, and was shaking hands with Guy Bradford. He looked well, somewhat brown from his sea voyage and journeying, but so handsome, so bright, so cordial in his greeting, that the doctor could not find it in her heart to feel any resentment against him.

" I am glad to see you back, Guy," she said, as they sat down ; " and yet I have been vexed at you ever since you ran away, for going off as you did."

" I know it was foolish," replied Guy ; " but if you could realize how much I have suffered from my own rashness, you would not blame me. Oh, Mrs. D'Arcy, you know how deeply I have cared for Laura ; tell me, how is she ? " with an eagerness that proved the strength of his feelings.

"She is well," said the doctor.

"And where is she?"

"Before I answer that question, you must let me ask you one."

"Well, what is it? I know I deserve punishment; but please don't make it very bad—I have endured a good deal already."

"I will make my homily as brief as I can," answered Mrs. D'Arcy; "but first you must explain some things to me. When I told you last Spring that Laura was not engaged to Frank Heywood, you made me the confidant of your sentiments towards her ; are they unchanged?"

"Entirely ; except that I love her a hundred times better than I did then," replied Guy, fervently.

"But if you loved her, why did you outrage her as you did, at that last interview? She told me of it some time after it took place."

"I know I behaved abominably," replied Guy, penitently ; "after awhile I realized it; at first I was so wretched that I tried to blame her and cure myself of caring for her, but it was impossible; I could not believe that she had ever done any thing of which she need be ashamed."

"Of course not; any sensible man would have known that, at once," said Mrs. D'Arcy, indignantly. "But you were in a state of mind in which your natural good sense was for a time obscured ; " she added, with a smile.

"I suppose so," acquiesced Guy ; "I know I was well nigh crazed. After that night at the Academy, I was so happy until the next morning, when I received a letter insinuating a horrible charge against Laura, and bidding me ask her where she spent her first night in the city."

"An anonymous letter?" asked the doctor.

"Yes, I ought not to have heeded it, perhaps, and I would not, if she had answered my question at once. I told myself all day long that it was nothing, but when she refused to reply to what seemed so simple a demand, I was maddened into distrust. If I had stayed here I should have gone to see her once more; but before night had come again, it was too late, and I was away on the ocean."

"You behaved like the impetuous fellow you always have been," said the doctor.

"Too rashly, I can see now; but Mrs. D'Arcy, do you know where Laura spent that night?"

"Yes."

"Why didn't she tell me?"

"Guy Bradford," said the doctor, very solemnly—"have you any right to ask?"

"What do you mean?" he demanded, a slow color rising to his honest face.

"I mean this; suppose she were to catechize you, would you tell her where *you* have spent all the nights of *your* life?"

The young man dropped his head. "I am no scoundrel," he murmured; "but I am not worthy of her."

"You are like other men," Mrs. D'Arcy said; "you think that you have a right to demand from the woman you wish to marry, a strict account of every act of her life, while you hold that your sins are a matter which do not concern her. Do you believe that this is fair?"

Guy had risen and was walking about the room. "No, it is not fair," he exclaimed. "In the sight of God, men and women are equal, and measured by that standard, I have no right to ask her to marry me. But, Mrs. D'Arcy, I have been absolutely true to her since I first saw her, and I love her so dearly!" And he turned upon the kind lady a look so full of honest pleading, that it touched her heart.

"And you think you will always love her?"

"So help me God, I will love her and be faithful to her, so long as we both shall live."

"I believe you, Guy, and knowing you as well as I do, I think you may be trusted."

"And now, won't you tell where she is?" beseechingly.

"She is in the library."

"Here!" with a glad light springing to his eyes.

"Yes."

" And I may go to her ? "

" Yes."

He waited for no other word; but dashed out of the room and across the hall. There he paused a moment. The door of the library was ajar, and looking in he saw Laura, seated in a low chair near the fire. The light from a shaded lamp fell on the noble head and the beautiful face, where it seemed that a shade of sadness lingered. Her hands were crossed on her lap over the book which had fallen from her clasp, and her gray eyes were looking thoughtfully into the fire; among the fancies she was reading there, could it be possible that his image had a place ? The young man tapped very lightly, and Laura turned her head :

" Come in," she said.

He stepped across the threshold, and she started up with a glad cry—" Guy ! "

" My darling ! My love ! Forgive me ! Oh, Laura ! Sweetheart ! You do care for me ! "

She was in his arms now, her face wet with happy tears hidden on his breast, and there was a dimness in her lover's eyes as he bent to win from her own lips an answer to his question.

" And you will be my wife ? " he asked, presently, as he held her in his embrace.

" Yes, Guy"—

Then after a moment she added ; " For I believe that you will not ask me to surrender my liberty entirely, and will permit me to follow out my own career in life ; " looking up at him with trustful affection.

" My own darling," he replied, " your obligations to me shall be no greater than mine to you. We will make life's journey hand in hand, equals in all things, by God's blessing travelling together to the end, and finding an immortal happiness in an eternal heaven."

THE END.

AFTERWORD
by Grace Farrell

When, in *Fettered For Life*, the protagonist Laura Stanley announces, "'I am here like a little girl in a fairy tale, to seek my fortune'" (35), her friend Flora Livingston expresses the shock of a whole era: "'To do what!' exclaimed Flora, . . . looking at her friend in amazement. 'What put such a thought in your head?'" (40). In 1874—more than fifty years before Virginia Woolf, in *A Room of One's Own,* recast Shakespeare in an equally gifted but feminine form—Lillie Blake reversed the protagonist's sex in an archetypal fairy tale of a youth who goes out into the world to seek his fortune and—like Woolf long after her—imagined the consequences. As we know, little girls in traditional fairy tales do not seek their fortunes; they remain in states of trancelike passivity until awakened by a prince.

Fairy tales are the stories a culture tells us about ourselves. They perform cultural work by defining models of propriety, obedience, patience, and courage and by clarifying social roles expected of men and women. They form the patriarchal script that we are expected to enter, to save us, so to speak, from having to write our own. But Lillie Blake shows us that only through the dangerous enterprise of constructing her own story can a woman escape the deadly confinement of the male text. Blake challenges the stories which fairy tales tell women about patience and love, about awaiting rescue by men who will fulfill their every wish and make life meaningful, about living happily ever after. She positions her reader to question fairy tales, including the fairy tale of her novel's own ending, with its romance plot. She alludes to tales of rescue, of patient Griseldas, of hardworking Cinderellas, but her stories of marriage reveal that "happily ever after" exists more in hope than in reality.

A culture's stories shape how its men and women read themselves and are read by one another. Lillie Blake's project was to undermine those readings of women which were based on a presumption that womankind was radically different from mankind, and thus fated only to certain gender-appropriate destinies. Recasting a traditional story with a female rather than a male protagonist was one way of disrupting a cultural script which prescribed roles by gender and which limited the life-scripts available to women.

Another way in which Blake disrupted her culture's rigid boundaries between male and female spheres was to create a character who successfully transgresses those boundaries through crossdressing. Blake creates a cross-dresser whose success in keeping her disguise a secret exposes as insubstantial the many gender differences that society ascribed to biological differences. Blake believed that differences between the sexes were a result not of biology, but of the pervasive stories of our patriarchal culture—stories through which we have learned to define ourselves.

Blake makes the writing of male cultural stories and the erasure of female voices the central political issue of her novel. In the opening chapter, a chorus of old men in a courtroom gaze at Laura Stanley, shaking their heads knowingly at "the old, old story"(8). That old story, the old men's story, is the titillating patriarchal story of seduction and possession.[1] It is a story which the novel's antagonist, Judge Swinton, has tried to impose on several women in the novel. In Laura Stanley, Blake presents a woman who is attempting to construct a different story for her life, one in which she can inscribe a self which is independent and artistically empowered.

However, to re-envision a woman's story rather than encode once again patriarchy's version of the feminine is a perilous enterprise. Several women in the novel face death as the only alternative to their prescribed scripts. Laura Stanley must negotiate her way between her story of success and adventure and the marriage plot which awaits her by the novel's end. And in her crossdresser, Blake presents a woman—as talented and successful as any man might hope to be—who can function in the world only when she steps into a male script and allows herself to be read as male. She can fulfill her talent and satisfy her ambitions only by erasing her female identity. If Blake's mysterious crossdresser could come out from behind her imprisoning disguise—which is the male script containing her—and write her own story, then she might achieve real selfhood. If, as she moves into the patriarchal marriage script, Laura Stanley can withstand the pressure to give up the life story that she wants to write for herself, then she too might accomplish her dream. As French feminist Hélène Cixous puts it: "Woman must write her self: must write about women and bring women to writing, from which they have been driven away as violently as from their bodies—for the same reasons, by the same law, with the same fatal goal. Woman must put herself into the text—as into the world and into history" (244).[2] However, Blake does not indicate that the world in which her women moved would ever willingly allow them to write their own selves—or to enter history without entering *his*-story. Instead we find women contained within male-defined worlds and denied the freedom necessary to be authors of their own lives.

Published three years after the famous meeting of another pair named Stanley and Livingstone, the novel makes clear that the primitive Congo which Blake's Laura Stanley and Flora Livingston enter at the risk of their own selves is that of American society at large.[3] Within the heart of Flora's Fifth Avenue home lies a conservatory filled with exotic flowers and jungle birds, a gorgeous yet primitive enclave, which provides ironic comment on her parents' practice of the barbarous but socially sanctioned ritual of enslaving their daughter in a cruel marriage. Other women, across class lines, suffer various forms of duress. Maggie Bertram and Rhoda Dayton, seamstresses forced to take second jobs as barmaids, are trapped in an economic system that denies them living wages and are harassed by men who rape them and then, in another instance of male scripting, scorn them as fallen women. Molly Bludgett is a long-suffering, romance- and bible-reading, battered housewife who takes in boarders who are really young women her husband procures for his boss, the well-known Judge Swinton. Unlike the wife-beating John Bludgett, the solidly middle-class husband of Agnes Moulder practices more conventionally subtle forms of abuse—overworking, undercutting, and invalidating his wife.

Blake provides several links among the various social strata she depicts. One is Cornelia D'Arcy, M.D.—seemingly the model for what any woman might be, given both freedom and education—who dispenses medical care and espouses the suffrage cause to women of all classes. Another is the immigrant washerwoman Biddy Malone, who bundles her way in and out of various households. And on the periphery is the crossdresser who, in order to escape rape and find fulfillment in work, has had to disguise herself as a man.

Disguise lies at the heart of Blake's fictional enterprise. In order to be published, she knew that she had to camouflage opinions that contradicted the status quo. It would seem that only by disguising her very self could a woman safely participate in the public world, and only by disguising her fiction could an author like Lillie Blake find her way into a middle-class readership. So Blake crossdresses her fiction, outfitting it with traditional plot elements and a conventional ending palatable to that readership, giving it the acceptable patina of the patriarchal script. But Blake's novel contains a hint for the reader that hers is a "cunningly-devised fiction," as her crossdresser says of her "dear little [fake] moustache" (367). With the use of the phrase "cunningly-devised fiction," Blake challenges her readers to see beneath her novel's camouflage. As the story of Molly Bludgett reveals, books in the hands of women are considered dangerous. By implication, *this* book, *Fettered For Life,* is dangerous. While Molly carefully hides her books from her husband, this book contains a carefully hidden agenda. Like its crossdresser, it is in disguise; it is really about something other than what it seems to be about.

NINETEENTH-CENTURY REFORM ISSUES

On its surface, *Fettered For Life* is about reform movements. It interweaves abolitionist, temperance, and women's rights issues with the plight of urban working women (especially poor women) and problems of women's personal freedom. It addresses in detail the post–Civil War status of women, including the restrictions on their use of public space, whether on the lecture circuit, on public streets, or in newspapers; issues of women in the workforce, their housing arrangements and their limited vocational options; the various forms of sexual harassment to which they were subjected; their educational options; and the push for reform in matters of property rights and marriage and even of female attire and exercise. The novel also documents broad social concerns resulting from industrialization, immigration, and an increasing urban population.

Fettered For Life's association of abolitionist, temperance, and women's rights issues reflects the historical interconnectedness of these movements. The American Temperance Society, formed in 1826, and the Female Anti-Slavery Society, formed in 1837, were two of the first large-scale social reform movements in post–Revolutionary War America to significantly engage women in reform struggles. In fact, the major reform movements of the nineteenth century relied heavily on the already existing structure of women's church-affiliated club networks for their organization and, as a consequence, their ideology became religiously or morally based; they were then seen as quite socially suitable for women's involvement. Reformers saw the complex interrelationship among these social issues and those that particularly affected women's lives, and often they devoted their time to more than one major issue. Lucy Stone began her career as a paid orator for the antislavery movement, while Susan B. Anthony was a temperance activist.[4]

The title of *Fettered For Life* is a conflation of allusions to nineteenth-century reform movements. "Fettered" was a familiar code word for black slavery, a word which came to signify for antislavery feminists their own link with their sister slaves,[5] and it also refers to marriage. The novel's subtitle, "Lord and Master," doubles both meanings, and the theme of female constriction and imprisonment underscores them. A third meaning of "fettered," which emerges thematically with Blake's exploration of disguise and the freedom gained when a woman appears in male form, is that of femaleness itself as a fetter which, in a patriarchal social order, enchains a woman for life, limiting her fulfillment as it circumscribes her freedom. Cornelia D'Arcy tells Laura, "It has been in some ages the worst curse that could fall on a human soul, to be imprisoned in a female form" (64).

After the Civil War, having put their own suffrage concerns in abeyance in favor of the antislavery cause, many women who had organized for abolition expected that women would be a part of the new postwar voting citizenry. But they were mistaken. The success of the abolitionist movement resulted in a serious setback for the women's movement. Most abolitionists considered support for woman suffrage a liability and an added burden that might imperil the fight for black male suffrage.[6] Woman suffrage was a threat to the existing system of political bosses and to those opposed to prohibition, who feared a women's voting bloc might support temperance measures.[7] It is in this context that we can place *Fettered For Life*'s indictment of the political organizer Judge Swinton and his band of liquor dealers. Also, through the anti-woman rhetoric of the immigrant Malone family, the novel reflects the opposition of new immigrant groups, most of whom had no tradition of woman suffrage.[8] In the post–Civil War milieu, when feminist disappointment over the denial of universal suffrage was keen, Blake resurrected in *fettered* a word sure to inflame feminist anger as well as to encode anew both the historical affiliation of the suffrage, temperance, and abolitionist movements and the forms of enslavement each fought against.

Reform novels were not unusual in the nineteenth century. American culture, open to voices of dissent, tends to incorporate calls for reform into its national life, and in so doing lessens their threat to the status quo.[9] Reform novels, in revealing how social institutions do not live up to an ideal, do not subvert those institutions at all. Rather, by showing deviations from unquestioned norms, these novels implicitly uphold those norms.[10]

Fettered for Life is a subversive, rather than simply a reform novel. Subversive novels not only reveal social ills, but also challenge underlying cultural presumptions. They must do so covertly, however, for to publish such challenges in a literary form intended for a middle-class readership requires subversive strategies.[11] What a writer could forthrightly criticize and what she had to hide can reveal what most threatened dominant social attitudes. Lillie Blake was able to expose with impunity behaviors such as drunkenness in husbands and abuse of seamstresses because these abuses were under attack in the mainstream society by temperance societies and the settlement house movement. Her middle-class readership, positioned at a superior distance, could accept her depiction of brutality in lower levels of society. She could even expose the sexual corruption at the heart of middle-class institutions—the judicial and marriage systems. *Fettered For Life*'s revelation of corruption within the very system that purported to protect women was not out of the ordinary. In fact, in the early 1870s allegations of political corruption during the reign of Boss Tweed in New York City were so widespread that reformers split the Republican Party, and in 1873 newspapers reported sensational allegations of sexual improprieties by Henry Ward Beecher, one of the best-known leaders of the abolitionist and suffrage movements. Nor did the public perceive as sensationalized Blake's exposure of what amounts to sexual enslavement in marriage. For instance, much earlier, in 1835, Lydia Marie Child, in her *History of the Condition of Women,* had compared the contemporary marriage market to the sale of Circassian women in Turkey.[12]

In its May 6, 1874, review of *Fettered for Life*, the *Home Journal* emphasized the accuracy of the novel's portrayals:

> While the story makes several startling statements, and draws some very dark pictures of men, we believe none of them are stronger than the truth. The great merit of this story is its startling reality, its truthfulness to every day life. Mrs. Blake writes of what she knows and some of the characters introduced to the reader are easily recognized by people acquainted in New York. Those who once commence to read the story of Laura Stanley's struggles, trials, and triumphs in this city will hardly close the book until the end is reached. In describing such a place as Bludgett's den, Mrs. Blake must have taken council of some of her gentlemen friends. The Judge Swinton she puts upon the canvas is far more of a representative man than most people suspect, while Flora Livingston is one out of many of the unfortunately married belles of Fifth Avenue. "Fettered for Life" is a powerful book in its motive, and is too true to be easily upset.[13]

While perhaps "startling" or "dark," Blake's polemics on the popular reform issues of the day presented no serious threat to the status quo. What was threatening to the readership of 1874 was something else—something which is still controversial today. Blake's belief that womankind was not radically different from mankind and that gender differences are socially constructed called for a reconception of the nature of woman, and had to be presented covertly.[14] As Mary Putnam Jacobi, M.D., wrote in 1891:

> . . . women have in the mass, never been publicly and officially regarded as individuals, with individual rights, tastes, liberties, privileges, duties, and capacities, but rather as symbols, with collective class functions, of which not the least was to embody the ideals of decorum of the existing generation, whatever these might happen to be. These ideals once consigned to women, as to crystal vases, it became easier for men to indulge their vagrant liberty, while yet leaving undisturbed the general framework of order and society. But all the more imperative was it, that the standard of behavior, thought, and life for women should be maintained fixed and immovable. Any symptom of change in the status of women, seems, therefore, always to have excited a certain terror.[15]

Fettered For Life reveals that the exposure of the most serious of political corruptions was less of a threat to the social order than a re-examination of the nature and status of women.

NINETEENTH-CENTURY
IDEOLOGIES OF WOMANHOOD

Twentieth-century readers need to understand the social ideology of womanhood in nineteenth-century America in order to understand how Blake's views on women differed from those of mainstream thinking. Two intertwined ideologies pervaded nineteenth-century thought about women: simply put, "woman's separate sphere" held that a woman's acceptable tasks in life were linked to home and hearth and had to do with her caring for others; but because of "woman's moral superiority," which held that women were morally superior to men, her influence radiated out from the domestic space into every area of the social order.[16] "The influence of woman is not circumscribed by the narrow limits of the domestic circle. She controls the destiny of every community. The character of society depends as much on the fiat of woman as the temperature of the country on the influence of the sun," wrote Henry Wright in *The Empire of the Mother over the Character and Destiny of the Race.*[17] As Mrs. D'Arcy preaches to Biddy Malone, whose son has accused her of being "'only a woman'": "'As a woman, you are the fittest guide to virtue'" (31).

These ideas functioned reciprocally to keep women in their proper place by circumscribing and idealizing that place. But they also gave power to women even as they restricted them. They made more acceptable women's work for the rights of others (in the abolitionist movement) and against the moral improprieties of drunkenness and the resulting hardships for women and their families (in the temperance movement and in other philanthropic organizations). In fact, calling for reform was women's work. Men of the patriarchy, forced into the corruption of the world, depended upon the moral sensibilities of women to fight against flaws in the social order. Thus, even writing a reform novel, such as *Fettered For Life* appears to be, was an appropriate activity for a woman.

Nineteenth-century suffragists invoked the ideologies of "woman's separate sphere" and "woman's moral superiority" to authorize their public voice: they reasoned that to give the vote to those morally superior persons charged with the upbringing of the next generation would raise the ethical level of political discourse and insure a more moral world for the future. Such notions were useful to the woman suffage movement because they bypassed the issue of inferiority by stressing difference. They authorized women's claim to a role in political life and valorized the bonds of women's networking for the good of others.[18]

However, because these ideologies limited women's action in the world to their moral influence upon others, any ambition, any yearning for achievement, any strong definition of self was unseemly.[19] Thus, for instance, Flora Livingston's fault lay in her ambition, albeit an ever so slight ambition; it lay in her yearning for some definition of self beyond that of being chief ornament in her husband's house. That is why Laura can conclude with "passionate regret" that Flora's life "had been sacrificed to the dictates of the society in which she lived, and to the conventional ideas of 'woman's sphere'" (360). In this passage, Lillie Blake aligns herself with a small minority of post–Civil War suffragists, including Elizabeth Cady Stanton, who saw the dangers for women's progress in emphasizing gender differences. As Lori D. Ginzberg writes: "Unlike most nineteenth-century woman's rights leaders . . . [Stanton] believed that the ideology of female moral superiority could ultimately benefit only those who opposed their cause."[20] Ellen Carol DuBois places Stanton in a radical line stemming from Mary Wollstonecraft and Frances Wright, who based their suffragism on the principle that women and men share a common nature and thus must share common rights. For the most part, however, American suffragists followed the line of thought of Catherine Beecher and others who emphasized the distinctive nature of woman, her special needs, and her unique role. They sought to elevate woman's role within the domestic sphere and to extend that role into the public world.[21]

GENDER IDENTITY

Blake's premise that gender identity is secondary to human identity countered the very heart of the social ideology of womanhood in nineteenth-century America, for underlying the ideas of woman's separate sphere and woman's moral superiority was the presumption that the sexes were radically different.

Especially after the Civil War, this issue was crucial to only a few in the post–Civil War suffrage movement. When the rhetoric of universal suffrage, which was based on the concept of the commonality of human nature, failed to win women inclusion in the Fourteenth Amendment, suffrage leaders began to focus more on the particular grievances of women. DuBois writes: "In basic ways, the women's organizations of the 1870s and 1880s continued the prewar tradition of women's benevolent and moral reform activity. Their leaders tended to stress women's unique virtues and special responsibility to the community, rather than the identity of men's and women's public roles, which had been the distinguishing argument of women's rights."[22] Elizabeth Cady Stanton "was willing, as were few women then or now," states Ginzberg, "to argue that only in the rejection of the ideology of female difference lay the possibilities for the broadest vision of social change and for a true benevolence, based not on sex but on justice."[23]

Covertly in *Fettered For Life*, and insistently in her personal journals, Blake made statements in direct opposition to the prevailing attitudes concerning woman's essential nature.[24] Blake's premise in "The Social Condition of Woman," an early essay published anonymously in 1863, is that the characteristics of "true womanliness" are the result not of nature but of training.[25]

Blake's attitudes are contradicted by Cornelia D'Arcy, the novel's leading suffragist, who is really a diversion for Blake's most hidden agenda. Mrs. D'Arcy's preference for the use of her married title rather than her professional one is indicative of her privileging marriage over work. It undercuts her feminism, the limits of which are otherwise scarcely noticeable, but quite significant. Most importantly, while it is in her home that Laura's artistic talents are encouraged, it is also there that her ambitions are trivialized; clearly, for Mrs. D'Arcy, female ambitions must be limited in scope. While she appears to be the novel's spokesperson for Blake's own ideology, instead, she speaks the language of mainstream suffrage thought, which became increasingly conservative in the post–Civil War period. At the time that *Fettered For Life* was published, the Women's Christian Temperance Union and the Association for the Advancement of Women were formed. As DuBois notes, both groups stressed the "special needs and distinctive nature of women" and "heralded a new development in feminism, within which [Elizabeth Cady] Stanton increasingly found herself marginal."[26] Cornelia D'Arcy is the spokesperson, not for Blake or for the radical Stanton, whom Blake followed, but for the suffrage ideology of such groups as the WCTU and AAW— ideology confined to the nineteenth-century conception of woman as radically other *vis-à-vis* man. The differences between the sexes "'are radical and God-ordained,'" Mrs. D'Arcy says. "'Man represents in the world, the element of strength and force; woman that of love and spirituality; the cooperation of both is needed to form a perfect society or government'" (258). When Mrs. D'Arcy voices these mainstream suffrage sentiments of the time, Laura Stanley remains mute; she does not agree—nor does Blake. In her private and anonymous writing, Blake insisted that people share a common nature but are trained in gender roles, that gender differences should not be privileged over other differences among people; in other words that gender is socially constructed and historically contingent.

Thus, the hidden premise within *Fettered For Life* is that men and women are essentially the same; and the hidden story within *Fettered For Life* is the story of the crossdresser, the man who is a woman. On one level, like Virginia Woolf after her, Blake uses a switch of gender as a rhetorical device to reveal social injustices: reversing the gender of the youth in the fairy tale who goes off to make his fortune shows how, within the current social order, the story cannot work for a woman; and disguising a female character as a man reveals how a fully capable woman cannot make it in the world unless she dons a surface disguise. But on a more covert level, Blake's use of the gender switch infers that gender itself is a surface detail. The fact that the woman who crossdresses and the man she pretends to be are the same person suggests that the profound differences between the sexes, which are used to create a hierarchy and to justify social inequities, are themselves not preordained essences, but mere products of social circumstances.

This, her most radical agenda, Blake kept well hidden not only from her middle-class readership, but also from her sisters in the suffrage movement—to whom her vision would not have been a welcome one. Only a "small minority," writes DuBois, "called for radical transformation in women's lives . . . the great majority of suffragists . . . intended no such challenge."[27]

WOMEN'S WORK

During the last third of the nineteenth century, writing about women and work constituted one way of entering the intense social debate over the changing status of women. For example, the year before *Fettered For Life* appeared, Louisa May Alcott published *Work: A Story of Experience,* a novel that provides a survey of various professions available to middle-class women. Alcott's insistent interpretation of women's work in the public world as a continuation of their duties in the home reasserts the notion that woman's essential nature is connected to a separate domestic sphere, and skirts the issue of the appropriateness of women working outside that sphere. Here we see the strategy typical of advocates for women's rights throughout the century. This strategy called for the expansion of women's options without questioning the underlying presumptions and attitudes about woman's essential nature which had limited those options to begin with. *Work* is a reform novel, but unlike *Fettered for Life,* it is not a subversive one; it upholds the status quo because it makes clear that for a woman, success in a career is unseemly, if not disreputable and selfish, unless her career involves working for the good of others. Only when Alcott's actress-heroine, Christy, sacrifices herself to save another can the reader begin to answer Alcott's central question: "A fine actress perhaps, but how good a woman?" We watch as illness and misfortune bring about a passivity in Christy, and we are told that her better self is emerging. When Christy looks back over her life, her proof of its success are her dead husband's presumed approval, her subordination of her own work to his, and the self-sacrificial (i.e. womanly) nature of her work. Alcott's need to domesticate her public women is indicative of the disease with which the middle class approached any change in the status of women.[28]

Eight years later, William Dean Howells's *Dr. Breen's Practice* rehearsed what had come to be standard fare in the novelistic treatment of women physicians. Unlike Blake who, reflecting her hope for a future of equality, treated Cornelia D'Arcy's position as a physician as ordinary, Howells saw women physicians as both unconventional and undesirable. His novel's treatment of female doctors—and by implication, women professionals in general—centers on questions of their motivation, their lack of physical and emotional fitness, and the conflict between their profession and the possibility of marriage. Howells's Grace Breen enters medicine "in the spirit in which other women enter convents"—that is, in response to a failed love affair, her fiancé having married her best friend. From the beginning of the novel, Grace is associated with helplessness, failure, and arrested development. The only time her "strength" is referred to is when she haltingly admits her "failure": "'I wished to be a physician,'" she confesses to her mother, "'because I was a woman, and because—because—I had failed where—other women's hopes are.' She said it out firmly, and her mother softened to her in proportion to the girl's own strength."[29] Clearly, a woman is here affirmed as strong when she is most vulnerable. In return for her declaration of failure, Grace is finally afforded her mother's affection. As the novel concludes, Howells paints the picture of a helpless woman who is rescued, through marriage, from what is viewed as the ridiculous predicament of having a profession. It is her weakness that allows her to be loved, and her rescue allows her, at last, to complete her arrested development and fully mature into a married woman.

Elizabeth Stuart Phelps's *Dr. Zay* was an answer to Howells's novel. In this 1882 work, Phelps depicts a fully mature, self-possessed professional, a new type of women who demands a new type of man if the conflict between marriage and a woman working is to be resolved.[30]

Throughout the nineteenth century, the need for women to fill industry's demands for cheap labor coexisted uneasily with the need for an ideal of domestic true womanhood. A split along the lines of class and marital status enabled both needs to be filled without a resolution of the contradictions involved. Working-class women like Biddy Malone, Rhoda Dayton, and Maggie Bertram—married or not, mothers or not—were in the labor force. Middle-class women, especially once they married, served as society's crystal vase, reflecting its ideal of woman in her domestic sphere.

From the beginning of industrialization early in the century, women were increasingly present in public, working outside the home and living outside the traditional family. By 1870 close to 325,000 women were factory workers, many crowded into the sewing trades "where their situation was desperate."[31] During the Civil War, the phenomenon of middle-class women in the workforce increased. In the North, women were mobilized in nursing units and in the Sanitary Commission. In post–Civil War society, although not ordinarily expected, it was not unusual for an unmarried, middle-class woman like Laura Stanley to be working and living on her own. It was assumed, however, that a suitable marriage would end her public career and begin what was considered to be her far more important, domestic role.[32]

In *Fettered for Life*, however, Blake exposes not only the oppression of working-class women and the difficulties of single, middle-class women in the labor market, but also the vacuity of the lives of middle-class and upper-middle-class married women. As the newly married Flora LeRoy laments, "I have literally nothing on earth to do. . . . no way of filling up the endless hours" (264). In "The Social Condition of Woman," Blake foregrounded the repetitive minutia of middle-class domestic life:

> . . . the endless sewing that fills up all the leisure of woman's life is a fearful degenerator. I know of nothing more cramping to the mind than this perpetual setting of minute stitches. . . . the utter weariness, the heart-sickness of many a poor lady who feels each morning when she wakes the lack of any stimulus in life! and sees existence stretching before her an endless world of petty conventionalities and wearisome repetitions (385).

Never does Blake suggest, as most of the domestic novelists do, that motherhood will solve Flora's ennui. Instead she seems to share the views of Laura, who encourages Flora to write and to publish what she writes. One of the radical ideas that Blake articulates in *Fettered*

For Life is that women need to work for their own self-fulfillment. While working-class women had to work for survival, and middle-class women could work for economic independence until marriage brought them better duties and other means of support, Blake insisted on a third function of work—that of a vital activity which brought meaning to life and definition to self. This idea countered the notion that women should only work for the good of others and not of self, it undermined the primacy of marriage in the fulfillment of women's lives, and it posed a threat to the dominance of husbands through whom wives were defined.[33] Blake's ideology was a precursor of that which enabled the next generation of writers, like Charlotte Perkins Gilman and Kate Chopin, to depict with sympathy women who awakened to their own selves and desires in the face of a culture that acknowledged in them no needs beyond fulfilling the needs of others, and no voice save that which the patriarchal culture might script for them.

FAIRY-TALE ENDINGS

The story Blake wanted to write—a story in which a woman might marry and not give up her self—was one that, in 1874, was scarcely imaginable. In fact, despite all Laura Stanley's assertions concerning the importance of self-fulfillment, of financial independence for women, and of equality in marriage, in the end, her promising art career is reduced to flower painting on commission, her earning power is domesticated (rather than earning a living, she can "settle her small debts . . . and [buy] a new dress" [279]), and she becomes engaged to marry a man who has difficulty filling the role of the new man Elizabeth Stuart Phelps would call for. This conclusion for the novel is a traditional fairy-tale ending, with a hardworking Cinderella rescued through marriage; it would seem to stand as a serious inconsistency in a novel which articulates the importance of woman's fulfillment and independence through work. But it is at the very point where an author seems to violate her own precepts that we are witness to a clash between a socially precribed norm and that which poses a threat to it. We come to the boundary beyond which the author can proceed only via disguise. Blake's fairy-tale ending is part of a cover plot which subversive fictions intentionally provide to reassert the status quo in order to make their work palatable to the literary marketplace.

Blake turns to the same cover plot when Laura wins first prize in the Academy of Design's art exhibit and her story of success—a threat to the patriarchal marriage script for women—is immediately recast into a more socially acceptable, gender appropriate romance, which leads Laura to see that life's best prize is a happy marriage. Blake uses this cover as a disguise for her radical idea that women as well as men have a need for self-fulfilling action in the world, an idea she first expressed in "The Social Condition of Woman." There Blake not only argued that social customs deny women meaningful work, but defined marriage, in a social order that limits women from other means of earning a living, as institutionalized prostitution. If all women were allowed employment, then no woman would "ever be reduced to the degrading necessity of marrying for a support—that is, selling herself because she sees with despair that, as society is at present constituted, and from the defects of her education, there is no hope of earning an honest livelihood."[34] *Fettered For Life* makes clear that there is little difference between the sweatshop seamstress, so underpaid that she is forced into prostitution, and the wealthiest of wives, who is permitted no activity save sewing and who, if married to a tyrant, soon finds that neither her life nor her body is her own.

While subversive writers construct cover plots to hide their radical ideas, they also, as Susan K. Harris has explained so well, form counterplots that serve to undermine the cover plots. These counterplots raise questions that encourage readers to form private conclusions more consistent with the narrative.[35] By revealing flawed marriage after flawed marriage, Blake undermines, even as she seems to prepare the way for, the possibility of a union of equality for Laura Stanley and Guy Bradford. We see an alcoholic wife-beater; a husband who at every chance dominates and demeans his intellectually superior wife; a stern, cold tyrant; a marriage that seems conventionally happy only because the wife has given up any claim to fulfillment of her own; and a marriage of enslavement. Suggesting how difficult it was to imagine the possibility of a successful middle-class marriage of equal partnership, Blake provides us with only two inadequate examples of such a union. We are told how just and happy the Bradford marriage is, but are provided with barely a glimpse of it in practice— a mention of the warm touch of hands and the meeting of eyes, the congeniality of their home; and we see a product of that marriage, Guy Bradford, having to struggle to accept the woman he loves on equal terms. The only "profoundly happy" marriage in the novel is Cornelia D'Arcy's—but her husband is dead! A marriage based on remembered happiness, without the possibly irritating intrusions of a live partner, seems to be the easiest to imagine.

In addition, Blake encourages skepticism regarding Laura's intended marriage by steering us towards a different match. Most readers see the more active and interesting Frank Heywood, who is committed to Laura's feminist precepts, as the more appropriate marriage partner. Guy is a nice guy, but rather an ordinary one, who espouses equality in the abstract but has an obviously difficult time accepting it on a personal level.[36] By playing with realistic and sentimental styles, Blake also undercuts Laura's reveries of a life with Guy. When Laura has "reflections [which] were as golden as the bright rays that the setting sun was casting over the city," Blake breaks the spell by having her "descend from the fairy realms in which she had been dreaming, to the prosaic realities of common life. The place seemed more than usually dingy" (209). Throughout the conclusion, Blake switches from a realistic to a sentimental style, alerting her readers that this too is another fairy tale, an entrapment which the culture of sentiment holds for women. In a continuing push to undermine her own publishable ending, Blake does not bring the novel to closure with the formulaic certainty of a wedding, but rather ends it with an engagement and a promise, leaving room for the reader to revise the ultimate outcome. In such ways, Blake provides her audience with an ending that upholds the public value of the primacy of marriage, even as she subverts it. She leaves Laura with the challenge of continuing to write her own life story in the face of patriarchal scripting which could erase that story altogether.

PATRIARCHAL SCRIPTS VS. WOMEN'S SELF-POSSESSION

The opening scene of *Fettered for Life* foregrounds the issue of female containment within the legal space of patriarchy. Questioned by Judge Swinton as to why she is in the city and where she plans to stay, Laura is befriended by Frank Heywood, who promises to keep her name out of the papers and warns her not to let anyone know that she has spent the night in the police court. Later in the novel, Guy Bradford, her otherwise unremarkable suitor, exiles himself on a trip abroad rather than face the uncertainty of Laura's where-abouts on her first night in New York. Unaware of the depth and breadth of the social restrictions imposed upon women, contemporary readers may be puzzled as to what all the fuss is about. However, an account of an actual event dating from almost a generation later illustrates the depth of the restrictions imposed upon women and the implications for a nineteenth-century woman of being out alone, particularly at night. Twenty-one years after the publication of *Fettered For Life*,

> on the night of December 6, 1895, the police of New
> York City arrested Lizzie Schauer, a young working-
> class woman, on a charge of disorderly conduct.
> She had, according to her own account, been looking
> for the house of her aunt and had stopped to ask
> directions of two men. This behavior—as well as
> the fact that an unaccompanied woman was out
> at night—was presumptive evidence that she was
> soliciting prostitution in the eyes of the arresting
> police officers and of the judge who sent her to the
> work house. . . . [She was released] only after a
> doctor's examination had shown her to be a "good
> girl."[37]

Such medical and judicial intrusions into a woman's very person as well as into her personal life are indicative of the level of social control exercised over her. The marriages which Blake exposes in *Fettered For Life* are the private manifestations of such public norms. When Ferdinand LeRoy tells his reluctant bride Flora that he has the right of entrance to all parts of his house (304), the sexual implications and the pervasiveness of control are clear; a married woman did not belong to herself. In the latter half of the nineteenth century, "'self-ownership,'" writes Margit Stange, "signified a wife's right to refuse marital sex—a right feminists were demanding as the key to female autonomy."[38]

When projected onto the larger canvas of the novel, the picture that Blake draws of Laura, detained against her will in the police court, implicates society as a whole in a broad range of actions that seek to control women. Laura has had to "escape" (35) her father; in his attempt to procure her for Judge Swinton, Bludgett threatens to drag her into his house; and later she is kidnapped. But these are the more violent forms of imprisonment she faces; sexual harassment of any degree restricts a woman's freedom, and just the threat of Judge Swinton's unwanted attentions results in Laura's self-confinement: "She made it a rule to be at home every day before twilight fell, and avoided going out, except on the ordinary round of her duties" (193). When she tries to earn a living as a book agent, the harassment she endures just entering commercial establishments is enough to force her to give up the job.[39]

Other women experience similar forms of confinement. Molly Bludgett is not allowed outside her home. In despair at the control her employer has over her, Rhoda wonders if she is "to be forever an utter and abject slave!" (122). Agnes Moulder, by metaphoric implication, is a caged bird whose escape throws her husband into a murderous rage.[40] Mrs. Livingston colludes in the patriarchal socialization of her daughter, although she "had at one period of her life protested against her destiny as bitterly as did ever any revolted slave; but having for years past been contented with her chains, she could endure no thought of revolt in others" (102–103). Flora Livingston is imprisoned like a pinned butterfly, and then "bartered away" (102) by her parents, although "if they had read an account of how certain savages deck out their young daughters with beads and feathers, and then offer them to some great chief for sale, they would probably have been shocked at such unchristian and barbarous practices" (103). Ferdinand LeRoy calls her "my sweet trembling little prisoner," and Flora is "unable to escape" (128). She is drawn through elegant salons like "some fair Grecian captive led in chains to adorn the triumph of a victor" (195).[41] Not only is the social order constructed in such a way that women are always in need of protectors, but those protectors—fathers, husbands, judges— are often the very people from whom they must escape.

Only the woman who has disguised herself as a man has unharassed access to the city any time of day or night.

Covering up her womanhood protects the novel's cross-dresser from, among other things, male proprietary gazing, which Blake constructs as another form of fettering.[42] It is the men of power who impose upon women the unrelenting, possessive gaze of patriarchy. Ferdinand LeRoy watches Flora "with a gaze which never relented. She was gay with her gay companions, she laughed with the rest; but there was with her all the time, a feeling of oppression, a sense that she was not one moment free from that cold, yet devouring regard" (127). Laura is violently startled when Judge Swinton gazes at her, but even after she turns away from him he looks after her from his position of power, amused and "with a smile on his lips" (38). Men look upon Laura as she stands before the police court, and an "almost imperceptible glance of intelligence" (10) is exchanged between the judge and his procurer, John Bludgett. A power network exists among these men, filled with "knowing winks" (338), so that often not a word need be spoken for an exchange to take place.

If the power of men is so great that words can be dispensed with, the suppression of women's voices, on the other hand, is a central form of patriarchal control. To be fettered in this society meant not only that women were confined in various ways, and not only that they were objects of intrusive viewing, but, in addition, that their freedom to speak was restricted. Although women were encouraged by a culture that valued the "feminine" orientation toward working for the good of others, it was clear that they were to be unobtrusive in doing so; they were to be neither seen nor heard. "'Women should be shrinking and modest, avoiding the public gaze'" (251), Mr. Glitter, the principal of a school for girls, informs Laura Stanley. To gaze at a woman is a possessive act reserved for a privileged male.

While women were the bedrock of the important reform movements of the century, they infrequently held positions of leadership, and those who appeared or spoke in public paid a public price. Even the 1848 Seneca Falls convention, one of the first meetings on women's rights, which produced Elizabeth Cady Stanton's famed *Declaration of Sentiments,* was chaired by a man. Nathaniel Hawthorne worried about women writers displaying their "naked minds" in public. And women like Sarah and Angelina Grimké who, in the late 1830s, publicly lectured against slavery were vilified in the press with innuendoes concerning the sexual impropriety of "exhibiting" themselves. As an antislavery orator, Lucy Stone, one of the most revered of the first generation of suffrage workers, was doused with water from a fire hose; pelted with eggs, "dried apples, smoked herring, beans, and tobacco quids"; and hit over the head with a hymnbook.[43]

By the time of the Civil War, women appearing in public forums had become a more frequent feature of American life, and where once only a woman's marriage and death were considered appropriate for a press notice, their activities and achievements began to take up space in the press.[44] Thus, while Ferdinand LeRoy is enraged at seeing his wife's name in print, a point is made of having Laura Stanley's first prize at the Academy of Design announced in the local paper. *Fettered For Life*'s most obvious allusion to the question of a woman's lecturing in public occurs in a confrontation between Laura and Mr. Glitter, who maintains his position that woman's place is in the home and not at the podium even as he sends his overworked wife out of the home and into the rain to run all his errands.

The real question here concerns the source of control over language, and *Fettered For Life* presciently plays out this question in ways that reflect contemporary feminist question of voice and authorship. Laura points out to Mr. Glitter that his position implies that while an actress is socially acceptable because she repeats other people's words, a female orator is not because she repeats her own words (107). The power of words, and the ownership of that power, is made clear when Judge Swinton abducts Laura. Chloroformed, she is "quiet as a lamb" (190). Frank Heywood's threat to use words, to give voice to Laura's outrage by reporting it for his newspaper, is sufficient to foil the judge, whose only response is the utterance of yet another word, "a very ugly word, which he gave under his breath, but with great force as he turned on his heel" (190).

Giving breath to any word with great force was not considered appropriate to women. When Laura first appears in the novel, she is described as "quietly self-possessed" (8), but ultimately *Fettered For Life* reveals that phrase to be an oxymoron; to be quiet, to give up one's voice, is finally to give up oneself. One can only be quietly dispossessed. Laura may "prefer the quiet paths of art and study to the angry strife of politics" (68), but her very choice of that quiet path of art is political, for when it is explained that Laura wants to be a serious artist, the idea is greeted with laughter. It seems that there is no quiet way for women to possess themselves. To be quiet, whether out of fear or the need to please another, is to erase one's own desires and to give up the power necessary to script one's own life. Out of fear of displeasing her father, Flora Livingston suppresses her desire to be more than an ornament. Agnes Moulder has spent years consciously silencing her yearnings for something beyond the domestic drudgery of her life (105). Molly Bludgett, who spends her days reading sentimental fictions like "Berenice the Beautiful," knows that to give voice to her dreams will result in nothing but a brutal beating. Indeed, to break the silence can be terrifying, and in several incidents, when Laura has incited her friends to speak up for themselves, she herself is frightened by the sounds they make and seeks to silence them: "'Oh do try to be more quiet,'" Laura urges Agnes

Moulder after her husband has killed her uncaged bird
(291); and "'It is perhaps better not to speak hardly of
him,' Laura said quietly" to the newly married Mrs.
LeRoy, leaving Flora silent and alone to guard "the secrets
of the prison-house" (263).

Female silence is essentially a matter of the erasure
of the female self. The most powerful and lordly of men,
Ferdinand LeRoy, makes clear that men of his ilk demand
quietness in women. With the dehumanizing gaze of one
who possesses a new toy, he looks at Flora "as one might
at a doll one was attiring," and says, "I can see that your
nature is quietness itself!" (23–32). When her father tells
her that "a true woman is willing to lose her own identity
in her husband's," Flora's "suppressed wrath . . . burst[s]
forth into words" (101). When she declares that her
marriage has killed her, and her mother cautions her,
"Don't say such wild words, and the doctor has forbidden
you talking much," Flora replies, "They are not wild
words, and it will not hurt me to talk" (351). Words are
what Flora chooses as the instrument that will make her
life her own, but upon the appearance of her first
publication, her husband burns all of her remaining
manuscripts. When she pleads with him, saying, "I need
an object in life," LeRoy's response is, "women should be
quiet" (343–44). To keep a woman quiet, to deny her the
use of words, is to keep her from scripting her own life
rather than following the dictates of the patriarchal
text. The burning of Flora's manuscripts, like Laura's
humiliating job of bookselling, becomes a trope both for
the erasure of women's attempts to write their own lives
and for the suppression of women's literary tradition.

Blake's motifs of voice and quiet, words and books,
converge with the death of the female self when the
silenced Flora—after dismissing her maid with a request
to go to a bookstore to get a book, any book—walks to the
sea, follows the voice of the waves which she hears "calling
to her, calling to her, with their hollow voices," and with

her own "strange wild cry" tries to drown herself. Suicide reduces the self to silence. When Flora dies "there was silence in the room; silence except for the faint sigh of the wind, and the chant of the waves that was like a requiem!" (352).

And when Molly Bludgett's life violently ends, it is significant that she is silenced with a boot heel in her mouth. Her life brutally connects the motifs of words and books, voice and silence. From her first appearance in the novel, Mrs. Bludgett has alerted us to the fact that, for a woman, reading is a subversive activity. A voracious reader of sentimental stories,[45] she quickly and guiltily hides from her husband whatever novel or illustrated story paper she happens to be reading. "Bludgett he don't like it," she explains (16). The last book she hides from her husband is "no showily-covered romance, but a poor, worn copy of the Bible," the appearance of which "seemed to stimulate his rage to madness; he snatched it from her and smote her down again, silencing that pleading voice by a stamp of his heavy boot-heel on the helpless mouth" (374–75). Significantly, the subsequent chapter finds Laura Stanley in Cornelia D'Arcy's library, where books are freely read and ideas are given voice.

However, whose books and whose voices are permitted expression in the world of *Fettered For Life* is an issue which the novel continuously exposes. Within its male-inscribed and predatory world, a covert circle of female storytellers creates a community of women which, at least temporarily, breaks through both the borders created by the hierarchical class lines of patriarchy and the silences imposed upon women. Laura asks Molly Bludgett, "tell me all about yourself" (18), and so begins a secret solidarity based on women's storytelling. Frank asks for Laura's story; she asks for Rhoda's and gives hers to Cornelia. Flora is a poet, the crossdresser loves to write; each speaks out of a silence that imprisons her. Everyone is careful to whom she tells her story, for in the patriarchal order a woman is not permitted to have her own story. The most secret story, the hidden story of disguise, becomes emblematic of the novel itself—for it not only keeps its most subversive story well hidden; it also makes clear that the very act of writing the self is a woman's most subversive activity. Coming to know to whom one can tell one's story and how much one can safely reveal is part of the process of survival for Blake's characters. Coming to know what was safe to write about openly and what was not is crucial to the formation of a paradigm for reading subversive novels like *Fettered For Life*. And coming to understand the complexity of the process which suppressed woman's literary tradition is not only part of the contemporary feminist project; it was also the project of writers like Lillie Devereux Blake, who wrote "cunningly-devised fictions" in hopes that their stories might be heard.

LITERARY-HISTORICAL CONTEXT

Fettered For Life was first published in 1874, at a time when America's national literature was gradually moving away from sentimental forms into realism and naturalism. Reflecting these cultural shifts and trends, *Fettered For Life* is an historically complex document positioned at a pivotal point in American literary history. As a realistic novel in transition, it looks backward towards the sentimental novel, with its emphasis on plot, and forward to the naturalistic portrayal of the industrialized world's class struggle. Like reform novels, it intentionally participates in the forward thrust of its transitional age. As a subversive novel, *Fettered For Life* suggests ways in which literature in transition manages to challenge outright some aspects of its society's status quo while seeming to acquiesce in other aspects. The combination of its outright challenges and its acquiescences diverts attention from the novel's most radical agenda, which remains disguised, hidden, and thus ever more subversive.

In her journal, Blake writes that the subtitle, "A Story of To-Day," was her initial choice for the title of her novel. "A story of to-day" was a commonplace term for an accurate history of the day as distinguished from a romance, with its focus on the past. Later both William Dean Howells and Hamlin Garland, the ordained fathers of American realism, would define realism and romanticism in such terms.[46] Blake's use of the subtitle indicates her intention to write a realistic novel rather than a sentimental romance.

Traces of the sentimental novel survive in Blake's densely populated plot. But unlike the sentimentalists, Blake exposes the harsh realities of economic and sexual exploitation unrelieved by the prettiness of downtrodden maidens rescued by more privileged men. Her depiction of lower-class and lower-middle-class characters in a commonplace, unheroic world is typical of realism and naturalism. And like the realists, she draws parallels among divergent social classes, stressing elements of commonality and revealing middle-class values of loyalty, hard work, and sacrifice in lower classes as well as primitive practices in the most cultured levels of society. Unlike her sentimentalist predecessors and more like the naturalists who came after her, Blake incorporates sensationalism into a realistic mode: violence and heroism exist within a framework of the probable. John Bludgett beats his wife to death in an alcoholic rage; Maggie Bertram dies of consumption, a tubercular condition not at all untypical of the times, which was associated with impoverished living conditions;[47] and Rhoda Dayton sacrifices her life by drowning so that another might live—another whom Rhoda thinks has a better chance to succeed in the struggle of life. Heroism displayed by characters in the lower social orders became a hallmark of realism, and Rhoda displays a nobility of character in several incidents in the novel. It is she who is instrumental in rescuing Laura from Judge Swinton, thus saving Laura from Rhoda's own unhappy fate.

Howells saw realism as intrinsically democratic because, in giving a view of the commonplace and the common person, it provided its readership with the basis upon which to understand the commonality of all people. Blake, in her novel, provides glimpses of a variety of social classes. Laura Stanley is one of five young women who begin their adult lives in the city—each from a different class, each with a different strategy for survival, sharing some similar adventures, but suffering different fates. Like the realists and naturalists who followed her, Blake's idea of fate was not the notion of cosmic inevitability familiar to the Romantic movement, but rather a socio-economic construct. She did not apply the moral judgments made by the sentimentalists, for whom character largely determined fate. Given a different set of circumstances, any of Blake's five women could end up like any other. Both Rhoda Dayton and Laura Stanley are the objects of Judge Swinton's abductions. He is successful with the one, but not with the other, whom he harasses at every opportunity; his success, however, has everything to do with circumstance and nothing to do with character, although Rhoda is perceived by society as a "fallen woman" after her abduction. Both Maggie Bertram and Flora Livingston are the objects of the wealthy Ferdinand LeRoy's obsessions: the first he seduces and betrays, the second he marries. While Maggie is left to waste away in a garret, Flora is expected to do much the same, but in more regal apartments. The fifth woman, also once the object of Judge Swinton's designs, escapes only by giving up her womanhood altogether and disguising herself as a man. The world in which these women find themselves is one in which they are prey and in which survival means renouncing the self.

The realists saw their enterprise not only as democratic but as intrinsically reformist, because, in providing its middle-class readership with a view of the life struggle

of the common person, their work encouraged empathy
across class lines and inspired a passion for redressing
social ills. Unlike the sentimentalists, Blake portrays the
social ills of nineteenth-century America as products of
a socioeconomic system that can be changed.

In "Tradition and the Female Talent," her alternative
to T.S. Eliot's New Critical ideology, Elaine Showalter
has traced a distinctively female literary tradition
through the nineteenth century.[48] Pre–Civil War women's
fiction was largely sentimental, aesthetically restricted,
and not self-consciously artistic; after the war, local
colorists began to assert themselves as artists, and, with
a nostalgia for the postwar decline of "women's culture,"
to mythologize domestic imagery. Later, the "New Women
writers of the 1890s no longer grieved for the female bonds
and sanctuaries of the past. Products of both Darwinian
skepticism and aesthetic sophistication, they had an
ambivalent or even hostile relationship to women's
culture."[49] Showalter cites Kate Chopin's *The Awakening*
as the first aesthetically successful novel by an American
woman, which, had it not been ignored for over half a
century, might have had profound effects upon women's
literary tradition in America.

In 1874, *Fettered For Life* dealt with issues which
Showalter cites as elements of the brave New Women's
fiction of the 1890s and beyond. While it may not be able
to claim the inward turn of such narratives as Chopin's,
it may well have helped paved the way for them. A
generation before *The Awakening* and Charlotte Perkins
Gilman's *The Yellow Wall-Paper* appeared, Blake depicted
the struggles of women bent upon telling their own
stories in a world that sought only to contain them within
male scripts. She creates a woman as artist in a losing
battle with patriarchal suppression. Unlike the sentimentalists, she does not venerate motherhood nor infer
that only though it can a woman find her natural
fulfillment. While Showalter cites the caged songbird as

the sentimentalist's representation of the "creative woman in her domestic sphere,"[50] Blake foregrounds not the singing bird, but the cage; she stresses woman's need to escape domestic confinement and at the same time depicts, with a portrayal of murderous male rage directed at the free-flying bird, patriarchy's investment in female confinement.[51] In attempting to re-envision a woman's story rather than encode anew patriarchy's version of the feminine, Blake, like the New Women novelists of the next generation, uses disguise and crossdressing.

Blake's novel stands within the masculine-defined traditions of sentimentality and of realism and naturalism; but it also takes its place within the literary traditions traced by Showalter. *Fettered For Life* is one of the important missing links of women's literary tradition.

BIOGRAPHICAL NOTE

Lillie Devereux Blake, fiction writer, journalist, essayist, and lecturer, was a cultural critic who commented on a wide range of social conventions, especially those regarding women. Her work, stretching over half a century, includes five novels, a collection of short stories, a collection of essays, and hundreds of uncollected short stories and essays.

Born Elizabeth Johnson Devereux on 12 August 1833 in Raleigh, North Carolina, Blake lived for the first four years of her life on her father's plantation in Roanoke, Virginia. When her father died in 1837, her mother returned to her family in Connecticut. There Blake attended school until she was fifteen and then was privately tutored in the Yale undergraduate curriculum. In 1855 she married Frank Umsted, a lawyer from Philadelphia, and settled briefly in St. Louis, where, after the birth of her first daughter in February 1857, Blake began writing. She sent her first story to *Harper's Weekly,* vowing to herself that if it were rejected, she would give up her dream of being a writer. It appeared in November 1857. A second story and a poem appeared in the *Knickerbocker* the following spring.

After moving to New York City, where her second daughter was born in July 1858, Blake began her first novel, *Southwold,* which appeared on 5 February 1859. Three months later, Frank Umsted killed himself with a pistol shot to the head. Whether his death was a suicide or an accident, Blake, traumatized by loss and by memories of the incident, was abandoned to support two children under the age of two and a half. Yet her journals reveal both a refusal to define herself as a victim and a resistance to remarriage as a solution to both her widowhood and the precarious financial situation that resulted from it.

The "degrading necessity of . . . selling herself" was not for her.[52] Instead she began writing again.

Although Blake published an early story in the elite *Atlantic,* in order to earn a living she turned almost exclusively to popular magazines and began writing for the mass market. Under her own name and a variety of pseudonyms (Essex, Charity Floyd, Violet; and later, Aesop, Tiger Lily, Di Fairfax, Lulu Dashaway), she routinely sold stories to Frank Leslie's publications, as well as to *Harper's Weekly,* the *Saturday Evening Post,* the *New York Leader,* the *Sunday Times,* and a wide variety of other periodicals. She contracted with the *New York Evening Post,* the *New York World,* and the *Philadelphia Press* to serve as a Washington-based Civil War correspondent during 1861–62 and again during 1865–66. Much later, while she was active in the National Woman Suffrage Association, led by Susan B. Anthony and Elizabeth Cady Stanton, Blake would become a regular columnist for the *Woman's Journal,* the voice of Lucy Stone's and Henry Blakewell's American Woman Suffrage Association. These two associations had split over the Fourteenth Amendment, which granted suffrage to African American men but excluded women from the vote. In 1890 they would merge into the National American Woman Suffrage Association. Blake's columns played a conciliatory role as these two sides of the woman's movement began to come together.

In 1866 Blake married Grinfill Blake, a New York businessman several years her junior, and continued to support herself through her writing. By the 1870s Lillie Blake, no longer anonymous, had also found her voice as a lecturer for the suffrage movement. During this period of her life, when she wrote *Fettered For Life*, Blake became a highly successful political organizer for the suffrage movement. She was president of the New York State Woman Suffrage Association (1879–90) and of the Civic and Political Equality Union of New York City (1898–

1900), and she founded and served as president of the National Legislative League. During her career in New York, she organized legislative action which proved instrumental in modifying many laws that discriminated against women. Through her leadership, Civil War nurses became eligible for pension benefits, women became eligible for civil service positions, mothers were made joint guardians of their children, and for the first time women were allowed to serve on school boards and work in public institutions in which women were incarcerated.

Blake even initiated actions which eventually led to the founding of Barnard College of Columbia University. Blake's great-great-grandfather had been Columbia's first president when it was known as Kings College, and her great-grandfather had been the first president after the American Revolution, when its name was changed to Columbia College. Yet she and her daughters were excluded from admission. In 1873, beneath portraits of her ancestors, Blake hand-delivered a written application to President F.A.P. Barnard for admission of five female candidates, and prepared a plea which Barnard proposed to the Board of Trustees. The board referred the proposal to committee, effectively halting action on it. But as a result of Blake's action, President Barnard would renew the plea over the course of several years until, in 1883, as a first step, women were admitted to the Columbia Collegiate Course for Women. In 1889 Barnard College was formed as an annex to Columbia. Blake was opposed to this latter course of action because she wanted women to be admitted to Columbia on an equal footing with men, and not relegated to a separate institution. The argument between Blake and her opponents on this issue reflects the argument between those nineteenth-century feminists who wanted women integrated into the public world without regard to sex and those who emphasized femaleness in their struggle for women's rights.

In 1883, Blake's public lectures in response to Dr.

Morgan Dix's Lenten lectures on "Woman" earned public recognition for her and drew ignominy down on him.[53] Her lectures were collected and published by popular demand under the title *Woman's Place To-day*. The book, writes Elinore Hughes Partridge, "created a sensation in the contemporary press and did much to awaken women into active workers for suffrage."[54]

Blake attained such prominence in the woman suffrage movement that Elizabeth Cady Stanton supported her to succeed Susan B. Anthony as president of the National American Woman Suffrage Association in 1900. However, Blake had incurred the displeasure of Anthony by persisting in her work for civil rights legislation for women rather than focusing solely on suffrage. At the same time, she had aroused ill will in a younger generation of more conservative suffrage leaders by collaborating with Stanton on *The Woman's Bible* and defending her against an 1896 NAWSA resolution denouncing the book. Thereafter, Blake was systematically marginalized by the NAWSA, and her contributions to it were minimized in its official records. Kathi Kern notes that Carrie Chapman Catt—with whom Anthony would replace Blake as the NAWSA organizer in Delaware, and who would then succeed Anthony as president of NAWSA—"strongly urged delegates to repudiate *The Woman's Bible*." Blake and other Stanton supporters were, as Kern has documented, "virtually ostracized" and "essentially disempowered in the wake of the controversy."[55]

Blake lived until 1913, continuing to write for the popular press through her seventh decade. Constructed over an undercurrent of private grief and dedicated to the eradication of social injustices, her work is well worth remembering.

NOTES

1. This kind of "happily ever after" marriage plot is, of course, a primary plot of the sentimental novel—a patriarchal plot that is allowed expression by women, and then, in a literary Catch 22, dismissed by the literary establishment as trivial. See note 45.

2. "The Laugh of the Medusa," trans. Keith Cohen and Paula Cohen, *Signs* 1 (1976): 875–893. In her insistence that women must write out of a female identity, Cixous holds what is usually referred to as an essentialist position. Blake contested the nineteenth-century essentialist view that women differed radically from men along an immense personal and social spectrum. As the profound sadness and isolation of her crossdresser suggests, Blake did not believe women should submerge their identities in the patriarchal order. Here, I believe she and Cixous would find common ground.

3. The novel uses many onomastic devices, from the allegorical Swinton and Bludgett to the flower names for women. In her personal journals, Blake notes the emphasis on fragility that naming women after flowers implies and relates how, to avoid association with the lily, she changed the spelling of the name her father called her to Lillie.

4. For discussions of women's involvement in these movements see Eleanor Flexner, *Century of Struggle: The Woman's Rights Movement in the United States* (Cambridge: Harvard University Press, 1959, 1975); Glenna Matthews, *The Rise of Public Woman: Woman's Power and Woman's Place in the United States, 1630–1970* (New York: Oxford University Press, 1992); and Ellen Carol DuBois, *Feminism and Suffrage: The Emergence of an Independent Women's Movement in America 1848–1869* (Ithaca: Cornell University Press, 1978). For further discussion of the relationship between the abolitionist and the women's rights movements see DuBois, "Women's Rights and Abolition: The Nature of the Connection" in Lewis Perry and Michael Fellman, eds., *Antislavery Reconsidered: New Perspectives on the Abolitionists* (Baton Rouge: Louisiana State University Press, 1979).

5. For work on this subject see especially Jean Fagan Yellin, *Women and Sisters: The Antislavery Feminists in American Culture*

(New Haven: Yale University Press, 1989) and Karen Sanchez-Eppler, "Bodily Bonds: The Intersecting Rhetorics of Feminism and Abolition" in Shirley Samuels, ed., *The Culture of Sentiment: Race, Gender, and Senti-mentality in Nineteenth Century America.* (New York: Oxford University Press, 1992). The association of women's condition and slavery was useful rhetorically for the middle-class white women in the suffrage movement. However, this association gave a distorted view of the realities of slavery, and its use belies the troubled relationship between white woman suffrage leaders and African Americans. In this regard see Angela Davis, *Women, Race and Class* (London, 1982).

6. It was not until the passage of the Fourteenth Amendment, which gave the vote to former male slaves, that the Constitution inserted the word *male* to specify the gender of the enfranchised. As Flexner puts it in her standard account of the nineteenth-century women's rights movement, suffrage leaders were "appalled at the appearance, for the first time, of the word 'male' in the constitution. Its three-fold use in the proposed Fourteenth Amendment, always in connection with the term 'citizen,' raised the issue of whether women were actually citizens of the United States" (*Century of Struggle,* 146).

7. The most important post–Civil War temperance society, the Women's Christian Temperance Union, was instituted the year of *Fettered For Life*'s publication, 1874.

8. See Alan P. Grimes, *The Puritan Ethic and Woman Suffrage* (New York: Oxford University Press, 1967). It should also be pointed out that Blake used the ethnic stereotypes of her day when depicting the Irish immigrant Malone family.

9. For further discussion of America and dissent, see Sacvan Bercovitch, *The Rites of Assent: Transformations in the Symbolic Construction of America* (New York: Routledge, 1993), particularly the final chapter.

10. America's tradition of didacticism, which goes back to its Puritan roots, had long since shifted from sermons and poetic prescripts into novels. The late–nineteenth-century novels of reform and subversion differed greatly from reform novels of early- and mid-century America, which revealed human suffering but preached the efficacy of faith and good Christian conduct rather

than social change. The novel of reform at mid-century, best illustrated by Susan Warner's *The Wide, Wide World* (1850; reprint,
New York: The Feminist Press, 1987), was sentimental both in its
relentlessly idealized view of the victim (of whatever hardship
was the object of the reformer's passion) and in its moral vision,
which was grounded in an optimistic faith in progress and human perfectibility. Characterized by emotional inflation, extreme
pathos, and a focus on a reality beyond the material world, a cosmic sympathy lying behind the often difficult reality of everyday
life, sentimental novels were widely popular and enjoyed excellent sales in the 1850s and well into the 1880s. The heroine,
prototypical and prescriptive of female behavior, deserves to be
saved from her pain because she endures it with quiet patience.
Her rescuer, inspired by that goodness and patient endurance,
will have the means to take care of her every need. Thus, while
the heroine will escape her particular plight, the institutional
underpinnings of a world in which such a plight might develop
are not examined and the status quo is not questioned. The assumption is that those who are good enough to deserve escaping
the hardships of life will do so; those who do not probably are
appropriately situated in life. One shares both blame and responsibility for one's own hardships. This attitude toward the
unfortunate has a long history in American culture. Clearly rooted
in Calvinism —with its doctrines of predestination and of the Elect—
material wealth, bestowed by God upon the deserving, became a
signifier of salvation. Blake's novel is an early, realistic novel of
reform. See the discussion in Literary-Historical Context.

11. For the politics of publishing see Nina Baym, *Woman's
Fiction: A Guide to Novels by and about Women in America, 1820–
1870* (Ithaca: Cornell University Press, 1978); Jane Tompkins,
*Sensational Designs: The Cultural Work of American Fiction 1790–
1860* (New York: Oxford University Press, 1985); and Susan
Coultrap-McQuin, *Doing Literary Business: American Women
Writers in the Nineteenth Century* (Chapel Hill: University of
North Carolina Press, 1990).

12. Boston: J. Allen & Co., 1835.

13. Praised by the New York *Herald* and *World, Fettered For
Life,* Blake's fifth novel, sold 1,300 copies on the day of its publi-

cation. It was declared a "thrilling story . . . a powerful book,"
vivid, vigorous, "among the most readable and notable books of
the year" by contemporary reviewers and "a feminist classic" and
"the most comprehensive women's rights novel of the nineteenth
century," by its twentieth-century critics. See the *Home Journal*
(May 6, 1874); *New York World* (April 13, 1874); Virginia Blain et
al., *The Feminist Companion to Literature in English* (New
Haven: Yale University Press, 1990): 103; and David Reynolds,
Beneath the American Renaissance (Cambridge: Harvard University
Press, 1989): 401. The novel was reprinted by its original
publisher in 1885.

14. The debate on gender differences continues. See Naomi
Schor and Elizabeth Weed, eds., *the essential difference*
(Bloomington: Indiana University Press, 1994) for a collection of
essays on gender difference, the politics of essentialism, and the
significance of these issues for feminism. For a discussion of
the biologically and historically based assumptions underlying
the notion of radical difference between the sexes see Naomi Schor,
"Reading Double: Sand's Difference" in Nancy K. Miller, ed., *The
Poetics of Gender* (New York: Columbia University Press, 1986):
248–69. Also see Elizabeth L. Berg, "Iconoclastic Moments:
Reading the *Sonnets for Helene,* Writing the *Portuguese Letters*"
in *The Poetics of Gender*: 208–21. Berg writes, ". . . it is important to
insist on the partial nature of sexual identity, to remind oneself
that gender is not the only difference among people, nor even the
essential difference, that the move to privilege gender as the primary defining characteristic of people participates in the same
logic of oppression as the masculine philosophy one criticizes, for
by that gesture one subsumes what is different from oneself (a
different color, a different class, a different sexual orientation, a
different belief) into a universal that denies that other even as it
pretends to represent it. Feminism, if it is to escape the phallo-
centric, or egocentric, appropriation of all representation, must
be partial; more than that, it must be a continual reminder that
there is nothing impartial" (220).

15. "Women in Medicine" in Annie Nathan Meyer, ed., *Woman's
Work in America* (New York: Henry Holt & Co., 1891):
195–96.

16. Because it was based on the notion that there was an essential woman whose nature could be well defined, the rhetoric of nineteenth-century discussions of women usually called for the singular form: woman suffrage, the woman's movement or the woman movement, the nature of woman, the woman question, the social condition of woman.

17. Boston: B. Marsh, 1870: 4.

18. As Nancy F. Cott notes, "For women who previously held no particular avenue of power of their own—no unique defense of their integrity and dignity—this [social power based on women's special female qualities] represented an advance." *The Bonds of Womanhood* (New Haven: Yale University Press, 1977): 200.

19. Judith Lowder Newton writes, "To have influence, in effect, meant doing without self-definition, achievement, and control, meant relinquishing power for effacement of the self in love and sacrifice." *Women, Power and Subversion: Social Strategies in British Fiction 1778–1860* (Athens: University of Georgia Press, 1981): 5.

20. *Women and the Work of Benevolence: Morality, Politics, and Class in the 19th-Century U.S.* (New Haven: Yale University Press, 1990): 213.

21. *Elizabeth Cady Stanton / Susan B. Anthony: Correspondence, Writings, Speeches,* Ellen Carol DuBois, ed. (New York: Schocken, 1981).

22. DuBois in *Stanton / Anthony,* 172.

23. Ginzburg, *Women and the Work of Benevolence,* 213.

24. Blake's unpublished journals and personal papers are housed in the Missouri Historical Society, St. Louis.

25. *The Knickerbocker Monthly* 61 (April 1863): 381–388. The historian of journalism Frank Luther Mott, called "The Social Condition of Women" "a startling article . . . demanding for women 'entire equality on every point-politically, legally and socially.'" *History of American Magazines 1850–1865,* Vol. II (Cambridge: Harvard University Press, 1930–68): 49. This article remained unattributed for over 125 years; I have located evidence in Blake's archives in the Missouri Historical Society which attests to her authorship.

26. DuBois in *Stanton / Anthony,* 109.

27. DuBois in *Stanton / Anthony,* 193.

28. Boston: Roberts Bros., 1873; reprint, New York: Schocken, 1977. Excerpts are available in *Alternative Alcott,* Elaine Showalter, ed. (New Brunswick: Rutgers University Press, 1988).

29. William D. Howells, *Doctor Breen's Practice* (Boston: James R. Osgood, 1881): 12, 43. Readers might want to consider the tone of the following excerpt from Edwin H. Cady, *The Road to Realism: The Early Years 1837–1885 of William Dean Howells* (Syracuse: Syracuse University Press, 1956): "Along with other signs of the new age, Howells was a great deal concerned in the late seventies with feminism, the place of women in the emergent society. . . . Even before Howells resigned from the *Atlantic,* having scheduled *Dr. Breen* for the summer of 1881, Elizabeth Stuart Phelps Ward told him about her similar theme for *Dr. Zay* and he had compromised on engaging to have hers follow right after his serial. Then came another such outline from a hitherto unknown girl [*sic*], whom Howells visited with his proofs in a book bag to convince her that he was not stealing her idea. And shortly after that a real 'doctress' proposed her autobiography to Aldrich—all in the space of a few months" (206–207).

It should not be assumed that a proliferation of novels about middle-class women and work indicated social acceptance of the phenomenon. To give but one illustration, in her chapter on "Women in Medicine" in *Women's Work in America,* Mary Putnam Jacobi outlined the following: In the Colonial period, women were limited to mid-wifery; before and during the American Revolution, "the first achievement of the new-born interest in medical art and education was the expulsion of 'females'" (142). There followed a period of reaction, based on decorum, against male intrusion into midwifery. The nineteenth century, during which medical schools and hospitals were formed, was a period of struggle for women. Jacobi documents difficulties for women gaining admission to medical schools: White males at Harvard were outraged when three African American men and a white woman were admitted in the 1850s and the pressure was such that the woman withdrew. In 1859, the Philadelphia County Medical Society passed a resolution which excommunicated any member physician (all were male) who consulted with a female physician. Not until 1869 were "the Drs. Blackwell . . . accepted as members of a voluntary 'Medical Library and Journal Association.'" Harvard seems to have been a holdout: As Jacobi notes, "On Oct. 9, 1879, an editorial in the *Boston Medical and Surgical Journal* says: 'We regret to be obliged to announce that, at a meeting of the councilors held Oct 1, it was voted to admit women to the Massachusetts Medical Society'" (187).

When reading *Dr. Breen's Practice* along with *Fettered For Life,* readers can see how easily Howells, as spokesperson for the prevailing view, can dismiss the suffrage movement with a single word (Grace Breen is not a feminist—rather, she held "sane" opinions [15]), while Blake, to explain what is not accepted as prevailing "common sense," must devote pages to arguments on women's issues, thereby opening herself up to the criticism of being didactic.

30. Boston: Houghton Mifflin, 1882; reprint, New York: The Feminist Press, 1987.

31. Flexner, *Century of Struggle* 134. Popular accounts of the wonders of a new inventive age of convenience sanitized the squalid, brutalized lives of workers who served as cogs in the wheels of other men's progress. In 1861 The *Atlantic* published Rebecca Harding Davis's evocative fictional exposé of the deadening poverty and exploitation of "Life in the Iron Mills" (reprint, New York: The Feminist Press, 1972). Davis's view of the life of "operatives" in the mills, like Blake's of the urban seamstresses in *Fettered For Life,* was the vision which impassioned the settlement house movement that created middle-class homes for working women in slum neighborhoods. Other examples of important nineteenth-century novels that opened factory life to the scrutiny of a middle-class readership include Rebecca Harding Davis, *Margaret Howth* (1862; reprint, New York: Feminist Press, 1990) and Elizabeth Stuart Phelps, *The Silent Partner* (1871; reprint, New York: Feminist Press, 1983).

32. Barbara Bardes and Suzanne Gossett write: "Given the strong cultural proscription against married women entering the public sphere in almost any capacity, few accounts of married women in wage work appeared either in fiction or nonfiction. . . .

it was widely believed that such economic power as women gained through wage earning might be detrimental to marital relations. The harmful impact on the family was seized on by the labor unions as yet another argument against the entry of women into the craft unions." *Declarations of Independence: Women and Political Power in Nineteenth Century American Fiction* (New Brunswick: Rutgers University Press, 1990): 105. For a discussion of other novels of the period which deal with women's work and for background on controversies surrounding female physicians see Bardes and Gossett, chapters 4 and 5.

33. Indicative of the persistent perception of woman's work as an extension of the domestic model of doing good for others, even at the century's end, *Women's Work in America* includes eight chapters ranging over education, literature, journalism, medicine, ministry, law, government, and industry, and seven chapters on various areas of philanthropy alone. Although *Women's Work* argued for the importance of women in public life, Bardes and Gossett point out, in *Declarations of Independence,* that this "was the minority view; most Americans considered woman's importance as the linchpin of domestic life undiminished" (106).

34. "Social Condition of Women," 382–83, 387.

35. Susan K. Harris, *19th-Century American Women's Novels: Interpretive Strategies* (Cambridge: Cambridge University Press, 1990). Another way to approach the shift in the ending of subversive fictions is to consider Peter Brooks's contention that the middle of a fiction is the site of most importance and is never superseded by the ending. See *Reading for the Plot: Design and Intention in Narrative* (New York: Knopf, 1984).

36. Blake's onomastics are here again worthy of note. Guy, whose name is also a word for a generic male, constitutes Blake's assessment of the ordinary man struggling to accept the "new woman."

37. Lisa Duggan, "'Sexual Secrets Revealed': Sex, Scandal and Tragedy in the Popular Press, 1890–1900," paper read at the Organization of American Historians Annual Meeting, New York City (April 1986). As quoted by Matthews, *The Rise of Public Woman,* 3.

38. "Personal Property: Exchange Value and the Female Self in *The Awakening*," *Genders* 5 (1989). DuBois writes: "At first Stanton's insistence that feminists declare for individual freedom and equality in marriage as well as in politics was not well received. The notion that woman should have 'sovereignty' over her sexuality, that her own wishes should take precedence over her husband's or that of any other external authority, seemed even to some feminists to spell the end of marriage and family" (*Stanton/Anthony*, 97). In fact, another century would pass before a woman's right to exclusive ownership of her body would be legally recognized, for even in recent decades husbands were still protected from prosecution on the charge of marital rape.

39. In her journals, Blake relates similar forms of harassment when she entered editorial offices to pick up her paychecks. For another account by a woman bookseller see Anonymous, *Facts, by a Woman* (Oakland, CA: Pacific Press, 1881)

40. The caged bird became an increasingly popular image in late-nineteenth-century writing; for examples see *The Awakening*, Frank Norris's *McTeague*, and Mary Wilkins Freeman's "A New England Nun." See also Lorenz Eitner, "Cages, Prisons, and Captives in Eighteenth-Century Art" in Karl Kroeber and William Walling, eds., *Images of Romanticism: Verbal and Visual Affinities* (New Haven: Yale University Press, 1978): 13–38 for a brief history of the imagery of the caged bird, moving from French rococo erotic painting, in which the cage signified secure possession (from the male's perspective) through eighteenth-century political ideology, in which the uncaged bird signified freedom. See also Victor Brombert, "The Happy Prison: A Recurring Romantic Metaphor" in David Thorburn and Geoffrey Hartman, eds., *Romanticism: Vistas, Instances, Continuities* (Ithaca: Cornell University Press, 1973): 62–79 for a discussion of the cage as a nostalgic place of security and a metaphor of interiority.

41. Blake's allusion must surely be to the most famous statue of nineteenth-century America, *Greek Slave* by Hiram Powers. Jean Fagan Yellin writes: "The *Greek Slave*, Powers' most famous work, signifies slavery by using the iconography that the abolitionists had popularized. But while it incorporates the nudity, the piety, and the chains of the supplicant slave emblem, the *Greek*

Slave presents a version of womanhood that counters the model of the Woman and Sister advanced by the antislavery feminists. . . . The antislavery feminists read the supplicant slave emblems as encouraging women to overthrow the despotisms of slavery, racism, and sexism through public struggle, and in their discourse they endlessly replicated the emblems in an effort to win adherents to their cause.

"In contrast, Powers' female slave was interpreted by everyone who saw her as a victim, variously identified as a slave or a woman who, through Christian resignation, transcended the tyranny of slavery or of patriarchy," *Women and Sisters,* 123.

42. In their critique of patriarchal authority, contemporary feminists often center on the gaze, claiming that "woman's place in culture is constructed by man's view of her, by a look that emanating from his position of self-identity seeks to circumscribe hers," as Mary Ann Doane suggests in "Woman's Stake: Filming the Female Body," *October* (Summer 1981): 34. For other discussions of gazing see E. Ann Kaplan, "Is the Gaze Male?" in Marilyn Pearsall, ed. *Women and Values: Readings in Recent Feminist Philosophy* Belmont, California: Wadsworth Publishing, 1986): 231; John Berger, *Ways of Seeing* (London: Penguin 1972); Nancy K. Miller, *Subject to Change: Reading Feminist Writing* (New York: Columbia University Press, 1988), especially chapter 7, "Performances of the Gaze"; and Mary Devereaux, "Oppressive Texts, Resisting Readers and the Gendered Spectator: The **New** Aesthetics," *The Journal of Aesthetics and Art Criticism* 48:4 (Fall 1990): 337–347.

43. Andrea Moore Kerr, *Lucy Stone: Speaking Out For Equality* (New Brunswick: Rutgers University Press, 1992): 54.

44. Matthews, *The Rise of Public Woman,* 113. Bards and Gossett in *Declarations of Independence* discuss the social forces mitigating against women finding a voice; see especially chapter 2.

45. Written primarily by women for women, sentimental fiction can be viewed as doubly threatening to any system of control. Such literature was not only introduced by male writers but embodied patriarchal values. Yet, when usurped by female writers, it was trivialized by the male establishment, which felt it necessary to undermine it by means of either parody or deni-

gration. This very attitude betrayed a mounting insecurity in the face of the emergence of an anticanonical literature, which was construed in the negative mode of the predominant "other." Paradoxically, although nineteenth-century women's fiction made an impact which called for suspicion, ridicule, and outright rejection, such reactions constituted an acknowledge-ment of an emergent and ever-widening threat that would eventually, with the feminist reassessment of women's literature, claim its own identity and authority.

46. For discussions of realism and naturalism see George J. Becker, "Modern Realism as a Literary Movement" in *Documents of Modern Literary Realism* (Princeton: Princeton University Press, 1963): 3–38; Edwin H. Cady, *The Light of Common Day: Realism in American Fiction* (Bloomington: Indiana University Press, 1971); Charles Child Walcutt, *American Literary Naturalism, A Divided Stream* (Minneapolis: University of Minnesota Press, 1956); Donald Pizer, *Realism and Naturalism in Nineteenth-Century American Literature* (Carbondale: Southern Illinois University Press), 1984; and Amy Kaplan. *The Social Construction of American Realism* (Chicago: University of Chicago Press, 1988).

47. Tuberculosis could attack the spine, skin, or blood-stream, but the most common form ate away at the lungs, leading to a feverish wasting away. Although it is often dismissed as a stereotypical disorder of sentimental heroines, Blake's use of it is a realistic detail. The form of the disease known as consumption spread especially among the overcrowded, undernourished poor. It was a mass killer which engendered the kind of fear which today is associated with AIDS. See Frank Ryan, *The Forgotten Plague* (Boston: Little, Brown, 1993).

48. In addition, it is a distinctly white, middle-class tradition; this is the tradition of Blake and her presumed readership.

49. "Tradition and the Female Talent: 'The Awakening' as a Solitary Book" in Wendy Martin, ed., *New Essays on "The Awakening"* (New York: Cambridge University Press, 1988); reprinted in Nancy A. Walker, ed., *Kate Chopin: The Awakening* (Boston: St. Martin's Press, 1993):175.

50. Showalter, "Tradition and the Female Talent," 173.

51. On caged and uncaged birds, see note 40.

52. "Social Condition of Women," 387.

53. A few years later Dix would support the formation of Barnard College. He opposed what he considered to be Blake's radical idea that women should be integrated into the student body of Columbia College.

54. Elinore Hughes Partridge, ed., *American Prose and Criticism, 1820–1900* (Detroit: Gale, 1983): 192–93.

55. Kathi Kern., "Rereading Eve: Elizabeth Cady Stanton and The Woman's Bible, 1885–1896" in *Women's Studies* 19 (1991): 377, 378, 382, n. 32.

ACKNOWLEDGEMENTS

The process of recovering a lost novel and making it accessible to the public and to academic discussion is one which takes much time and the generous support of many people. I would like to thank Elaine Hedges, Florence Howe, and Susannah Driver for their belief in this project; Jean Casella, senior editor at the Feminist Press, for her thought-filled editing; Feminist Press staff members Sara Clough, Sarah Stovin, Rachel Weiss, Susan Cozzi, and Kim Mallett, and interns Jesse Souweine and Maya Kremen for their contributions to the book's publication and success; Richard Kopley and Kent Ljungquist for indirectly sending me to Lillie Blake; David S. Reynolds, Alfred Bendixen, and Susan Gubar for reading the manuscript; Terence Martin and Lois Cuddy for support and encouragement; G.R. Thompson for refusing to let me give up; Nancy Manning of Buck Creek Books for searching for Blake's novel; my colleagues in the Department of English at Butler University who granted me a course reduction to do a portion of the research that led to this afterword; the Butler University Academic Grants Program for research support; Lois Cuddy, Greg McNabb, and my colleagues Aron Aji and William Watts for help with technical matters in a crisis; and my Butler students, whose enthusiastic reception of *Fettered For Life* over the course of several semesters convinced me of its importance for classroom use.

My thanks especially go to my family: my daughter Elizabeth, who reminds me that even women aged twelve have strong voices and strong minds; my son and personal computer consultant Matthew, who reformatted my Macintosh disks for The Feminist Press's IBMs (no small task); my stepdaughter Lisa, for becoming part of my life; and my husband Giancarlo Maiorino, with whom I have the kind of equal and loving partnership which Lillie Blake wished for, but, fettered as she was to the nineteenth century, could scarcely imagine.

Grace Farrell
August 1996